AFTER THE SHADOWS

SECRETS OF SWEETWATER CROSSING,
BOOK 1

AFTER THE SHADOWS

AMANDA CABOT

THORNDIKE PRESS
A part of Gale, a Cengage Company

LIBRARY OF CONGRESS CIP DATA ON FILE.
CATALOGUING IN PUBLICATION FOR THIS BOOK
IS AVAILABLE FROM THE LIBRARY OF CONGRESS.

ISBN-13: 979-8-88578-940-0 (hardcover alk. paper)

Published in 2023 by arrangement with Revell Books, a division of Baker Publishing Group.

Printed in Mexico
Print Number: 1   Print Year: 2023

For Peggy Jo Wells,
whose love of the Lord
shines through everything she
says and does

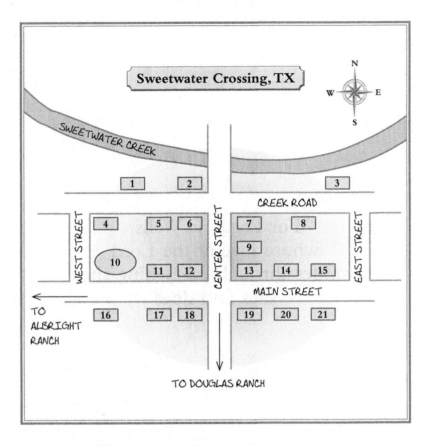

1 - Mrs. Sanders's Home
2 - Cemetery
3 - Finley House
4 - Saloon
5 - Mrs. French's Home
6 - Mrs. Locke's Home
7 - Mrs. Adams's Home
8 - The Albrights' Home
9 - Mrs. Carmichael's Home
10 - Park
11 - Alice Patton's home/Library

12 - School
13 - Church
14 - Mayor's Home and Office
15 - Mercantile
16 - Livery
17 - Sheriff's Home and Office
18 - Ma's Kitchen
19 - Dr. Sheridan's Home and Office
20 - Post Office
21 - Dressmaker

CHAPTER ONE

August 19, 1882

Everything looked the same. The live oaks in the park still shadowed this block of Main Street, providing a welcome respite from the early afternoon sun. In the schoolyard, two boys vied to see who could swing higher, while another scuffed his feet, impatiently waiting for his turn. Beulah Douglas raced down the street, her single blond braid flapping against her back. It wasn't the first time Emily had seen the twelve-year-old hurrying, but today she was moving faster than Emily remembered, probably because she'd spent more time than usual with Father's horse and knew her parents would be looking for her. Other than Beulah's uncharacteristic speed, nothing appeared to have changed, but Emily Leland knew otherwise. Everything had changed. Or perhaps only she had changed.

She guided her horse onto Center Street,

trying not to frown at the memories the sight of the small church sent rushing through her. All those Sundays sitting sandwiched between her two younger sisters in what everyone called the preacher's pew, not daring to fidget even when Father's sermon lasted for what seemed like hours. The Christmas and Easter services when well-meaning parishioners pinched her cheeks and told her mother that even though Emily was shorter than her sisters and might not be as talented, she was the prettiest of the Vaughn girls, that her blond hair and blue eyes made her look like an angel.

She was no angel, but she'd been a happy girl. And when she'd left Sweetwater Crossing, she'd been a bride smiling at her groom and dreaming of the life they'd share. Now . . . Emily adjusted the sleeves of the black dress she'd found in the attic and had hastily altered to fit, ensuring that neither the sun nor prying eyes would see her skin.

Mama had insisted that the hallmark of a lady was her lilywhite complexion. Mama had said . . . Emily bit her lip. She wouldn't cry. After all, tears solved nothing. If there was anything she'd learned in the last year, it was that.

She kept her gaze fixed firmly ahead as she approached the corner of Creek, refusing to look at the cemetery. The wrought-iron gates would be open; the cypress trees had probably grown an inch or two, and somewhere within the fenced area was a new grave. Since it was too soon for grass to have covered it, it would be what Mama called a raw grave. The grave wasn't the only thing that was raw. So too was Emily. This was far from the homecoming she'd dreamt of.

"We're here." There was no need to tell the horse, for Blanche's ears had perked and she'd tossed her head in apparent delight as they'd approached town. While Emily dreaded what faced her, Blanche was happy to have returned. For her, the barn behind the house that still looked out of place in this small Hill Country town was home. Blanche was probably anticipating a reunion with Father's horse, never questioning her welcome, while Emily wondered what awaited her within the stone mansion.

She looped the reins over the hitching post on the side of the house, then returned to the front. Fourteen months ago, she would have entered through the closest door, but today she felt the need to climb the front steps as if she were a visitor. For she was. She wouldn't knock on the door, but she also would not use the entrance that had been reserved for family. The harsh tone of her sister's letter after all those months of silence had made her cautious.

As she stepped inside, Emily took a deep breath, savoring the familiar scents of floor polish mingling with the lavender of Mama's sachets. The house was blessedly cool compared to the summer sun, the silence normal for a Saturday afternoon when everyone spoke in hushed voices lest they disturb Father while he was writing his sermon. Only parishioners were allowed to interrupt him, and the majority knew his schedule well enough to time their visits for the morning.

It was an ordinary Saturday afternoon, or as ordinary as one could be without the woman who'd turned this house into a home. For a moment, Emily let herself believe that everything would be fine. Then, mustering her courage, she called out, "Father! Joanna! Louisa! I'm here." By some small miracle, her voice did not tremble, nor did it reveal the grief that threatened to overwhelm her.

There was no sound from the library that had been Father's office for as long as she could recall, but Emily's youngest sister emerged from the kitchen, an apron tied around her waist, a frown on her normally smiling face.

"I wasn't sure you'd come." Louisa's voice radiated anger, sorrow, and something that might have been fear.

Emily had been wrong in thinking she was the only one who'd changed. So too had her sister.

"I left as soon as I received your letter." The letter whose tone had worried her as much as its content. Though Emily wanted nothing more than to gather her sister into her arms, hoping that a warm embrace would lessen their grief, Louisa's forbidding expression stopped her. If she wanted comfort, Louisa would have to take the first step. As it was, she stood there stiffly, her hands clenched into fists, and shook her head, loosening a strand of medium-brown hair from her chignon.

Four inches taller and with more curves than Emily, Emily's half sister shared only one characteristic with her: deep-blue eyes, a legacy from their mother. Right now, those eyes were as angry as her voice.

Trying to calm her thoughts, Emily glanced around the spacious foyer whose twin staircases mirrored those of the house's exterior. Mama had once confessed that she found it all a bit ostentatious, but Father would not consider leaving the home he'd promised his closest friend he'd care for, especially when he realized Clive would never return.

"We owe it to Clive," he'd told Mama. She'd nodded, her resignation apparent.

But Mama would nod no more.

The enormity of the situation hit Emily with more force than she'd thought possible, turning her legs to jelly.

"I can't believe it's true," she said, her voice no longer steady. "Father always said he'd be the first to go."

"But he wasn't. Father's lost without her," Louisa continued as she led Emily into the parlor. In the past, they might have sat in the kitchen, sipping cups of coffee as they talked. Today, however, Louisa appeared to want more formality. She perched on the edge of one of the least comfortable chairs in the room and gestured toward the one facing it, telling Emily this would be a confrontation, not two sisters comforting each other.

"He walks around in a daze, and when he leaves, he doesn't tell me where he's going." Louisa glanced through the open doorway into the hall. "He had lunch with me, but he must have gone out again. It's awful, Emily, awful. He won't even sleep in the room they shared." She closed her eyes, clearly

14

attempting to control her emotions. "It's been horrible trying to be strong for him." And that was a role Louisa, as the youngest, had never needed to assume. Perhaps that was part of the reason for her uncharacteristic coldness.

"Where's Joanna?" Though their sister had sometimes seemed capricious, declaring nothing was as important as playing the piano, she'd also helped Mama keep the house spotless. The layer of dust on the spinet made Emily wonder whether Joanna's grief was so deep that she, like Father, was in a daze.

Louisa's eyes flew open, sorrow replaced by anger. "As if you care!"

Emily cared. Oh, how she cared. She'd written letters to the family every week, asking about each of them, hoping their lives were happier than hers, but there'd been no response.

"Joanna's in Europe with her grandmother. They left a couple months ago and are supposed to be gone for a year, maybe longer." Louisa's voice was harsh. "Her dreams are coming true, just like yours did. You got a handsome husband; Joanna's studying music with a master, and I'm stuck here alone." Louisa glared at Emily. "You should have been here. Mama asked for you at the end, even though she knew you wouldn't come."

The words ricocheted through the room before piercing Emily's heart. "Why would she think that?"

"Don't pretend you don't know. That letter George wrote for you was very clear. You may have scalded your hand, but that didn't stop you from telling us you were a Leland now and didn't need any of us Vaughns, so we shouldn't bother writing to you or coming for a visit."

Emily bit down the bile that threatened to erupt at the evidence of George's cruelty. She'd known something was wrong when she'd found Louisa's letter in his pocket — *"I'm not sure you'll care,"* her sister had written, *"but I thought you should know that our mother died"* — but she hadn't realized the extent of her husband's depravity.

"Mama couldn't believe you'd written that letter," Louisa continued. "She said she was going to visit you, no matter what you'd said, but Father told her you needed time to adjust to being a wife. He was convinced you'd change your mind, but when three months went by and you didn't answer any of our letters, even he gave up."

No wonder Emily had received no response to the letters she'd written. In all

16

likelihood, George hadn't mailed them any more than he'd given her the ones her family had sent. It was probably only chance that he hadn't destroyed Louisa's last letter. Or maybe he'd meant to torment Emily with it, promising she could visit her family once she gave him what he wanted. She'd never know.

"Mama was devastated," Louisa continued, "and Father looked like he'd been bludgeoned. You know he always tried his best not to treat you differently from his real daughters."

Emily winced. She was the offspring of Mama's first marriage, while Joanna was Father's daughter from an earlier marriage. Only Louisa had been raised in a home with both of her parents. Even though Joseph Vaughn was the only father Emily remembered, for as long as she could recall she'd known he wasn't the man who'd sired her. Most days it hadn't mattered, but when one of the girls was angry and wanted to hurt her sisters, parentage was a convenient weapon.

"It was bad enough that you didn't answer Mama's letters, but I never thought you'd ignore the one I sent you, telling you she was failing and wanted to see you."

Ignoring Emily's gasp, Louisa continued.

"How could you-leave me to do everything by myself? When we were girls, you promised you'd always be there for me, but when I needed you most, you stayed on your ranch with your husband. I'll never forgive you for that."

No wonder Louisa was so angry. She believed Emily had willingly abandoned her. And that, like sending a hateful letter, was something Emily wouldn't do.

"I never received your letters."

Louisa scoffed. "You can say that, but I don't believe it."

"Believe it, Louisa, because it's the truth. I didn't write that awful letter, and the only one I received from you was the one announcing Mama's death."

Her sister's eyes flashed with disdain. "A likely story and one you can't prove, especially since you admit you received the last one. As for the one you sent us, I know you didn't write it. George wrote that letter, but you dictated it."

Emily hadn't. She would never have written, dictated, or had any part in something like that, for it was as far from the truth as east was from west. Surely her family knew that. But it appeared that whatever George had written had convinced them that Emily no longer wanted to be part of the family.

Knowing she had only one defense that Louisa would accept, she held out her hands, turning them so her sister could see both sides. "Look. There are no scars. I never scalded my hand."

Though Louisa studied Emily's hands, she still appeared dubious. "You must have said those things. Why else would George have written them?"

Because he wanted me totally dependent on him. Even though it might exonerate her, Emily wouldn't say that. When she'd left the ranch that had been her home for over a year, she had vowed that no one would know the truth of her marriage. Some things were too horrible to put into words. Besides, she didn't want pity or even sympathy. All she wanted was to forget.

Louisa raised her head and met Emily's gaze. "Where is George? I'm surprised he'd let you travel alone."

He wouldn't have. He hadn't even let Emily go into town unless he accompanied her, and by telling everyone she had delicate nerves and was easily disturbed by visitors, he'd ensured that the neighboring ranchers' wives stayed away. Visits, he'd told her, would be her reward when she fulfilled her mission. But she hadn't. Fortunately, George could no longer control her life.

19

Emily squared her shoulders, knowing there was no need to cower. "George is dead."

"Dead?" The blood drained from Louisa's face as the word registered.

"He was killed in a fight at the saloon." The anger that his hopes for a son had been dashed again had been more intense this time than any other month, leaving bruises that had yet to fade. Emily thought he'd gotten himself under control before leaving the ranch, but it appeared he hadn't. The sheriff said he'd started the fight.

Louisa shook her head, dumbfounded. "I don't know what to say other than I'm sorry."

I'm not.

"Food."

Craig Ferguson smiled when his son's stomach rumbled, confirming his hunger. Though the boy frequently claimed to be famished, perhaps because eating helped alleviate the boredom of their journey, this time the need was real.

"You're right, Noah. It's time to eat." Craig nodded when he saw a row of trees ahead. They'd provide welcome shade from the August sun, and if his assumption that they lined the banks of a stream was accurate, he and Noah would also have a source of water. This part of Texas might be cooler than Galveston, but it was still hot, and fresh water was always welcome.

Even if there was no stream, stopping would give Noah a chance to run. That too would be welcome. Craig knew it was hard for a two-and-a-half-year-old to sit in a wagon for so long. It was also hard for him. He and Noah shared more than the same dark brown hair and eyes. Being a school-master might not involve heavy labor, but it kept Craig on his feet most of the day. The extended periods of sitting involved in traveling halfway across the state were dif-ficult for both of them, but the result would be worth it: a new home, a new beginning, and — if his prayers were answered — the end of Noah's nightmares.

"Me eat?" Noah darted an anxious look at the back of the wagon when Craig brought it to a stop.

"We'll both eat." And so would Hercules, thanks to the lush grass. "But let's see who can reach those trees first." Craig lifted Noah and set him on the ground, knowing his son needed to release some energy. Noah had slept better since they'd been on the road, bolstering Craig's belief that the change, which many had considered extreme, would hasten the healing process, but that extra sleep meant the boy had an even greater need for activity.

"Me! Me run!"

As Noah scampered toward the trees, Craig grabbed the bag that contained their food and followed at a leisurely pace. Noah might fall in his hurry to win the race, but the thick grass meant he wouldn't hurt himself, and he'd feel independent. Rachel would have been proud. She'd claimed that the most important things parents could do were ensure that their children knew they were loved and give them the freedom to make mistakes.

"They'll learn from them," she'd declared.

"Who's the teacher here, you or me?" Craig had asked, feigning annoyance, though he knew Rachel would see through his pretense. They'd rarely argued, and when they did, it was usually because Craig thought she was being too impulsive. But there was nothing impulsive that day, simply a shared desire to raise their soon-to-be-born child the best they could.

"We'll both teach our baby," she'd said. "That's the reason God gave children two parents."

But now Noah had only one.

"Water, Pa, water!" Noah shrieked in delight.

Craig, who was only one step behind him, moved to his side, ready to catch him if he seemed likely to tumble into it, then smiled when he realized the stream was only a few inches deep. It would provide water to wash down the bread and cheese he'd bought in the last town but wouldn't be a threat to his son's safety.

"Me wade."

Craig's smile broadened at Noah's use of the word he'd learned the day before they'd left Galveston. "I thought you were hungry." He rubbed Noah's stomach, then bent down to listen to it. "Yep. You're hungry. Let's eat first, and then you can wade."

He wouldn't deprive his son of the simple pleasure of splashing in a creek, particularly when there was no need to rush. The journey had taken less time than he'd expected, and unless they encountered a major delay, they'd arrive in Sweetwater Crossing two days earlier than he'd arranged with Mrs. Carmichael. He hoped that wouldn't create a problem, but if she wasn't ready for them, he and Noah could sleep in the wagon as they'd done every night since they'd left home.

"Good." Noah reached for the bag of

food, confirming Craig's priorities.

What was good was that his son had not had a single nightmare since they left Galveston.

"He'll forget," the minister's wife had told Craig a week after Rachel was laid to rest. "Children that young forget quickly."

But Noah had not, not even after a year had passed. He still refused to be separated from Craig, even though he was too young to spend his days in a schoolroom. He still woke screaming at least once a week . . . until they'd left the house that held tragic memories. The difference was dramatic, proof that God still answered prayers.

Craig hoped Noah's healing would continue once they reached Sweetwater Crossing. The gently rolling hills with their sandstone and limestone outcroppings, the roads canopied with live oak branches, and the open fields carpeted with wildflowers filled his heart with joy and the sense of peace that had been missing for too long. That and the hope that Noah had begun to heal made him more confident that the decision to come to the Hill Country had been a wise one.

Though he'd balked at the thought of leaving the home he and Rachel had shared, Noah's problems convinced Craig there was little choice but to change their lives, and so he prayed for guidance. His prayers were answered sooner than he expected. Only days after he'd first prayed about his future, the minister mentioned a letter he'd received, saying a town in the Hill Country would need a new schoolteacher because the current one was about to marry.

In less time than Craig had thought possible, everything was arranged. The decision makers had been impressed with his credentials and had offered him the position of schoolmaster, a position that included room and board as well as a small salary. Craig and Noah would live with a widow who claimed to love children and whose house was catty-cornered from the school. It sounded ideal, a chance to put the past behind them. And maybe, just maybe, both he and Noah would find peace in the Hill Country.

"I wish Father were back," Louisa said as she glanced at the clock.

So did Emily. After Louisa's grudging welcome, she needed the comfort of his smile and a hug. Where was he? In the past, unless one of his parishioners had an emergency, their father spent most of Saturday afternoon writing and rewriting his sermon.

A year ago, he would not have left without telling someone where he was going. But according to Louisa, their father was greatly changed.

"Do you want to help me make supper?" Louisa rose and smoothed her apron, further evidence that it wasn't only Father who was changed. The Louisa Emily knew would not have left the kitchen without removing her apron. But, then again, the Louisa Emily knew would have acknowledged their shared sorrow, not treated Emily like an adversary. "You always were the better cook, and you know how Father depends on a hot meal served precisely at six."

"Of course, I'll help." Emily accepted the olive branch her sister had extended.

As they passed the library, she glanced inside. The desk was cluttered with papers, the two chairs in front of it turned sideways, evidence of visitors. Both were common occurrences. Father's absence was not.

As if she'd read Emily's thoughts, Louisa paused and stared at the empty desk chair. "He's different. Nothing's been the same since Mama . . ." Louisa's voice broke, and tears filled her eyes.

"How did it happen?" Like her sister, Emily wouldn't pronounce the word *died*, but she needed to know. While Emily and her sisters had had measles, chicken pox, and other ailments, she could not recall Mama ever being ill.

"Doc Sheridan claimed it was a virulent fever. He bled her, but that didn't do any good. She just kept getting worse." This time Louisa shuddered, her grief visible. "Oh, Emily, it was awful watching her waste away. I tried to help, but no one would listen to me."

And that refusal would have made the situation even worse for Louisa. Not only was she left alone to care for their mother, but her knowledge of the healing arts, while not as extensive as Doc's, had been dismissed. It was no wonder she was lashing out in anger.

Hoping her sister wouldn't reject her attempt to comfort her, Emily wrapped her arms around Louisa. "I'm sorry I wasn't here. There's nothing I could have done to save her — you know far more than I do about healing — but I could have helped in other ways. I could have —"

Emily stopped, her thoughts arrested by the unexpected odor wafting through the hallway. She'd closed the front door behind her, but all the windows were open in an attempt to cool the house. She sniffed the air again. "It smells like smoke." And fire was one of the town's greatest threats. Though many of the houses were made of stone, others and almost all the outbuildings were wooden structures.

Their grief shoved aside for a second, the sisters ran to the front porch, searching for the source. Billows of dark, acrid smoke rose from Center Street, turning the clear blue sky an ominous gray.

"It's either the church or Mrs. Carmichael's house." Louisa stared at the smoke, appearing frozen by shock.

"We've got to help." Emily touched her sister's arm. "They'll need water. You take the kitchen pail." At this time of the day, it was sure to be almost full.

The urgency in Emily's voice seemed to break through Louisa's shock. "There are two," she said. "We'll go together. Come on, sister."

Though it took an emergency to reunite them, for the first time since she'd returned home, Emily felt as if they really were sisters.

CHAPTER TWO

An hour later, Emily, Louisa, and the others who'd attempted to fight the fire conceded defeat. The flames had been extinguished, but all that remained of Mrs. Carmichael's house were charred beams.

Exhausted by the effort, Louisa returned home, leaving Emily to follow after the final ember was doused. When the last of the volunteers dispersed, Emily headed back to Finley House, her heart heavy as she thought about the destruction and what it would mean for the widow who'd lived there for almost two decades.

"Emily Vaughn, why, it is you. I didn't know you were back in town."

Emily turned, recognizing the voice of the woman whose home was now no more than smoldering ruins. Mrs. Carmichael was sitting on her neighbor's porch, her arm wrapped around Clara Adams's shoulders, giving comfort though she was the one who needed it. How typical of the gray-haired widow. Though she was close to seventy, Mrs. Carmichael had always impressed Emily as being much younger, perhaps because her light blue eyes normally seemed to sparkle with happiness. She doubted they were sparkling now.

"I arrived this afternoon," Emily said as she approached the older women. "I'm sorry about what happened to your house." It was a day no one in Sweetwater Crossing would soon forget.

"I wish I knew what happened. I didn't leave anything cooking on the stove, but someone said embers might have started the fire."

"Now, Mary, it doesn't matter." Mrs. Adams shook her head, strands of white hair escaping from the knot at the back of her neck, her gray eyes solemn. The widow was the shortest of Mrs. Carmichael's friends, like Emily only five feet two inches tall, but what she lacked in height, she made up for in girth. "All that matters is that you're safe."

"The timing is terrible." Mrs. Carmichael's voice was steady, but Emily saw the pain in her expression. "Clara said I could stay with her, but she doesn't have room for Mr. Ferguson and his son. Lottie and Betty don't either."

Emily recognized the names of Mrs. Carmichael's three closest friends, all of whom lived in what Hill Country residents called Sunday Houses, small dwellings that ranchers built so they'd have a place to stay overnight when they brought their families into town for Saturday shopping and Sunday services. The houses were functional but tiny. Emily understood Mrs. Carmichael's need for lodging, but as far as she knew, there was no one in Sweetwater Crossing named Ferguson.

"Who's Mr. Ferguson?"

"The new schoolmaster. When the town hired him, the mayor arranged for him and his son to stay with me. He's supposed to arrive in a day or two." Mrs. Carmichael raised an eyebrow. "Didn't anyone tell you that Gertrude Albright is married?"

In a day that had been filled with surprises, at least this one was pleasant. Like most of the town, Emily had believed her former teacher was a confirmed spinster. She only hoped that the woman who'd tried to instill proper behavior as well as knowledge in her pupils had been wiser in her choice of a spouse than Emily.

"Louisa didn't have a chance to tell me all the news, but that doesn't matter. What's

31

important is that you need a place to stay until your house is rebuilt."

The small house between the church and Clara Adams's home had been the town's parsonage until the War Between the States. Then, when Clive Finley, the man from Alabama who'd fallen in love with Texas and planned to bring his sweetheart here as soon as he'd convinced her father that the house he was building was worthy of her, left to join a regiment from his home state, he'd asked Emily's father to move his family into his newly completed mansion until Clive returned with his bride.

But though Father had returned after serving as a chaplain in the horrible war that had left him with serious injuries, Clive had not come back, and Finley House had remained the Vaughns' residence, leaving the parsonage empty until Mrs. Carmichael's husband died. When she sold their ranch, the church elders offered the parsonage to her at a minimal rent, since, unlike her widowed friends, she had no Sunday House. She'd lived there ever since.

"Rebuilt? Who knows when the church will have time and money to do that?"

Emily wished she could offer the widow the assurance that that would happen quickly, but that seemed unlikely, since

32

Finley House was serving as the town's parsonage. Until Father retired, there was no need to construct another. Meanwhile, Mrs. Carmichael and the new schoolmaster needed a place to live. There was an answer, an obvious one. Though Emily cringed at the thought of offering a man — any man — a room in her home, she knew it was the right thing to do.

Tamping back her fears, Emily addressed the widow. "Let me talk to my father. I'm sure he'll agree that you and the schoolmaster should stay with us. You know we have plenty of room."

The tension that had made the widow's shoulders rigid began to dissipate, but her voice held concern. "Are you certain? Small children can disrupt a household. Noah's only two and a half. His mother died a year ago, and you know that children that age can be a handful."

It wasn't the child who worried Emily. It was his father. What would she do if Mr. Ferguson was like George? He was a stranger, someone no one in town had met. And even if they had met him, there was no telling what he was truly like. The masks some people wore could fool anyone. George's certainly had.

Emily bolstered herself with the reminder

that there were ways to keep herself safe. She would ensure that she was never alone with the schoolmaster, and when they were in the same room, she would keep her distance. She couldn't let fear rule her, for opening her home to people in need was what Mama and Father would have wanted. How many times had they reminded their daughters of Jesus's command to care for widows and orphans? Mrs. Carmichael was a widow, and while Noah might not be an orphan, he had no mother.

"Let me talk to Father," Emily repeated.

But Father had not returned, and when Emily told Louisa what she'd suggested, her sister shook her head.

"It's a terrible idea." She and Emily were seated at the table in the kitchen, trying to wash the taste of smoke from their throats by sipping glasses of water. "Mrs. Carmichael can stay here, but why would you invite total strangers to live with us, especially now? Mama's not here to be the hostess. Besides, she used to tell me that guests should stay no more than a week." Louisa's frown deepened. "What will Father say?"

"I expect he'll welcome Mrs. Carmichael and the schoolmaster." Emily took another sip of water, her thoughts roiling as she realized she hadn't seen her father fighting the fire. That wasn't like him. Even though his leg pained him, he would have done everything he could to help save Mrs. Carmichael's house.

"Where is Father?" she asked.

Louisa shrugged. "I don't know. Maybe he took Horace for a ride. Sometimes when he's having trouble with his sermon, he does that."

"I'll look for them." Knowing Father was the only one who could convince Louisa, Emily headed outside. Horace was in the corral, but there was no sign of Father. That left the barn. Though she would have expected the door to be open, it was not. She slid the door to the side, then entered, pausing for a second to let her eyes adjust to the darkness.

"Father?"

There was no answer, and the building felt empty. Emily blinked once, twice, then a third time. When she opened her eyes again, she stared in horror, praying that her mind was playing tricks on her, knowing that it wasn't.

"No, Father! No!"

Emily stood motionless, paralyzed by shock while she struggled to make sense of what she was seeing. The noose. The overturned crate. Those lifeless eyes. It couldn't be true. It couldn't. She shuddered as horror warred with disbelief. Father would never, ever have taken his own life. He'd told them that while life might sometimes be painful, it was a precious gift. He would never, ever have thrown that gift away.

Oh, Father, how could you? The last time Emily had seen him, he was smiling. Now . . .

"What happened?"

Emily swiveled, not wanting her sister to witness the horrible sight, but she was too late. Louisa stood in the doorway, her face a mask of grief and disbelief as she screamed. "Take him down! We have to take him down! No one can know what he did!"

Desperate to comfort her, Emily placed her hand on her sister's shoulder and gave it a little squeeze. When they were children, that had calmed Louisa. Emily could only pray the gesture would be as effective today. "You know we can't do that. The sheriff needs to see what happened."

"But he can't!" Louisa's voice cracked. "If anyone knows, they won't let us bury Father next to Mama. You know what happened when Chauncey Clinton shot himself. Father said he couldn't be buried in consecrated ground."

Emily closed her eyes, trying to forget the

anguish on Chauncey Senior's face when Father had told him his son's grave would have to be outside the cemetery fence.

"I wish it were otherwise," she told her sister, "but you know Father wouldn't want us to lie. It would be lying to hide the evidence." She forced herself to look at the man she'd loved so dearly, trying to understand what had driven him to such an unspeakable act. "Besides, there will be rope burns. Doc will see them."

"And then everyone will know." Louisa shuddered, her face contorted with anguish. "How could he do it? How could he leave me alone?"

Emily's heart ached at the evidence of Louisa's grief and wished there were something she could do to comfort her. "You're not alone. I'm here."

But Louisa refused to be comforted. As tears rolled down her cheeks, she stared at the man they'd both loved. "You're wrong, Emily. He did leave me alone. He didn't know you were coming, but he did this anyway. It was his choice." Though her voice was muffled by the tears, there was no mistaking her anger. "Don't you see? Father didn't love me enough to stay with me. Maybe he didn't love me at all."

"Of course he loved you."

Louisa shook her head. "No, he didn't, and nothing you can say will convince me otherwise. He wouldn't have done that if he loved me."

Knowing Louisa's cries were those of a woman trying to grapple with almost unthinkable tragedy and that nothing she could say would help, Emily remained silent, letting her sister sob and rail at their father's final decision. Although it seemed like an eternity had passed, it was perhaps only five minutes later when Louisa said, "Someone needs to notify the doctor and the sheriff." She turned her tearstained face toward Emily. "Will you do that? I can't."

Feeling that she'd been transported back to their childhood when unpleasant tasks had always fallen to her as the eldest, Emily nodded slowly. "Of course."

Half an hour later, the two men she'd summoned stood in the barn, their faces solemn. They were both the same height, a couple inches less than six feet, but that was the only physical characteristic they had in common. The sheriff's hair was darker brown and had yet to develop the gray that colored the doctor's, perhaps because he was in his early forties, while Doc Sheridan was over fifty. And while the doctor was thin, the sheriff had begun to develop a paunch.

Sheriff Granger spoke first, his brown eyes reflecting his shock. "If I hadn't seen it with my own eyes, I wouldn't have believed it, but the evidence seems straightforward." He turned to his companion. "Get him down, Doc. The girls don't need to look at this any longer."

At Emily's side, Louisa sobbed while the doctor stood on the crate to lower their father to the ground. Doc Sheridan's normally ruddy face was paler than Emily had ever seen it. "There's no question about it. I wish it weren't so, but the cause of death is obvious. Your father died by strangulation."

"His neck's not broken?" The sheriff seemed surprised. "Let me see the rope." He mounted the crate and shook his head as he inspected the noose, then untied it and removed it from the beam. "He used a figure-eight on a bight to make a noose. I would have expected a hangman's knot."

"The result is the same." Doc ran a hand over his face in an apparent attempt to calm himself. "When I saw Joseph last night, he seemed in pain, but I didn't realize it was so severe. If he'd come to me, I could have helped him."

The sheriff nodded as he addressed Louisa. "I know Emily didn't arrive until later, so she can't help me, but did your father say or do anything unusual today?"

Brushing the tears from her cheeks, Louisa said, "He complained that his leg hurt, but that's not unusual. We all know he's had almost constant pain ever since the war."

"When did you see him last?" The sheriff continued his questioning, his manner more formal than Emily had ever seen.

"We had lunch together. He was quiet, and I thought he might be troubled about something, but he wouldn't tell me what it was."

The sheriff nodded as if he'd expected that. "Did anyone come to see him today?"

Louisa shrugged. "He must have had visitors, because the chairs in his office weren't in their normal position, but I didn't see anyone. Saturday mornings are my time to clean the upstairs. I don't look outside while I'm doing that. As I told you, he was quiet at lunch." Her lips trembled as she added, "That was the last time I saw him. I don't think anyone came after that, but I can't be sure."

"Anything else?" Though the sheriff seemed content with Louisa's answer, he continued to question her.

"It's no secret that Father hasn't been

himself since Mama died."

"I saw that too." Tears welled in the doctor's gray eyes, reminding Emily that he'd been one of her father's closest friends and that he would grieve his death. "I wish things hadn't gotten so bad." Doc picked up the rope the sheriff had discarded and wrapped it around his hand before dropping it back onto the ground. "Oh, Joseph, if only there'd been another way."

As Emily stared at the rope, a memory resurfaced, and a shiver made its way down her spine. "Father didn't kill himself."

The sheriff patted her arm, much as he might have an overwrought child's. "I know you don't want to believe it, but what happened is very clear. Either your father didn't want to live without your mother or the pain from his war wounds was unbearable. In either case, he chose to end his life."

"No, he didn't." Emily picked up the rope. "You said the knot was a figure-eight."

Both the sheriff's and the doctor's expressions left no doubt they thought she was on the verge of hysteria. She wasn't.

"You don't understand. No matter how hard he tried, Father could never master that knot. Don't you see? Someone killed him."

CHAPTER THREE

The town was charming, except for the lingering smell of smoke. Even with the lengthening shadows, it was easy to see that Main Street was lined with stores interspersed with what appeared to be offices. The church on the corner directly across from the school where he'd be spending his days dominated the block, and the school itself was appealing. Everything was as Mrs. Carmichael had described it except that the church's white steeple was now sooty and the air reeked.

"Phew! Tink."

Craig smiled at his son's attempt to say *stink*. Though his speech was improving, with new words being added on an almost daily basis, Noah was still unable to pronounce *s*'s. Craig had given up trying to teach him to say "Mrs. Carmichael" and hoped the widow wouldn't be offended when she was called "Mcar."

After they'd had their supper, Noah had been quieter than normal, perhaps the result of fatigue, perhaps anxiety because Craig had told them they'd reach their destination before the sun set. Now he rubbed his eyes and wrinkled his nose at the unpleasant odor.

"Tink," he repeated, touching Craig's arm to ensure he had his father's full attention.

"I know, son, but the wind will blow it away." The smell would dissipate at some point. What worried Craig was whether the house that was supposed to be his and Noah's home might have been damaged. As he turned the wagon onto Center Street, his spirits plummeted. The lot next to the church no longer contained the house Mrs. Carmichael had described as "small but more than sufficient for the three of us." Instead, there were only charred beams and two women staring at the ruins, one white-haired and only an inch or two over five feet, the other with gunmetal gray hair.

"Good evening, ladies." Craig stopped the wagon and doffed his hat in greeting. "I wonder if one of you could direct me to Mrs. Carmichael. I'm Craig Ferguson. She wasn't expecting us yet, but the trip took less time than I'd thought."

The gray-haired woman stepped forward.

43

"I'm Mary Carmichael, and this is my next-door neighbor — my former next-door neighbor, that is — Mrs. Adams. We were just talking about when Emily and Louisa would have Finley House ready for us." She gestured toward the burned-out site. "As you can see, my house is no more."

Craig climbed out of the wagon, marveling at how calm his future landlady seemed. The fire must have been very recent, but the fact that she could display such composure under extraordinarily difficult circumstances confirmed his belief that she was the right woman to care for Noah. It appeared she'd even arranged temporary housing.

"You needn't worry about Noah and me right now when you have so many other things to do." The poor woman had lost not only her home but all her belongings. "We've grown accustomed to sleeping in our wagon."

Noah, who'd moved to the edge of the bench and was listening intently, pointed to the sky. "Tar."

Before he could explain that Noah was speaking of sleeping under the stars, the widow nodded. "Why, of course, you saw stars when you were in the wagon, but a bed would be more comfortable, wouldn't it?"

Noah nodded.

Mrs. Carmichael turned back to Craig. "It seems your son would like a bed. You needn't worry about being early. People from Pastor Vaughn's former church come to visit occasionally, so the Vaughns are used to having guests. Finley House has more than enough room for all of us."

"That's for certain," her companion said. "There are ten bedchambers, and that's not counting the attic. I've heard there are six more there." The white-haired woman shook her head in apparent dismay at the size of the home. "I never did understand why Clive Finley wanted such a large house or so much land. You could have built four or five houses there, but I heard tell he wanted to keep the prettiest section of the creek for himself and his wife. That sweetheart of his must have been an extra-special woman." The woman who obviously enjoyed the sound of her own voice clucked her tongue. "It's a shame what happened to him."

"Now, Clara," Mrs. Carmichael chided her friend, "Mr. Ferguson doesn't need to hear old stories. He and his son need somewhere to sleep tonight." She turned to

Craig. "If you follow me, I'll introduce you to Pastor Vaughn and the girls."

"Emily's not a Vaughn any longer." Clara Adams appeared to have made it her mission to ensure that Craig was fully informed about his future residence and its occupants. "She's a Leland now. I don't know why that husband of hers didn't come with her. It was only right, seeing as how her mother just died."

The comfort Craig had felt about coming to Sweetwater Crossing began to dissipate. How could he bring Noah into a home where the family was grieving? His son was sensitive to others' emotions. Would the Vaughns' sorrow trigger a recurrence of his nightmares? Craig wished there were an alternative, but it appeared there were none. He and Noah couldn't continue living in the wagon indefinitely. He'd have to trust Mrs. Carmichael when she said Finley House was the right place for them.

"I imagine ranching kept George Leland busy," Mrs. Carmichael told her friend, "but it's none of our business why he didn't accompany Emily." She paused, then nodded, having made a decision. "Thank you for offering me a bed, but I think it best if I stay at Finley House tonight. I can help the girls get the rooms ready, and Mr. Ferguson might need help with Noah."

"Are you certain we won't be imposing on them?" Craig had to be certain his arrival wouldn't create any problems. In a town the size of Sweetwater Crossing, first impressions were even more important than they were in a large city.

It was Clara Adams who responded. "The Vaughns will welcome you."

"But we'd best get there before the sun sets," her companion added.

"I hope you'll ride with us," Craig told Mrs. Carmichael when she started to walk away.

"It's only a block. I've walked farther than that many times."

But not on the day her house was destroyed. Though the widow might not be aware of it, he'd noticed that her gait seemed less than steady. "Please. I'd feel better."

"Oh, all right."

Craig helped her into the wagon, then took his seat on the bench with Noah between them. "Noah, this is Mrs. Carmichael. Remember, I told you about her."

His son grinned. "Ni lady."

Mrs. Carmichael seemed to understand that she'd been called a nice lady because she smiled at Noah. "I can see we're going to get along just fine." When they reached the corner, she directed Craig to turn right, then remained silent until they approached a house that had to be Finley House. "There it is."

The number of bedrooms had told Craig it would be large, but he was still surprised by the size and magnificence of what would be his temporary home.

Though the other houses he'd seen had been set close to the street, this one had been built far back, giving it an extensive front yard, a yard that was surrounded by a stone wall. Two pillars topped by stone balls marked the end of the wall and flanked the curved drive that led to the house itself. And what a house it was!

The symmetry of the design and the elegance of the four columns supporting the second story verandah impressed Craig, but what riveted his attention was the way guests approached the front porch.

While many of the houses he'd seen had only one story, this one boasted two and an attic, all placed on a raised foundation whose purpose seemed to have been to require an elaborate staircase rather than two or three steps to reach the front door. Instead of a single, utilitarian set of steps leading directly to the entrance, Finley

House had two staircases, one on either side of the porch, each with eight steps leading from the drive. Those staircases ended on twin landings, turned ninety degrees, and were followed by five more steps to meet at the center of the front porch. The stairway was beautiful, probably unnecessary, and unlike anything Craig had seen on his journey.

"Big."

"Yes, it is." Mrs. Carmichael smiled at Noah, then turned to Craig. "You can see there's plenty of room, and I'm sure you'll like the Vaughns. Joseph is our minister. A nicer man you'll never meet. It's a shame you never met Mrs. Vaughn because she was just as welcoming as her husband." The widow appeared to be taking over her friend's role as town crier, making certain Craig knew his host family's history. "The two of them raised their daughters the right way," she continued. "As soon as she saw what had happened to my house, even though it was her first day back in town, Emily insisted we all stay here."

Her litany of praise helped relax Craig, making him more confident that he and Noah would be welcome, despite the family's mourning. He helped Mrs. Carmichael out of the wagon, then walked up the right-hand staircase with her, while Noah insisted on climbing the other, beaming with pride as he reached the top. When Craig knocked on the door, Noah formed a fist and pounded on it a second time, his grin growing at the new evidence of his maturity.

Craig smiled. The smile faded when the door opened, revealing one of the Vaughn daughters. His first impression was that she was as different from Rachel as any woman he'd met. This woman was a blue-eyed blond, whereas Rachel had been a brunette with chocolate-brown eyes. This woman was four or five inches shorter than his wife, slender in contrast to Rachel's more sturdy build. The biggest difference was in their expressions. While Rachel had almost always worn a smile, though this woman attempted to smile, grief and something that looked like fear etched her face. Sorrow was only natural, but fear? Surely he was mistaken. But as Craig lowered his gaze, he saw that her hands were fisted to control their trembling.

Mrs. Carmichael was wrong. They should not have come. He and Noah were intruders, not welcome guests.

The widow took a step forward. "I'm sorry for the surprise, Emily. I know you didn't expect us tonight, but Mr. Ferguson and his son arrived sooner than I'd thought. They have nowhere else to stay."

Before Emily could respond, a second woman strode across the massive foyer and stood at her side. Though she was taller than Emily and had brown hair rather than blond, the resemblance was unmistakable. This must be the other sister, Louisa.

The brunette glared at Craig. "You couldn't have picked a worse day to come. Our father died this afternoon."

CHAPTER FOUR

Before anyone could react to Louisa's blunt statement, the boy whose dark hair and chiseled nose made him a miniature version of his father wrapped his arms around his father's leg and began to wail.

Though she had no idea what was causing his distress, the cracks in Emily's heart that had been formed when she received the news of Mama's death widened at the sight of the child who, like her, had lost his mother. Just as she had no memory of her first father, Noah probably had none of his mother. But, unlike Emily, who'd grown up surrounded by her adopted father's love and her mother's, he had only one parent.

"It'll be all right, Noah." Mr. Ferguson stroked his son's head. "Everything will be all right."

Though his voice was calm, designed to soothe an overwrought child, Emily saw the anguish in Mr. Ferguson's eyes and knew that he was suffering even more than his son, for he'd lost his wife and now faced the daunting task of raising their child alone.

She took a deep breath, trying to slow her racing heart as she told herself that no matter what fears she harbored, she could not turn Mr. Ferguson away. He and the boy needed a home.

"You're all welcome to stay here as long as you need," Emily said firmly, and as she did, a sense of rightness settled over her.

Louisa glared at her, her anger once again apparent. "You're making a mistake," she said as she stalked toward the staircase.

It might be a mistake, but Emily doubted it. She studied the man she'd invited to share her home. Taller but not as handsome as George, he had dark brown hair and eyes, while George had been a blue-eyed blond like her. "We'll have pretty blond babies," he'd told her, punctuating his statement with one of the smiles that had captured her heart. *No!* She wouldn't think about George. He was her past. This man would be part of her present. As for the future, only God knew what that would bring.

Mr. Ferguson didn't look dangerous, and the child gripping his leg certainly wasn't. Noah was a boy who'd been uprooted from what was probably the only home he remembered. Then there was Mrs. Carmichael, the woman who'd always been kind to Emily, the woman who had lost her home, probably permanently. They all needed Emily.

George may have considered her a failure — and she had failed at the thing he wanted most — but Emily knew she had succeeded in turning his house into a home. She could and she would give these people what they needed: a home.

"Please excuse my sister. Let's sit down for a moment." Emily gestured toward the parlor. When they'd taken seats, Noah perched on his father's lap, she continued. "Louisa's right. Today has been a difficult day for us, but it hasn't been easy for you, either. You need a place to stay. Fortunately, we have plenty of room for you here. All of the bedchambers have been aired, so you can have your choice."

Emily had been surprised when she'd gone to what had once been her room and discovered that nothing had changed. Even the tattered quilt that she had loved simply because it had been made by her paternal grandmother was still on the bed, though she'd thought Mama would relegate it to the rag bag as soon as Emily left. She hadn't expected it, but the house seemed to have been waiting for her.

She nodded at Noah as she addressed his father. "Your son can have his own room if you'd prefer. I can also set up a table in your room so you can work there." Emily remembered Miss Albright carrying papers home from school each day. Though Finley House's library was the logical place for the new schoolteacher to work, Emily wasn't ready to offer what had been Father's domain to anyone.

"That's very kind of you, Mrs. Leland, but Noah can stay with me." Though Mr. Ferguson did not raise his voice, it carried clearly, probably the result of making himself heard above the chatter of unruly pupils. It wasn't his voice, though, that caught Emily's attention but the way he'd addressed her. Mrs. Carmichael must have told him she was married.

"Please call me Emily." That was easier than being reminded of her mistakes. For, without a doubt, marrying George was a mistake.

"I'm Craig and, as you know, this is Noah." Craig Ferguson put his hand on his son's head and ruffled his hair. The boy was once more calm, his earlier outburst seemingly forgotten. "He'll never admit it, but he's tired, so I'd appreciate it if you'd show

55

us to whatever room you think is best for us."

"Certainly. Would you like to see yours too, Mrs. Carmichael?"

When they reached the top of the stairs, Emily turned right and opened the door to the first room facing the backyard. "I thought you might like this, Mrs. Carmichael. It's the largest one on this side of the house." Father had said it was the room Clive Finley had intended to share with his bride and, rather than appropriating it for himself and Mama, had reserved it for honored guests.

The widow took one look at the sumptuously furnished room and sighed softly. "It's beautiful. Thank you."

"I can't offer you the largest room on the front," Emily told the schoolteacher. He didn't need to know that it had been her parents' room and still held their possessions. She opened another door. "This one also has a door leading to the verandah. You'll find that helps keep the room cool."

"No!" Craig practically shouted the word, the vehemence of his reply making Emily cringe and take a step backward. Perhaps she'd been wrong in offering him a home; perhaps he was more dangerous than she'd realized, for his reaction reminded her of

George. But as she stared at him, though she couldn't identify the emotion she saw flitting across Craig's face, she realized it wasn't anger.

"Do you have one without access to the verandah?" His voice was once more pitched normally, and the fear that had caused her heart to pound subsided.

"Yes, of course. Both end rooms on the front side have only normal windows."

"We'll take one of them. It doesn't matter which."

Emily led the way to the room farthest from hers and opened its door. Although it was the same size as the one Craig had rejected, she'd always thought it felt smaller, perhaps because it lacked the additional light that the French doors provided.

The schoolteacher appeared to find no flaws. "This will be perfect." He touched his son's back, urging him into the room. "Look, Noah. A real bed."

His previous distress seeming to have evaporated, the boy giggled and ran to the bed, pounding the mattress to test its softness. "Good," he declared.

His father smiled at his son's exuberance. "Thank you again, Mrs. . . . . Emily."

Craig walked into the room, then turned, waiting for her to follow him. She wouldn't.

The room wasn't small, but if there was one thing she had learned during her marriage, it was to avoid being in a place with only one exit when she was with a man. Instead, she said briskly, "Breakfast will be served at 8:00. Church begins at 9:00." Emily had no idea who would lead the service, but she knew one thing: she and Louisa needed to be there.

Her guest nodded. "Again, thank you for opening your home to us at such a difficult time. If there's any way I can help you, you need only ask."

"There's nothing anyone can do."

Skittish. Craig wasn't sure why, but Emily Leland seemed skittish around him. If he hadn't known better, he would have said she was afraid of him, but that made no sense. She had no reason to fear him. Admittedly, he'd been a bit vehement in his refusal to have a room with access to the verandah, but her wariness had begun before then.

A frown crossed his face as he doused the lamp. Perhaps she was simply devastated by her father's death. That was to be expected. Craig had only vague memories of the first days after Rachel died. Somehow, he'd gone through the motions of living, but it was a poor imitation. He'd been numb and over-whelmed by the realization that he would have to raise Noah without Rachel.

Craig looked at the boy he loved so dearly curled up on the bed, fast asleep and likely to remain there until morning unless he had another nightmare. Noah had been ex-hausted and ready for bed. Craig was not. After Noah had fallen asleep, he'd unloaded the wagon, left Hercules contentedly chew-ing hay in the barn alongside the Vaughns' two horses, and stashed his and Noah's belongings in the room that would be theirs for some time.

There was nothing more to do, but Craig wasn't ready to retire for the evening. With a quick nod, he grabbed his hat. Daylight would have been better for exploring his new home, but the half-moon would provide enough light for him to walk around the town and get his bearings. And perhaps by the time he returned, he'd be relaxed enough to sleep.

As he descended the stairs, he heard voices coming through the partially closed parlor door. Though he knew the perils of eavesdropping, Craig could not stop himself from pausing and listening.

"I hope you'll let me help prepare your father for burial." Widow Carmichael's voice radiated concern as well as the willingness to assist the sisters in an undeniably difficult process. Even though two ladies from the church had chosen the clothing and dressed Rachel's body, Craig had been the one who folded the handkerchief she'd carried on their wedding day between her fingers, his heart breaking at the finality of the act.

"Thank you, but there's no need," Emily said firmly. Craig suspected that she was the older sister by the way she assumed the leadership role. She might be shorter than her sister, shorter than most women, but when she spoke, it was with authority. That made her skittish reaction to him all the more perplexing.

Craig took another step as Emily continued her explanation. "Doc Sheridan took Father. He claimed it wasn't fitting for Louisa and me to do that."

If Louisa was in the room, she made no reply. Instead, it was the widow who spoke. "I don't always agree with Roger Sheridan, but this time he's right. Have you and Louisa decided who'll perform the funeral?"

"There won't be a funeral." Louisa joined the conversation, her voice harsh with anger. Though it might be wrong to judge based on such a brief acquaintance, Craig wondered if anger was Louisa's primary emotion or if it was only the day's events that had made her so prickly. She was certainly different from her sister, for if he'd had to characterize Emily in one word, it would have been *compassionate.*

"What do you mean, no funeral?" The widow's confusion mirrored Craig's.

"Our father killed himself. That means he can't be buried in consecrated ground." Once again, it was Louisa who spoke.

Craig gripped the railing, trying to make sense of her statement. Even in the depths of his grief after Rachel's death, Craig hadn't considered ending his own life. Noah needed him, and while Joseph Vaughn's daughters were grown, surely he had realized they still needed him.

"I find that hard to believe," Mrs. Carmichael said. So did Craig.

"I don't believe it." Emily was quick to answer the widow. "I don't care what the doctor and the sheriff said. I know my father wouldn't have killed himself." Her voice, which had been firm when she'd declared her father's innocence, trembled as she added, "No one will listen to me."

"That's because we've accepted the truth." Louisa made no effort to soften her words. "I don't understand why you keep denying what happened. We both saw him with the rope around his neck."

The image burned into Craig's brain. No wonder Emily was so skittish and Louisa so angry. As horrible as Rachel's death was, Craig had had the consolation of knowing it had been an accident — a terrible, possibly avoidable accident, but an accident nonetheless. The sisters had no such comfort.

"But he didn't tie that rope." Emily's voice left no doubt of her conviction. "He couldn't have."

Craig's assumption that the scoff he heard must have come from the sister was confirmed when Louisa said, "Stop deluding yourself, Emily. You've been gone so long that you don't know what Father could have done."

"You poor dears." The widow was clearly trying to mediate. "There'll be talk, of course, but it'll die down. I'll do what I can to stop it, especially for your sake, Louisa." She paused for a second, the rustling of her skirts making Craig suspect she'd risen to be closer to the younger sister. "Emily has her husband, but you're alone."

"She's not the only one who's alone, Mrs. Carmichael." Emily's voice was once more firm and clear. "So am I. George is dead."

Craig closed his eyes as the magnitude of

Emily's situation washed over him. She was a widow — a recent one, he surmised, since Mrs. Carmichael hadn't been aware of her husband's death — who'd lost both parents and was now living with an angry sister. How horrible for Emily!

Craig clenched his fists at the realization that the situation wasn't good for him, either. He'd come to Sweetwater Crossing expecting a peaceful town where he could put sorrow behind him, and Noah could heal. Instead, he had been thrust into a greater tragedy than the one he'd endured.

Why, dear Lord? Why?

"That was awkward." Louisa gripped Emily's arm as they descended the church steps, their black skirts brushing the ground. "I don't know why I let you convince me to come."

"Mama and Father would have wanted us to be here." Her determination to come to church had wavered during the mostly sleepless night when images of the day's events had continued to flash through her brain, but as she'd dressed this morning, Emily was filled with renewed resolution. No matter what had happened to her family, Sunday was still a day to worship her Lord and Creator.

"It'll get better," she told Louisa. Today was the first time since the war ended that the pulpit had been occupied by someone other than Father. Though the mayor had done his best to lead the congregation through hymns and prayers, he'd made no attempt to preach a sermon, replacing it with five minutes of silent prayer.

"How will it get better? What do you think will change?" Louisa lowered her voice and led the way to the large oak tree that had survived yesterday's fire. Emily had expected her to want to go home immediately, but she appeared to be clinging to their tradition of meeting friends under the old oak.

So far, no friends had approached them. Many of the congregation had clustered around Craig and his son to welcome them to Sweetwater Crossing, but Emily and Louisa remained alone. Even Phoebe Sheridan, the doctor's daughter and Louisa's closest friend, had avoided them, though her gaze had darted toward the oak tree as she'd headed home with her parents.

"Didn't you see the way everyone was looking at us?" Louisa demanded. "Didn't you hear what they were saying? Everyone knows what Father did, and they pity us. Even Phoebe! I hate being pitied."

So did Emily, which was one of the reasons she'd resolved that no one would know the truth of her marriage. "We need to give people time to adjust. Father's death was a shock for everyone, but it'll get better." That wasn't what her sister wanted to hear, but it was the only comfort Emily could offer.

Louisa pursed her lips. "It's easy for you to say that. You can go back to your ranch. I'm stuck here, listening to gossip. I can't do it, Emily. I *won't* do it. Somehow, I'll find a way to leave this horrible town. And don't you try to stop me."

Emily sighed as her sister stormed away. Determined to give Louisa some time to calm down, Emily looked around the churchyard, searching for a friendly face. Most of the congregation had left, but Gertrude Albright — Gertrude Neville now — had cornered Craig, probably to give him some advice. Father had claimed Gertrude was a born teacher and had predicted she'd remain in the classroom until the Lord called her home, but he'd been wrong. According to Louisa, Gertrude had married Thomas Neville, the man whose ranch adjoined her parents'. Because the Albrights' house was larger than Thomas's, they were living on Gertrude's family's ranch, while her newly retired parents stayed in their town house.

Even from a distance, Emily could see that something — perhaps marriage — had changed Gertrude. She no longer wore her light brown hair in a severe bun; instead, soft curls framed her face, making her appear younger than when she'd presided over the schoolroom. Nothing could change her stature. She was still only a couple inches taller than Emily, but now her shoulders appeared less rigid, perhaps because she was no longer trying to control unruly pupils.

Emily started toward Gertrude as much because she wanted to spare Craig a long dissertation as to renew her acquaintance with her former teacher, but before she'd taken three steps, a young woman carrying a baby approached her.

"Alice! Alice Newberry!" Emily smiled as she recognized the almost painfully thin redhead who'd been her lifelong friend. When she'd hugged Emily after her wedding, Alice had whispered that she hoped to be the town's next bride. It appeared her wish had come true.

Emily's friend grinned. "It's Alice Patton now. Cyrus and I were married a month after you." Alice shifted the baby in her arms so that Emily could see her. "This is Jane."

"She's adorable." The bright red fuzz that covered her head told Emily Jane had inherited her mother's hair color, and there was no doubt which parent had given her those freckles. Though Jane's eyes were closed, Emily guessed they were the same shade of green as Alice's.

Emily tried to tamp down the spark of envy that seeing Jane had ignited and looked for Alice's husband. "Where's Cyrus? I want to congratulate him." Cyrus had always been a quiet boy, and though Emily had long suspected he was attracted to Alice, as far as she knew, he'd never mustered the courage to say more than two words to her. Apparently, that had changed.

The smile that had wreathed Alice's face disappeared. "Cyrus is gone. He died two months after our wedding. Just keeled over in the fields. Doc said it was his heart."

The jealousy that had stabbed Emily vanished, replaced by sorrow over the magnitude of the pain Alice had endured. First, her parents died of the influenza that had swept the county early last year, leaving Alice alone, and then she'd lost Cyrus too.

Emily wanted to hug her friend but was afraid of crushing the baby, and so she contented herself with saying, "Oh, Alice."

Alice's eyes glistened with unshed tears.

"It was hard, but fortunately Jane was on the way." She bent her head to press a kiss on her daughter's nose, then looked up at Emily. "She's been a blessing, but what about you? How are you and Louisa holding up, and where's George?"

It seemed the rumor mill had been so busy spreading the story of Father's death that they'd missed the other Vaughn family announcement.

"He died last week." No one needed to know more than that.

"How awful for you, losing both of your parents and George too." Alice was silent for a moment, perhaps at the realization of how similar their situations were. Then she gave Emily's midsection a speculative look. "Any hope of a little one?"

Emily shook her head. "No."

"I'm so sorry . . . about everything." Alice tightened her grip on her daughter, clearly fearful of losing her. "I know what you're going through, and it's not easy, but I'm glad you're back. We widows need to stick together."

CHAPTER FIVE

"Tink." Noah wrinkled his nose as they passed the charred remains of Mrs. Carmichael's house. Even though they were on the opposite side of the street and upwind from the ruins, the odor was still noticeable.

"Yes, Noah, it does stink, but it'll get better." The smell of smoke and burnt wood was less pronounced than it had been after church yesterday. It was so strong then that Craig was surprised by how many members of the congregation lingered to introduce themselves and welcome him and Noah to Sweetwater Crossing.

Everyone was friendly, although the former schoolteacher's conversation consisted of carefully worded explanations of what parents expected rather than a simple welcome. Craig wasn't surprised by that because he knew Mrs. Neville was trying to prepare him for his first day in the classroom just as he'd given advice to the woman who was replacing him in Galveston.

What did surprise him was the way the parishioners avoided the Vaughn sisters. It wasn't a true shunning — more like fearful citizens keeping their distance from those suspected of carrying the plague. But suicide was not contagious, and anyone with an ounce of empathy should have realized that Emily and Louisa needed comfort. He, however, was not the one to provide that. The sisters had made that clear, although in very different ways.

Noah tugged on Craig's hand, then pointed to the stone foundation of the widow's former home. "Fire?" he asked.

"Yes, it was a fire. But don't worry, it's not burning any longer." Remembering how Noah had worried when he'd seen a house in Galveston burn, Craig wanted to reassure him that their temporary home wasn't in any danger. His son nodded, and the way he loosened his grip on Craig's hand told him the boy had accepted the comfort he offered. If only he could have given the Vaughn sisters a similar measure of comfort.

Louisa's anger at having to share her home with him and Noah had not abated, and she'd all but ignored them at meals, which were the only times he saw her. Emily was different. She was unfailingly polite to him and did everything she could to make Noah's first days in a strange place happy ones. Had it not been for the way she flinched when he'd inadvertently brushed against her, Craig would have said that she welcomed his presence as much as she did Noah's and Mrs. Carmichael's. But there was no ignoring her wariness. If he'd had an alternative, Craig would have left Finley House.

Fortunately, Noah seemed oblivious to the tension that filled the air there. He'd slept well both nights since they arrived and had wakened cheerful and full of energy. He hadn't even protested when Craig had left him alone with Mrs. Carmichael for half an hour yesterday afternoon, hoping he'd gradually become so comfortable with her that he wouldn't insist on accompanying Craig to school each day. Though he'd accepted that, Noah's unbridled excitement when Craig suggested they take a walk this morning told him his son still needed to be close to him.

"I think you'll like what I'm going to show you next," he told his son, hoping he wasn't making a mistake by taking him to the schoolhouse.

Mrs. Carmichael had offered to care for

Noah as soon as the funeral — if you could call it that — was over, but Craig hadn't wanted to wait that long to go inside. The school was locked when he'd walked past it on Saturday evening, and although the mayor had given him the key after church yesterday, he'd cautioned him that the town frowned on anything that had the appearance of work on Sunday. Entering the schoolhouse, it seemed, would constitute work, and so Craig had tamped down his curiosity. Soon it would be satisfied, but first, there was one more thing to do.

"Wing! Me wing!"

Craig grinned at his son's excitement over the presence of two swings in the schoolyard. This was one of the reasons he'd wanted to bring Noah with him, to give the boy a chance to enjoy a simple pleasure. Because, no matter what else happened, he was determined that somehow, someway his son would have a happy life in Sweetwater Crossing.

As he'd expected, Noah's interest in swinging waned after a few minutes, and he was content to accompany Craig into the schoolhouse. It was larger than the one where he'd taught before, but the interior design was similar: a small cloakroom with hooks for coats and shelves for lunch pails close to the outside door, then a second door leading to the classroom. The large teacher's desk stood at the far end in front of the chalkboard and the president's and governor's portraits.

As he'd expected, a tall stool occupied one corner. He'd have to find a place to store that, perhaps under the schoolhouse, because if there was one thing Craig knew, it was that a dunce stool had no place in his classroom.

Ignoring the offending piece of furniture, he studied the room. Three rows of desks filled the remaining space: doubles on the two sides, smaller ones designed for only one pupil in the middle. When he realized there was barely enough room for him to walk between the rows of desks, Craig frowned. It appeared Sweetwater Crossing was on the verge of outgrowing its schoolhouse, and while growth was good for the town itself, crowding was not good for his pupils. It would add to the challenge of trying to keep them engaged. If Rachel were here, she'd say that was good for him because challenges kept people from stagnating.

Noah had no problem with the cramped quarters. He ran down one aisle and up the other, then amused himself by sitting in different desks. Predictably, his attention soon wavered, and he tugged on Craig's hand, urging him to leave. Craig had seen all that he needed to at the school. They could explore the town, beginning with the building next door.

When he'd strolled the streets Saturday evening, he thought it nothing more than a private residence until he saw the sign on the front: Sweetwater Crossing Library. That had been one of the most encouraging parts of the day. A town that valued books enough to have a library would surely be a good home for him and Noah.

"Come on, son. Let's go inside." Craig's impression that this was a converted home was confirmed when he opened the door and discovered that the library appeared to consist of one room, probably the former parlor. Floor-to-ceiling shelves were filled with books, giving the room the unmistakable scent of paper and ink, while an official-looking desk sat in the middle of the room.

"Welcome to Sweetwater Crossing's library, Mr. Ferguson. I'm Alice Patton." The redheaded woman who'd spoken with Emily after church yesterday rose from her chair. "Are you looking for books for yourself or your son?" She gave Noah a warm smile, but Noah had no interest in another

74

grown-up. He'd spotted an open crate behind the desk and scampered toward it.

"Baby!"

Alice Patton nodded. "Yes, young man. It's a baby girl. Her name is Jane."

Noah stared at the infant, obviously fascinated as Jane batted her hand against her cheeks and chuckled. "Me want," he declared as he bent to touch her.

Craig reached for Noah, intending to stop him, but when Alice shook her head, he contented himself with saying, "Be gentle, Noah."

"She's sturdier than you might think," the librarian assured Craig, "but you didn't come here to discuss my daughter. How can I help you?"

"I wondered what your lending policy is and what books might interest my pupils."

As Alice explained, Craig kept an eye on Noah, who was clearly entranced by the baby. Little Jane held his son's attention longer than anyone or anything he could recall, making him wonder if he'd been wrong in dismissing the advice he'd been given about remarrying. The women who'd told him he owed it to Noah, some going so far as to suggest potential wives for Craig, had meant well. He knew that, just as he knew no one could replace Rachel. She was the woman he'd loved with all his heart, the only woman he could imagine loving.

Emily looked at the two women who shared the parlor with her. Though she had placed cups of tea and a platter of small cakes in front of Louisa and Mrs. Carmichael, neither had taken more than a sip, and that sip was probably out of politeness rather than any desire for refreshments. She couldn't blame them. She wasn't hungry or thirsty, and she dreaded the conversation she was about to initiate.

Emily inhaled deeply, trying to erase the memory of being forced to lay Father to rest outside the cemetery instead of in the plot next to Mama, with only six people in attendance. After Phoebe Sheridan had spent half an hour with Louisa yesterday afternoon, leaving Louisa in a better mood, Emily expected the doctor's daughter to accompany her father, but Doc Sheridan came alone. Fortunately, Mrs. Carmichael insisted on accompanying Emily and Louisa and held their hands while the mayor read the funeral service and the doctor gave a brief eulogy for his friend. The sheriff said nothing.

If this were a normal funeral, there would have been a church overflowing with mourners, and Finley House would now be filled with people sharing stories of Father, doing their best to console Emily and Louisa. But this had not been a normal funeral. There was nothing normal about what had happened or what Emily had to tell her sister and the widow.

She picked up one of the cakes and took a bite, trying to encourage the others, then focused her attention on Mrs. Carmichael.

"I know I promised you a home for as long as you and the schoolmaster needed it, but I may not be able to keep that promise." Emily had been living minute to minute since she arrived back in Sweetwater Crossing, dealing with the seemingly unending series of crises as they occurred, and hadn't thought too far into the future. The reality of that future had come crashing in on her before she'd left her father's gravesite.

"The mayor reminded me that taxes are due soon and that the church will no longer pay Father's stipend." She should have realized at least the latter, but she hadn't, and if Louisa had thought of it, she had said nothing. Emily turned to her sister. "Unless something has changed since I left, I doubt we have enough money to continue living here." Finley House was the largest building in the town and had an equally large as-

Louisa flushed, then shook her head. "I don't know. Father never discussed money with me. He said that was his responsibility."

"But Mama was always very frugal. I remember her saying this house was expensive to maintain and that she had to be careful about what she spent. That's why we didn't have as many clothes as some of our classmates." Emily had hated that, as well as the effort required to alter clothing that parishioners' children had outgrown. Being short and thin had meant that everything needed substantial modifications.

For the first time today, a faint smile crossed Louisa's face. "I was lucky that Phoebe's almost the same size as me. She used to share her dresses with me." And while the Sheridans might not be wealthy, they indulged their only daughter. At least as far as clothing was concerned, Louisa had indeed been luckier than either of her older sisters.

Emily doubted she'd feel lucky much longer. "I'll see what I can find in Father's records, but I'm afraid we may have to sell the house."

Louisa's reaction was immediate. "You have no right to do that!" Her eyes narrowed as she glared at Emily. "You were gone for over a year. You have no idea what it was like for me once both you and Joanna left, but now that you're back, you're trying to take over. Just because you're the oldest doesn't mean you're in charge." The words came out in a torrent.

Though Mrs. Carmichael said nothing, she nodded slowly, perhaps recalling the decisions she had had to make when her husband died. Emily was thankful that someone understood the predicament she and Louisa faced.

"I was trying to help," she said. Just as she'd tried to help by agreeing that she would be the one to write the letter to Joanna, telling her what had happened. When she and Louisa had discussed their absent sister last night, Emily suggested they encourage Joanna to complete her studies. It was a once-in-a-lifetime opportunity that should not be squandered. At the time, Louisa agreed. Now it appeared she disagreed with everything Emily said.

"How can you help when you live in a fantasy world?" Louisa shot her a scornful look. "You won't even accept that Father killed himself."

"Because he didn't."

"There you go again. Face the facts, Emily. Father was in pain and couldn't bear it any longer, so he decided to end it all."

But he wouldn't have. Emily knew that as surely as she knew that what had happened on the bloody battlefield called Gettysburg had wounded more than Father's leg. She had no idea whether he'd spoken of those horrible July days to Louisa, but he'd told her that war seared a man's soul and that seeing the destruction it wrought made him cherish life all the more.

"If the pain was so bad, he would have gone to Doc," Emily insisted. "You know Doc kept a supply of morphine for him."

"He may not have had time." The widow spoke for the first time since Emily began her explanation. "Lorena Albright and I were sitting on her front porch, and it seemed your father had a constant stream of visitors that morning."

"He wouldn't have turned them away, no matter how he felt," Louisa said.

"You're right, Louisa. Father put his parishioners' needs above his own, but that doesn't help us pay the taxes."

Once again, Louisa glared. "If we need money, why don't you sell your ranch? George said it was a big and profitable one. That should tide us over for a few years."

Emily swallowed deeply as memories of

the first time she'd seen the ranch flooded her brain. It was a prosperous ranch with an attractive house just as George had promised, and she'd envisioned a long, happy life there. The possibility that it might become a prison had never entered her mind.

As much as Emily hated admitting the truth and what it revealed about her marriage, this was not the time to dissemble. "The ranch isn't mine to sell. George left it to a cousin."

"Oh!" Louisa was silent for a moment, clearly startled. "Didn't he leave you anything?"

Bruises, which were already fading, and memories that she hoped would also fade, but those were not things Emily would tell her sister. "Other than Blanche, no." The horse had been a gift from her parents and so had not been included in George's estate.

Emily turned to the widow. "I'm sorry to have involved you in this discussion, but I couldn't bear the thought of having it twice." And perhaps in the back of her mind, she'd hoped that Mrs. Carmichael's presence would mute Louisa's reaction. Unfortunately, it had not. The widow was now privy to the ever-widening rift between two of Joseph Vaughn's daughters.

Taking a moment to collect her thoughts, Mrs. Carmichael picked up her teacup and sipped. When she'd carefully placed the cup back on the saucer, she looked from Louisa to Emily. "There may be a way to save your house. I've been thinking about this ever since I learned of your father's death and realized that I'd need more than temporary housing. Since the town needs a new minister, when it rebuilds my former home, it'll become a parsonage again."

She took another sip of tea. "If you agree that we can stay here permanently, the money the town is paying me for Mr. Ferguson and his son's room and board should be yours. After all, you're the ones who are providing them a place to stay and food to eat."

Emily was pleased that Mrs. Carmichael had included Louisa in her statement, though her sister showed no signs of being mollified.

"Aren't they also paying you to care for Noah during the day?"

The widow gave Emily a brief nod but said, "I don't need to be paid for that. Harry and I weren't rich, but we weren't destitute, either. There's one more thing. You'll be giving me room and board too, so it's only fair that I pay you for that." She closed her eyes for a second, her lips moving in what appeared to be silent calculations, then opened them and said, "Here's what I can offer you."

When she named a sum that was exactly equal to Father's stipend, Emily knew it was no coincidence. Like most of the townspeople, Mrs. Carmichael would have known what the church paid him and, whether or not she could afford it, she was offering to match that. The widow was both kind and generous.

"I hope that will be enough."

"It should be. Like my mother, I'm frugal."

"You're doing it again, Emily." Louisa frowned in obvious frustration. "You're making all the decisions just because you're the oldest. You married your handsome rancher and deserted us for a year. Now you're back and planning to turn *my* home into a boardinghouse."

Louisa's frustration was understandable, but she was wrong about one part. Finley House was no longer only her home. It was once again Emily's too.

"What else would you suggest? Mrs. Carmichael's offer means that we don't have to sell our home." Emily emphasized the plural pronouns ever so slightly. "I thought that would make you happy." Or if not happy, at least more comfortable with the future. Running a boardinghouse might not have been Emily's idea of the perfect life, but it was preferable to being homeless. And it was something she could do. She might not have Louisa's skills as a healer or Joanna's musical talent, but she was a good cook and housekeeper.

Louisa shook her head vehemently. "None of this makes me happy, but I shouldn't have expected you to understand. Don't you see? Everything has changed. Mama, Father, the house . . . I don't recognize my life anymore." Louisa sprang to her feet and stormed out of the parlor, pausing in the doorway to say, "I hate what's happened, and I hate . . ."

You. The unspoken word hung in the air. Emily couldn't blame her. As the youngest child, Louisa had been, if not pampered, at least protected. Now the foundations of her life had been shaken, leaving her bereft of more than her parents. She'd lost her sense of stability and safety.

"She'll calm down," the widow said softly.

Emily wasn't so certain.

"No!" Noah kicked his legs and began to shout when Craig lifted him into the high

84

chair. He'd had tantrums at home, but this was the first time Noah had protested about anything in Sweetwater Crossing. For the life of him, Craig couldn't imagine what was bothering his son. The food had yet to be placed on the table, so it couldn't be the prospect of an unfamiliar dish. That left the high chair, but it was where it had been every day, placed between Craig and Mrs. Carmichael.

"No!" Noah gestured wildly, then pointed at Emily, who'd brought in a pitcher of milk. The two sisters sat on the opposite side, leaving the chairs at the head and foot of the table empty. "Em!"

"That's Mrs. Leland," Craig corrected.

"Em! Me Em." Once again, Noah pointed at the spot next to Emily.

"You know better than to shout indoors, Noah. If you don't behave, you won't get supper tonight."

"Em!" Craig's threat had no effect.

"I think he wants to sit next to me." Though her voice was neutral, it was obvious Emily was trying to stifle a smile. "It's all right, Craig. I don't mind." She turned toward Noah. "Would you like to sit here?"

A vigorous nod confirmed Noah's agreement. His son might be happy, but Craig was not. "I don't like indulging him when

85

he's having a tantrum."

"He's been through a lot of changes in a short time. If it makes him happy to sit beside me, let's indulge him this once."

Despite himself, Craig was impressed by Emily's insights. "You may be right. It's been a difficult year for him since Rachel died." Noah beamed with pleasure when Craig moved the high chair, but when he reached for Noah's bowl and began to cut his food as he had for every meal since Rachel's death, his son shouted "No!" again.

The look Emily gave Craig urged patience. "Let me."

He did. To Craig's surprise, Noah ate every bite without complaining, though he'd balked at carrots the last time Craig had served them. His son cleaned his bowl, then stared at Emily the way he had at Alice Patton's daughter, his fascination apparent.

His son was happy, but that could not be said for everyone in the room. While Emily and Mrs. Carmichael did their best to keep the conversation flowing, nothing could disguise the tension between the sisters. Louisa spoke only when addressed, and even then, her replies were grudging.

Craig understood her anger toward him — he was an interloper — but he did not understand her treatment of her sister. He might have believed she was sulking, but the problem appeared to be deeper than that. Though he would have thought that grief would have united the sisters, it seemed to have opened an unbreachable chasm.

Through it all, Emily maintained her composure, attempting to soothe Louisa while she made Noah feel like the most important person at the table. The woman was truly remarkable. When the meal ended, Mrs. Carmichael turned to Craig.

"Mr. Ferguson, I wondered whether you and Noah would like to walk to the creek with me."

Though she said nothing more, Craig sensed that she wanted to have a private conversation with him, perhaps about the obvious discord between the two Vaughn sisters.

"We'd enjoy that, but please call me Craig." He helped Noah down from the high chair. "We're going for a walk with Mrs. Carmichael."

"Mcar."

When the widow chuckled, Craig realized this must be the first time Noah had addressed her that way. "That's one way to say it." She was still chuckling when they reached the door leading to the rear verandah. "Would you like to hold my hand, young man?" Noah nodded and walked contentedly between her and Craig.

When they reached the small creek that formed the north boundary of Finley House's property, Noah began to run in circles. "He'll be happy for a little while," Craig told Mrs. Carmichael. The last few minutes before the sun set were among Noah's favorites.

"Good. As you might have guessed, I wanted to talk to you without anyone overhearing us. I trust that you'll keep what I'm about to tell you in the strictest confidence."

"Of course." Craig nodded, both in agreement with the widow's request and confirmation of her assumption. Though he'd strolled along the creek the day before and found it a peaceful spot, the widow's words left little doubt that this conversation would not be a pleasant one.

Mrs. Carmichael watched Noah scampering before she turned back to Craig. "I'm glad your son likes it here. That helps. You see, I had thought our stay at Finley House would be temporary, but what I learned today tells me we need to remain here permanently. If we don't, those dear girls will lose their home."

Though he had a dozen questions, the

foremost being what would happen to the sisters if they found themselves homeless, Craig simply nodded, encouraging the widow to continue.

"They have no money for taxes or anything else. Their father's stipend has ended, the family has few savings, and Emily inherited nothing from her husband."

It was indeed a dire situation. At least when Rachel died, though he'd been bereft emotionally, Craig had had no financial worries.

Mrs. Carmichael continued her explanation. "What the town is paying for your lodging and the little extra I can offer will let them keep their house. I hope you'll agree and will not seek another place for you and Noah."

Craig was silent for a second, absorbing all that the widow had said. Finley House was not the perfect place for him and his son. The danger of the verandahs, Emily's wariness, and the discord between the sisters all concerned him, and yet what alternative did he have? If he refused, two innocent young women would be homeless. How could he refuse when the room he and Noah shared was more than adequate, the meals were excellent, and — most importantly — Noah seemed happy here?

"What about you?" Craig looked at the woman who'd lost her home and was now trying to keep others from losing theirs. "Won't this hurt you?" While he had no knowledge of her financial situation, he assumed the reason Mrs. Carmichael had volunteered to house him and Noah was because she needed the money. Now, not only would she not have that income, but she'd have to dip into whatever savings she might have to pay for her own room and board.

She shook her head. "I'm not worried about it. Doc Sheridan keeps reminding me that the Good Lord only intended us to live seventy years. I don't believe him, but I've two more until then and enough money to last years longer."

She laid a hand on Craig's arm and gave it a little squeeze. "It was kind of you to worry about me, but it's those poor girls who worry me. The three of them were so close growing up. You'd never have known they weren't all Prudence and Joseph's natural children. But now there are deep rifts. Joanna's in Europe, and as you saw at supper, Louisa barely speaks to Emily."

Mrs. Carmichael paused and shook her head again, this time in apparent dismay. "Oh, listen to me. I must sound like a gossiping old woman."

It was Craig's turn to shake his head. "What I heard wasn't gossip but a kind woman's concern for her friends. What do you think caused the rift?" Perhaps he shouldn't have asked, but if he was going to live here, the more he knew about his landladies, the better.

"I don't know, but looking back, it seems everything changed when George Leland came to town and swept Emily off her feet. Of course, she wasn't the only one who fancied him. That man could have charmed the rattles off a snake. I probably shouldn't say this, seeing as how he's dead, but I never did quite trust him. But that didn't matter to anyone else. It seemed every girl in town set her sights on him."

And if Louisa had been one of those who fancied him, perhaps she'd resented her sister's marriage. Craig didn't pretend to understand a woman's mind, but he would have thought the losses Louisa and Emily had shared would have overcome any past jealousy. Apparently, they hadn't been enough.

CHAPTER SIX

She wasn't sure how much longer she could tolerate the situation. Emily pounded the dough she was kneading with more force than necessary. When she was finished, she'd have a perfectly shaped loaf of bread. If only she could have a perfectly shaped life.

It had been three days since she'd told Louisa they would have to turn their home into a boardinghouse, three days since Louisa had spoken a word to her other than "please pass the gravy," three days of ever-increasing tension. Though Emily had tried to talk to her, Louisa had ignored her, once going so far as to plug her ears with her index fingers, acting no older than Noah.

Noah. Emily smiled as she gave the dough a final thump, then formed it into a loaf and placed it in the greased pan. The boy had been the one bright spot in the week. His insistence on sitting next to her at the table and following her around the house even when Mrs. Carmichael tried to distract him had helped assuage the pain of Louisa's rejection, and knowing that she'd never have a child of her own made her savor the time she spent with this one. Noah was a reminder that life continued, that there could be happiness even after unspeakable sorrow.

As she covered the bread with a cloth for its final rise, Emily heard the door open. Turning, she saw her sister, her head held high, her eyes sparkling with excitement. This was the Louisa Emily remembered.

Louisa tugged off her gloves and flung them onto the table, then faced Emily, her expression defiant as she untied her bonnet strings. "I'm leaving."

"What do you mean?" Though Louisa had threatened to leave, Emily had believed it to be an empty threat.

"Exactly what I said. I'm leaving this horrible town. You can do what you want with Finley House until Joanna returns, but I won't be a party to this travesty. I'm leaving."

Emily leaned back against the counter, trying to brace herself for what she feared would turn into a tirade. "Where are you going?" she asked as mildly as she could.

"Cimarron Creek. Phoebe's mother wants

to visit relatives there. One of Phoebe's cousins is getting married, and another is expecting a baby. Mrs. Sheridan says she can't miss either of those, so they'll be gone for a few months. They've agreed that I can accompany them." Louisa paused for dramatic effect, then fired her final salvo. "I may never come back."

This was Louisa, the impulsive Vaughn sister. She saw only the possibility of escape from a difficult situation and hadn't considered the practicalities. "What will you do there? You can't expect Mrs. Sheridan's family to let you stay with them permanently."

"I'll find a job." Louisa waved a hand, dismissing Emily's concerns. "The town has a doctor. I'll see if he needs a helper. Doc Sheridan wouldn't let me do anything, even though I know I could have kept his records and helped him with simple procedures, but maybe Cimarron Creek's doctor is more modern. Maybe he'll care that I've always dreamt of becoming a healer. Maybe he'll teach me."

"And if he doesn't?" Though Emily hated to be the one to discourage her sister, someone needed to temper Louisa's unfounded optimism and remind her how unlikely it was that Cimarron Creek's physician would be any more amenable to her assistance than Doc Sheridan.

"I'll find something else. Anything will be better than staying here." Louisa narrowed her eyes and glared at Emily. "Don't try to change my mind. It won't work. I'm leaving."

There was only one question left. "When?"

"Tomorrow."

"I can dry those for you."

Emily turned, startled by Craig's offer. She'd been so intent on washing the Sunday dishes that she hadn't heard him enter the kitchen, but there he stood, less than two feet from her, his expression mirroring the sincerity of his words.

"I can't let you do that. You're a paying guest." Besides, drying the dishes would put him close to her. Too close.

He shrugged, dismissing her excuse. "You're an overworked landlady. Furthermore, this guest has nothing else to do right now. Noah's napping."

Without waiting for her approval, Craig picked up the towel Emily had laid on the counter and began to dry the dishes. Perhaps he somehow realized how nervous she felt being alone in a room with him because he took two steps backward and stood at the other end of the counter as he wiped the last drops of water from the plate.

"You needn't worry that I'll break them," he said. "I've had a lot of practice."

"Since your wife died." It made sense that as a widower Craig would have had to assume many of Rachel's responsibilities.

He shook his head. "Well before then. I helped Rachel with the dishes every day."

Emily couldn't mask her surprise. Father had rarely set foot in the kitchen, and the thought of helping her would never have crossed George's mind. It appeared that Craig Ferguson was very different from the men she'd known. Surely there was no need to fear a man who'd help his wife with something as mundane as dishes. Emily eyed the distance between them, trying to convince herself that she would be safe. It would be all right, she told herself, especially if she kept the conversation light.

"Most men believe the kitchen is a woman's domain."

"And it is. Rachel was the queen. I was her lowly servant." To punctuate his words, Craig took an obsequious bow.

The unexpected gesture turned Emily's chuckle into a full-fledged laugh. "That sounds like an exaggeration, but thank you. I appreciate your help, just as your wife must have. She was a fortunate woman."

Craig shook his head. "I was the fortunate one. From the first time I saw her, I knew Rachel was special. Of course, it took me twelve years to grow up enough to convince her."

"You're joking."

"Nope. Rachel was six the day she came to school. I was an ancient seven-year-old who thought he knew everything, including how to woo a girl." Craig feigned a heartbroken expression. "Stealing her apple turnover may have gotten her to notice me, but it did nothing to win her heart."

Emily laughed again, picturing the young girl's outrage. "But you did eventually."

"Eventually." Craig reached for another plate. "We were married the day after her eighteenth birthday. That was the happiest day of my life until the day Noah was born. Nothing could compare to that."

Emily bit back a sigh at the realization of how different their lives had been. The only thing she and Craig had in common was the loss of a spouse, but while that had been a tragedy for Craig, George's death had been a blessing for her.

"Mrs. Carmichael said your courtship was shorter than mine." Though he made it a statement, there was a hint of a question.

Emily scrubbed the last plate with more force than it needed as she tried to form a response. She should have realized that the widow would have shared at least a bit of her past with Craig and that he might be curious. Rather than raise his suspicions by refusing to answer, she said, "George came to Sweetwater Crossing because the Albrights were selling part of their cattle herd. He wanted some cows."

Craig smiled. "It seems he found more than cows here."

Emily tried to match his smile. "Louisa claimed that the cattle were only an excuse and that what George wanted was a bride. She always was one for romantic tales."

"Even though it's only been a couple days, I imagine you miss your sister."

Emily frowned at the memory of the last week — the anger, the silence, the refusal to do anything around the house.

"I miss the closeness the three of us shared. We used to call ourselves the Three Musketeers, but then everything changed."

Craig's nod said he understood. "It's only natural that your lives would change as you matured."

"Matured is an interesting word." Emily paused for a second. "I probably shouldn't say this — I'm not sure why I'm even having this conversation with you — but you can't have helped noticing that before she left, Louisa was acting more like a child than a mature woman." And that had bothered Emily as much as the hurtful words she'd flung at her and the days of silence.

Reaching for the pan Emily had just rinsed, Craig said, "Everyone reacts to loss differently. After Rachel died, if it hadn't been for Noah and my pupils, I'm not sure what I would have done. They gave me a reason to get out of bed every morning and helped break the shackles of grief."

Shackles. The word reverberated through Emily's brain, reminding her of how often she'd felt like a prisoner at the ranch. There'd been no shackles, but George had made certain she had no way of leaving unless he accompanied her. That and the fact that she'd felt relief rather than grief when he died were things no one needed to know. Besides, they were speaking of Louisa.

"You could be right. I have the work of running this house to keep me occupied." But even that had not banished the memory of finding Father in the barn. She doubted anything other than proving he hadn't fastened that noose would lessen her grief, for no matter what anyone said, she knew he had not.

Louisa did not have that comfort. In addition, she had been at their mother's side when she took her last breath. Perhaps those memories were part of the reason for her behavior.

"I hope Louisa finds what she's seeking in Cimarron Creek." No matter what Louisa had said and done, Emily could not wish anything but happiness for her sister.

"What's that?"

"To become a doctor. You might not believe it, but Louisa has a tender heart. When she was a child, she tried to help wounded animals. Now she wants to heal people."

Craig looked at the wall for a second before he said, "That's a noble ambition, even if not a typical one for a woman. What about you? What's your dream?"

There'd been only one, and it had burst as easily as the soap bubbles that floated in the air. Emily struggled to meet Craig's gaze while the picture of herself standing next to a smiling husband and holding an infant flitted before her. "It doesn't matter. I've stopped dreaming."

Craig looked around the schoolroom, assuring himself that everything was in order, knowing it was, since he'd arrived an hour ago to verify that. The first day of school was always a challenge as he tried to keep his pupils' attention focused on learning when they'd rather be anywhere else. He couldn't risk having them distracted by missing primers or broken pieces of chalk, especially today when he was in a new school with a new set of students.

Fortunately, everything was going well. The dunce stool was gone, stashed under the schoolhouse. His carefully printed welcome message was legible even from the back of the room. Best of all, Noah seemed content to remain at Finley House.

He'd pouted when Craig had told him he was going alone, but the pout had turned into a grin when Emily promised that Noah could help her cook lunch. Craig suspected Noah's help would mean more work for Emily, but he wouldn't argue with the result. His son's happiness was an auspicious start to the day.

It was time. He rang the bell, then returned to his spot at the front of the classroom, nodding as the pupils filed in. Some were hesitant, some wore friendly smiles, two swaggered and smirked. Craig took note of the last two, knowing they'd be his biggest challenge. When all twenty-two children were seated, he tapped his pointer on his desk and waited for silence.

"Good morning, boys and girls, and welcome to the first day of school. I'm Mr. Ferguson." Though he tried to look directly at each pupil, the shy ones kept their gaze fixed on their desks, and the boys he'd identified as probable bullies looked only at each other. "We're going to go around the room. I want each of you to tell me your name, your age, and one thing you hope to learn this year."

There were few surprises until he reached the smirkers. "He's Mitch Sanders," the brunet said, pointing his thumb at his friend.

"And he's Harlan Miller," the stocky boy whose sandy brown hair needed a good wash chimed in. "We're twelve."

Though Craig suspected the names were correct, he knew neither was that old.

"Perhaps you didn't understand my instructions. I expect you to introduce *yourself* and tell me your correct age as well as your educational goals for the year."

"They're ten," Susan Johnson, the twelve-year-old with medium brown hair and green eyes who appeared to be the brightest of Craig's pupils, announced.

"Thank you, Susan, but I want each student to speak for himself."

The girl flushed at his reprimand and lowered her gaze to her desk.

"You gonna make her sit on the dunce stool?" Mitch demanded. "She oughta sit there." He glanced at the front of the classroom. "Where'd it go?"

"We have no need for it." Craig kept his voice firm. "There are no dunces here, only children who are eager to learn." He waited until the low murmur his declaration had caused subsided before he addressed Mitch and Harlan again. "I still need to know your educational goals."

"Ed-you-kay-shun-ul go-als." Harlan drawled each of the syllables. "Them's big words, but I ain't got none."

"Me neither," Mitch agreed. "There ain't nothin' you can teach me."

"I see." As he had for each of the other pupils, Craig wrote notes next to the boys' names.

"What you writin'?" Harlan demanded. "We don't need nothin'."

"We'll start with basic grammar and diction."

When a flurry of giggles erupted from three of the older girls, Harlan glared at them and hissed, "You gonna be sorry."

It was precisely the kind of intimidation Craig expected from bullies. He'd dealt with them before; he'd do it again, but now was not the time. Instead, he proceeded with the pupils' introductions. When he reached the last one, he nodded.

"All right, boys and girls. I want you all to line up along the walls. I'm going to give your assigned seats."

Mitch groaned. "Miss Albright let us sit where we wanted."

Though Craig suspected that was a lie, all he said was, "I'm not Miss Albright." Gertrude, as she'd insisted he call her, had warned that some of the pupils would respect him only after he'd given them a sound caning, but Craig had no intention of using that form of discipline.

By the end of the day, he was tired but exhilarated. Other than Mitch and Harlan, the pupils had appeared willing and in some cases eager to learn. While he didn't like the crowding in the classroom, he had an idea for a partial solution, and that added a spring to his step as he walked home. All things considered, it had been a good first day.

"Pa!" Noah raced toward him the moment he entered Finley House, his arms raised in a wordless appeal for Craig to pick him up.

"Did you miss me?" he asked as he swung Noah into his arms, hugged him, then deposited him back on the floor.

His son nodded. "Me cook."

Mrs. Carmichael, who'd followed Noah into the massive foyer, confirmed Noah's assertion. "Emily gave him a wooden spoon and a small pan. Noah's now an expert at stirring imaginary pudding."

"Is that real chocolate pudding I smell?"

"Yes, indeed." The widow's eyes sparkled, and the corners of her lips curved into a smile. "Your son tasted it and pronounced it acceptable for us."

"I can only imagine what his face looked like." Craig directed the last comment to Emily, who'd joined the conversation. Still wearing an apron, her face wreathed in a smile, she was the picture of a happy woman, or at least a happy cook.

"Not just his face," she confirmed. "His hands too, but he had fun. Didn't you, Noah?"

Noah gave her a big nod. "Em fun."

But she was also a woman who'd lost her husband and abandoned her dreams.

"It's kind of you to allow my friends to meet here."

Emily straightened the knife she'd just placed on the table, ensuring that it was lined up with the spoons. "I'm happy to have them come." When Mrs. Carmichael had mentioned that it was supposed to be her turn to host the weekly luncheon for her three widowed friends, Emily had offered to serve as their hostess.

"Lottie, Betty, and Clara have been my closest friends for as long as I can remember. We used to play together as children back in Illinois, and once we were married and moved here, we instituted the luncheon tradition. I wasn't sure how we'd continue once Noah came, but you've solved that problem."

Emily had suggested that Noah remain with her in the kitchen while Mrs. Carmichael was entertaining her friends. She'd already discovered that he was easily entertained with cooking utensils and that he understood he wasn't allowed to go into the dining room unless Emily or Mrs. Carmichael took him.

"Our luncheons remind me a bit of your father and his cronies," the widow continued. "The four of them used to have supper together every Saturday night."

Emily had heard stories of the foursome, who were now only a duo. "Father said they didn't let age come between them. Mr. Albright is more than a decade older than Father and Doc, but he claimed that didn't matter."

"Clive Finley was a year or so younger than your father and a dashing young man. He wasn't as handsome as your George, but he was the kind of man no woman could ignore." Mrs. Carmichael pretended to swoon. "Every unmarried girl in town set her cap for him."

That was part of the story Emily hadn't heard. "But he was engaged to a woman back in Alabama."

"You would have thought that would have discouraged the girls here, wouldn't you, but it only added to his allure." The widow shook her head. "Oh, listen to me, rambling on about things that happened long ago. I should know better. Besides, the ladies will be here any minute. You're welcome to join us, you know."

"Noah would be a distraction, and I'd be a fifth wheel. You don't need that."

"We all need friends." The widow wagged her finger at Emily. "I'm going to sound like a meddling woman again, but true friends are treasures. Sometimes they're even more valuable than siblings because we've chosen them. Don't neglect yours."

As she prepared plates of food for the four widows, Emily's thoughts churned. She was forging a new life here, but although it brought her a measure of comfort to know she was helping Mrs. Carmichael, Craig, and Noah, it was a far-from-perfect life.

When George was alive, Emily's days had been focused on making him happy. As much as she'd missed her family, she had found comfort in picturing them going about their normal activities here. But now they were all gone, leaving Emily alone in the house they'd once shared. Joanna was somewhere in Europe, and Louisa . . . ah, Louisa. Memories of the way she and her youngest sister had parted were almost as painful as the knowledge that Emily would not see her parents again this side of heaven.

Was Mrs. Carmichael right in saying friends could be more valuable than siblings? Emily wasn't certain, but she couldn't dismiss the possibility, nor could she dismiss the thought that perhaps the woman who'd been her closest friend needed Emily as much as Emily needed her. Hadn't Alice said they should stick together?

Even though the library kept her busy during the day, Alice's evenings must be lonely. Emily knew hers would be if she didn't have Noah, Craig, and Mrs. Carmichael living here.

Mrs. Carmichael was right. They all needed friends. Tomorrow morning as soon as lunch was in the oven, Emily would visit the library, not just to check out a book but to invite Alice and little Jane to have supper with them. It was the least she could do for her friend.

CHAPTER SEVEN

"This is the best roast I've ever tasted." At Emily's urging, Alice helped herself to another piece of the tender meat and a second potato. "I'd ask for your secret, but it wouldn't make any difference. Cyrus loved me dearly, but even he admitted that I'm a terrible cook."

Emily smiled, pleased by both the compliments and the way the others had reacted to her friend's presence. Mrs. Carmichael had beamed her approval when Emily told her about the invitation, and Craig had insisted he didn't mind being outnumbered by women. "Adult conversation is always welcome," he'd told Emily.

Alice had done her part to provide that, proving to be the perfect guest as she recounted amusing stories of her library patrons.

"Children are the biggest problem," she admitted. "Many don't understand the difference between borrowing and owning."

Craig did not appear surprised. "I'll add that to one of next week's lessons. Is there anything else they need to learn?"

"You might remind them that the library is open. It's been less than a year, and some people still don't seem to remember."

Sweetwater Crossing's residents had always been slow to adapt to change, even when it was a positive one. Had Father been among the reluctant ones?

Emily handed Noah another roll, then turned to Alice. "How did my father feel about no longer being the town's unofficial librarian?" For as long as she could recall, people had borrowed books from the Finley House library. Father never kept records, saying he trusted his fellow citizens, and the informal arrangement had appeared to work well. As far as Emily knew, the adults had had no difficulty understanding the difference between borrowing and owning.

"He told me he was relieved." Mrs. Carmichael laid down her fork and smiled at Emily. "Even though he knew Clive Finley would never return and his book-loving fiancée would never see the collection he'd amassed for her, your father confided that he worried whether he was being a good steward."

And that, like so many other things, was something he had not shared with his daughters. What he had shared was the story of how he'd become the caretaker and eventually the owner of Finley House.

"Has anyone told you about Clive Finley?" Emily asked Craig.

When he shook his head, Mrs. Carmichael said, "It's both romantic and tragic — something Shakespeare might have written."

"I agree." Alice smiled as she forked a piece of potato. "I know some of what happened, but Emily should be the one who tells the story."

Though she suspected both her friend and Mrs. Carmichael would interrupt, Emily began. "The way my parents tell it, Clive arrived in Sweetwater Crossing about a year after my father, and the two men became the closest of friends, possibly because they were both relative newcomers."

When Emily paused to take a breath, Alice continued. "The romantic part is that Clive wanted to marry a woman from his hometown in Alabama and bring her to Texas, but her father wouldn't agree to the marriage unless Clive could give her a home that equaled the one she'd grown up in. From what I heard, he was a wealthy plantation owner, and his house was similar to

Finley House."

"Similar but smaller, or so the legend goes." Mrs. Carmichael's smile said she knew no one was letting Emily tell the story.

"That much is true." Emily had seen drawings of the Alabama mansion and the original plans for Finley House. "The house was finished and Clive was ready to return to Alabama to claim his bride when Abraham Lincoln was elected and the South began to secede from the Union. Before Clive left to fight alongside his fellow Alabamians, he asked my father to move into Finley House and take care of it until he returned. Mama was expecting Louisa at the time, and the parsonage was on the verge of being overcrowded."

"But Clive never returned. That was the tragedy." Alice mimed brushing tears from her eyes.

"My father claimed the real tragedy was that he never knew where Clive died. Everyone assumed it was on the battlefield, but once the war was over and Father began searching for his friend, he realized he'd never known the name of Clive's hometown."

"And so the Vaughns continued to live here. End of story."

Since Craig appeared satisfied, Emily did

not contradict Mrs. Carmichael, but she knew it wasn't the end of the story. Both Mama and Father had lived with the hope that someday they would learn what happened to the man who'd built the house that had become their home. That hope had not been fulfilled.

With the subject of Clive Finley finished, the conversation continued to flow easily as Alice sought Mrs. Carmichael's advice on growing hollyhocks, then engaged Noah in a lively if largely unintelligible discussion of carrots' sweetness. This was the Alice Emily remembered from her childhood — gregarious and genuinely interested in others.

She'd expected that. What she hadn't expected was Noah's fascination with Jane. He'd paid little attention to anyone else and persisted in wanting to share his food with her, even though Alice had told him Jane was too young.

"She doesn't have any teeth," Emily explained, "so she can't chew meat." The baby gave a toothless grin, confirming Emily's words. "See?"

When Noah bared his teeth, pointed to them, then toward Jane's mouth, and said, "Hurry," the adults chuckled, reminding Emily of the camaraderie she'd experienced so often around this table. Oh, how she missed her parents and her sisters!

As a pang of sorrow washed over her, she tried to force it away. She was fortunate — more than fortunate, she was blessed — to have these friends who were making it possible for her to keep her home, but she worried about her sisters. Were they happy? She hoped so. And while she wasn't certain it would bring either of them happiness, she resolved to write them each a letter every week, keeping them abreast of the Sweetwater Crossing news and telling them how much she missed them. For she did.

"Seriously, Emily," Alice said as she forked the last bite of pie, "everything has been delicious. Much better than Ma's Kitchen."

Ma's was the town's sole restaurant, and though Emily had had few occasions to sample it, the food had an excellent reputation.

"Do you eat there often?"

Alice wrinkled her nose. "Most nights. I wasn't joking when I told you I was a terrible cook. I'm lucky Sweetwater Crossing has a restaurant almost across the street from my house." She wrinkled her nose again. "Ma's food is good, but it can't compare to yours, especially now that Mrs. Webster isn't there."

Emily blinked in surprise. "Where is she?"

Though Emily was a child when Mrs. Webster had opened the restaurant after her husband's death and their daughter's marriage, she recalled Mama saying that Ma's Kitchen was what both Mrs. Webster and the town needed.

"Lillian died a few weeks before your father. It was less than a month after the big celebration for her seventieth birthday, and it was so sudden that it was a shock for everyone." Mrs. Carmichael took a sip of water before continuing. "We're fortunate that Ada Tabor was willing to take over." Mrs. Tabor, Emily knew, was Lillian Webster's daughter.

"She's trying her best," Alice agreed, "but her cooking can't compare to her mother's or Emily's."

Emily had never considered herself an impulsive person, and so she was startled when she heard herself saying, "You're welcome to join us each night. I know coming here isn't as convenient as going to Ma's, but if you don't mind the longer walk, I hope you'll accept the invitation."

After Mrs. Carmichael nodded her approval, Craig chimed in. "Speaking for myself and my son, I think it's a good idea. Noah's been shy around other children, but he's certainly not shy with Jane."

Though Alice was rarely tongue-tied, she appeared unsure of how to respond. Finally, she nodded. "It's a wonderful offer, but I'll accept only if you let me pay you."

"I was inviting you as a friend." The thought of money had not crossed Emily's mind, and it seemed wrong to accept payment from her closest friend.

"I know, and I appreciate your generosity, but I also know that you need to support yourself. It's only fair for me to pay my share." Alice turned to the widow for support. "Right, Mrs. Carmichael?"

Placing her cup back on its saucer, the widow inclined her head in agreement. "Alice is right. It's only fair." She smiled at Emily. "I was going to wait until later to bring this up, but since we're talking about your delicious meals, I might as well tell you that my friends and I enjoyed yesterday's luncheon so much that we're hoping you'll agree to be our hostess every week. And of course we'll pay you for our food. It'll save us the trouble of cooking and will let the four of us enjoy every minute we spend together."

Without waiting for Emily's agreement, Alice declared, "It's settled. Mrs. Carmichael's friends and I will pay you what we would have spent otherwise."

An hour later, Noah was in bed and Craig had joined Emily in the kitchen for their nightly dishwashing. Though it had been only two weeks since he'd arrived in Sweetwater Crossing, Emily's wariness about him had lessened. Craig had been a perfect gentleman, never coming too close, never touching her, never giving her any reason to fear him. Instead, he'd treated her the same way he did Mrs. Carmichael. That was reassuring.

"How do you feel about having a second business?" he asked.

"Truthfully, relieved. I don't like worrying about money." That had been one of the good aspects of her marriage. George might not have been wealthy, but he was generous with what he had . . . for the first few months.

Pushing those memories aside, Emily said, "I'm hoping I won't have to worry about taxes or what I'll do if there are unexpected expenses." She ran her dishrag over the last plate, then rinsed it and handed it to Craig. "Louisa won't be pleased, and I don't know how Joanna will feel, but turning Finley House into a boardinghouse and serving meals to others feels right."

"Like this was what God had in store for you?"

Emily turned, startled by the question. It was the first time Craig had spoken of God other than when he gave thanks for their food.

"Yes," she said, surprised by both the peace that had settled over her at Alice and Mrs. Carmichael's offers and the realization that she'd never felt that peace during her marriage. Was that because it hadn't been part of God's plan? Emily had been so fascinated by George and so flattered by his pursuit that she hadn't taken time to ask for guidance. And because she hadn't, she'd paid the price. This was different.

Craig looked around the classroom, assuring himself that everything was in its proper place before he left for the day. The second week of school had begun well. The students were settling in, and Mitch and Harlan were more subdued now that they were no longer sitting together. That wouldn't last forever. Craig knew there'd be another outburst or another attempt to subvert his authority, but he was enjoying the relative calm.

Locking the door behind him, he reflected that he was also enjoying living at Finley House. Emily seemed more relaxed, perhaps because of her renewed friendship with Alice. The young librarian had a wonderful sense of humor and seemed to know when to interject an amusing anecdote. Though Craig doubted Noah understood why the adults were laughing, he always joined in, sometimes even clapping his hands in apparent delight. No doubt about it: Noah was blossoming in Sweetwater Crossing.

Craig was smiling as he crossed Center Street.

"Mr. Ferguson. You're just the man I wanted to see." The mayor's booming voice made Craig stop. Though there was nothing impressive about Malcolm Alcott's appearance — he was medium height with medium brown hair, medium blue eyes, and appeared to be in his midforties — his voice was deep, distinctive, and designed to impress.

"Good afternoon, Mayor Alcott." Craig walked toward the man who governed Sweetwater Crossing with an iron hand. "Shall we dispense with the formalities? I'd prefer that you called me Craig."

A frown crossed the mayor's face, making Craig regret his friendly overture. He should have realized that Alcott would insist on being addressed by his title.

The frown deepened. "I trust you don't encourage such informality with your pupils."

"Of course not. They need to respect me." The mayor wasn't the only one who was aware of his position in town.

"That's what I need to talk to you about." Alcott looked up and down both Center and Main Streets. Though there were only a few pedestrians strolling along the boardwalks, he appeared uncomfortable. "Let's go to my office." It was a command, not a request.

"Yes, sir." Craig repressed his urge to salute.

When they were both seated inside the spartan office, the mayor steepled his hands and fixed his gaze on Craig. "You're new to Sweetwater Crossing. I understand that. I also understand that things might have been different at your last school, but I'm concerned by some of the reports I've heard."

"What have you heard?" The mayor's children were all too old for school, making Craig wonder about both the source of the complaints and why, if parents were disturbed by some aspect of his teaching, they hadn't contacted him directly.

"Some parents are worried that you don't understand how important discipline is." As Alcott's voice resonated through the office, Craig suspected the commanding tone was his form of discipline.

"There have been no disciplinary problems." Harlan and Mitch's efforts to disrupt the class the first day hardly counted as a problem.

"Not yet, perhaps, but how will you handle them when they occur, because they most assuredly will?" The mayor's blue eyes darkened. "I understand you removed the dunce stool."

They'd reached the heart of the matter. Though there had been no further discussion of the missing stool, Craig had heard several students snickering about its absence, and Mitch had mocked Craig's declaration that there were no dunces in Sweetwater Crossing. Undoubtedly, some parents had heard those stories.

"I did." Craig would not apologize, although that was clearly what Alcott expected. "I do not believe that public humiliation is the best way to correct misbehavers."

The mayor appeared surprised. "Then you will not cane pupils in front of their classmates?"

"I won't cane them at all."

Surprise turned to shock, leaving Alcott speechless for a moment. When he regained his faculties, he was practically sputtering. "Every other teacher in Sweetwater Crossing has recognized that sparing the rod means spoiling the child."

Craig had known his stand would raise some eyebrows and perhaps even elicit some complaints, but he hadn't expected to face criticism so soon, nor expected it to come from this source.

"I cannot control how parents discipline their children at home, but nothing in my contract requires me to hit a child." Craig wouldn't have signed it or come here if it had. "The contract merely says I must maintain appropriate discipline in the classroom. I've done that and will continue to."

"Time will tell." The mayor rose, his face ruddy with anger as he ushered Craig to the door. "I hope we didn't make a mistake in hiring you. Time will tell," he repeated.

Craig bit back his retort. The only mistake the town had made had been in allowing this man to think he spoke for everyone, but nothing would be gained by saying that. Instead, Craig nodded curtly. "Good day, Mr. Alcott." He wouldn't address him as Mr. Mayor until his own anger subsided.

By the time he reached Finley House, Craig had convinced himself that the unpleasant time with the mayor was an aberration. The town had not made a mistake in hiring him, and he had not made a mistake in bringing Noah here. It was nothing short of miraculous that his son had not had a nightmare since they'd left Galveston. Though the churchwomen had warned him not to uproot Noah, that a young child needed the familiarity of his home, Noah seemed to be thriving in his new surroundings.

Noah was healing, and so was Craig. The emptiness deep inside him no longer felt as overwhelming. He still missed Rachel — he always would — but the pain had become more bearable, the future less bleak. All of that was good. He would think about that rather than the mayor's heavy-handed attempt to dictate disciplinary methods.

Craig was smiling as he entered Finley House. Though normally Noah greeted him with open arms, demanding to be picked up and whirled around, the house was quieter than usual with no sign of Noah and Mrs. Carmichael. The delicious aromas filling the foyer suggested Emily was in the kitchen. Craig headed that way, certain she'd know where his son was.

As he strode toward the back of the house, he glanced into the library and stopped abruptly, fear paralyzing his limbs. *What on earth? Doesn't she recognize the danger? Doesn't she know she could fall like . . . ?*

Refusing to complete the sentence, Craig did the only thing he could: he forced his legs to move and raced into the room, determined to save Emily from her foolishness.

For there she was, reaching for a book on the highest shelf while the chair she'd used instead of a ladder wobbled precariously. If she snagged the book, the action would cause the chair to topple over, taking her with it. She'd fall. She'd hit her head. She might . . . The final thought was unbearable. Craig couldn't — wouldn't — let that happen.

He crossed the room in three swift strides, grabbed Emily around the waist, and lifted her off the chair. "What were you thinking?" he demanded, his voice harsher than usual.

She spun around, her eyes wide with terror. "Don't touch me!"

CHAPTER EIGHT

"I was such a fool." Emily tried to keep her voice from trembling lest she frighten the horses. There was no reason to be speaking aloud. Neither Blanche nor Horace would respond, but the terror she'd felt — the ridiculous, unfounded terror — had thrust her back to her childhood when she would flee to the barn, seeking solace when she'd argued with one of her sisters or when a schoolmate had hurt her feelings. Somehow the simple act of pouring out her heart to whichever horse was closest had assuaged her pain. Perhaps that would happen again today.

"I was acting like a ninny just because he touched me." Emily stroked Blanche's nose, taking comfort from the soft fur and her mare's whinny. "Craig wasn't like George. He wasn't going to hurt me. It was the exact opposite. He was trying to keep me from being hurt."

126

She closed her eyes for a second, remembering the instant when she'd felt the chair begin to wobble. "I should have known better than to climb on it, but when I saw three of my favorite children's books on the top shelf, I thought Noah would like them." She shook her head. "I didn't get the books, and now I owe Noah's father an apology."

Blanche whinnied again and tossed her head, as if telling Emily the apology was overdue. "I know, Blanche. I know."

Emily started to leave the barn, then paused as she passed Horace's stall. Poor Horace. He must miss the daily rides he and Father used to take. Father had claimed they were important because they gave the gelding exercise while he visited parishioners who lived out of town. And in some cases, people confided their problems to Horace rather than directly to Father, much as Emily had confided in Blanche this afternoon.

"Some people are more comfortable with animals than people," Father had told her.

That had certainly been the case with Beulah Douglas. The girl most folks called simple used to insist on visiting Horace each week when she and her parents came to town. More often than not, she'd slip away while her mother was occupied and come here. Her parents, who soon learned where to look for their daughter, would find her standing next to Horace's stall and chattering away, pretending the horse understood the speech that others found almost incomprehensible.

Where was Beulah? Unless her family had changed their routine, they came to town to shop once a week and rarely missed Sunday services, but Emily hadn't seen the girl since the day she'd returned. When she had a chance, she'd ask Alice if something had happened to Beulah, but right now, she needed to find Craig and apologize before Mrs. Carmichael and Noah returned from their walk. Emily could only hope he'd accept the apology and wouldn't ask any questions.

"Why. That's the question we should ask." Craig stood in front of the schoolroom, his gaze moving from row to row, watching his pupils' reactions. Today was the first day he was going to deviate from the pattern of memorizing and reciting facts that Miss Albright and her predecessors had considered the foundation of their teaching.

"It's been more than a hundred years since the colonists fought for freedom," he continued. "We've reaped the benefits of their fight, but to fully appreciate the significance of the revolution, we need to understand the reasons behind it."

And he needed to understand why Emily had been so frightened. She'd apologized for her outburst, saying he'd startled her, but he knew there was more to the story. Though he'd wanted to probe, to ask why the way he was encouraging his students to do, Emily's expression had been so guarded that he'd realized she wouldn't answer. Instead, he'd claimed he understood. But he didn't. Not fully.

"Why do you believe our forefathers thought independence was worth risking their lives?"

Craig wasn't surprised when Susan raised her hand. The twelve-year-old was one of his brightest pupils and typically the first to respond. "Yes, Susan."

"They didn't like paying taxes."

He nodded. "No one does, but there was more to it than simply paying taxes."

The girl looked down at her textbook. "They wanted repre–"

Before she could finish, Harlan shouted, "It was cuz they didn't wanna wear them powdered wigs."

The class burst into laughter.

Craig frowned at Harlan. "There will be no interruptions in this classroom. Continue, Susan."

"They wanted representation. No one in England asked them if they wanted to pay taxes on tea."

"They wanted to be real men and drink coffee, not tea." Mitch punctuated his statement with a loud guffaw.

The bullies were at it again, trying to disrupt the lesson. Craig had known this moment would come, but he hadn't expected it so soon after the mayor's warning. Alcott had said, "Time will tell." It was time — time to teach a different lesson, time to prove that his form of discipline was effective.

Craig fixed his gaze on first Mitch, then Harlan. "I said there would be no interruptions, and I meant it. I expect every one of you to be polite and to respect each other. If you don't, there will be repercussions."

"Like what?" Harlan demanded. "I ain't seen no ree-per-cuss-es. I reckon it's cuz you're a coward."

Craig heard a gasp followed by nervous laughter. Before he could respond, Mitch grinned. "Harlan's right. You ain't man enough to cane us."

The bullies were daring him to act, betting that he wouldn't. They were wrong.

"That's enough. I will not tolerate rudeness in this schoolroom." Craig glanced at the clock on the wall behind him. "We'll take our morning recess a few minutes earlier than normal today. You're dismissed, all except Mitch and Harlan."

The boys eyed each other, clearly trying to decide whether or not to challenge him further by leaving with the others. To Craig's surprise, prudence won, and they remained in their seats.

"What you gonna do to us?" Mitch demanded.

"I'm going to show you the repercussions of your behavior." Craig paused, wanting the boys to have a few seconds of wondering exactly what he had in mind. When they exchanged puzzled glances, he continued. "Since you obviously do not respect your fellow classmates, you will be happy to know that you will not have to spend recess or lunch with them for the next week. Instead, you will spend that time with me."

The boys' eyes widened as the implications registered.

"Furthermore, your recesses will be spent reading aloud, and when school is dismissed for the day, you will remain. Today you will scrub the floor. Tomorrow you will polish the stove."

Anger colored Harlan's face. "You can't

make us do that."

"I not only can, but I will. Every time you protest, I'll add a day to the length of the repercussions."

"That ain't fair." The way Mitch sulked reminded Craig of Noah when he'd been corrected, but Noah was only a toddler. Mitch and Harlan were old enough to know better.

Harlan nodded. "Caning would have been easier."

"I heard you gave a lesson on repercussions today," Alice said as she passed the mashed potatoes to Craig. When she'd arrived for supper, she'd told Emily that today appeared to have been an eventful one in the schoolhouse, but she'd refused to say anything more.

"I wondered how long it would take for the story to spread."

"What happened?" Emily looked up from the chicken leg she was preparing for Noah.

"Two of my pupils decided rules were for everyone else. I tried to teach them otherwise."

Mrs. Carmichael laid her fork on her plate and fixed her attention on Craig. "Did you use the dunce stool, the cane, or both?"

To Emily's surprise, Craig shook his head.

"None of the above. I don't believe in public humiliation or physical punishment."

The relief that rushed through her startled Emily with its intensity. She had never seen Craig strike Noah, but she had assumed he used the same forms of classroom discipline that Miss Albright had. First offenses, unless they were particularly serious, resulted in time on the dunce stool. Boys were caned for second offenses; girls had their palms beaten with a ruler. All discipline was administered in the front of the classroom, adding humiliation to the punishment. But Craig had not done that.

"How did you discipline them?" she asked.

"I took away their privileges for a week, in this case recess and lunch with the other children."

Mama had done that too when Emily or her sisters misbehaved. She'd claimed that they'd remember that punishment far longer than they would a switching.

"I also put them to work cleaning the schoolhouse. They scrubbed the floor today. Tomorrow's stove polishing day."

Emily could only imagine how the boys — for she was certain the misbehavers had been boys — had reacted to what most considered girls' and women's work.

"If they behave, that will be all for now."

Craig smiled. "The windows need washing, but they can wait for the next time."

"You expect there to be a next time." Emily couldn't recall her or her sisters repeating their mistakes.

"Certainly. Boys rarely learn a lesson the first time. I can almost guarantee they're going to challenge me again."

"How did they react to their punishment?" Mrs. Carmichael had been watching Craig carefully, her expression guarded, saying she wasn't convinced of the efficacy of his approach. It was certainly unheard of in Sweetwater Crossing.

"It wasn't punishment. Those were the repercussions of poor behavior."

"That's not the way I heard the story." Alice spoke for the first time since initiating the discussion. "The children who came into the library said Mitch and Harlan wouldn't tell them what happened. They were sure you'd tanned their hides."

Craig's smile was almost smug. "One of them told me he would have preferred that. My hope is that several days of hard work will make them think twice before misbehaving. If not, there will be other repercussions. They need to know that I'm in charge." Though he'd been speaking to Alice, Craig turned to Emily as he said, "I

134

want their respect, not their fear."

She had been right. Craig was a good man, kind but firm. She had no reason to fear him, for he was nothing like George.

CHAPTER NINE

Emily took a deep breath and laid her hand on the railing, willing herself to climb the stairs. She'd waited a full month, thinking it might become easier, but it hadn't. Instead, her dread had grown, telling her she needed to do this today. It was time to clear out the room Mama and Father had shared and decide what to do with their belongings.

Though Mama's clothes wouldn't fit any of her daughters because she'd been even shorter than Emily, Emily couldn't bear the thought of giving them all away. Instead, she decided as she took another step, she'd store the best ones in the attic. Perhaps Louisa or Joanna would have a daughter who'd appreciate them. As for Father's suits . . .

The sight of the open door stopped Emily's thoughts in midsentence. When she'd come downstairs this morning, it had been tightly closed, but now it was more than ajar. It was fully open. She hurried across the hallway and entered her parents' room, her surprise turning to shock at the sight of Noah on the opposite side of the room attempting to open the door to the verandah.

"You shouldn't be here, Noah." He was supposed to be napping. "This isn't your room."

Though he'd turned at the sound of her voice, he pointed toward the verandah. "Mama falled."

"Oh!" So that was what had happened to Rachel. Emily hadn't wanted to ask Craig for fear of reopening deep wounds, and he hadn't volunteered the information, but Noah's expression left no doubt that his mother had lost her life by falling from a porch or verandah. No wonder Craig had been so adamant about not having a room with access to the verandah.

Had Noah witnessed the fall, or was he simply repeating what he'd been told? Emily's heart ached at the thought that the boy might have been present and hoped that hadn't been the case. Either way, she needed to know so she could comfort Noah if memories of that day resurfaced. Even though it might verge on prying, something Mama had insisted was wrong, she would ask Craig about Rachel's death when he came home today. In the meantime, she needed to distract Craig's obviously upset son.

Emily took Noah's hand and gave him a reassuring smile. "Let's go downstairs and find Mrs. Carmichael." The widow had gone to visit Mrs. Adams while Noah was supposedly napping, but she should be back soon. And before Noah climbed the stairs again, Emily would make certain the door to every room that opened onto a verandah was locked.

Craig opened the front door and began whistling "Oh! Susanna," his signal to Noah that he was home. The song had been one of Rachel's favorites — he'd made her laugh when he'd changed the lyrics to "Oh! Rachel" — and though he no longer sang it, his son always came running when he heard the whistled tune. Today was no exception. Noah raced from the kitchen into the hallway.

"Me no fall."

Noah's pride was evident. Craig hoped his alarm was not. "That's good," he said as he led his son back into the kitchen. Years of masking his emotions in front of his pupils had taught Craig how to maintain a neutral demeanor no matter what he was feeling. "Let's see if Emily has a cookie for you." And an explanation for him.

As he'd expected, Emily was standing near the stove, stirring something that would have made his mouth water had he not been so concerned. *We need to talk,* he mouthed. She gave a short nod, then turned her attention to Noah. "You've been a good boy, so you may have a cookie."

Wise Emily. She knew that devouring the treat and then chasing the crumbs he'd dropped would keep his son so occupied that he would pay no attention to the adults' conversation.

"Why was Noah talking about falling?" Craig heard the intensity in his words, and the way Emily's eyes darkened told him she did too.

"I'm still not sure how it happened. Noah was supposed to be napping, but I found him in what used to be my parents' room. That's the center one on the front of the house," she explained. "That's the first time I've known him to open a door. Usually, he waits for Mrs. Carmichael or me, but when I found him, Noah was inside the room and trying to open the door to the verandah." As if she realized how distressing Craig found this news, Emily added, "You needn't worry. All the doors are locked now."

He tried not to shudder at what might have happened. Though he took pride in his son's expanding vocabulary and physical growth, he hadn't observed the other skills he was developing. What kind of father was he to miss something so important, something that could have had such disastrous consequences? Rachel had been right when she'd said God had good reasons for giving children two parents.

Craig looked at his son contentedly munching a cookie. Thanks to Emily, Noah was safe. He nodded at her, knowing he owed her an explanation.

"I should have anticipated that. Noah's been fascinated with verandahs since he first started walking. He and Rachel used to play on the small one we had at our house." Except on the coldest of days, they'd wait there for Craig to return from school, Noah's giggles carrying to the street when he approached.

"He said his mother fell."

Though Emily's voice was as neutral as he'd made his earlier, Craig heard the unspoken question. "They were waiting for me on the verandah the way they did almost every afternoon. As best I can figure, Noah saw a butterfly and Rachel was reaching for it. That was Rachel. She would have done anything for our son, so if Noah wanted to touch a butterfly, she would have done her best to catch one for him."

Craig paused, tamping down the sorrow that memories of that afternoon always brought. He'd been close but not close enough to save her. "She leaned too far over the railing and lost her balance. Both Noah and I watched her fall to the ground."

It had taken mere seconds, but when he relived that day, Rachel remained suspended in the air for minutes while he raced toward her, desperate to reach her, ultimately failing.

"I don't know how much Noah remembers, but he kept trying to get to the verandah, even though I'd locked the door, and he had nightmares at least once a week until we left Galveston."

Emily blinked rapidly, trying to hold back the tears that spiked her eyelashes, and in that moment, Craig realized how painful this conversation must be for her. She too had lost a beloved spouse, and her loss was more recent than his.

Her voice wavered as she said, "I'm so sorry. It must have been horrible for both of you."

"In some ways, I think it was harder for him than for me. I knew it was an accident, but he was too young to understand anything other than that his mother was gone. The women at church told me children are resilient and that Noah's memories would fade, but he kept wanting to go onto the verandah."

As Emily nodded, Craig felt waves of sympathy emanating from her. "Maybe he was remembering that that was a place to play."

She understood. Others had told him that was unlikely, but somehow Emily, who had no children of her own, had a better understanding of his son than the women who'd raised half a dozen youngsters.

"Between that and the nightmares, I knew we had to leave. I didn't want Noah to grow up in the shadows of those memories."

Emily darted a glance at Noah, who was engrossed in chasing cookie crumbs around his plate. "Has he had any nightmares since you moved here?"

"No, and that seems like a miracle."

"Or the answer to prayer." She turned her attention back to him, her eyes still dark with emotion as she looked at Craig. "You needn't worry. The doors are locked now, and Mrs. Carmichael and I will make sure Noah doesn't go onto the second-story verandahs. I wonder, though, if he might benefit from playing on the first-floor one. That wouldn't be dangerous, and it might help him form new memories."

Craig started to object, then reconsidered. "You could be right." Once again, Emily had impressed him with the depth of her understanding. It was no wonder his son wanted to spend so much time with her. "Noah's fascination with porches might diminish if playing on one becomes part of his daily routine."

"But only a small part." Once again, Emily had anticipated what Craig was planning to say. "I want to find new things for him to do."

That wasn't her responsibility, but Emily didn't seem to mind assuming more of a role in Noah's life.

"Mrs. Carmichael takes him on walks every day," she continued, "but he keeps asking about rides and wants to spend time with the horses. He's told us that he wants a horse and refuses to listen when we say he's too young. In that respect, he reminds me of Beulah Douglas. She used to sneak away from her parents to spend time with my father's horse."

Craig made a mental note to take his son on a horse ride at least once a week. All three of them — Craig, Noah, and Hercules

— would benefit.

"Who's Beulah Douglas? I don't believe I've met her." Although Craig had not memorized the names of everyone he'd met, he felt confident he had not been introduced to anyone named Beulah.

Emily's expression, which had lightened when she'd spoken of Noah's time with the horses, once again turned solemn, making Craig wonder about her connection to the girl.

"She lives on a ranch south of town. Her parents used to bring her into town when they shopped — usually on Saturday — and then again on Sunday for church, but I haven't seen her since the day I returned. I'm worried about her."

The woman was amazing. She'd suffered great personal loss, and yet while some might have wallowed in their grief, Emily continued to feel responsible for others.

"How old is Beulah?" Though Emily hadn't mentioned an age, Craig had the impression that Beulah was a child and wondered if she'd be a playmate for his son, especially since they shared an affinity for horses.

"Twelve."

Older than he'd thought. "Then she ought to be in school."

When Noah started fussing, Emily lifted him out of the chair and pointed toward the wooden blocks he'd brought into the kitchen. "Why don't you show your father what you can build?" she suggested.

Once Noah was occupied with his task, she turned back to Craig. "Many in Sweetwater Crossing wouldn't agree with you. Beulah's different from other children. She's very slow to learn things, and sometimes it's difficult to understand her speech. She looks different too. Her eyes are almond-shaped, and her face . . ." Emily paused, searching for the correct word. "It's hard to describe, but she doesn't look like the other children."

"Which means they tease her." Craig could imagine the pleasure Mitch and Harlan would find in tormenting a child who was in all likelihood unable to defend herself.

"The adults weren't much better. My father preached more than one sermon about us all being God's children, but they didn't listen. They told Beulah's parents she shouldn't be allowed to leave the ranch."

And they'd probably done that in the child's hearing, causing confusion and more anguish.

"The Douglases didn't care what the others said," Emily continued. "They brought Beulah into town and attended church almost every Sunday, although they arrived just as services began, sat in the last pew, and left before everyone else."

Craig nodded. "They're as protective of her as I am of Noah."

"It's different, though. You know Noah will grow up and become independent. Even though Beulah's body continues to grow, her mind will always be that of a child." Emily looked at Noah, perhaps envisioning him as an adult. "Beulah's a truly loveable girl."

Craig had no experience teaching children others called simple, but his heart ached at the thought of a girl being shunned by those who should have known better. As Emily's father had told his congregation, God created and loved all of his children.

"I wish there were something I could do to help Beulah."

The sweet smile Emily gave him warmed his heart. "You're a good man, Craig."

"I try."

"I miss your father's sermons." Mrs. Carmichael took a seat at the table while Emily continued preparing breakfast. Since it was Sunday morning, they would eat half an hour later than on weekdays, when Craig had to be at school before his pupils, or Saturdays, when Emily wanted an early start at cleaning the house, but the widow was not one to lie abed. Or perhaps she sensed that Sundays were difficult for Emily, bringing back memories of her family gathered around the table, enjoying the cinnamon rolls that Mama served only on the Lord's Day.

The rolls had been delicious, as were the scrambled eggs they accompanied, but Emily's most vivid memories were of each of the girls trying to guess the subject of Father's sermon. Mama must have known what he'd chosen, but she feigned ignorance, even on the rare occasions one of them guessed correctly.

The half hours they spent before Father returned to the library for a few minutes of private prayer were filled with love and occasional laughter as well as good food and fellowship. Most of all, they were times when the family was united. Those times were gone forever. The sisters were separated, leaving Emily alone to endure the rumors and innuendos that continued to swirl as townspeople speculated about Father's death. "Why?" they asked. "Why did he kill himself?" But he hadn't.

Oblivious to the direction Emily's thoughts had taken, Mrs. Carmichael continued. "Mayor Alcott and the others try, but they don't have the same knowledge of Scripture your father did."

Few did. Father had not been a gifted orator, but he had spent years studying the Bible. As a result, his sermons had rung with conviction.

Emily cracked another egg into the bowl before she responded. "Alice said they're searching for a new minister. Everyone wants someone here before Advent."

"I hope whoever they find is half the man your father was. Joseph was a fine preacher and a fine man."

The widow's praise brought tears to Emily's eyes, making her wonder if she'd ever be able to hear her father's name without wanting to cry. Why wouldn't anyone believe her when she said that he would not have taken his own life, that he loved life too much to end it?

Perhaps to stem Emily's tears, Mrs. Carmichael changed the subject. "What were services like in Cranston?"

It was a different subject and a more distressing one. Though Emily didn't want to discuss her life with George, she owed the widow a response. "They were different.

Not as many hymns, and the minister preached mostly about fire and brimstone." He'd been a strong advocate of punishment. Perhaps that was part of the reason George had been the way he was.

"I don't think I would have liked the Cranston preacher," Mrs. Carmichael said. "Your father warned of the consequences of sin, but he emphasized love."

And love was one thing that had been lacking in Emily's marriage.

With the pancake batter ready, Emily rose to her tiptoes and reached for the china pitcher Mama used on special Sundays. Though today was not a special occasion, something deep inside her longed for the connection to her mother. Perhaps serving syrup in Mama's pitcher would remind her of good times, not Sundays on the ranch near Cranston and her father's death.

"Let me get that. I'm taller." Mrs. Carmichael matched her actions to her words and stretched her arms toward the pitcher. "It's lovely." She grabbed the handle, then turned.

Afterward, Emily wasn't certain what happened. Perhaps the widow had caught her heel on the braided rug in front of the sink. Perhaps she'd simply lost her balance. All Emily knew was that she fell, hitting her head on the corner of the table, and lay on the floor surrounded by shards of china while blood dripped from the back of her head.

"I'm so sorry." Emily grabbed a towel and knelt next to Mrs. Carmichael, trying to staunch the bleeding. "It was all my fault. I never should have let you do my work."

"Nonsense. I'm the one who tripped, and look what I did — I broke your pitcher."

The pitcher didn't matter. What did was that this woman who'd brought sunshine into the house was injured.

The widow tried to sit up, then moaned again. "Ooh, that hurts."

"You need to stay there until the bleeding stops." If it stopped. Emily was alarmed by the amount of blood Mrs. Carmichael had lost. "I'm going to fetch Doc Sheridan." If Louisa were here, she might have been able to help, but Louisa was in Cimarron Creek. Doc was Emily's only choice.

The widow grabbed Emily's hand, squeezing it so hard that it hurt. "Don't you dare. Head wounds always bleed a lot. It'll stop in a minute or so, and if Doc comes, he'll want to give me morphine. I don't need that." She was adamant in her refusal.

"Sometimes morphine is the only way to bear the pain. My father relied on it."

"That doesn't mean I plan to." The stern tone reassured Emily as much as the slowing flow of blood. "Your father received a serious wound during the war. This is simply a bump on the head." The widow released her grip on Emily's hand and touched her head. "Look at it, Emily. Isn't it bleeding less?"

"Yes."

"Then I was right." This time she sounded triumphant. "I don't need Doc." Moving more slowly than usual, she sat up. "I'm going to rest today. You can make my excuses at church. A little rest is all I need, but don't talk to Doc. I won't risk what happened to your father happening to me."

"What do you mean?" The conversation had taken an unexpected turn.

"I know you don't want to believe that your father killed himself. I understand that, and I agree that if he'd been in his right mind, he would not have done that, but what if he wasn't in his right mind?"

What did Mrs. Carmichael mean?

"Louisa said he was despondent over Mama's death, but that wouldn't have been enough for him to put a noose around his neck. Someone killed him. I know that." Emily simply didn't know how to prove it.

The widow shook her head, then moaned.

151

"Everyone knew he took morphine for the pain, but what if Doc didn't give him enough? What if your father's pain was so horrible he couldn't bear it? People in extreme pain will do things they wouldn't have under ordinary circumstances."

A frisson of fear made its way down Emily's spine. Had she been wrong? Had Louisa been right? Had Father changed more than she realized?

"Is that what everyone thinks happened?"

"I don't know about everyone, but it seems possible to me."

Chapter Ten

Emily was still thinking about the widow's theory hours later. It had distracted her during the sermon, and each time she saw parishioners looking at her, she wondered if they believed the same thing Mrs. Carmichael did. Now that the service had ended, she wanted nothing more than to go home, but she needed to talk to Doc. He wasn't simply Father's physician; he'd been one of his closest friends. He would tell her the truth about Father's pain and whether he'd been despondent.

"Emily, you're just the person I wanted to see." Emily's former schoolteacher laid a hand on her arm, seeming to sense her desire to flee and wanting to stop her.

"Good morning, Miss Albright. Sorry, Mrs. Neville." Emily tried to smile at the woman who'd been such an important part of her growing up. The blue eyes that had once flashed with annoyance when a pupil disobeyed were filled with concern today as she fixed her gaze on Emily.

"I'm no longer your teacher, so why not call me Gertrude? That'll avoid the confusion."

"All right, Gertrude." It felt awkward, but perhaps that would change with practice. "Marriage agrees with you." The impressions she'd had the first time she'd seen Gertrude since her return were confirmed. Her former schoolteacher had a new softness and an undeniable sense of happiness about her.

Smile lines creased Gertrude's face. "Marriage is wonderful, but that's not why I wanted to talk to you. It's such a beautiful day that I was hoping you and Alice would come to the ranch. As dearly as I love Thomas, there are times when I crave female companionship. Please come." She lifted her hand from Emily's arm and touched her shoulder. "Alice has already accepted. I hope you will too."

"I'd like to, but there's something I need to do."

Gertrude gave her one of the looks that had never failed to quell unruly pupils' exuberance. "Can't it wait?"

Emily hesitated, then nodded. It had already been more than a month since

Father died. One more day would make no difference. And so, she found herself hitching Blanche to the buggy and driving Alice and Jane to the Albright ranch.

The last time she'd headed west on this road, she and George were newlyweds on their way to his home. George had been playfully affectionate, leaving Emily filled with anticipation of the joys of married life. And then . . . She bit the inside of her cheek, determined to think of something — anything — else.

"It still seems hard to believe Miss Albright — Gertrude," Alice corrected herself, "is married."

"I thought she was a confirmed spinster."

Before she spoke, Alice gave her daughter one of the loving looks that made Emily more than a little envious, knowing she'd never have a child of her own.

"Thomas was in love with her for years. Rumor has it that he proposed at least once a year, but she always refused."

"I didn't know that."

Alice shrugged. "You missed a lot of gossip. Everyone knew your father didn't approve, so we were careful what we said around you."

For a second Emily considered asking Alice what the townspeople were saying about

Father's death, but she stopped, unwilling to dwell on that again today. What others thought and said didn't matter. Emily *knew* he had not taken his own life, and when she saw Doc tomorrow, he would confirm that. Even though he'd appeared to accept Father's death as suicide when he and the sheriff had come to the barn that awful day, now that he'd had a chance to reflect, surely the doctor would feel otherwise.

Emily took a deep breath and resolved to savor the beautiful September sunshine and the opportunity to be with friends. Instead of talking about Father, she'd ask for Alice's insights into Beulah Douglas.

"I noticed that the Douglases haven't been in church since I came home. Do you know whether something's wrong?"

Alice gave a short nod. "Someone said Mrs. Douglas — the older Mrs. Douglas, that is — has had some kind of stomach ailment. They're staying out of town in case she's contagious."

As the explanation eased Emily's concerns that something might have happened to Beulah, she turned her attention to today's destination. She'd driven past the entrance numerous times and had heard that the house where the wealthiest Sweetwater Crossing family lived was the largest in the county, but this was the first time she had been invited to the Albright ranch.

As she guided Blanche along the carefully maintained road, Emily saw that the rumors were indeed accurate. The house was only one story and lacked the elegance of Finley House, but it sprawled across an expansive yard. Why, she wondered, had Mr. and Mrs. Albright built such a large house when they had only one child? Perhaps they'd been like Clive Finley and had expected to have a dozen children to fill all the rooms.

"Oh, girls, I'm so glad you came." Gertrude rose from one of the rockers on the front porch and hurried down the steps, her hands extended in welcome. "I shouldn't call you girls, should I? After all, you're both grown up. And you, Alice, are a mother."

Her gaze moved to Jane cradled in Alice's arms. "May I hold her?" When Alice transferred her to Gertrude, Gertrude's smile broadened. "You're so sweet." She started to rock the baby, then stopped abruptly when Jane began to cry. "I guess I'm not meant to be a mother," she said as she handed Jane back to Alice, bitterness coloring her words. "Come, let's sit on the porch for a while. I have tea and cakes for us, but it's too early for them. Let's just enjoy the day."

She pointed to the sky, where puff white clouds drifted slowly, casting shadows on the ground. "Aren't those cumulus clouds beautiful?"

For a second, Emily was back in school, listening to Gertrude explain the difference between cumulus, cirrus, and stratus clouds. Alice's mind did not appear to have taken the same detour, because when they were all seated and Jane was once more quiet, she turned toward Gertrude. "You'd be a good mother. Remember how you told us you were *in loco parentis* and explained that that meant you were like a parent to us? You were a good teacher, so I expect you'd be a good mother."

Gertrude's expression became wistful, but she shook her head. "I'm probably too old. After all, I'm thirty-seven."

Only thirteen years older than Emily and Alice, and yet in that moment, Gertrude seemed old enough to have been their mother.

"What do you think of my replacement?" she asked as she set her rocker to moving. "I hear he has very different ideas about discipline."

The hint of censure in her former teacher's voice made Emily say, "Good ones as far as I can tell."

Gertrude's eyes narrowed, reminding Emily of the times she'd misbehaved in school. A scolding was sure to follow, but this time she'd done nothing wrong. Defending Craig from criticism was the right thing to do.

"Are you sure your head hasn't been turned by his handsome face? I know you're a recent widow, but everyone deserves a second chance at love. Your George wouldn't want you to spend the rest of your life alone. You should marry again and have children. That's what he would have wanted."

Gertrude had no idea what George would have wanted or that Emily knew there were worse things than being alone. Though she was tempted to tell Gertrude that, she remained silent.

Undeterred, the former schoolteacher turned to Alice. "Don't you agree, Alice? Don't you want to marry again?"

Emily's friend hesitated. "I miss Cyrus terribly, but you're right. I loved being married, and I want to find another man to love, but I won't do that unless I'm convinced he'll love Jane like his own." She turned toward Emily. "One of the things I admired most about your parents was that they treated all you girls the same. That's what I want for my daughter. Some days I'm convinced I'm destined to remain a widow."

"Maybe not." Gertrude's gaze moved from Alice to Jane. "What about the schoolmaster's son? What's his name?"

"Noah."

Gertrude nodded at Emily's response. "That's right. Noah. He needs a mother just like Jane needs a father. Perhaps I was wrong in thinking Emily was the right one for Craig." She smiled at Alice. "Marriage might be the perfect solution for you and the schoolmaster. You both love your children, and I imagine you'd love each other's child just as much."

It was a perfectly reasonable observation, a logical solution to two problems. It shouldn't have bothered her, and yet Emily found herself troubled by the thought of her friend and Craig together.

"Would you show us around?" she asked Gertrude, as much to avoid thoughts of other people's marriages as anything else. "I've never been here."

"Of course." Gertrude rose. Though Emily had expected her to move toward the front door, she stepped off the porch. "The first thing you need to see is my special flower bed. My mother always says flowers are a waste of good ground, that we ought to grow vegetables, but I insisted on planting flowers."

She led the way over a small rise to a part of the ranch that wasn't visible from the house. There, close to a spreading live oak but far enough away that the branches did not shade it, was a beautiful flower bed. It was small — perhaps three feet wide and seven feet long — but covered in a brilliant array of flowers.

"Oh, Gertrude, this is gorgeous. When did you plant it?"

Emily's hostess turned away for a second before responding. "A long time ago. Before the war broke out. It reminds me of my first love."

Emily exchanged a look with Alice, silently asking if this was some of the gossip she'd missed. An almost imperceptible shake of her head told Emily Alice hadn't heard this story, either.

"What happened to him?" Emily asked.

"He died."

"Oh, how sad, but you have Thomas now."

Gertrude nodded. "Yes, I do. Thomas is proof that everyone has a second chance at love, so don't either of you give up. The right men are waiting for both of you."

Chapter Eleven

"Two apple pies. What's the occasion?" Mrs. Carmichael sniff then smiled as she and Noah entered the kitchen after their morning visit to the horses.

"I'm going to take one to Doc Sheridan." Mama had claimed that gifts of food were always appreciated and that they made people more willing to talk. Emily hoped that would happen today.

"What a good idea. I doubt he's had a home-baked pie since his wife and Phoebe left." Mrs. Carmichael settled Noah on the floor with his bucket of blocks. "I do hope Honor doesn't stay away as long as she did the first time."

When Emily raised an eyebrow, indicating she was curious, the widow continued. "She was gone for six or seven months before Phoebe was born. You can imagine how tongues wagged when Honor returned with a baby, but Doc took it all in stride. Said he'd wanted his wife to be attended by a midwife. It's a shame we still don't have one in Sweetwater Crossing. I've heard ladies say they're more comfortable with another woman."

Emily had no trouble understanding that. When she'd thought about childbirth, she'd always imagined her mother at her side. Mama would have known what to do. But Mama was no longer here, and even if she were, Emily would never share that special experience with her. But Emily was only one woman, and there were others who craved a woman's assistance. Mrs. Carmichael was right: the town needed more than Doc Sheridan.

"Maybe Louisa will become a midwife." Though Emily's sister's dream was to be a physician and heal those who were in pain, perhaps because she'd seen how much Father suffered, helping women bring new life into the world was a noble calling.

Mrs. Carmichael smiled, her approval obvious. "She'd be a good one. You might try to encourage her."

Emily mulled over the widow's advice as she carried the still-warm pie to the doctor's office. If she thought Louisa would listen to her, she'd urge her to work with Cimarron Creek's midwife, but after the way they'd parted, Emily suspected her sister would dismiss anything she suggested. Still, it was a good idea.

"Good morning, Emily." Doc gave her an appraising look when she closed the door behind her. "Unless my olfactory nerve is mistaken, that's an apple pie in your hands. I'm afraid I don't treat pies." He waggled his eyebrows.

"No treatment needed. I'm hoping you'll eat it." Emily handed him the pie, then sat in one of the chairs in front of his desk and looked around the room. Like Doc's manner, it hadn't changed since her childhood. The desk still had two journals, one that the doctor used to record visits, the other listing the medications he'd prescribed. The same potted plant stood in the far corner, although it was taller now than it had been ten years ago. The glass-fronted cabinet still held bottles of tonics and other remedies. The brown jar of the foul-smelling salve Doc insisted was the best cure for a congested chest stood next to the blue bottles of morphine he'd used to treat Father.

"It's strong medicine," Father had told her, "but it's the only thing that makes the pain bearable. I pray you girls will never need it." So far, none of them had. The question was whether Father had been in so much agony that even morphine could not assuage it.

"I'll eat this with pleasure," the doctor assured Emily. "I miss my wife's cooking almost as much as I miss her company. But tell me why you came. I doubt it was only to deliver a pie." The comment proved Father's claim that Doc had good insights into people.

"I want to talk to you about my father."

"Are you still insisting he couldn't have killed himself?" Doc fiddled with one of the journals.

"The father I knew wouldn't have done that, but as many have reminded me, I was gone for more than a year. It's possible he changed during that time." But surely not that much. "Louisa said his leg was paining him more than usual the day he died. Did he come to you for morphine?"

As Doc shook his head, a lock of hair tumbled onto his face. Looking annoyed, he brushed it back, then shook his head again. "Joseph did not come here that day. When I saw him the night before, he was obviously distressed about something. I wish I'd asked him what was bothering him, but as much as I hate to admit it, I'd been at the saloon and had too much whiskey. My mind wasn't as clear as it should have been."

Doc's gray eyes darkened. "You can't imagine how many times I've wished I could turn back the clock to that night. I wouldn't have drunk as much, and maybe Joseph would still be alive."

Emily understood his wish, for she had her own. Hers was that she'd arrived earlier that Saturday. Perhaps then she could have stopped her father from entering the barn. But neither she nor the doctor could go back in time and undo what had been done.

"Do you believe Father was in so much pain that he would have wanted to end his life?"

Doc was silent for a moment, his expression troubled. "I wish I could say no, but I've seen patients hurting so much that they were pleading with God to take them. My grandmother was one of them. I pray to God you never see anything like that."

Emily heard the anguish in the doctor's voice and realized how deeply his grandmother's condition had affected him, but that didn't explain what had happened to her father.

"If Father's pain had been that severe, wouldn't he have come to you? He knew you'd help him."

"Of course, I would have helped him. I would have done anything for him because he was more than simply a patient. Joseph was my friend. I don't know why he didn't come here. All I can tell you is that when the pain becomes too intense, people don't think clearly. They do things they would not have done under other circumstances."

Doc regarded Emily for a long moment. "I'm sorry, Emily. I know that isn't what you wanted to hear."

"No, it isn't."

Today was the day. Though he kept his expression neutral, Craig was smiling internally as he glanced out the window. He hadn't wanted to try the experiment yesterday, knowing his students were always more difficult to control on Mondays when they'd been away for two days, but everything seemed to be cooperating today, including the weather.

"All right, boys and girls," he said when they'd completed their first lesson of the day. "We're going to do something different. Bring your slates and follow me." He headed for the door.

"It's not recess time." Trust Susan to state the obvious.

"We aren't having recess."

Craig waited until all the children had filed out of the schoolhouse, the last closing the door behind him as he'd been taught, then led the way past the library to the park. Though there was quiet speculation as they walked, no one — not even Harlan and Mitch — got out of line. When they reached the large live oak Craig had chosen as his temporary classroom, he nodded.

"I want you all to sit down. This is where we'll have this morning's history lesson."

"Under a tree?" Mitch's lip curled in scorn. "What we gonna do — count leaves?" He picked up one that had fallen and crushed it between his fingers. "Can't count that one."

Ignoring the boy's attempt to rile him, Craig said, "We'll continue our discussion of the American Revolution. During the winter of 1777 to 1778, George Washington and his troops camped at Valley Forge. Who remembers where Valley Forge is?"

Predictably, Susan thrust her hand into the air. She was always the first to respond, eager to show off her knowledge. Craig waited until a second pupil raised his hand before nodding. "Yes, James."

"Pennsylvania."

"Correct. What do you think winters were like there?" As he posed the question, Craig saw a woman and a girl emerge from the livery. Though Craig guessed her to be ten or eleven and old enough to be in school, the girl clutched her mother's hand as they prepared to cross the street.

"Cold." Mitch feigned shivering, then apparently aware that he was no longer taunting anyone, he scowled. The scowl was classic Mitch, but his response was not. This was the first time he'd provided a correct answer to a question.

"Exactly." Craig infused the word with both enthusiasm and approval. "There was snow. A lot of it. Many of the soldiers' boots were so worn they had holes in their soles. Some didn't have any boots at all."

"No boots!"

"That's awful."

"How did they survive?"

While his pupils tried to imagine ways that Washington's troops had coped with the harsh winter, Craig's attention was drawn to the girl and her mother. They wore matching calico dresses, but while the girl had a blond braid, the mother's hair appeared to be light brown. The girl tugged her mother's hand and gestured toward the children seated under the tree, her posture declaring that she wanted to join the class. Her mother shook her head, her voice carrying clearly. "No, Beulah. You can't go there."

So this was Beulah Douglas. From this distance, Craig could see no physical differences, although her dependence on her mother appeared to confirm Emily's statement that the girl was slow to develop.

He rose and approached them, his eyes cataloging Beulah's features. As Emily had told him, there were unmistakable differences between Beulah's face and that of his other students. Her face was flatter, her eyes almond-shaped, her nose and ears smaller than most children's. She would have a difficult time in school because children were often cruel to anyone they perceived as being different, and yet . . .

"Beulah's welcome to join us." The invitation came out seemingly of its own volition.

Mrs. Douglas shook her head again. "Thank you, but no. Come, Beulah. We have errands to do while Blackie is being shod."

As the two of them made their way along Main Street, Beulah kept turning around, her eagerness to be part of the class apparent. If only all his pupils were so enthusiastic.

"I was worried when you missed church, Mary. Emily told us about your fall. You know they can be serious." Clara Adams's voice carried into the kitchen, where Emily

170

was watching Noah eat his lunch and listening for cues that it was time to serve the ladies' next course.

Today was Friday, the day Mrs. Carmichael's friends joined her for a meal and an hour of conversation. Even though the women had urged Emily to share the meal with them and to bring Noah into the dining room, she'd refused. They needed their time together, and Mrs. Carmichael needed a respite, even a brief one, from caring for the active toddler.

"Have you been having dizzy spells? Doc warned me they can happen at our age." Betty Locke sounded more concerned than Mrs. Adams, perhaps because her worries over her own health caused her to consult the town's doctor on a regular basis. Emily had heard the other women chiding her for her dependence on Doc Sheridan, but no one seemed to doubt that the pain she suffered from her lumbago was real.

"Betty's right." Lottie French joined the conversation. "You were always the healthiest of us, Mary. Maybe it's because you're a few years younger, and age will catch up with you. I hope that's not the case." Mrs. French paused to cough. "Between Clara's gout, Betty's lumbago, and my coughs, we all have something wrong with us, but you've never complained about any ailments. The fall you took worries us."

"It wasn't a dizzy spell. I simply tripped." Mrs. Carmichael flashed a smile at Emily as she entered the dining room to clear the soup bowls. "I was fortunate Emily was here. I don't know what I'd have done if I'd been alone, but she took care of everything."

"Living alone worries me. I won't deny that," Mrs. Adams admitted.

While Emily carried the bowls back to the kitchen, Mrs. Carmichael began the proposal she'd discussed with her. "I worry about all of you. You're my dearest friends. What happened to me made me wish you'd move here so we could help each other. I know Emily wouldn't charge you too much."

When she'd first broached the subject, Emily had suspected that Mrs. Carmichael knew Emily could use additional income and was as eager to help her as her friends, but she'd seemed sincere when she insisted that her primary concern was her friends' health.

"I can't. Mr. Locke and I built our Sunday House together. Leaving it would be like losing him again."

Though Emily had had no trouble, no trouble at all, leaving the house she and

George had shared, her marriage had been far different from the Lockes'.

"My gout would make it hard to climb the stairs." Emily heard the regret in Mrs. Adams's voice. "It's a good idea, Mary, but I think I should stay in my own home."

"I agree." Mrs. French was the last to respond. "I've gotten used to solitude. I'm not sure I'd like having a young boy around." She chuckled. "I still remember how much mischief my Todd got into when he was a youngster."

Mrs. Carmichael had predicted that the other women would need a while to get used to the idea. "I hope you'll think about it. These lunches are wonderful, but I'd still like you to live here. As you keep telling me, we're not getting any younger. We don't know how much time we have left."

It was a sobering reminder. Mama's illness had given Louisa and Father some warning, but Emily had not expected George's life to end so abruptly. And Father . . . No matter what anyone said, she was certain he hadn't planned to die so soon.

"It was an ambush. That's the only way I can describe it." Craig wrinkled his nose as he passed the mashed potatoes to Alice.

173

Though the conversation — *confrontation* might be a better word — had been unpleasant, there was no reason to burden his dinner companions with the story. If Alice hadn't asked, he would have said nothing at all.

"I was afraid something like that would happen when I saw the mayor approaching with the Millers and Mrs. Sanders," Emily said as she finished cutting Noah's roast into bite-sized pieces.

No matter how many times Craig told her he could do that, she always refused, saying she enjoyed helping Noah. That was fortunate because Noah still insisted that Emily be the one to help him eat. There were times when Craig felt like the bystander while Emily was the parent.

It was ridiculous to feel that he was being replaced. He wasn't. Besides, one of the reasons he'd brought Noah to Sweetwater Crossing was to give him a feminine influence. Mrs. Carmichael and, to an even greater extent, Emily were providing that. The question was, how would Noah react when the situation changed? If Emily remarried — and Craig had no doubt that she would — she would no longer need to rent out rooms. Either she'd move to her husband's home or Finley House would once again become a private family residence. The thought was oddly disturbing.

"Miller and Sanders. Aren't their sons the troublemakers?"

Mrs. Carmichael's question brought Craig back to the present. "It wouldn't be professional to describe them that way, but they are my most difficult pupils." What had surprised him about the ambush was that Harlan and Mitch had been better behaved this week than any other time since school had begun.

"What did the parents want?" Alice asked as she poured gravy over her potatoes.

"According to the mayor, they objected to my teaching outdoors."

"One piece, Noah. One piece at a time." Emily stopped Noah from piling three bites of meat onto his spoon, then turned to Craig. "You only did it once."

"True, but I told everyone that if they behaved, we'd do it again."

"A new kind of repercussion? Potential rewards rather than punishment."

Craig smiled, not surprised that Emily had understood his reasoning. While he'd sometimes had to explain his actions to Rachel, Emily seemed to think the same way he did.

"Exactly," he said. "So far it's been working. Even Mitch and Harlan have been less troublesome than usual."

"Then why did their parents complain?" The widow's question echoed Craig's reaction when the quartet had approached him.

"The mayor was their spokesman. He claimed being outside was too distracting, that children could not learn when other people were walking by and talking to them."

All the three parents had done was nod, making Craig wonder whether the mayor had approached them rather than vice versa. Though the stated complaint had been the lesson under the tree, Craig suspected that Beulah's presence, although very brief, had bothered the mayor.

"I asked Mrs. Sanders what Mitch told her about the lesson. She said he was glad he lived in Sweetwater Crossing rather than Valley Forge because it's warmer here. I got the impression this was the first time he'd volunteered information about school."

A triumphant smile lit Emily's face. "In other words, you accomplished more than one thing that day."

"I've always felt sorry for Mitch," Mrs. Carmichael said. "From what I've heard, his mother's so busy entertaining her gentlemen callers that she doesn't have much time for him. Betty and Lottie say it's scandalous how many different men spend their evenings with Hazel Sanders."

Craig helped himself to another serving of potatoes as he absorbed the gossip that appeared to have shocked Emily. Whether or not it was exaggerated, he suspected there was a grain of truth in the story, and that changed his perspective of Mitch Sanders. The boy needed more than a teacher. He needed a father, but that was something Craig could not give him.

"I hate to impose on you when you're already doing so much, but I wondered if you'd watch Noah for a few minutes." Mrs. Carmichael kept a firm grip on the boy's hand as she entered the kitchen. "I want to check on Clara. She said her gout was worse than ever yesterday, and she wasn't sure she'd be able to come to lunch today."

Emily nodded. The widow's request was no imposition, particularly since the roast chicken she planned to serve the four women today was already in the oven.

"That'll be fine. Noah can help me make piecrusts." Pie was not on the menu, but he wouldn't know that. Ever since Emily had discovered that he enjoyed playing with the rolling pin, she brought it out whenever she needed to distract Noah. He'd spend long minutes kneeling on a chair and pretending to roll out piecrusts on the table.

"Thank you. I shouldn't be gone more than half an hour."

But it was less than that when the widow reentered the kitchen, her face ashen, tears filling her eyes.

"What's wrong?" Afraid that Mrs. Carmichael might collapse, Emily pulled out a chair and helped her sit. "Would you like a glass of water?" Louisa used to claim that calmed people.

The widow shook her head. "I can't believe it. Clara's dead." The tears that had hovered on her lashes began to fall. "The house was so quiet that I knew something was wrong, but I never thought . . ." Mrs. Carmichael took a deep breath, apparently trying to marshal her emotions. "I found her in bed, already cold. Oh, Emily, I can't believe it."

Emily wrapped her arms around the widow's shoulders, wishing there were something she could do or say to ease her grief. At times like this, words were small comfort, and yet she had to try. "I know how much you loved her. She was more than your neighbor; she was a dear friend." The four widows had been friends for decades, and now one was gone, a reminder that life was indeed short.

"It makes no sense." Mrs. Carmichael shook her head again, and this time her voice was filled with anger. "Other than her gout, she seemed perfectly healthy."

CHAPTER TWELVE

"There've been too many funerals." Mrs. Carmichael raised a crumpled handkerchief to her eyes and dabbed at the tears that continued to leak from the corners.

Emily nodded. "Far too many." Mama had said life had its seasons. That might be true, but this season of funerals was unwelcome. Emily said a silent prayer that this would be the last time she stood outside the church waiting for pallbearers to load a coffin onto a wagon for the short drive to the cemetery.

Mrs. French and Mrs. Locke made their way to Mrs. Carmichael's side. "We need to be strong, Mary," Mrs. French declared. "Clara wouldn't want us to grieve."

But it was normal to grieve. Father had reminded his parishioners that sorrow was part of life, that everyone — even Jesus — wept when a loved one died. Emily knew that was true. The three older widows had mourned their husbands' deaths, and now they mourned their friend. Alice and Craig grieved for their spouses. Only she was different. She'd lost both parents and her husband, but rather than unmitigated grief, hers was mingled with anger — anger that her marriage had not been a happy one, anger that so many believed her father had taken his own life, anger that she had not been with Mama when she'd breathed her last, anger that the quartet of widows was now a trio.

She took a deep breath, reminding herself that anger accomplished nothing positive, then blinked at the sight of a girl hurrying toward the school. The single blond braid and the almost furtive way she was moving left no question of her identity. The question was why Beulah wasn't with her parents. Emily looked behind her and saw the elder Douglases deep in conversation with two other couples.

Knowing the widows wouldn't miss her, Emily crossed the street and approached the girl, who was now standing underneath the window, listening intently to a young boy reciting a multiplication table.

"Hello, Beulah," Emily said softly, not wanting to startle her. "You remember me, don't you?"

The girl turned and smiled. "You're Miss Emily. Your pappy has Horace. He's a nice horse, but he falled dead."

It appeared Beulah was confused. "Horace is still alive, but I think he misses you." The horse had been off his feed ever since Father died. Perhaps seeing Beulah would remind him of better times. "You're welcome to visit him whenever you're in town."

The girl shook her head, then pointed at the schoolhouse. "I want school."

Her calm statement confirmed Craig's impression. When he'd told Emily about seeing Beulah, he'd said her interest in the school appeared to be more than fleeting. He was right. Beulah was as fixated on joining the class as she'd once been on visiting Horace. Unfortunately, while no one objected to her sneaking away to talk to the horse, attending school was not so simple.

Though Emily's heart ached for the girl, she couldn't promise Beulah that her wish would become reality. Instead, she laid her hand on the girl's shoulder. "Your parents are probably worried about you. Let's go back to them."

To her relief, Beulah nodded. "Okay."

Emily was still thinking about Beulah and her wistful expression when she'd looked at the schoolhouse as she headed home with

Noah. He'd accompanied them to the church, but she and Mrs. Carmichael had agreed that he should not attend the interment. Even if it did not raise memories of his mother's burial, lowering a coffin into the ground was something no small child needed to witness.

Mrs. Carmichael needed to go to the cemetery, but Emily did not, and so she took the long way home, stopping at the post office to pick up the mail.

Noah, who normally chattered while they walked, was silent. Perhaps he'd absorbed the solemnity of the funeral. Perhaps he somehow sensed that Emily's thoughts were focused on Beulah and that she was wracking her brain, seeking a way to help the girl. It seemed wrong that someone who wanted to learn was being denied the opportunity simply because she would not learn as quickly as the others. Emily was no closer to finding a solution when they reached Finley House.

"All right, Noah," she said as they entered the front door. "Let's get you something to eat."

After he'd happily slurped his soup and gone upstairs for his nap, Emily began sorting the mail. The majority of the letters came from former parishioners who maintained a correspondence with her father. She'd need to tell them of Father's death. It was a task she dreaded, but that dread paled compared to what she felt about opening the remaining envelope, one addressed to her in Louisa's handwriting. Unsure what to expect after the way they'd parted, Emily found her hands shaking as she slit the envelope and withdrew the closely written sheets.

Dear Sister. That was a positive beginning. *The three of us arrived in Cimarron Creek without delays other than a rainstorm that left the road so muddy we had to stop for several hours to let the ground dry. That was one day I was grateful for the Texas sun.*

Emily smiled and remembered all the times Louisa had complained about the sun, claiming it gave her freckles.

Cimarron Creek is not what I expected, but it's charming in its own way. I was surprised to discover three homes almost as large as Finley House. The townspeople call them founders' houses, because they were built by members of the two founding families.

Louisa might have aspirations of being a doctor, but if that didn't work out, she would make a fine schoolteacher. Perhaps it was because she was the youngest, but she seemed to relish every opportunity she had to teach her sisters something.

We're staying in one of them that belongs to one of Mrs. Sheridan's cousins. Everyone has welcomed me, but the best news is that I've met the town's doctor and its midwife, and they both agreed to let me work with them. Oh, Emily, I'm so happy. I may never leave here.

Emily felt the tension that had knotted her neck when she'd recognized her sister's handwriting begin to subside as she realized that two of her prayers had been answered. The Louisa who'd written this letter was the exuberant Louisa of their childhood, not the angry, resentful woman who'd made their final days together so difficult. And, just as importantly, Louisa was considering midwifery as well as doctoring. That would be an easier road for her to travel and one with a greater probability of success.

Emily hoped — oh, how she hoped — that her sister would return to Sweetwater Crossing and that they could once again be the best of friends as well as sisters, but if that didn't happen, she would still give thanks that Louisa had found people who were encouraging her desire to help others.

Now, if only she would hear from Joanna.

"You'll probably think I'm a meddling old

woman," Mrs. Carmichael said as she passed the bowl of peas to Alice, "but standing by Clara's grave today made me realize how short life can be and how we shouldn't waste a single moment."

Alice nodded. "My mother used to say the same thing."

"My friends and I were fortunate," Mrs. Carmichael continued. "Our marriages lasted for most of our lives. We grew old with our husbands."

The way her gaze moved from Alice to Craig and then to her made Emily uncomfortable. What was the widow going to say? Whatever it was seemed to involve the three of them.

"You've each lost a spouse, and you may believe you've lost your only chance at love, but I assure you that love can come more than once. You weren't here, Craig, and Emily and Alice weren't yet born, so it's unlikely they know this, but I was married twice. Fred died only two years after our wedding, leaving me devastated."

The look Alice gave Emily confirmed that she was as surprised by this story as she'd been by the news that Gertrude had loved a man before Thomas.

Mrs. Carmichael's gaze moved around the table. "I was certain I'd never love again, but then I met Harry. I won't tell you that it was the same love I had for Fred. It wasn't, but it was equally strong and wonderful. Don't give up on love. You're all young enough to marry again."

It was the same advice Gertrude had given Emily and Alice.

Other than Noah's chortling as he mashed his peas, the room was silent. Finally, Alice spoke.

"My situation is different from yours because I have Jane. I know some would say that she needs a father, but she needs more than that. She needs one who'll love her as if she were his own child. That's harder to find."

"That's nonsense," Mrs. Carmichael was quick to say. "Any man would love Jane. Wouldn't you agree, Craig?"

Emily hated the way Mrs. Carmichael was putting them in such awkward positions. It wasn't like the normally sensitive widow, but as she'd said, today had not been a normal day. Still, it was Emily's responsibility to ensure her guests were comfortable.

"I don't believe this is an appropriate discussion for tonight or any night."

The widow shook her head. "I warned you that you might think I was meddling. I won't ask Craig whether he plans to marry

187

again because he already knows how much Noah needs a mother, but what about you, Emily? Don't you dream of children of your own?"

More than almost anything, but dreams didn't always come true.

"I'll never remarry. Never."

"When we're finished here, would you join me on the porch? I need your advice about something."

It probably wasn't the best time, especially after the disturbing conversation at supper, but Craig knew he wouldn't sleep well until he spoke to Emily. Though they talked each night while they washed dishes, those discussions were casual. This was more serious, and he didn't want her to be distracted.

"As long as it has nothing to do with Mrs. Carmichael's suggestion that we all remarry, I'll come."

Craig hadn't been surprised by Emily's adamant refusal to consider a second marriage. Like him, she was still mourning.

"I assure you it has nothing to do with that, although I do wonder what prompted Mrs. Carmichael to be so outspoken."

"My father used to say that people did things they would never have done otherwise during the first few days of grieving. I imagine that's what happened."

Craig considered his own behavior after Rachel died. He couldn't recall having done anything odd, but that might be because he had so few memories of those days.

"From everything you've told me, your father was a wise man, so he might have been right about that."

Emily ran the dishrag over the last of the plates, then rinsed it. "Will you give me a hint about tonight's discussion?"

"No. I want your full attention."

"And whatever it is is more important than sparkling pots and pans."

"Exactly."

A quarter of an hour later, when they were both seated in rocking chairs on the front porch, Emily wrinkled her nose at him. "I'm sure you know that I've been trying to imagine why you could possibly need my advice."

"That's easy. You're an intelligent woman who doesn't rush to judgment. You consider all sides of an argument before you decide which one to espouse."

"I try," she admitted, "but my family can tell you that I have my impulsive moments."

"Everyone has those moments," Craig said, glad that her mention of impulsiveness gave him a way to introduce his subject. "I thought that's all it was the first time, but now I believe it's more than an impulse. I think she wants — no, want isn't strong enough — I believe she needs to come to school."

"Beulah?"

"Yes. How did you know that's who I meant?" He'd deliberately neglected to mention the girl's name, wanting to ease into the discussion.

"I talked to her today. Mrs. Douglas usually keeps Beulah at her side, but she managed to escape after the funeral. I found her standing under the schoolhouse window, listening to someone recite a multiplication table. She told me she wants to be there."

Craig wasn't surprised. "She got farther than the window the next time. I looked up, and there she was in the back of the classroom. Her mother arrived a few seconds later, but Beulah was there long enough for me to see the hunger in her eyes." A hunger that had haunted him. "I want to help her, but I'm not sure what to do, based on everything you've told me."

Though her foot had been moving rhythmically, rocking the chair, Emily stopped and fixed her gaze on him. "Mrs. Douglas tries to teach her at home, but she's not trained. I don't think she had more than six years of schooling herself."

Craig wasn't surprised. Girls' education was frequently abbreviated, since many parents believed their daughters had no need for more than basic reading and writing skills. Cooking, sewing, and caring for children were often prized above academic pursuits.

"I don't think the issue is her mother's qualifications. From what I've observed, Beulah wants to be part of a group. Does she have any siblings?"

"No. There were other children, but none of them lived past infancy." The way Emily shuddered told Craig this was a subject close to her heart and made him wonder whether she had had a child that died at birth.

Emily resumed her rocking. "Beulah lives with her parents and grandmother. I can see where she'd be lonely without other children nearby."

The girl's plight touched Craig as nothing other than Noah had in the months since Rachel's death. "I want her to be able to attend school," he said firmly. "I believe it would be good for the other pupils as well as Beulah." Learning to accept people who were different from them was at least as important as being able to read.

Though she nodded slowly, signaling her understanding, Emily was cautious. "Some of the parents won't agree with you."

Craig had no doubt of that. If they objected to classes being held outdoors, it was unlikely they'd be in favor of something as unusual as having a child like Beulah in the schoolroom.

"I read my contract again." That was the first thing he'd done when he'd returned to Finley House. "There's nothing in it that prohibits me from accepting Beulah as a pupil. We know she's eager. The question is whether her parents would allow her to attend school."

"They might." Doubt colored Emily's response and slowed her rocking. "I know they want the best for her, but there could be another problem. The Douglases live half an hour out of town. Beulah can't ride by herself, and I doubt her parents can afford two hours out of their day to bring her back and forth."

That was a valid concern, but there had to be a solution. "Do any of the other pupils live near the Douglases? Maybe she could ride with one of them."

"Only Simon James."

Craig frowned. "He rides a horse. Do you think Beulah would be comfortable riding with him?"

"I don't know. I've never seen her on a horse. Still, there must be a way." When Emily began to rock faster than before, Craig wondered if she believed the speed would help her think more clearly. She closed her eyes for a few seconds, then smiled as she opened them. "I have an idea that might work."

"What?"

"I was thinking about how the ranchers built Sunday Houses to give them a place to stay overnight when they came into town on weekends."

"Do the Douglases have one?"

"No, but it doesn't matter. Even if they did, Beulah couldn't live there alone. Thinking about the Sunday Houses made me realize I could offer Beulah a weekday house." She pointed to the verandah above them. "You know I have empty rooms. If her parents agree and if Beulah is willing, I could offer her a room here during the week. Her mother could bring her to school Monday morning and pick her up Friday afternoon. In between, she could stay here. What do you think?"

Before he could respond, a small frown crossed Emily's face. "Would it be awkward to have one of your pupils living here with you and Noah?" she asked.

Craig thought for a moment, trying to envision Beulah at the supper table as well as in the classroom. Under normal circumstances, he would have avoided even the slightest hint of intimacy with a student, but these were not normal circumstances.

"It might be a problem if Beulah were an ordinary pupil," he admitted, "but she's not." He paused for a second, then gave Emily a warm smile. "I knew I was right to ask for your advice. You're not just thoughtful, Emily; you're brilliant."

Brilliant. No one had ever called her that. As she headed toward the Douglas ranch the next morning, Emily was still smiling at the idea that Craig, a man who chose his words carefully, would use that term to describe her. The time she had spent with him last night had been extraordinary. That was the only way to describe it. The heady feeling that he valued her opinion enough to consult her about something had only increased as they'd worked together, exploring possible ways to help Beulah. Throughout their discussion, Craig had treated her like a partner — an equal partner — and that was not simply extraordinary, it was unprecedented.

George had never done that. From the moment he'd carried her over the threshold, he'd made her role clear. She had her responsibilities; he had his, and his were more important. Father and Mama had had many discussions with her, but in each case, they'd been telling her something, not asking her opinion. The relationship with her sisters had been different. As the oldest, she'd been the leader, the one giving advice. There had always been a hierarchy. Until Craig. Until last night. And oh, how wonderful equality had felt.

Mrs. Carmichael hadn't been as effusive as Craig, but she'd agreed that inviting Beulah to live with them was a good idea. Now all that remained was learning whether Beulah's parents were willing to let her attend school and — more importantly — spend her weeknights at Finley House. Emily knew it wouldn't be easy for them to be separated from their daughter, even if they believed that schooling would benefit her. The question was whether they would trust Emily enough to permit it.

When she reached the farmhouse, Emily saw Beulah and her mother near the chicken coop. Though she was surprised neither of them had heard her approach, she dismounted and hooked Blanche's reins over the porch rail, then smiled when Beulah spotted her.

"Miss Emily!" Beulah's cry of delight left no doubt that she welcomed her. She dropped the tin plate of food she'd been scattering for the chickens and tugged on her mother's skirt. "Mama! Miss Emily is here."

Mrs. Douglas turned, concern etching her face. "Is something wrong?"

"No, no. Nothing at all." Emily hadn't realized that her unannounced arrival might alarm the Douglases. She gave Mrs. Douglas a reassuring smile while Beulah wrapped her arms around her waist. "I'd like to talk to you and Mr. Douglas. Privately," she added, tipping her head toward Beulah.

Though Mrs. Douglas's expression still radiated concern, she nodded. "Certainly. Hiram's in the barn." She touched Beulah's shoulder. "Miss Emily is probably thirsty. Mama's going to be busy for a few minutes, so I'm trusting you to help Grandma get tea and some cinnamon rolls ready for us. I know you can do it."

A wide grin split Beulah's face. "Yes, Mama. Can we use the pretty dishes?"

"There's no need to fuss," Emily protested.

But Mrs. Douglas did not agree. "That's

196

a good idea, Beulah. Tell Grandma I said we should do that." When the girl skipped toward the house, her mother led the way to the barn. "Hiram, we have a visitor. Emily Vaughn." She paused as her husband emerged from the building, blinking at the bright sunshine, then said, "That's not right. It's Emily Leland now."

"Just Emily is fine."

She hoped her smile would reassure Beulah's parents. Though she knew them to be around the same age as Gertrude, they appeared older, the gray hairs already salting their light brown hair and wrinkles at the corners of their blue eyes making Emily wonder whether those visible signs of aging were the result of caring for Beulah.

After she'd greeted Mr. Douglas, she said, "I'd like to talk to you about your daughter."

"Has she done something wrong?" Mr. Douglas's voice was harsh with worry.

"Not at all. I'm here for a very different reason." Emily waited until Mr. Douglas relaxed enough to lean his shoulder against the barn door before continuing. "Has Beulah said anything to you about going to school?"

Mrs. Douglas nodded. Unlike her husband, her posture remained stiff, telling Emily she was still worried. "She talks about it all the time. I've told her she can't attend school, but she doesn't understand."

Emily wasn't surprised by either part of Mrs. Douglas's response. "What if she could go? Would you agree?"

Mr. Douglas exchanged a look with his wife before he spoke. "What do you mean?"

Emily explained the plan she and Craig had devised, finishing by saying, "Both Craig and I believe this might be good for Beulah. We're willing to try it if you are."

The parents' expressions were ones that Emily could not decipher. "We've never been apart," Mrs. Douglas said. "It would be hard for us, but I'm afraid it would be even worse for Beulah. I'm not sure how she'd handle sleeping in a strange house."

Mr. Douglas wrapped his arm around his wife's shoulders. "You know, Miriam, there's only one way to find out."

"Then you think we should?"

"Yes." He squeezed her shoulder. "Everything I've heard about Mr. Ferguson tells me we can trust him, and we've known Emily her whole life. Her parents raised her well." Mr. Douglas turned his gaze to Emily. "I can practically hear your father telling us this is the right thing to do."

That appeared to be all the encouragement Mrs. Douglas needed. Though her smile was strained at the thought of being separated from Beulah, she nodded. "You're right, Hiram. We owe it to Beulah to give her a chance at school. I'll drive her into town tomorrow." She blinked, trying to hold back tears. "Thank you, Emily. If there's ever anything we can do for you, you need only ask. Now let's go into the house and tell Beulah."

CHAPTER THIRTEEN

"I can go to school?" Beulah's expression of awe and wonder was so intense that Emily felt tears well in her eyes. She'd known the girl would be excited, but her reaction was stronger than she had expected and confirmed the wisdom of the plan she and Craig had developed.

"Yes. Your parents have agreed that you'll stay with me during the week." Emily took a bite of the cinnamon rolls that Beulah and her grandmother had arranged on a china plate. They were delicious, with a slightly different flavor from the ones she made. She'd have to ask Mrs. Douglas which spices she used, but not now. There was only one thing to discuss now.

"You'll have the room across the hallway from me," she told Beulah. "It's very pretty, and I'll be close by if you need anything during the night."

"I'll sleep there?" Beulah's enthusiasm

seemed to wane.

When Beulah's mother raised an eyebrow, signaling that this was a private discussion, Beulah's grandmother rose and addressed Emily. "I want to show you the quilt I'm fixin' to finish." Though she might have once been taller than Emily, Mrs. Douglas's back was now curved, subtracting a few inches. While her gray hair bore further witness to her age, her blue eyes still seemed youthful.

"This used to be for storage," the older Mrs. Douglas explained as she ushered Emily inside a room that opened off the kitchen and closed the door behind them. "My rheumatism got so bad that I couldn't climb the stairs no more, so Miriam and Hiram reckoned this should be my bedroom. All that's left is that." She gestured toward a large wooden cabinet with an intricately and inexpertly carved door. "My son figured he'd try his hand at carving. It's plain as the nose on my face that he ain't a very good carver, but I got me a place to store my quilt supplies."

She opened the door, revealing a rainbow of fabrics. Emily's mother, who'd enjoyed quilting, would have loved this. She'd claimed that piecing a quilt was like painting with fabric.

"Here's the one I've been workin' on." Mrs. Douglas pulled a folded quilt from the cabinet and laid it across her bed.

Emily stared at a design unlike any she'd seen on a quilt. Instead of a geometric pattern that was repeated in different blocks, bits of fabric had been sewn together to form a single scene. Somehow, Mrs. Douglas had captured the beauty of spring in the Hill Country. A field of bluebonnets and Indian paintbrush in the foreground was balanced by spreading oak trees and granite and limestone hills in the background. There was even a large prickly pear cactus in one corner.

"This is incredible. My mother would have called it a fabric painting."

Mrs. Douglas stroked the prickly pear, smiling at the spines that were far softer than real ones. "That's what she said when she showed it to me."

"Mama made this?" Emily stared at it with new eyes. The quilt was different from anything her mother had done, and yet now that she knew to look carefully, she recognized some of the fabric. "That's one of my dresses." She touched the piece. "And that looks like one of Father's shirts."

Mrs. Douglas nodded. "She said the whole family was on it. That was mighty important to her. Your mama done finished the piecin' afore she became so ill, but we both knew she couldn't quilt it. That's when I brung it here." The older woman gave Emily a piercing look. "Do you like it?"

How could she not like something so exquisite? "It's the most beautiful quilt I've ever seen."

"That's good. You see, your mama was gonna give it to you for your birthday."

Craig kept a close eye on the door. Recess had ended, and if everything went according to the plan, Mrs. Douglas would bring Beulah to school in the next ten minutes.

Emily had been practically glowing when she'd recounted her visit to the Douglas ranch, telling him everyone had agreed to let Beulah try attending classes. There'd been a bounce in her step and a softness in her expression that he hadn't seen before, making him wonder exactly what had happened at the ranch, but he hadn't asked. It was enough to know that Beulah would have a chance for the schooling she craved.

Emily had suggested Mrs. Douglas take Beulah to Finley House first to show her her room, then bring her here. As if on cue, the door opened, revealing the young girl clinging to her mother's hand.

"Good morning, Beulah." When he smiled and walked to the back of the room, Beulah dropped her mother's hand and took a step forward, her fear turning to awe as she looked around.

Craig heard muffled gasps when he escorted his new pupil into the classroom and gestured toward an empty desk. "You'll sit with Susan." The two girls were the same age but had very different levels of intelligence. Though he had not spoken to Susan about her seatmate, Craig's instincts told him she would be kind to Beulah, and the smile she gave the newcomer confirmed his decision.

He nodded at Mrs. Douglas, wordlessly telling her she could leave, then spoke firmly. "Boys and girls, please welcome Beulah."

Harlan and Mitch exchanged looks that didn't bode well for peace in the classroom.

"She ain't never come here before," Mitch observed.

"There's a first day of school for everyone. This is Beulah's." Craig walked to the front and gestured toward the map that he'd unrolled for their next lesson. "It's time for geography. Who can find South Carolina?"

Beulah watched intently as one of the youngest girls rose and pointed toward the state's location, earning Craig's approval. She said nothing during the rest of the morning, but when he dismissed the group for lunch, she remained behind, staring at the map.

"Is there something you want?" he asked.

She nodded, then approached the map and pointed at it. "South Carolina."

The warmth that filled Craig's heart threatened to overflow. It was as he'd suspected. While Beulah might not learn at the same pace as his other pupils, she was like parched soil, eager to absorb life-giving nutrients.

"That's right, Beulah. Good job."

The rest of the day went smoothly, but Craig found himself more tired than normal as he walked back to Finley House. As much as he'd like to believe otherwise, he wasn't naïve enough to think there would be no problems. Beulah's presence was a major change in the classroom, and not everyone welcomed change.

"I went to school." Beulah grinned as Emily brushed her hair and prepared to braid it for sleep. "It was good."

So many good things had happened today. Craig had reported that Beulah's first day in the classroom had gone well. Noah had welcomed her, apparently considering her a better playmate than Jane since she could walk and talk. Although she'd shed a few tears after supper when the reality of spending the night without her parents close by had hit her, Beulah had regained her usual cheerfulness and was prattling about her time at school.

The one sour note had been Alice. She'd been uncharacteristically quiet and had rarely directed her gaze to Beulah, even when the girl was speaking. Emily could only hope that her friend would be more comfortable with Beulah after she spent more time with her.

"Granny made this quilt." Beulah pointed toward her bed, where a red, white, and blue quilt had replaced the light green spread. Her mother had suggested bringing the quilt so that Beulah would have a bit of her home here. "They're Texas stars," the girl explained.

"I see." Mrs. Douglas had used elements of the state flag to create a distinctly Texan covering. "It's beautiful." But not as beautiful as the quilt Mama had designed for Emily. Tears still filled her eyes when she thought of it.

"You were her firstborn," Mrs. Douglas had explained. "She tole me she wanted you to have something special." Beulah's grand-mother had pointed to two pieces of fabric that Emily didn't recognize. "This here was part of the dress she wore when she married your father, and this 'un was from his wedding suit."

Mama had incorporated every aspect of Emily's life except her wedding to George. Was that because she had nothing from that day, or had she somehow sensed that the marriage was a mistake? Emily would never know. All she knew was that, despite the cruel letter George had sent, her mother's love had not faltered. That knowledge was an even more priceless gift than the quilt itself.

"Are you expecting an ambush today?" Emily asked after breakfast the next Sunday. They'd be leaving for church in a few minutes, but Craig and Emily had lingered at the table for a second cup of coffee while Mrs. Carmichael brushed Noah's hair for the tenth time, trying to tame his cowlick.

"It wouldn't be an ambush if I expected it, would it?"

As he'd hoped, Emily laughed. "I stand corrected, Mr. Schoolmaster. I should have asked whether you were expecting an attack."

"I am." Despite the relative calm, he suspected at least a few parents would have something to say about Beulah attending school. "I'm surprised the mayor hasn't talked to me. Perhaps he's waiting for some parents to complain."

"But no one has."

Even Alice, who'd tried but failed to hide her discomfort over sharing the dinner table with Beulah, had admitted that no one who'd come into the library had commented on the new pupil.

"Not so far. The students have been more accepting than I expected. Some treat Beulah like she carries the plague and shy away from her, but others have included her in their games at recess." And that had pleased both him and Beulah. She'd returned from recess with a grin on her face and color in her cheeks.

"She's happy." Emily's smile said she was as well. "Every night when I tuck her into bed, she tells me how much she likes school. When she prays, she thanks Jesus for making you her teacher. She thinks you're an angel."

The thought was so ludicrous it made Craig laugh. "Hardly! We'll see what happens after church. I doubt the word *angel* will be part of the conversation."

As he'd expected, the mayor led a contingent of parents toward him once services had ended. As he'd expected, there were more than there'd been the day they'd complained about outdoor classes. What Craig hadn't expected was that Susan's parents stood close to the mayor.

"I'm sure you know why these people want to talk to you." Mayor Alcott gestured toward the people who'd formed a semicircle behind him.

Before he could respond, Emily spoke, her voice pitched so that no one could fail to hear her. "If you're here to compliment Mr. Ferguson on the way he maintains discipline without resorting to corporal punishment, I agree with you."

The reaction was immediate. Several parents murmured. The mayor frowned. "No one asked for your opinion, Emily," Alcott declared.

"Be that as it may, I'm a concerned citizen. I have every right to be here."

Though Craig appreciated her support, he needed to control the situation. He took a step toward the group of parents, keeping his expression as neutral as he could. "Is there a problem?"

"Yes." A dark-haired man Craig recognized as Clarence Braxton's father practi-

209

cally shouted the word. "We don't like having Beulah Douglas in the same room as our children."

"And why would that be?" Craig's only other interaction with the man had been amiable, when he and his wife had explained that Clarence was deaf in one ear. They'd seemed pleased when Craig said he'd ensure that Clarence was seated where he could best hear him.

Mr. Braxton scowled. "Because she's simple. She don't learn like my Clarence do."

Craig forbore pointing out that Mr. Braxton hadn't learned the finer points of grammar, but before he could make any reply, Clarence's father continued. "You agree with me, don't you, Miss Albright? You wun't let Beulah come to school when you was the schoolmarm."

Craig sensed Emily's surprise that the former teacher had joined the ever-growing crowd. The first time he'd met her, Gertrude had advised him about the best ways to ensure that Sweetwater Crossing's children continued to advance their learning. Her expression made him suspect she would not be supportive today, perhaps because he hadn't followed her advice in several matters.

210

"I'm Mrs. Neville now." The correction was delivered with all the solemnity of a lesson. "You're right, though, Mr. Braxton. I felt that Beulah's presence in my classroom would not be beneficial for my other students."

Her classroom. Her students. Craig wanted nothing more than to remind Gertrude Albright Neville that she was no longer in charge of the school, but he knew that would accomplish nothing positive. Instead, he merely inclined his head, acknowledging her comment but not agreeing with it.

"Mr. Ferguson is the teacher now," Emily said firmly. "The decision is his."

The former teacher gave Emily a look designed to quell what she obviously viewed as rebellion, but Emily refused to back down. "You know I'm right, Gertrude."

Emily had mentioned that she and Alice had spent at least one afternoon with their former teacher and that their relationship seemed to be changing from teacher-student to friends. That she was willing to jeopardize her fledgling friendship spoke volumes about Emily's integrity.

"You ain't got no children, Emily. You got no right to be here."

Craig saw her flinch at the attack from a

dark-haired man he didn't recognize, but she said nothing, simply raised her chin and glared at the man who'd shouted at her.

"We're payin' you to educate our children." The dark-haired man clenched his fists, making Craig wonder if he planned to use them.

Wanting to defuse the situation but refusing to accede to the unspoken demand that Beulah be banned from the classroom, Craig turned to the mayor. "It's my understanding that my salary comes from taxes. Is that correct?"

Mayor Alcott nodded. "Yes."

"Do the Douglases pay taxes?"

"Yes." The mayor's discomfort with Craig's questions was obvious.

"Then they have the right to expect an education for their daughter."

Mr. Braxton shook his head. "Not at the expense of my Clarence. He needs to learn his letters."

"I agree, and he's making good progress. I don't understand your concern."

The dark-haired man clapped Mr. Braxton on the shoulder in a show of solidarity, then glared at Craig. "You're spending time with the simple gal that oughta be spent with our children."

"Did Clarence say he was being neglected?" Craig directed the question at the boy's father.

"No, but . . ."

As the man's response trailed off, Craig turned toward Susan's parents. "Does your daughter feel neglected?"

"No, but . . ."

Before Mr. Johnson could complete his sentence, Emily spoke. "Today is the first day I'm glad my father is dead. I wouldn't want him to see this. It's disgraceful. You claim to be Christians, but you're not acting the way Jesus would. You seem to have forgotten that God created each and every one of us. Only he knows why Beulah is slower to learn than most children, but just because she's slow is no reason to deny her a chance to learn."

Her eyes flashing with anger, Emily pointed a finger at Mr. Braxton. "How would you feel if Mr. Ferguson refused to teach your son because Clarence is hard of hearing?"

"It's not the same."

Emily shook her head. "You're wrong, Mr. Braxton. It is exactly the same."

CHAPTER FOURTEEN

"Can we go for a walk tonight?" Beulah gave Emily a hopeful look as she finished her last bite of spice cake.

"If you want to." The girl's enthusiasm seemed almost as boundless as Noah's, perhaps because she spent most of the day seated in a classroom rather than helping her mother with tasks at home. By evening Noah's energy would flag, but Beulah's seemed rekindled. Trying to find something that would help her sleep in a still-unfamiliar bed was the reason Emily had suggested their first evening walk. Now Beulah appeared to expect them to be daily events.

"I do. Noah likes walks."

Craig chuckled. "Noah likes the cookies he gets when we come back."

Noah, who'd been listening intently, clapped his hands. "Cookie."

"I'll have them ready for you. Maybe some

214

warm milk too."

Emily tried to refuse Mrs. Carmichael's offer. It wouldn't take her long to heat the milk when they returned, and she hated for the older woman to work after supper. Though Mrs. Carmichael never complained, Emily saw signs of fatigue each evening. "You're not supposed to be helping in the kitchen. You already do so much."

The widow shrugged. "Warming milk is easier on my knees than walking." She winked at Craig. "Some days I'm sure your son could outrun a racehorse."

"Don't give him any ideas." Craig lifted Noah from his chair. "C'mon, little man. We need to wash your face and hands. We don't want you to scare people." At least as much of the cake's frosting had made its way to Noah's cheeks as into his mouth.

Though there were only a few crumbs on Beulah's face, Emily sent her upstairs to wash, leaving her alone with Alice and Mrs. Carmichael.

"Will you join us for the walk?"

Alice shook her head. "Not tonight. Jane has been fussy."

It was the response Emily had both expected and dreaded. The first night Emily had suggested walking with Beulah, the four of them accompanied Alice and Jane home,

215

then came back to Finley House. Though she said nothing while they walked, Alice was visibly nervous, glancing around in apparent fear that others would see her.

Yesterday she suggested Emily and Craig take the children in the opposite direction, ostensibly to give Beulah and Noah some variety, but declined to accompany them. Tonight there was the feeble excuse of Jane's fussiness, which no one had seen. If Mrs. Carmichael hadn't been present, Emily would have asked Alice what was really bothering her, but she didn't want to embarrass her friend in front of someone else.

"Do you think she's teething?" Emily asked, throwing out a plausible excuse.

"Possibly." Alice seized on it. "She didn't take a long nap today, so she could be tired. I'd best get her home." Scooping her baby into her arms, Alice left.

"You know that wasn't the problem." The widow waited until Alice was out of earshot before she spoke.

"We don't know how long Jane slept." Emily wasn't certain why she was defending her friend, but it seemed disloyal to do otherwise.

"That's true, but neither of us saw any sign of crankiness. What are you going to do about Alice?"

"I'm not sure," Emily admitted. "Right now, though, I plan to enjoy my walk."

When Craig, Noah, and Beulah appeared, their faces clean and shining, Emily smiled. "The ground is dry. I thought it might be a good day to walk along the creek."

Noah grinned. "Me wade!"

"I'm afraid not, son. It's too cold, but you might see frogs or fish." Despite Noah's protest that he was old enough to do it without assistance, Craig held his hand as they descended the steps to the backyard.

Emily studied the sky for a moment, noting the clouds that were rolling in. While she doubted it would rain, darkness could fall before they returned.

"We should probably take a lantern." Since Beulah was always offering to help, Emily turned toward her. "There's one hanging inside the barn. Would you get it for us?"

Horror and something else, something Emily thought might be fear, crossed Beulah's face. "No! No barn! Bad man!" She raced behind Craig and stood there, visibly shaking.

The look Craig gave her told Emily he was as puzzled as she. "That's all right, Beulah." Emily used the same tone she used to soothe horses. "There are no bad men there, but you don't need to go into the barn. I'll get the lantern."

When she returned with it, Beulah appeared to have forgotten her outburst. She held Noah's hand and led him toward the creek, leaving Emily and Craig to follow.

"What do you think frightened her?" Craig kept his voice low, though Emily doubted Beulah was paying any attention to the adults. She seemed engrossed in a conversation with Noah.

"I have no idea. I don't know what happened while I was gone, but Beulah used to spend time here when her parents came into town. We'd find her talking to my father's horse. Sometimes Horace was in the corral. More often, though, he was in the barn. Father used to say his horse was afraid of getting sunburned."

Emily thought about the interactions she'd seen since Beulah had moved to Finley House and realized they were different. "She still talks to Horace, but only when he's outside."

Craig looked thoughtful. "I suppose Beulah could have heard people talking about your father's death in the barn and saying they thought suicide was wrong. That might make her believe he was a bad man."

Though the explanation was plausible,

Emily bristled. "Father wasn't a bad man. I know he didn't kill himself."

Craig slowed his pace and placed his hand on Emily's arm, perhaps to calm her. "Beulah only knows what she heard."

Before Emily could respond, Noah raced toward them. "Look, Pa!" He gestured toward the creek.

"Fish." Beulah confirmed the sighting. "We saw fish."

After Emily and Craig had admired the fish and the children's attention began to wander, they resumed their walk, Beulah and Noah once again leading the way and setting the pace.

Emily smiled at the memory of how often her family had strolled along the creek after supper. She and her sisters had searched for fireflies rather than fish while Mama and Father followed, speaking of things that held no interest for their daughters, but the scene was the same: a family enjoying an evening walk.

Emily's smile faded. If strangers saw the four of them tonight, they'd probably believe they were a family, sharing a perfect moment in a perfect life. That was all an illusion. This wasn't Emily's family, and it never would be her life. A loving husband and two children — maybe more — had been her dream for as long as she could recall, but it was one dream that would never, ever come true.

She couldn't put it off any longer. The pot roast was cooking; the pie was cooling; Mrs. Carmichael was watching Noah. Emily could easily leave Finley House for an hour, and so, though she wasn't looking forward to the next few minutes, she donned her hat and gloves and headed for the library.

As she'd hoped, the room was empty save for Alice and Jane. Perhaps it was only her imagination that Alice's smile seemed a bit strained, or perhaps Alice knew why she'd come.

"I wish you'd stayed last night. You might have enjoyed the walk," Emily said after she'd declined Alice's offer of a cup of coffee. "Noah and Beulah were so excited when they saw fish and a frog that I was afraid they wouldn't sleep. But they did." It was Emily who'd had difficulty falling asleep.

Alice shook her head slowly. "I wouldn't have enjoyed it." She paused for a moment. Then, seeming to realize Emily was waiting for an explanation, she continued. "You've probably noticed that I'm not comfortable with Beulah. I try, but I can only understand half of what she says."

Emily had had the same problem the first few days Beulah had spent at Finley House, but as her ears became accustomed to Beulah's speech, Emily found she was having less difficulty. Moreover, she knew Alice couldn't always understand Noah, and that didn't seem to bother her.

"It's more than that, isn't it?" The reason Emily had come here was to understand her friend's concerns and how they might affect her guests. Though she hated confrontation as much as Alice did, Emily knew she couldn't ignore the strain that characterized supper the days Beulah was there.

"You don't think Beulah should be at school or staying at Finley House, do you?"

Alice recoiled slightly from Emily's blunt statement, then nodded. "You're right. I don't. Children like her make others uncomfortable."

"And so they should be hidden away."

Alice nodded again. "That's the way it's always been."

Alice wasn't saying anything Emily hadn't heard before, and yet the fact that it was her friend who was saying it angered Emily. She'd expected more tolerance from Alice.

Emily took a deep breath and exhaled slowly, trying to control her emotions. "Just because it's always been that way doesn't make it right. Beulah's happy at school, and she obviously enjoys spending time with you and Jane." Like Noah, Beulah was fascinated by the baby.

When Alice did not reply, Emily continued. "She would miss you if you didn't come to dinner, and so would I." Though Alice hadn't said anything, Emily knew her well enough to realize that she was considering no longer having supper at Finley House.

"I know." Alice turned to look at her daughter. When she was satisfied that Jane was content playing with her rag doll, she turned back to Emily. "I don't want to give up your wonderful meals or seeing you every day, but having Beulah there makes it hard for me. I guess I'm not as good a person as you."

Emily wished there were something she could do to lessen the pain she heard in Alice's voice. Her friend was struggling, her head and her heart battling for supremacy. "I'm not judging you, and I won't ask you to do something that makes you uneasy." Emily laid her hand on Alice's in an attempt to comfort her. "We've been friends for a long time, so I don't want Beulah to come between us, but I can't hurt her, either."

Emily hoped she wouldn't be forced to choose between them, but if she were, there was no question of what she'd do. Alice was a grown woman, fully capable of caring for herself, while Beulah was a girl who needed others to care for her and protect her from those who didn't understand her limitations.

"I know." Alice's face crumpled. "I'm trying, Emily. I really am. I want to continue having supper with you — all of you — but I won't join you for walks."

Though she didn't say it, Emily knew the reason was that Alice feared others would see her with Beulah. She was like some of the pupils Craig had described, acting like Beulah carried some communicable disease.

"I understand." While she would have preferred that Alice spent the entire evening with them, she would accept the compromise her friend had offered. "Of course you're welcome to eat with us."

Alice let out a sigh of relief. "Oh, I almost forgot. Gertrude came in first thing this morning to invite us to have tea with her next Sunday. Do you want to go? It'll give us a chance to spend some time together."

Without Beulah.

Craig mounted the stairs, wondering why

his son hadn't greeted him when he'd come home from school. Most days, Noah was waiting for him, but when he'd called out, there'd been no response. Perhaps he was still napping. More likely, he and Mrs. Carmichael were outside. The widow had started taking Noah with her when she visited her elderly friends, saying the other widows enjoyed seeing a youngster and that Noah was well behaved in their homes.

When he reached the top of the stairs, Mrs. Carmichael emerged from her room. "If you're wondering where Noah is, come out to the verandah and look."

The verandah. Craig fought the dread that welled up inside him at the sound of that word. It was foolish, he told himself. The widow knew that Noah was never to be left alone, especially on a verandah, but fear wasn't so easily conquered. Even though Mrs. Carmichael hadn't broken the rule before, there was always a first time.

"Look." The pleasure in her voice told Craig his son was in no danger, and indeed he was not. When he reached the verandah and looked down, he saw Noah and Beulah seated under one of the live oaks, gazing intently at the book on Beulah's lap.

"Don't worry. I've been watching them." Mrs. Carmichael addressed Craig's unspoken worry. "I didn't realize Beulah could read, but she insisted on taking the book with her. They've been out there for half an hour now." There was a hint of wonder in the widow's voice at the realization that Noah had remained in one place for so long.

"Beulah can't read very well, but Noah won't know the difference as long as the story is interesting." Craig suspected Beulah was looking at the pictures and inventing a story. Or, if the book was one her parents had read to her, she could have memorized it. In either case, his son was content and Beulah appeared happy. That was what mattered.

The widow turned around, leaning against the railing as she addressed Craig. "I didn't share my concerns with Emily, but at first I wasn't sure about having Beulah here. Now I see that she was right. Beulah seems to be thriving."

"And Noah enjoys her company." His son didn't understand why she went home on weekends and asked about her each day she didn't join him for breakfast and supper. Though he didn't mope, there was no denying that Noah was happier when Beulah was here.

Mrs. Carmichael's eyes narrowed, the calculating look she gave Craig telling him he might not like whatever she planned to say next.

"I know I may sound like I'm meddling again, but Noah needs a mother. It becomes more apparent to me each day. Emily and I do our best, and Alice helps when she's here, but it's not the same." She looked up at him. "You know how I feel about second marriages. It would be good for you as well as Noah."

Craig's instincts had been accurate. Mrs. Carmichael had steered the conversation in a direction he didn't want to travel. It wasn't as though he hadn't considered everything she'd said both the night of Mrs. Adams's funeral and now. He had. It was simply that he wasn't ready and possibly never would be ready to take the steps she advised.

Though he was tempted to tell the widow she was indeed meddling, Craig did not. Her questions were motivated by concern and genuine affection for his son, and they deserved answers.

"If I marry again, it will be to give Noah a sibling or two. That's the only reason." And it was a compelling one, for he knew that children benefited from having the company of brothers and sisters. Though his childhood had been a happy one, he'd always felt that he was missing something important when he saw his playmates' interactions with their siblings.

"There'll never be anyone like Rachel," he said.

Mrs. Carmichael nodded. "You wouldn't want another Rachel, but what about someone very different? Second loves can be good. You've heard my story, but it's not the only one. Look at Ruth in the Bible. If she hadn't found a second love, King David would not have been born."

Craig had to smile. "I'm not Ruth."

"No, you're not," she agreed, matching his smile. "But you're a man with abundant love to give."

"And you're a would-be matchmaker. Next thing I know, you'll be telling me to marry either Emily or Alice." He'd seen the speculative looks Mrs. Carmichael gave both of them whenever he engaged them in conversation.

"Would that be so bad?"

Craig shrugged. He couldn't imagine himself married to Alice, particularly after the way she was treating Beulah. There was no overt hostility, but the way she shied away from the girl made his stomach turn.

Then there was Emily, a woman with the abundant love Mrs. Carmichael claimed he had. She treated his son like her own child.

She championed Beulah. She even made Craig feel like part of the family rather than simply a boarder. Emily was an intriguing woman who dominated far too many of Craig's thoughts. She was also a woman who'd made it clear she had no intention of remarrying. There was no point in thinking about something that would never happen.

"When I invited you, I didn't realize we'd have such exciting news to discuss." Gertrude bubbled with enthusiasm as she poured tea for Emily and Alice. "We're getting a new minister!"

The mayor had made the announcement at the end of the service this morning, outlining the man's qualifications but cautioning that he was coming to Sweetwater Crossing on a provisional basis, giving both him and the town three months to determine whether this was the right congregation for him.

"Pastor Dietrich has been an interim minister for a number of years," Mayor Alcott had explained, "but he's ready for a permanent calling. I'm certain everyone in Sweetwater Crossing will do their best to convince him this is the place he and his family are meant to be. Y'all know how much we need a minister."

"He sounds perfect — married with a daughter." Alice was almost as enthusiastic as their former schoolteacher. "Family men make the best preachers."

Since the only minister Alice had known was Emily's father, she wasn't certain how Alice had formed that opinion, but Emily wouldn't dispute it.

Gertrude passed the plate of small sandwiches to her before taking one. "My father said Pastor Dietrich's credentials are impeccable and that the trial period is a mere formality. The committee is convinced he's the right man for Sweetwater Crossing. Apparently, his only concern is that we have no parsonage for him."

Though Emily had been surprised when the mayor had approached her about providing rooms for the new minister and his wife and daughter and had suspected the only reason the committee had chosen Finley House was because of its undeniable elegance, she had agreed to take the new boarders.

"Living in a boardinghouse isn't the same as having your own home, but they should be comfortable with us until the town can rebuild the parsonage." Emily had already designated the three empty rooms on the front of the house for the Dietrichs, reasoning that in addition to bedrooms for the couple and their daughter, the minister might want a separate office. Perhaps she was being sentimental, but Emily did not want someone else using the library. That had been Father's domain.

"I heard the new parsonage is going to be larger than before," Alice said. "There's some talk about making it two stories tall."

Emily didn't know where Alice had learned that, but it made sense.

Gertrude agreed. "That's a good idea. The Dietrichs may have other children."

"Or visitors. Father used to welcome people from his first congregation." Though she had no memories of life in the original parsonage, Mama had told stories of how crowded it became when whole families came to see their former pastor.

"My mother said you needed more room." Gertrude's expression changed, becoming wistful. "Your family was fortunate that Clive Finley left the house to your father."

"Did you know Clive?" Alice asked the question that was echoing through Emily's brain.

"Oh yes." Gertrude's voice was filled with emotion. "He was a wonderful man. It was a terrible shame that he died, but let's not dwell on that." She turned toward Emily. "I assume you plan to move Beulah to one of the rooms in the attic."

Emily blinked at the unexpected and unwelcome suggestion. "Why would I do that?"

"You wouldn't want the Dietrichs to be uncomfortable, would you? I know you and Craig think it's a good idea to treat Beulah like any other child, but you can't ignore the fact that she isn't like them." That had been Gertrude's argument five years ago when Beulah's parents had asked whether she could attend school.

Emily tried not to bristle. "I'm not going to argue with you, Gertrude. We'll never agree on this, so there's no reason to even discuss it. Beulah will stay in the room she already has at Finley House for as long as she and her parents want her to."

"Sometimes you amaze me." Gertrude's look bordered on patronizing. "I saw it even when you were one of my pupils. I know he wasn't your real father, but there are times when you're just like Reverend Vaughn. He had strong opinions and would share them, even when he knew it would stir up others. I heard someone say that it was just a matter of time before he'd get folks so angry that they'd run him out of town or worse."

She chose another sandwich and laid it on

her plate, her expression softening as she looked at Emily. "But that isn't what happened, is it? I wonder if his ideals became too much of a burden for him and that's why he did what he did."

Emily dismissed Gertrude's last speculation as pure fantasy, but her other comments were worth pondering. Emily knew her father wasn't afraid to express his opinions. To the contrary, he believed it was his duty. She knew he'd riled some people when he'd taken an unpopular stance, but it was hard to believe that he'd angered anyone so greatly that they would resort to violence. Still, someone had put that noose around Father's neck.

Who? And why?

CHAPTER FIFTEEN

Craig was almost as relieved as his students when the day ended. There had been no unusual problems this week, but he was still glad to have reached Friday afternoon and have two days without worrying about anyone's behavior other than Noah's. He gathered his satchel, locked the door, and was heading for home when he spotted a fancy buggy parked across Center Street in front of the church.

"Good afternoon. Can I help you?" As he approached the vehicle, Craig saw that the front seat was occupied by a dark-haired man and woman, while a young girl sat behind them. The man's clothing was unremarkable, as was his appearance, but his wife and daughter wore what Craig would have called Sunday clothes. Rachel would have scoffed at those fancy dresses, pointing out that they were impractical for traveling.

The man nodded in response to Craig's

question. "I certainly hope so. I'm Anthony Dietrich, Reverend Dietrich. I expected to meet the mayor, but he's not in his office, and no one's inside the church."

Anthony Dietrich's voice was warm and mellow, the kind of voice Craig had always associated with ministers. He could imagine it consoling or confronting parishioners or perhaps simply persuading them to listen to God's Word. Though Craig did not normally make quick judgments, his instincts told him this man would be an effective preacher.

He gave the man and his wife what he hoped was a welcoming smile. "There must have been some kind of emergency that called him away, because I know Mayor Alcott was looking forward to welcoming you to Sweetwater Crossing." He would undoubtedly be annoyed that Craig had been the first to greet the town's new minister. "On his behalf and on behalf of the whole congregation, welcome."

Though the man's expression was friendly, his wife sniffed in obvious annoyance, her dark eyes radiating scorn as she assessed Craig. "Who are you?"

The hair on the back of Craig's neck rose at her imperious tone. "My apologies, Mrs. Dietrich," he said as mildly as he could.

"I'm Craig Ferguson, the town's schoolmaster." He looked more closely at the girl in the backseat and guessed her age to be around twelve. Physically, she resembled her father, but the way she eyed Craig was remarkably similar to her mother's scrutiny, and the sniff she gave when Craig failed the test was an echo of Mrs. Dietrich's disdain.

Refusing to be annoyed, Craig addressed the parents. "I know it's premature, but once you're settled in your rooms, I'd like to discuss your daughter's previous schooling." He knew nothing about the last town where they'd lived and the quality of education there. "I want to be certain she's placed with the right group." If there was one thing Craig had learned during his years of teaching, it was that age was not the only factor in a child's progress.

Mrs. Dietrich's expression verged on a glare. "My daughter takes after both of us and is very intelligent. She's been at the top of her class in every school."

Every school. That was right. Alice had said that Reverend Dietrich had been an interim pastor for a number of years. Craig could only hope the girl had learned as much as her mother claimed and that Mrs. Dietrich's superior attitude was the result of travel fatigue, for she was far different from the other ministers' wives he'd met. They'd been warm and welcoming, their concern about their parishioners evident in everything they said and did. Mrs. Dietrich seemed to have come from a different mold.

Forcing himself to keep his voice neutral, Craig said, "It will be a pleasure to have . . ." He let his voice trail off, waiting for one of the parents to provide their daughter's name.

"Lizzie." The girl spoke for the first time. "My name is Lizzie. That's short for Elizabeth. Elizabeth is my mother's name. They call me Lizzie because it would be confusing to have two Elizabeths in the same house."

Craig bit back a smile at the girl's pedantic tone. "It'll be a pleasure to have you in school, Lizzie. Since Mayor Alcott is otherwise occupied, I'd be happy to escort you to your new home." A home whose atmosphere was bound to change once they arrived. Craig hoped the changes would not be as unpleasant as he feared.

"Temporary home." Mrs. Dietrich pointed at the empty lot where the former parsonage had stood. "I see no sign of a parsonage."

Her husband laid his hand on top of hers. "Don't vex yourself, my dear. I imagine they wanted to consult us before beginning work."

Apparently mollified, the minister's wife nodded. "I'm sure you're right, Anthony. Let's let the schoolmaster show us where we'll be staying for a while."

As he walked alongside the buggy, Craig tried to see the town from the Dietrichs' perspective. Would they find Sweetwater Crossing as charming as he did, or would Mrs. Dietrich continue to find fault with everything? Though he attempted to engage them in conversation as he led the way, every comment met with disapproval. Craig said a silent prayer of thanks that Beulah had gone home for the weekend. Perhaps by Monday, the minister's wife would be in a sunnier mood.

"Here we are," he said, stopping in front of Finley House. There was a second of silence as the three Dietrichs gazed at Sweetwater Crossing's finest home.

"Ooh, it's big. I like it." Lizzie's enthusiasm seemed genuine.

"It is indeed an impressive building," her father agreed.

For the first time, Mrs. Dietrich smiled. "Quite nice. You were right, Anthony, when you said Sweetwater Crossing could be our permanent home. I like the double staircases and the verandah." She studied the impressive entry. "I see no need for the town to build another parsonage. Perhaps you can convince the mayor and the elders that this would do quite nicely."

Craig could only imagine Emily's reaction to that idea.

And she'd thought living with Louisa was difficult. Emily wielded the knife with more force than necessary to chop the last carrot into tiny pieces. The past weekend had been particularly troublesome. Reverend Dietrich seemed reasonable, but there appeared to be no way to please his wife. She'd found fault with almost everything. The pillows weren't properly plumped; the quilt had a loose thread; the wallpaper made the rooms gloomy.

Mrs. Dietrich's complaints reached new heights when Alice and Jane joined them for supper Friday evening. Though she said nothing while they were present, as soon as they left, she announced that only boarders should be allowed to dine here, and the look she gave Mrs. Carmichael, Craig, and Noah made Emily suspect she wanted to evict them as well as Emily and have Finley House to herself. That was not going to happen.

Emily reached for an onion, hoping the only tears she shed today were because of it, not the way Mrs. Dietrich might treat Beulah. Although she'd mentioned that one of the schoolchildren boarded here during the week, Emily had said nothing about Beulah being slower to learn than the other children. Perhaps she was a coward, but she hadn't wanted to add another item to the minister's wife's list of things that were wrong with life at Finley House.

The strangest part was that she had seen a very different side of Mrs. Dietrich at the social the town had held to welcome them on Saturday. She'd been smiling and gracious, telling everyone how much she liked living at Finley House, with Lizzie chiming in, saying she hoped she could stay there forever.

Mrs. Dietrich had been equally charming after church yesterday. As Emily had expected, the church was filled. Even distant parishioners came to town to meet the new minister and his family and hear his first sermon. It was a powerful one. With Psalm 118:24 as his basis, Reverend Dietrich urged them to rejoice in each day, since each day was a new gift from God.

Emily was rejoicing until she saw Mrs. Dietrich corner the mayor after the service.

"There's no need for the town to build a new parsonage," she told him. "Finley House will serve us as well as it did the former minister and his family. If Emily and the boarders move out, we'll have plenty of room."

"But, ma'am, perhaps you don't understand. Finley House belongs to Emily and her sisters. The man who built it gave it to their father, and now it's theirs. No one can ask Emily to leave."

To Emily's surprise, Mrs. Dietrich's smile did not fade. Instead, she patted the mayor's arm, acting like he was a child who needed soothing. "I have the greatest confidence in you, Mayor Alcott. I know you'll do your best to arrange this for us, especially since the house is much too large for Emily. Then my husband and I will truly be able to rejoice."

As she scraped the chopped onion into the saucepan, Emily reminded herself there were many reasons to rejoice, including an empty and peaceful house. Lizzie was at school; the reverend was at church; his wife was joining Gertrude's mother for lunch; Mrs. Carmichael had taken Noah with her to the mercantile, intending to purchase a birthday present for Mrs. French. Though her birthday was on Thursday, the widows would celebrate during their usual Friday luncheon.

"Something smells delicious," Mrs. Carmichael said as she and Noah entered the kitchen half an hour later.

Noah sniffed. "Chicken."

"You're right, Noah. It does smell like chicken." Mrs. Carmichael smiled at Emily. "You know how much I like chicken."

Emily returned the smile. The widow wasn't the only one who favored poultry. So did Beulah.

"I'm making fricassee for supper tonight. That way no one will have to cut Noah's food." And Emily could devote herself to making Beulah comfortable, for though she told herself not to borrow trouble, she feared the Dietrichs' introduction to the girl would be difficult.

"My mouth is already watering at the thought of your biscuits." Mrs. Carmichael reached into her reticule. "I stopped at the post office on our way back. There's a letter from Joanna addressed to your parents. I thought you'd want to read it."

Emily fingered the envelope, surprised that it was sent to Reverend and Mrs. Vaughn. Louisa had said she'd told Joanna of their mother's death, and Emily had written weekly letters since she'd been back in

Sweetwater Crossing, but it appeared those messages had not reached Joanna. Unsure what she'd find inside, Emily was unwilling to read in front of the widow. Instead, she retreated to the library and sat at Father's desk.

Dear Mama and Father, Joanna had written. *The tour was wonderful. Herr Ridel says my playing improved with every stop.* Emily paused, wondering who this man was, then surmised he must be the pianist who'd agreed to take Joanna under his wing. Louisa had mentioned Joanna studying with a maestro.

I'm not sure I believe him, but I do know I've learned even more than I expected. Being in Europe and studying with masters is wonderful. Emily smiled at her sister's repetition of "wonderful." That had always been one of Joanna's favorite adjectives.

My only regret is not seeing you and Louisa. I miss you and wish you could be here with me. I had hoped to have a letter or two waiting when I returned to Munich, but there were none. Please write soon. I long for news of you. There was no mention of Emily.

Emily brushed the tears from her eyes, the pain that Joanna did not miss her overshadowed by the happiness that her sister was finding what she sought in Europe. She picked up Father's pen.

Dear Joanna, I think of you each day and wonder where you are and what you're doing, so I was relieved to receive your letter, although I'm concerned that the ones Louisa and I've sent you were somehow lost. Perhaps they're being held for you somewhere. In case they never reach you, here's what's been happening. There is no easy way to tell you this. Emily blinked, trying to keep the tears from falling and blurring her words, then recounted their parents' deaths. *If you're wondering why you're hearing this from me and not Louisa, it's because Louisa has gone to Cimarron Creek with Phoebe and Mrs. Sheridan. I'll forward your letter to her and imagine you'll hear from her.*

Emily paused, remembering the enthusiasm of Louisa's last letter and how it had assuaged some of the pain of their angry confrontations. *I don't want to spoil her story by telling you what she's doing. All I'll say is that her stay in Cimarron Creek appears to be as good for her as your time in Europe is for you.*

I rejoiced when I read how your talent is being developed and recognized. Mama always said you'd been blessed with the ability to heal people with your music. What a wonderful gift!

Mama had claimed each of them had been

given special talents. Louisa healed bodies; Joanna healed spirits, but she'd never told Emily what gift she had received. Refusing to dwell on that, Emily picked up the pen again.

It's strange to realize that none of us is where we were a year ago. My life has changed in ways I could never have imagined. I'm a widow now.

Emily rose and walked to the window, trying to calm her thoughts as she stared outside, but though the day was peaceful, she was not. Turbulent emotions washed over her, threatening to overwhelm her. This was the first time she'd put the news of George's death in writing, and somehow that brought memories she'd tried to repress out of hiding.

Her wedding day, so filled with hope. George's tenderness the first month. Her belief that their love was like Abraham and Mary Lincoln's — eternal. But then George had changed, or perhaps Emily had simply seen a side of him that had always been there. All she knew was that hope had turned to fear and that each month had been worse than the previous one.

That was over now, ended the day George had been killed. What remained were relief that the ordeal she'd endured was in the past and sorrow that her most cherished dreams would never come true. Emily had turned the last page of that chapter of her life. Now it was time to start a new one and discover why God had brought her back to Sweetwater Crossing.

"Miss Emily." Beulah stopped to catch her breath as she skidded to a stop in the kitchen. "New girl at school. Said she lives here."

Emily wrapped an arm around Beulah's shoulders and gently pushed her onto a chair. Though the Douglases normally attended church each Sunday, they'd been absent yesterday, which meant that Beulah's introduction to Lizzie had occurred at school.

"That's right. Our new minister, his wife, and their daughter will live here until the parsonage is built. Lizzie has the room next to you." When Beulah's eyes widened in what could have been either surprise or alarm, Emily added, "I hope you'll be friends."

As her breathing slowed, Beulah nodded. "Friends are good. Me and Noah are friends."

"Noah's waiting for you to read to him." Perhaps the normalcy of sitting under the tree and reading — or pretending to read — to Noah would further calm the child.

"Good. I like to read."

As if on cue, Mrs. Carmichael and Noah entered the kitchen.

"Come, Noah." Beulah took his hand and headed for the door.

"You forgot the book." Emily refused to smile at the evidence that Beulah was indeed reciting rather than reading.

"Book! Book! Book!" Noah punctuated each word with a hop.

"That's enough noise, Noah." Mrs. Carmichael laid a cautioning hand on his arm. "Remember how we talked about indoor voices."

Chastened, Noah nodded and whispered, "Book."

As the children scampered toward the oak tree that had become their reading spot, Mrs. Carmichael followed at a more sedate pace, telling Emily she wanted to keep a close eye on Beulah today. "I wouldn't want anyone to upset her."

Emily shared that wish, which was why she was waiting to greet Lizzie and her mother when they entered the house. Having seen how critical both of them could be, she wanted to caution them to be kind to Beulah.

"Did you enjoy your first day of school?" she asked, infusing her voice with enthusiasm.

Lizzie shook her head. "The other pupils are stupid, especially one girl. She's as old as me, but she can't even read."

Though she said nothing, Mrs. Dietrich wore the sour expression that seemed to be habitual when she was inside Finley House.

"That's Beulah," Emily explained. "God didn't give her the same gifts he gave you. It takes her longer to learn things, but she has the sweetest smile I've ever seen. You'll see that at supper."

Disgruntlement turned to horror, but to Mrs. Dietrich's credit, she said nothing in front of her daughter. "Lizzie, why don't you go outside and play? I need to talk to Mrs. Leland." When Lizzie was out of earshot, she took a step toward Emily. "Is this Beulah the girl you said stays here during the week?"

"Yes. She spends Monday through Thursday nights with us."

"You should have told me she was simple. Anthony and I would never have agreed to have her here."

Emily took a deep breath before she spoke, and when she did, she kept her voice low but firm. "It wasn't your decision, Mrs.

Dietrich. I have an agreement with Beulah's parents. I don't need your approval, but I do expect you and Lizzie to treat her with kindness. She is, after all, one of God's children." That was becoming a refrain.

For the first time since Emily had met her, Mrs. Dietrich appeared abashed. "Of course."

As she set the table, Emily was glad she'd thought about the seating arrangement before the Dietrichs arrived. For the first time, the chairs at the head and foot of the table were occupied, with her taking what had been Mama's seat and Mrs. Carmichael at the other end. She'd kept Noah's high chair on her right with Craig, Alice, and Lizzie on the same side. Beulah, the pastor, and Mrs. Dietrich sat on the other. That placed Beulah as far from Lizzie and her mother as possible.

To give Reverend Dietrich credit, though his wife's discomfort was obvious, he greeted Beulah politely. He did not, however, speak to her after that, instead keeping his attention focused on the opposite side of the table, engaging Alice and Craig in a discussion of the town's library while Mrs. Dietrich recounted Lizzie's academic achievements to Mrs. Carmichael. Whether or not it was intentional, Emily felt that she, Beulah, and Noah were being ostracized.

She refused to let the children suffer. "Did you enjoy the story Beulah read to you?" Emily asked Noah as he shoveled bits of chicken fricassee into his mouth.

He nodded vigorously. "Good book!"

"Which one was it?" Emily directed the question to Beulah, wanting to include her in the conversation.

"Children and a witch in the forest."

"Did she say *witch*?" It appeared Lizzie was paying more attention to this discussion than the other.

"Yes." Beulah smiled, oblivious to the disdain in Lizzie's voice.

"That's a bad book, isn't it, Father? She shouldn't be telling Noah about witches."

Before the minister could respond, Craig laid his fork down and fixed his gaze on Lizzie. "It's a fairy tale. I'm glad Beulah chose it because it was one of my wife's favorite stories to read to our son. Rachel used to say you could never start too early to teach children the difference between good and evil."

"I agree with the sentiment," Reverend Dietrich said slowly, "but surely there are more appropriate books." He looked across the table at Alice. "Perhaps you can suggest

249

some to Mr. Ferguson. I wouldn't want to think he was encouraging his pupils to read such stories."

Beulah turned to Emily, confusion erasing her smile. "Did Mr. Ferguson do something wrong?"

"No, he didn't. It's simply that he and Reverend Dietrich have different opinions about books. That's all right."

But Beulah was not satisfied. "Did I do something wrong?"

"Yes!" Lizzie's shout echoed through the room, destroying the last vestige of a pleasant supper.

Tears welled in Beulah's eyes, and she pushed her plate aside. "I stay quiet."

And she did. Not only that evening. Though Emily tried to encourage her, the only time Beulah would speak was when the Dietrichs were not present. She no longer volunteered to read to Noah, and she said nothing at meals. Even her conversations with Emily as she prepared for bed were subdued, perhaps fearing Lizzie might hear her and chastise her again.

To Emily's dismay, Beulah's silence was not limited to Finley House. Craig reported that she rarely spoke at school and no longer joined the other pupils for recess or lunch, instead remaining at her desk.

"I'm worried about her," he confided one night when they were washing dishes.

So was Emily. The girl whose sweet smile and gentle manner had won Emily's heart was suffering, and there was nothing she could do. If only she hadn't agreed to let the Dietrichs live here.

CHAPTER SIXTEEN

"Emily. Emily."

Dimly, she was aware of a voice calling her name. It must be a dream, though she wasn't aware that she'd been dreaming.

"Are you all right?"

The hand on her shoulder jolted Emily awake, and she blinked, trying to understand why she was sitting at the kitchen table with Mrs. Carmichael standing over her when the clock said it was midmorning. The last thing Emily remembered, she'd planned to rest her head on her arms for a moment, but it seemed that the exhaustion of too many nights worrying about Beulah and comforting her when she woke in tears had caught up with her, and she'd fallen asleep.

"I'm fine. Just tired," Emily assured the widow. "But you're not fine. What's wrong?" For there was no question that something was wrong. Mrs. Carmichael's face radiated worry. "Is it Noah?" The boy had complained of a sore throat last night, and he'd started coughing.

The widow nodded. "Do you have any honey?"

"A full jar. Mrs. Douglas gave it to me on Monday." Emily had protested that it wasn't necessary, particularly since the older Mrs. Douglas was finishing the quilt Mama had started for Emily, but the Douglases had insisted on paying her whatever they could for giving Beulah a home during the week. More often than not, that payment came in the form of food.

Emily rose and walked to the cupboard where she'd stored the honey. "What are you going to do with it?"

"I hoped he'd get better after breakfast, but Noah's cough is worse. He feels so bad that he agreed to take a morning nap."

Emily understood the widow's concern because that hadn't happened since he'd been here.

"I've got to do something to help that poor boy," Mrs. Carmichael continued. "My mother used to give me honey mixed with hot water to drink when I had a cough. I thought I'd try that for Noah."

Emily nodded, eager to do whatever she could. Mama's remedy had been wrapping hot towels around Emily's throat, but perhaps drinking something warm and sweet would be better. "We can try the honey water. If that doesn't help, I'll take him to Doc Sheridan while you and the ladies have lunch."

It was Friday, which meant the trio would expect their meal in two hours. Each week, Emily tried to serve something different so they would have the anticipation of a new meal in addition to the pleasure of each other's company. "I made meat loaf and plan to serve mashed potatoes and glazed carrots with it. Everything's easy to swallow, so we might be able to convince Noah to eat some." He'd complained that last night's roast had scratched his throat.

The widow appeared dubious. "Even if Noah doesn't improve, shouldn't we wait for Craig to come home and let him decide whether to consult the doctor?"

Emily shook her head. "It's Friday. You know what that means." Father used to implore his friend to stop, but more Fridays than not, the doctor spent his evenings at the saloon. It was common knowledge that the judgment of Sweetwater Crossing's doctor was impaired on Fridays and that patients should wait until at least midmorning on Saturday to consult him.

Mrs. Carmichael wrinkled her nose. "You're right. I heard Doc's starting earlier now that his wife and daughter are gone."

Unfortunately, the honey made no difference. By noon, Emily knew she had no choice but to take Noah to the doctor before whiskey dulled his senses. As soon as she'd served the ladies their desserts, she put Noah in the small wagon she and her sisters had once used. It was a measure of Noah's illness that he did not protest riding. On an ordinary day, he would have asserted his independence and attempted to walk. Today he didn't try to climb out even when Emily stopped at the schoolhouse to tell Craig what was happening.

When he saw her in the back of the schoolroom, Craig gave his pupils a brief assignment, then joined her, nodding when she explained about Noah's cough.

"Do whatever you think is best for him. I trust you."

Craig's words warmed Emily's heart and filled her with a sense of purpose. She didn't have Louisa's gift of healing, and she couldn't coax haunting melodies from the piano like Joanna, but she could ease Craig's worries by caring for his son.

Craig descended the steps and lifted Noah out of the wagon to give him a hug. "You do whatever Miss Emily says. She'll take care of you."

Another coughing spasm and a tightening of his arms around his father's neck were Noah's only response.

When he'd settled Noah back in the wagon, Craig turned to Emily. "I'm sorry you have to handle this by yourself."

The warmth that had surrounded Emily's heart spread through the rest of her body. Once again, Craig was treating her like a partner, not simply the woman who provided him and Noah with food and lodging. What a wonderful feeling!

She shook her head slowly, hoping to reassure him. "I don't mind taking Noah now that I know you agree the doctor should see him. I wish we could wait until you could come, but that's not a good idea. I'll tell you why later." There was no reason to burden Craig with stories of the doctor's fondness for whiskey when the truth was that Doc Sheridan was a competent physician when he was sober, which was most of the time.

"I trust you, Emily." Craig repeated the words that were like balm to her spirit. "There's no one I trust more."

Emily pulled the wagon diagonally across the street to the doctor's office, then lifted

Noah out. "Doc Sheridan's going to make you feel better," she said as she carried him inside.

"What do we have here, young man?" The doctor's gray eyes were clear, his voice as steady as ever, his expression concerned when he saw the child in Emily's arms.

Noah's response was a cough. The poor boy had coughed practically nonstop since they'd left the schoolhouse, confirming Emily's decision not to delay their visit to the doctor.

"It sounds like you need some of my special syrup." He gestured to Emily to lift Noah onto the examining table, then asked how long Noah had been coughing.

When she explained how the cough had begun as a sore throat, Doc nodded and began to examine his patient. His careful explanation of everything he was doing reminded Emily of how he'd reassured her in the same way when she was a child. Though she and her sisters hated being ill, they never feared the doctor's visits because he made even some of the more painful treatments easier to bear by preparing them for what was going to happen.

When the doctor completed his examination of Noah, he retrieved a clear glass bottle from the cabinet and handed it to

Emily. "There's nothing to worry about. The boy is strong enough to recover from the cough, and the syrup will help. Give him a tablespoon every four hours. If he's not better by Monday, bring him back."

Doc took the seat behind his desk and began to make entries in his journals, carefully inscribing Noah's name and diagnosis in one, the medicine he'd dispensed in the other. When he finished, he looked at Emily. "What do you hear from Louisa? My wife hasn't said much about her in her letters." He frowned and muttered something that sounded like, "I wish she'd come home. I need her."

Emily's heart ached for the man who was all alone. Even though she couldn't condone his drinking, she understood why he might seek companionship at the saloon.

"Louisa's happy in Cimarron Creek. She said she's learning from both the town's doctor and its midwife." There'd been no further letters despite the ones Emily wrote each week, but she cherished the conciliatory tone in the one she'd received.

"The midwife. That's a good idea." Doc nodded his approval. "Your sister said she wanted to work with me, but I couldn't let her do that. Girls aren't meant to be doctors. It's not ladylike."

Emily knew many — perhaps most — men would agree with him and hoped for Louisa's sake that she found satisfaction as a midwife. Her life would be easier if she chose that profession rather than becoming a physician.

Doc gave Emily an appraising look before he continued. "You're doing the right thing. Running a boardinghouse is something women are suited for. That and raising children. I'm surprised you don't have one. You were married for more than a year, weren't you?"

The pain she suspected would never fade assailed Emily, and she had to struggle to respond. "Yes, but it wasn't meant to be." Not wanting to continue the discussion, she lifted Noah into her arms and prepared to leave the doctor's office. "Besides the syrup, is there anything else I should do for Noah?"

"Just keep an eye on him."

That was one thing she could do.

Though he'd been tempted to dismiss school early, Craig did not, but he also did not linger once the last pupil left. Worries about Noah had weighed heavily on him all afternoon, even though he told himself that Emily was watching over his son.

Rather than enter Finley House through

the front door, he went directly to the one that led into the kitchen. If she followed her usual routine, Emily would be preparing supper. He wanted to talk to her before he saw his son, wanted to be prepared if Noah's life was in danger.

As Craig had expected, Emily was in front of the stove, stirring something. What he hadn't expected was the way the warmth of her smile reassured him even before he had a chance to speak.

"I know you're worried, but Doc said it's not serious, and Noah's coughing less, thanks to the syrup he gave me. That seems to have made Noah sleepy, so Mrs. Carmichael is sitting at his bedside in case he wakens and starts coughing again."

Relief washed over Craig at the realization that this was a normal childhood ailment, not a life-threatening illness. All afternoon he'd told himself that Noah had a cough, nothing more, but all afternoon memories of other parents burying their young children had flashed before him.

"The widow's a good woman, and so are you."

The flush that colored Emily's face surprised Craig. Was she unaccustomed to compliments? Surely her parents and her husband had lavished them on her. Emily was more than a good woman. Her combination of competence and compassion intrigued him. Though she had no children of her own, the way she treated both Noah and Beulah told him she had deep maternal instincts, and the way she did everything she could to maintain peace in a household whose equilibrium had been shaken by the Dietrichs' arrival demonstrated her skills as a peacemaker.

"I haven't done much, but I'm glad to help." Emily was characteristically self-deprecating.

Craig looked at her more closely, frowning when he saw the circles under her eyes. "You look as tired as I feel. Did Noah's coughing keep you awake last night?" That seemed unlikely, since their rooms were on opposite ends of the house, but he had to ask.

"It wasn't that. My mind kept whirling, so I couldn't relax."

He suspected he knew the reason. "Life's been different since the Dietrichs moved in. The only word I can find to describe it is *tense.*" Even Noah had sensed the difference the newcomers had made and had told Craig he didn't like Lizzie.

"Mean," he'd said. Craig had to agree.

"I wish the town would rebuild the parsonage."

Emily shrugged. "That would help, but it wouldn't resolve everything. Beulah would still be in school with Lizzie. She cries every night because she doesn't understand why Lizzie is mean to her." Emily appeared to be on the verge of tears herself. "It makes my heart ache."

"Mine too." As seemed to happen more and more often, he and Emily shared the same opinions. "I do the best I can at school, but Beulah's sensitive. She knows Lizzie scorns her." And Lizzie was smart enough to do nothing so overt that Craig would reprimand her.

"Maybe we should talk to her parents."

"The Dietrichs won't change."

Emily shook her head. "I meant Beulah's parents. Maybe they should take her out of school."

The thought had crossed his mind when he'd seen how unhappy Beulah was, but Craig had dismissed it as quickly as it appeared. "Do you want to let the bullies win? Because that's what Lizzie is. Her tactics are different from the boys', but the result is the same. Do you want her to win?"

"No."

"Neither do I. I keep telling myself there's a way to solve this problem, but I haven't been able to find it." And oh, how he hated that.

Emily smiled as Noah shoveled a spoonful of oatmeal into his mouth. Though she was no closer to solving the problem of Beulah and Lizzie, at least one problem had been resolved. The syrup Doc Sheridan gave Noah had eased his cough enough that he could sleep. Despite a noticeable improvement by Sunday morning, Craig had stayed home with Noah rather than disturb other parishioners, but by last night, the cough had virtually disappeared.

"It's good to see he's regained his appetite." Mrs. Carmichael handed Noah a glass of milk and watched carefully while he drank it. As proud as he was of being a big boy who could handle a glass, spills were all too frequent.

That was one of the reasons Emily had suggested that the widow, Craig, and Noah have their breakfast in the kitchen this morning. Lizzie never failed to laugh when Noah spilled something, and when Mrs. Dietrich had heard about Noah's visit to the doctor, she'd declared that children who were ill had no place in the dining room, where they might infect others. Maintaining a distance between them seemed like the better part of valor. They'd all eat together this evening, because Beulah, Alice, and Jane would be here, but Emily was happy to be in a different room now.

"I'll keep Noah inside today," Mrs. Carmichael told Craig. "You don't need to worry."

"I don't. I know you and Emily treat him like your own."

Emily had overheard Mrs. Carmichael telling Craig that Noah was the grandson she'd always wanted, but Emily had never admitted how deeply she loved Noah and how she wished he were her child.

The pang of longing that sliced through her was familiar, and yet it wasn't. For as long as she could recall, she'd wanted to be a mother, to carry a child beneath her heart, to guide it from birth to adulthood. She had believed that dream would come true when she married George, but each month was more difficult, more disappointing, more painful as the dream faded. George's fists inflicted physical pain. The inner pain caused by the realization that she was a failure was just as intense as that from the bruises.

When she left the ranch, Emily told herself it was time to let the dream die, to admit that motherhood was not part of God's plan for her. But dreams, she soon discovered, were not so easily dismissed. Each time she hugged Noah or cut his meat or watched him try to coax Jane to speak, the longing returned but with a difference. Instead of wishing she were the mother of a child — any child — she now wanted to be Noah's mother. And that was something she could never, ever admit, because becoming Noah's mother meant she would also be Craig's wife. He deserved more than she could offer.

Hoping her turbulent thoughts were not apparent, Emily forced a light tone as she said, "We do our best."

"That's all I could ask." Thankfully, Craig seemed oblivious to everything other than his son. He rose and stroked the boy's head. "Goodbye, Noah. Be good for Mrs. Carmichael and Miss Emily while I'm gone."

"Yeth."

When Craig had left, the widow poured herself another cup of coffee. "It warms my heart to see a man bestow so much love on a child."

"Noah's easy to love."

"That he is, and so resilient. His cough went away faster than I expected."

"Faster than Doc expected too." He'd told Emily it might take a week before Noah was completely recovered. "There's still half a bottle of syrup left."

After she'd wiped Noah's face, removing the last of the oatmeal from his cheeks, Mrs. Carmichael turned back to Emily. "Do you think Craig would mind if I gave the syrup to Lottie? She was coughing when she was here on Friday, and you heard her in church yesterday."

Emily nodded. Mrs. French's cough hadn't been as severe as Noah's, but it still disturbed Reverend Dietrich's sermon, earning her several disapproving glances.

"I'm sure Doc has more syrup." Emily had seen several bottles in the cabinet.

The widow shook her head ever so slightly. "But he'd charge her for it and the office visit. Lottie doesn't like to talk about it, but I know she worries about money. Our Friday lunches are the only luxuries she allows herself."

Emily took a sip of tea, trying to control her emotions. Had she been so concerned with her own finances that she hadn't realized others were also struggling?

"I'm sure Craig won't object," she said firmly. "I'll take the syrup to Mrs. French as soon as I get our lunch started."

An hour later, Emily headed west on Creek and approached the small Sunday

House, frowning when she noticed peeling paint on the front door. Mrs. Carmichael hadn't been exaggerating her friend's situation.

When her first knock wasn't answered, Emily knocked again. Again, there was no answer. Perhaps Mrs. French was still sleeping. Though she hated disturbing her, she wanted to explain about the syrup. As she'd expected, the door was unlocked.

"Mrs. French," she called as she stepped inside. "It's Emily Leland. I've brought you some cough syrup."

Once again, there was no response. Emily tipped her head to one side, listening carefully. The house was totally silent. More than that, it felt empty. Perhaps Mrs. French had judged herself well enough to visit friends or shop at the mercantile. Still, Emily couldn't leave without reassuring herself.

She looked around the main room. There was nothing cooking, no residual smell from the bacon and eggs Mrs. French had once declared were her preferred breakfast. If she'd left the house, she'd left early.

With a feeling of foreboding, Emily turned the knob on the bedroom door. A small form lay under the quilt, its stillness confirming what she had feared. Mrs. French was dead.

"I don't understand it." Mrs. Carmichael's sobs were so strong that her words were difficult to understand. "Lottie's cough wasn't as severe as Noah's."

"Doc said it wasn't that." When she'd realized what had happened, Emily had summoned the doctor. "He said her heart just gave out and that that was to be expected at her age."

"She wasn't much older than me." The widow wiped the tears from her cheeks and took a deep breath. "Betty and I are the only ones left. I don't know what we're going to do." She shuddered, then shook her head. "It seems wrong to continue our Friday lunches with only two. The four of us had so much fun together. Sometimes we'd reminisce. Sometimes we'd try to predict the future. Sometimes we'd tell silly jokes. It didn't matter what we did, as long as we were together. And now . . ."

Emily handed Mrs. Carmichael a fresh handkerchief when her tears resumed. "Don't you think your friends would want you to keep meeting? It would be a way for you and Mrs. Locke to honor Mrs. Adams and Mrs. French. I'll even set places for them if that will make you feel better."

The widow shook her head. "That would only remind us that they're gone. Betty and I don't need any reminders to keep Clara and Lottie in our hearts. But you're right, Emily. Betty and I'll continue the Friday tradition . . . as long as we're here. There's no telling how long that will be."

And that was the crux of the problem. Death was the one certainty in life. Emily bit her lip, trying not to think about Mrs. Carmichael dying and the hole it would leave in her life. Not only hers, but Noah's and Craig's too. She'd become important to all of them, and the idea of no longer having her soothing presence filled Emily with dread. There'd already been too many deaths in too short a time. Surely Mrs. Carmichael's wouldn't be the next.

When the widow had dried her tears, Emily announced that she was going to take Noah back to the doctor. "When I saw him, I told Doc that Noah's cough was much better, but he said he wanted to check on him. Why don't you rest a bit while we're gone?"

The widow's fatigue was evident in the speed with which she agreed.

When Noah awoke from his nap, Emily brought the wagon from the barn.

The boy frowned. "Me walk."

Emily doubted he was well enough to walk the entire distance, but she wouldn't argue. "I'll bring the wagon so you can give me a ride if I get tired." As she feigned climbing into it, Noah laughed. Oh, how good it felt to hear genuine laughter, particularly today.

This time Emily headed east, taking a different route to the doctor's office, one that didn't involve passing the cemetery. She needed no further reminders of death today. As she'd expected, Noah's energy flagged before they reached Main Street, and he agreed to ride the remaining distance.

"You're looking much better." The doctor confirmed Emily's assessment that the syrup had done its job well.

"Me no cough." The brave assertion was marred by a small cough.

Doc winked at Emily. Pulling out his stethoscope, he said, "Let me take a listen, Noah. All right. Now, open your mouth and let me take a look."

As the doctor continued his examination, Emily let her gaze wander around the room. Something seemed different, but she couldn't identify what had triggered that feeling. Both record books were still on the desk. The same plant still stood by the window. The cabinet shelves still held bottles. Everything looked the same. She must have been mistaken.

271

CHAPTER SEVENTEEN

"I'm worried about her." A frown crossed
Emily's face as she handed Craig a plate.

"Mrs. Carmichael?" Though she might
have meant Beulah, because the girl had
been visibly nervous at supper, he doubted
she was the object of Emily's concern tonight.

Emily nodded. "The funeral was awful.
Reverend Dietrich did his best, but he'd
only spoken a few words to Mrs. French, so
he couldn't say anything meaningful about
her. At least when Mrs. Adams died, Mayor
Alcott gave a good eulogy."

"And that's important." Craig remembered the comfort he'd received when their
minister had recounted several stories about
Rachel, revealing new aspects of his wife's
life. "Rachel claimed funerals were meant
to give loved ones strength to continue living."

As she slid another plate into the soapy

272

water, Emily nodded again. "My father used to say that too, but I'm not sure how much comfort Mrs. Carmichael found in the service. She was distressed after Mrs. Adams's death, but this was worse. Much worse."

Craig had no trouble believing that. The widow's light blue eyes had lacked their normal sparkle, and her responses at supper had been subdued. "Do you think it's because it's only been a short time since her other friend died?" It had taken months before Craig felt that his life had resumed any sense of normalcy, and while some might argue that a friend's death wasn't as devastating as a spouse's, the death of any loved one was a major change.

"It was exactly a month. Mrs. Adams died on October 6, Mrs. French on the sixth of November." Emily handed Craig the now-clean plate. "Mrs. Carmichael said she's not superstitious, but she's afraid of what December 6 might bring."

"We'll have to pray that it's an uneventful day."

"It has to be. I don't know what she'd do if something happened to Mrs. Locke."

Emily was still thinking about her conversation with Craig as she braided Beulah's hair that evening. Even though Doc had assured her that the two deaths were to be expected given the women's age, Emily took no comfort from that and hoped he hadn't said something similar to Mrs. Carmichael. The widow needed no reminders of her own aging.

"Your hair is pretty," Emily told Beulah as she tied a ribbon around the single braid Beulah preferred.

"My granny said hers was the same color when she was little. Now it's gray." Beulah pulled the braid forward, seeming to need to verify that it had not suddenly changed colors. Apparently satisfied, she gripped Emily's hand. "Granny said she's old. Is she gonna die?"

Craig slid the books into his satchel, then looked around the schoolroom as he prepared to leave for the day. Something felt different. It had been two days since Mrs. French's funeral and, as he'd known would happen, life had resumed its normal rhythm. He had no doubt that Mrs. Carmichael was grieving, but she gave no outward sign of her sorrow. If anything, she seemed more cheerful than before, telling stories that made Noah laugh and encouraging Beulah to speak at the dinner table. Though the

Dietrichs clearly disapproved, Beulah talked about helping her grandmother quilt and how she had pricked her finger.

"Pokes are bad," she declared. "Very bad." She looked at Emily and shuddered. "I don't wanna be poked."

"A good seamstress knows how to handle a needle," Lizzie informed everyone. "Blood will spoil fine fabrics."

Emily must have realized the unpleasantness that would result if the conversation continued, for she quickly changed the subject, asking Reverend Dietrich whether he had any new Christmas traditions that he planned to introduce here.

There had been nothing special about that discussion, just as there'd been nothing unusual about today. It had been an ordinary Thursday, and yet Craig couldn't dismiss the feeling that something was different.

He slung the satchel over his shoulder, one part of his mind registering the frayed corners while the rest tried to identify what had changed. He took another step toward the door, then stopped at the realization that the difference was inside him.

For the first time in a long while, Craig felt content. It was an unexpected and yet very welcome feeling. His life wasn't perfect.

It never would be. There would always be bullies like Mitch and Harlan to disrupt his classes. There would always be people like Lizzie to create tension at home.

Home. The word made Craig smile. When had he begun to think of Sweetwater Crossing and Finley House as his home? He couldn't identify the date and time any more than he could say exactly when contentment had begun to displace the emptiness that had plagued him since Rachel's death.

When he'd left Galveston, Craig had hoped his sorrow would ease, and it had. There were no longer the constant reminders of what he'd lost. Instead, there were new challenges, new problems to resolve. He'd expected that as well. What he hadn't expected was this feeling of, for want of a better word, rightness.

He could attribute part of it to his son. Noah had recovered remarkably quickly from his cough, reminding Craig of the many times Rachel had spoken of children's resilience. She'd been right. Wonderful, wise Rachel.

Craig's breath caught as he realized that the thought of his wife had not been followed by deep sadness. Instead of feeling that his heart had a hole in its center, he was filled with joy as he remembered the times they'd had together: her radiant smile at their wedding, the sense of wonder they'd shared when Noah was born, the thousands of small moments that had comprised their life together. Craig sank onto a chair as memories overwhelmed him. Then he smiled.

"Thank you, God." The memories were a gift, just as Rachel had been a gift. He bowed his head in a silent prayer, then rose as the breadth of his revelations swept over him. Rachel had been his first love, the woman who'd shared his dreams and helped make many of them come true. Craig knew she would always be a part of him, but as he looked around with newly opened eyes, he also knew she wouldn't want him to spend the rest of his life mourning her.

You can't go backward, Craig. You can't stand still. You need to keep moving forward and keep giving of yourself. The words that echoed through his brain were so clear that his beloved wife could have actually spoken them. Rachel was right, and in what might be her final gift to him, she'd shown him the path to follow.

"You're a dummy. Look at you. You don't even know how to eat bacon." Lizzie ges-

277

tured toward the slice of meat Beulah held between two fingers. "You're supposed to cut it with your knife and eat it with a fork. What a dummy!"

Emily gasped at the attack. Lizzie had been, if not kind, at least less cruel to Beulah this week, but the truce appeared to have ended. Before Emily could say anything, Beulah dropped the bacon as if it had burned her fingers. With a sob that wrenched Emily's heart, the girl pushed back her chair and raced from the room, ignoring Noah's cries of "What's wrong?"

Though Emily wanted nothing more than to reprimand Lizzie, comforting Beulah was more important. After a quick glare at Lizzie, she headed toward the girl, whose sobs were still audible. Beulah had reached the foot of the staircase when Emily intercepted her and put an arm around her shoulders.

"It's all right, Beulah. Lots of people eat their bacon the way you do. Lizzie had no right to say what she did."

Beulah shook her head. "I am a dummy. I do everything wrong."

Emily's heart ached at the pain she heard in Beulah's voice. "That's not true," she said, determined to do what she could to heal the wounds Lizzie had inflicted.

"It is. Nobody likes me."

Emily turned Beulah so they were facing each other, wanting the child to see as well as hear her sincerity. "That's also not true. I like you. More than that, I love you. So do Mr. Ferguson and Noah and Mrs. Carmichael."

There was silence for a long moment. Then Beulah's expression changed, revealing hope mingled with lingering doubts. "Really?"

"Really. Now, let's go back to the dining room so you can finish your breakfast." If Lizzie so much as opened her mouth to criticize Beulah, Emily would stop her.

"No! I'm not hungry."

Emily doubted that, since Beulah had eaten almost nothing before Lizzie began her attack. Even if she had momentarily lost her appetite, Emily couldn't send Beulah to school without breakfast.

"We'll go to the kitchen. I'll make some new pancakes, and we can eat there."

"You too?" Her almost incredulous tone told Emily just how much Beulah craved acceptance.

"Yes. It'll be our private party. Then you can walk to school with Mr. Ferguson."

Beulah nodded. "Good."

Half an hour later, after Beulah and Craig

had left for school, followed a few minutes later by Lizzie, Emily joined the elder Dietrichs in the dining room. The minister and his wife were drinking their second cups of coffee, apparently undisturbed by their daughter's outburst.

"What happened this morning cannot be repeated." Emily saw no need for a preamble.

"I agree." Mrs. Dietrich laid her cup back on the saucer and inclined her head in a regal gesture. "A child who lacks proper table manners cannot be allowed to dine with adults. If you insist on permitting Beulah to live here, she must take her meals in the kitchen."

Emily realized she shouldn't have been surprised by Mrs. Dietrich's view, since Lizzie had had her parents' tacit approval when she criticized Beulah, but it took her a second to calm herself enough to speak.

"You misunderstood me, Mrs. Dietrich. What cannot be repeated is Lizzie's behavior. It was unkind — and yes, I would say unchristian — of her to taunt Beulah. Lizzie is old enough to understand that Beulah did not choose to be the way she is."

"And you are old enough to know that simpleminded children should be kept away from those of us who are not so afflicted."

Reverend Dietrich laid his hand on his wife's arm. "Now, my dear, that's a bit harsh."

"How can you say that, Anthony? Lizzie was perfectly right to correct Beulah's table manners."

Emily shook her head. "Lizzie is a guest here, just as Beulah is. I did not reprimand Lizzie for her shameful behavior because I am not her parent. You two are. I expect you to ensure that she treats everyone in this household with respect. If she does not, I will have no recourse other than to ask you to find different accommodations."

"You would put a simpleminded child ahead of us?" Astonishment colored Mrs. Dietrich's words.

That was exactly what Emily was doing, but rather than inflame Lizzie's mother further, she settled for saying, "I am merely asking for civil behavior from everyone who stays here."

The minister's wife rose. "Come, Anthony. We must discuss this."

By suppertime, Emily's anger had faded. She had spent the morning preparing lunch for Mrs. Carmichael and Mrs. Locke, hoping that the roast pork and applesauce, which she'd overhead Mrs. Locke say was one of her favorite dishes, would be a bright spot in this, their first luncheon as a duo. The sporadic laughter coming from the dining room told Emily the widows were finding some measure of joy, and that buoyed her spirits.

She continued to be encouraged when supper that evening was uneventful, suspecting there were two reasons: Beulah's absence and Alice's presence. Beulah had gone back to the ranch for the weekend, and for some reason, Lizzie was always better behaved when Alice was present. Still, Emily did not miss the looks Mrs. Dietrich shared with her husband when Craig complimented her cooking. As irrational as it was, Emily had the feeling the minister's wife wanted her to fail.

The truce, for that was the only way Emily could describe it, continued through Saturday, with Lizzie saying almost nothing at meals and her parents directing most of their comments to either Craig or Alice. This morning there'd been more activity than normal before breakfast, but the calm persisted through the meal, and Emily approached the church hoping that the new week had brought new peace to all of them.

She followed Mrs. Carmichael into the same pew they occupied each Sunday, enjoying having Noah seated between her and Craig. Beulah and her family sat in their customary spot in the back, while Mrs. Dietrich and Lizzie were in the first pew, the one reserved for the minister's family. As she'd done on the previous Sundays, Lizzie kept turning her head to see who had entered the sanctuary. This time, though, she did not meet Emily's gaze.

Following the first hymn, Reverend Dietrich took his place in the pulpit, but instead of opening the Bible, he simply looked out at the congregation, his face solemn.

"I had a sermon prepared for today," he announced. "I had planned to talk about what Jesus called the second great commandment: love thy neighbor as thyself. That no longer seems appropriate."

He paused, waiting until the murmurs subsided. "My family and I have been here for two weeks. We had hoped that you would become more than our congregation. We had hoped you would become our neighbors, but that hope has been destroyed. I will not cite people by name, but there are those in Sweetwater Crossing who have not welcomed my family with open hearts."

Again, he waited for the murmurs to subside before he spoke again. "Because of that, we have decided to leave. This will be my last time in your pulpit." Reverend Dietrich let his gaze move throughout the congregation, then said firmly, "Let us pray." But before he could begin his prayer, the church was filled with shocked cries.

"Who was it?" Mayor Alcott demanded. "Who did this?"

The minister shook his head. "As I said before, I will not single out anyone. I will simply say that my family and I find ourselves in an untenable situation."

"Surely there is something we can do to change your mind." The mayor's tone was almost cajoling.

"At this point, no. My wife and I need to find a better town to raise our daughter. We are leaving this afternoon."

"Please, don't make any hasty decisions," one man shouted.

"We need you," another chimed in.

"I want to know who's responsible," a third declared.

When Reverend Dietrich refused to answer, Lizzie turned and pointed directly at Emily. "It's her. She's the one."

CHAPTER EIGHTEEN

She wouldn't hurl one of the plates against the wall. She wouldn't shout. Most of all, she wouldn't cry. Instead, she'd wash and dry the dishes, wishing it were as easy to remove memories from her brain as it was to scrub gravy from a plate.

Lizzie's accusation had been bad enough, causing some members of the congregation to glare at Emily, while others' derogatory comments were clearly meant to be overheard. Though Mrs. Carmichael patted her hand and Craig gave her a look that radiated support, Emily felt as vulnerable as she had the days George had vented his anger on her.

"We need to talk," the mayor said as she left the church. He took her aside but spoke loudly enough that others had no trouble overhearing his words. A deliberate choice, Emily was certain.

"What did you do to drive the minister

285

and his family away? You know how much the town needs a pastor."

Like Reverend Dietrich, Emily had no intention of discussing the events that had led to this morning's declaration. "His wife and I had a difference of opinion."

Mayor Alcott's frown began to soften. "That doesn't sound serious. I'm sure that if you apologize, they'll agree to stay."

Even if she were inclined to apologize, which she was not, Emily doubted that would satisfy Mrs. Dietrich. The woman wanted both Beulah and Emily gone so that her family could call Finley House their home.

"I'm not the one who owes anyone an apology."

The mayor frowned again. "Then who is? Surely you're not suggesting Reverend or Mrs. Dietrich did anything wrong."

"I'm not suggesting anything. All I'm saying is that I have no reason to apologize." And while Jesus called for his followers to turn the other cheek, he'd also told his disciples to bring children to him, saying, "for of such is the kingdom of heaven." Emily had no doubt that he would not want her to allow Beulah to be mistreated again.

Clenching his fists in what appeared to be an attempt to control his temper, the mayor glared at Emily. "The apple doesn't fall far from the tree. You're just like your father, convinced your opinions are the right ones. Be careful, Emily. You too might find yourself with enemies."

Mayor Alcott had stalked away, leaving his words echoing through Emily's brain. She'd spent the afternoon thinking about what the mayor said. Did Father have enemies? She hadn't been aware of them, but perhaps things had changed while she was gone. Gertrude had alluded to Father's beliefs alienating some people. Had resentment festered and become something more serious?

More disturbed than she'd been in a long time, she hardly spoke during supper and told Craig she would do the dishes alone. "I'm not good company," she'd said.

He waited until she'd hung the towels to dry and removed her apron before he entered the kitchen. "Let's take a walk. You look like you need to talk, and a change of scenery might help."

"I told you I'm not good company."

"I'll be the judge of that. Fetch your shawl, and let's go."

Though it sounded more like a command than a request, Emily complied. Craig was right. She did need to talk, and if he was willing to listen, she might be able to make sense of the thoughts that tumbled through her mind.

When they left the house, Craig crooked his arm so she could place her hand on it. It was a courtly gesture, one George had abandoned early in their marriage, and one Emily found comforting. The ugliness of the morning lessened as she and Craig strolled west on Creek, then turned right onto Center.

By unspoken consent, they stopped when they reached the middle of the bridge. At this time of the year, the creek was well below its banks, meandering rather than rushing downstream, and though there was no moon, the slowly moving water reflected starlight. A frog croaked; an owl hooted; the breeze stirred the oak leaves, creating a scene of infinite tranquility. Emily was far from tranquil, but she could feel her pulse slowing, and she took a deep breath, savoring the cool autumn air.

Craig leaned his arms on the railing and stared at the water. "This is the first time I've been here at night. I didn't realize how peaceful it would be. The one time I walked across the bridge was during the day, and I could still hear noises from the town." He chuckled. "Or maybe it was only Noah's chatter."

"I used to come here when I was a child and wanted to escape from my sisters. Sometimes I'd hide under the bridge, convinced I was invisible." Emily smiled at the memories. "I love them dearly, but there were times when I wished I was an only child. Now I'd give almost anything to have them back with me."

If they'd been here, her sisters might have been able to answer her questions about Father and potential enemies.

"I always wished I had brothers." Craig sounded nostalgic. "I wasn't so sure about sisters, but seeing the way Noah acts around Jane makes me wish I could give him a sister."

"Perhaps you'll marry again." Despite Mrs. Carmichael's less than subtle attempts at matchmaking, the thought was oddly disturbing.

"Perhaps, but I didn't come out here to talk about me." Craig's voice was once again firm. "I can't say I'm sorry the Dietrichs are leaving. I'm not. The way Lizzie and her mother behave makes me wonder whether they've stayed anywhere very long. I knew Reverend Dietrich was an interim pastor, but somehow I thought that meant they spent a year with each congregation. Now I wonder whether their tenures were much shorter and whether the decision to leave was always theirs."

Craig paused for a second before he added, "Lizzie told the class she'd attended more than a dozen schools. At the time I thought she might be exaggerating, but I suspect it was the truth. That would mean they spent only a few months in each place."

Though it was tempting to cling to the idea that this was not the first time Lizzie and her mother's behavior had caused the Dietrichs to leave a town, Emily found little consolation in it.

"Even if that's true, the town still blames me for their leaving." And that was a problem. A huge problem. "I don't regret what I said to the Dietrichs — Lizzie was wrong to treat Beulah that way — but it makes me wonder if I made a mistake by coming back to Sweetwater Crossing. At the time, I didn't think I had any alternatives, but now . . ."

She paused, thinking of what had happened since that August day. "First, my sister leaves. Now everyone believes I drove the minister away." Emily's conviction that this was where she was meant to be, that providing a home for the widow and caring for Noah were part of God's plan for her, had faded under the force of the townspeople's anger.

Craig turned so he was facing her. "You're not responsible for other people's behavior, and you shouldn't blame yourself for it. Louisa and the Dietrichs made their own decisions."

"But if I hadn't been here, things would be different." Like a rock tossed into the water, Emily's return had created ripples, and those ripples had reached farther than she'd expected.

"Different, but not better," Craig was quick to respond, his tone leaving no doubt that he did not agree with her. "If you hadn't been here, I doubt your sister would have considered turning your home into a boardinghouse. That would have meant that Mrs. Carmichael, Noah, and I wouldn't have a home. If you hadn't been here, Beulah would still be on the ranch, wishing she could attend school, instead of soaking up a surprising amount of learning."

Craig paused, his expression darkening. "Don't you see what a difference you've made in our lives? And, yes, I include myself in that list. You've done so many things to help us. The love you show to Noah and Beulah has given them more confidence in themselves, and the way you've supported me has made my time in Sweetwater Crossing infinitely easier. Those are priceless gifts."

Emily felt her cheeks warm. No one had ever given her such credit. "I didn't do much."

Craig shook his head. "That's where you're wrong. You've been a force for good in Sweetwater Crossing."

Was he right? Had the disturbance she'd caused, the ripples she'd created, resulted in positive changes? Oh, how Emily hoped that was true. Craig's words were balm on the wounds George had inflicted and the barbs Louisa had slung at her, giving her the confidence Craig claimed she'd given others.

"My father used to say each of us was responsible for making the world a bit better." Emily hadn't been doing it consciously, but if Craig was right, she'd succeeded on some level. Would Father have been pleased?

Her thoughts took an abrupt turn, erasing the momentary peace Craig's praise had provided, reminding her of the mayor's accusations. "Father tried to do that — I know he did — but look what happened. He's dead and no one believes me when I say it couldn't have been suicide. Even Louisa thinks I'm wrong."

292

Emily shuddered at the memory of her first day back in Sweetwater Crossing, the horror of finding Father's body, the pitying looks she'd endured when she questioned the doctor's verdict.

"I need to prove I'm right." She met Craig's gaze, willing him to understand. He'd sensed that she needed to talk, and this was why. "I'm such a failure. I've been home almost three months, and I haven't done anything to restore my father's reputation. What kind of daughter am I?"

"One who's been overwhelmed with the other changes in her life."

It would be easy to accept that, but she couldn't. "That's just an excuse. I don't like people who hide behind excuses, and I won't be one. Somehow, some way, I'm going to uncover the truth. I need to know who hated my father enough to kill him."

CHAPTER NINETEEN

There has to be something, Emily told herself the next morning as she sorted through the pile of papers Louisa had stuffed into one of their father's desk drawers when they'd cleaned the room. If it wasn't here, it was somewhere else, but there had to be something that would help her discover who'd killed Father and why. So far, she'd found nothing.

She pulled another sheet from the pile and frowned when she saw it was only an invoice from the mercantile. Mama had always preferred to pay cash, but this bill for a surprisingly large amount indicated that there had been at least one exception.

Was Louisa right when she said Emily hadn't realized how many things had changed while she was gone? And, if she was right, was it possible that not only circumstances but people had changed so greatly that what had once been unthinkable had happened? Could it be that Father took his own life?

Emily stared at the papers, hating the direction her thoughts had taken, then telling herself that no matter what anyone claimed, it wasn't possible. Her instincts weren't wrong, and knots didn't lie.

This was like one of the problems she had had to solve in school, where Gertrude had insisted they show each step they'd taken to reach their conclusions. Gertrude had described it as a methodical approach designed to identify any errors in logic. Where Father's death was concerned, there were no errors.

Emily pulled out a fresh sheet of paper and wrote.

Father was killed by a noose around his neck.
The noose was tied with a figure-eight knot.
Father was unable to tie a figure-eight.
Therefore, Father did not put that noose around his neck; he did not kill himself.
QED

A faint smile crossed her face as she penned the final three letters. Gertrude had explained that the acronym stood for *quod erat demonstrandum,* the Latin phrase meaning "that which was to be demonstrated."

Emily's logic was sound. She knew it. Father had not taken his own life. She didn't understand why neither the sheriff nor Doc had seen any sign of a struggle. Father would never have willingly let someone put a rope around his neck, which meant the killer must have stunned him. A blow to the head was possible, but until she found the person who'd fastened the noose, she wouldn't know what happened that day. The question was, how would she find the killer?

Emily let out a sigh of relief when she heard a knock on the front door. A distraction might be just what she needed. She smiled when she saw that her visitor was the woman who'd taught her how to solve problems logically. Though she and Gertrude had disagreed the last time they were together, Emily respected her former teacher and welcomed her company.

"Are you busy? I was in town visiting my mother and thought you might need a friend today."

She did. "Thank you. Would you like some coffee?"

Gertrude shook her head and smoothed

an invisible wrinkle from her skirt. While she'd worn only dark colors when she'd taught, today she was dressed in a light blue frock that highlighted her eyes. "Mother insisted I drink a cup with her. I came to talk." When they were both seated in the parlor, Gertrude turned toward Emily. "I'm sorry about what happened yesterday. It couldn't have been pleasant for you."

"It wasn't. Mayor Alcott made his opinion very public." His assertion that Father had enemies had concerned Emily even more than his condemnation of her actions.

"He always does. I sometimes wondered if he resented your father. People listened to him more than they did the mayor."

Though Malcolm Alcott had been mayor for as long as Emily could recall and had been a guest in this house countless times, she hadn't realized there was any rivalry between the two men. When he spoke of enemies, was it from personal experience? Emily tried and failed to imagine the mayor killing her father.

"Regardless of what Mayor Alcott or anyone else says," Gertrude continued, "you were right to follow your conscience. I don't know what happened, but I know you, Emily. You don't act impulsively. Whatever you did was warranted."

Emily gave her former teacher a grateful smile. "I appreciate your support, but how can you be so sure?"

"As I said, I know you. If I had to guess, I'd say Lizzie was unkind to Beulah and you felt the need to defend her." Though Gertrude phrased it as a supposition and not a fact, her tone was so definitive that Emily wouldn't have been surprised if she'd ended it by saying, "QED."

"That's exactly what happened, but how did you know?"

A little shrug was Gertrude's first response. "Years of teaching. I don't agree with you about having Beulah in the classroom, but if I were still the schoolmarm, I'd rather teach her than Lizzie."

That surprised Emily almost as much as Gertrude's insights into her father's relationship with the mayor. "Why?"

Gertrude's pursed lips made her look like she'd eaten a whole lemon. "The girl had the audacity to tell me I was too old to be a bride." While someone else might have been insulted, Gertrude's words were infused with sarcasm, leaving no doubt she'd ignored the barb. "Thomas and I had a good laugh over that."

Her expression became solemn as she laid her hand on Emily's. "Stay true to your convictions. That's what's important."

Though Gertrude was speaking of Beulah, the advice could also be applied to Emily's determination to uncover the truth of her father's death. No matter what happened, she would not abandon her convictions.

"Thank you, Gertrude. I'm glad you're my friend."

"I'm glad she's gone." Susan Johnson gestured toward Lizzie's empty desk as she returned from recess.

"Me too. She was mean."

Though Craig wasn't surprised by Susan's words, since Lizzie had usurped her role as the smartest girl in the class, Mitch's comment did surprise him. He'd thought Mitch had viewed Lizzie as a kindred spirit, but perhaps he as well as Beulah had borne the brunt of her scorn.

Craig hadn't fully realized how much of a disturbance Lizzie had been, but the classroom was noticeably calmer today. Breakfast had been peaceful, and were it not for his concerns about the town's anger toward Emily, he would have considered it a good day.

As the last student sat, Craig pulled down the map of Texas. "All right, boys and girls.

It's time for geography. Who can find Austin?"

A dozen hands shot into the air, and to Craig's surprise, one of those was Beulah's. This was the first time she'd volunteered an answer.

"Beulah, please show us."

She walked to the front and pointed to the state capital.

"That's correct. Thank you."

Her grin would have warmed even a January afternoon. "Not a dummy."

No, she wasn't. Craig watched the other pupils' reaction and was gratified there were no unkind comments. At least for the moment, Beulah had been accepted as a member of the class.

If only every problem were as easy to solve. Craig wished he could help Emily prove — or even disprove — her belief that her father had been killed. She needed answers so that she could begin the grieving process that Craig's minister in Galveston had told him was the first step in healing. Emily might dispute it, but Craig sensed that she was still struggling with the manner of death.

Perhaps it was because her father had died so soon after her mother and her husband. Perhaps Emily had been overwhelmed by the number of losses. Perhaps it had been easier to concentrate on turning her home into a boardinghouse than to grieve those losses.

Craig had questions, many questions. First and foremost, had Pastor Vaughn taken his life, or had someone else strung that noose around his neck? He couldn't answer that without knowing more about the man himself.

When he'd asked her, Mrs. Carmichael said that Joseph Vaughn was strong-willed but honest and that she'd been shocked by the news of his suicide. "I would never have thought that of him," she told Craig. "I know he was devastated by his wife's death, but still . . ." She had been shocked but unlike Emily had admitted the possibility that the minister had chosen to end his life.

There was no point in speaking to the mayor, since he was clearly not impartial, but Craig needed to talk to someone. Perhaps someone from a different generation would have different insights. After dismissing the students, he turned right when he left the schoolhouse. Alice was first on his list of people to visit.

She greeted him with a warm smile. "Are you looking for a new book?"

"Not today. I wanted to talk to you privately." Though he saw her each evening at supper, she wouldn't be able to speak freely in front of Emily and Mrs. Carmichael.

"About the Dietrichs?" Without waiting for him to agree, Alice continued. "I don't know what Emily did or said to them, but she made a bunch of enemies. People don't like being without a minister again. They said she must have overstepped her bounds. Some even said she's acting like her father, only she doesn't have his authority because she's just a woman, not a minister."

Craig had no trouble imagining how Emily would bristle if she heard that being female made her less valuable than a man. That was so far from the truth it was laughable. If there was one thing he had learned during his marriage, it was that women were not less than men. They might not have the same physical strength, but no one should underestimate them.

"I'm glad you mentioned Reverend Vaughn," he told Alice rather than addressing the ridiculous comments about Emily. "I wanted to ask your opinion of him."

Alice appeared wary. "In what regard?"

"As a man and a minister."

She was silent for a moment, obviously choosing her words. "He was a good man. I never felt that he treated Emily differently from the other girls, even though he wasn't her father."

"He wasn't?" Craig had a vague memory of Mrs. Carmichael saying the girls were not all Reverend and Mrs. Vaughn's natural children, but he had assumed that the minister was Emily's father.

"I thought you knew. Pastor Vaughn was a widower when he came here with his daughter. That's Joanna. You haven't met her, but she's the middle girl, a year younger than Emily. I was too young to remember, but I've heard people say that it was love at first sight when he met Emily's mother. She'd been widowed a bit longer than he, but according to the stories, they were two lonely people who found happiness together. Louisa was born a year later."

Craig tried to absorb what he'd learned and wondered whether it had any bearing on Joseph Vaughn's death. He doubted that the Vaughn girls' parentage mattered to anyone other than them, but he couldn't be certain.

"He sounds like a good man. What did you think of his preaching?"

A little shrug was Alice's first response. "I never had a problem with him, but I know some people didn't approve of his sermons. My pa didn't like it when he talked about the evils of whiskey. Pa claimed a glass or two never hurt anyone. Some thought Pastor Vaughn was too harsh in condemning other sins."

In Craig's experience, it was a minister's responsibility to remind his parishioners of the difference between right and wrong and the consequences of making the wrong choices.

"Do you think he was too harsh?"

Another shrug. "He always had Scripture to back up what he said. People just didn't like hearing that what they were doing was wrong."

"The truth is sometimes hard to accept." And the difficulty of accepting it might be another reason for Joseph Vaughn's death.

Buoyed by Gertrude's visit, Emily returned to her father's desk, more determined than ever to learn what had happened that final day. She filed the paid bill from the mercantile along with the receipt for last year's taxes, glanced at Father's notes for the sermon he hadn't lived long enough to deliver, and placed the letters from former parishioners in a separate pile. Tomorrow she'd begin responding to them, informing them of Father's death. Though it was a task she did not relish, it was one she should have done months ago.

She laid a paperweight on top of the letters, then looked up when she heard footsteps in the hallway.

"Did you find anything?" Craig asked as he entered the library.

"No." Emily wished she had a more positive answer for him. She'd been so certain she could find something before he returned from school, but if the answers were here, they'd eluded her. "I don't know why I thought it would be easy. All I know is that Father did not tie that rope."

Craig settled in one of the chairs on the opposite side of the desk. "How can you be so sure?"

As quickly as she could, Emily explained about the knots. "Louisa said he must have learned how to tie a figure-eight, but I know he didn't. I watched him try and try again, and that was one thing he could not master. Father was frustrated — it must have been hard for him to admit there was something he could not do — but he finally said he was done trying. He told me those knots were God's way of teaching him humility."

Emily smiled at the memory of that day and how her father's failure had made her realize that she didn't have to be perfect. It was a lesson both of them had needed.

"I wish I could have met your father. He sounds like a man I would have liked."

"I think you would have." Emily smiled again at the thought of her father and Craig sitting here discussing everything from the last book they'd read to the best way to raise children. They might not have agreed, but she knew instinctively that they would have respected each other's opinion. Respect, Father had said, was critical.

"Most people liked Father or at least respected him, but someone obviously hated him enough to kill him."

Emily could understand how disagreements could fester into resentment and resentment into hatred, but no matter how many times she read the story of Cain and Abel, she could not understand murder.

Leaning forward, Craig said, "I've been thinking about that. What if the reason wasn't hatred but fear? I've heard your father didn't shy away from confronting sin."

"That's true, but he never denounced people in public. If he saw someone heading down the wrong path, he'd counsel them privately. Father claimed that when someone believed he'd directed a sermon at them, they were hearing the voice of a guilty conscience."

306

Like the time he'd preached about not stealing. Convinced he knew she had taken Joanna's pink ribbon, Emily had burst into tears and raced out of the sanctuary. Afterward, when she apologized and returned the ribbon to her sister, Father told her he hadn't known about the ribbon, but that God had urged him to use that commandment for his sermon.

Craig's expression was somber as he said, "If they were guilty of something serious, maybe the fear of having that revealed was the reason someone wanted to silence your father permanently. Fear can be as powerful as hatred."

Fear rather than hatred. Emily thought for a moment before she spoke. "I suppose it's possible, just as it's possible that the mayor was right and Father had enemies, but I still can't imagine who could have been so fearful that he'd resort to murder. I wish I'd been here that morning."

"What morning?" Mrs. Carmichael stood in the doorway. "Excuse me for interrupting, but Noah and I just returned from our walk, and he's anxious to see his father."

Craig gave Emily a look that said they'd continue their conversation later, then left to greet his son.

As the little boy's giggles echoed through

the hallway, the widow stepped into the library and took the chair Craig had vacated, her fatigue evident. Though she did her best to disguise it, her friends' deaths had taken a heavy toll on her.

"You two looked like you were in the midst of a serious discussion," she said.

"We were talking about my father's death. I wish I knew what happened that day. Someone must have seen his killer."

Mrs. Carmichael reached forward and laid her hand on Emily's, her face reflecting concern. "Oh, Emily, why won't you accept that your father chose to end his life? You're only tormenting yourself trying to prove otherwise."

What was tormenting her was the knowledge that whoever had murdered her father was still free. She looked at the sheet of paper where she'd written QED and the steps she'd taken to reach her conclusion, wondering whether she should show it to the widow. Instead, she said, "Father didn't kill himself. He wouldn't have. He *couldn't* have. I know that, Mrs. Carmichael. I may be the only person in Sweetwater Crossing who believes it, but I know I'm right."

Frowning, the widow tightened her grip on Emily's hand. "I don't suppose anything I say will change your mind, will it?"

When Emily shook her head, Mrs. Carmichael pursed her lips. "All right. I'll tell you what I know about the people who came here that morning."

Emily didn't bother to hide her astonishment. She hadn't expected anyone to recall what had happened on a specific day several months ago, but it appeared Mrs. Carmichael did.

"I probably wouldn't have remembered it," the widow admitted, "but after my house burned, I tried to recall everything I'd done that day. I wanted to see if there might have been a way to stop the fire before it was out of control."

The regret in her voice made Emily realize she wasn't the only one bearing scars from that August day. "Surely you don't blame yourself for the fire. No one knows how it started."

"But if I'd been home instead of sipping cool tea on Lorena Albright's porch or spending the afternoon with Lottie, it wouldn't have happened. Those hours of pleasure cost me dearly."

"It wasn't a crime to leave your house. Everyone's entitled to time with their friends." Like the half hour Emily had spent with Gertrude this morning.

"Still, I wonder why I chose that particular

309

day to be gone." The widow shook her head. "But we were talking about your father and who visited him that morning. There were a number of people, one right after the other, or so it seemed."

"Who?"

"Alice came first. She was here about three quarters of an hour, as I recall. I saw her leaving when Chauncey Clinton arrived. His visit was much shorter. So was Adam Bentley's. The last person I saw was Hazel Sanders. I didn't see her leave."

Emily tugged her hand from Mrs. Carmichael's and scribbled the names on the same sheet of paper as her logic. Even though they'd all left before lunch, if they'd been angry enough with Father, they might have returned later and surprised him in the barn.

"Alice?" She couldn't imagine why her friend would have consulted Father. "Are you sure she didn't come to see Louisa?"

"It's possible, I suppose," the widow admitted, "but I doubt it. She entered the same way everyone else did, by the back of the house. If she'd wanted to see Louisa, wouldn't she have used the front door?"

"Probably. I'll ask her anyway." Though Emily knew Alice couldn't be the killer, because unlike the men she didn't have the strength to lift Father, she might recall something he'd said or done that would help Emily identify whoever had put that noose around his neck.

"I did visit your father that day." Alice seemed surprised when Emily took her aside before supper, but the way she responded without hesitation told Emily she had nothing to hide. "I wanted to return his copy of Chaucer. I thought it would be a short visit, so I didn't worry about leaving Jane while she napped, but it took longer than I'd expected and by the time I got back home, Jane was crying for her next feeding."

Alice wrinkled her nose. "She needed a fresh diaper too. When I heard what happened to your father, I wondered if I'd been the last person to see him before he . . ." She paused for a second. "I hope I didn't say anything that upset him."

"How could you upset him simply by returning a book?" Father had enjoyed sharing the contents of what he'd always referred to as Clive's library, though it had been his for decades.

"We disagreed. He thought *Canterbury Tales* was one of the best books ever written. I didn't. We talked — more like argued

— for a while. When it was over, he seemed sad that he hadn't convinced me."

The story was so familiar that Emily smiled. "It was all pretense. That was Father's way of trying to persuade you to agree with him. He used to do that with the three of us. He'd pretend we'd hurt his feelings, and at first we believed him. Eventually he'd admit that he was testing us, trying to discover how strongly we held our views. I'm surprised he didn't tell you that before you left."

Alice's frown turned to a smile, and her shoulders relaxed. "He might have, but I left rather abruptly because I started worrying about Jane. Afterward, I was worried about him, and then about you." Alice's smile widened. "I feel better now. I didn't want to say anything about that day because I was afraid that would only add to your burdens, but I was concerned. Thank you, Emily."

Emily was happy she could relieve her friend's worries. She was not happy that she was no closer to finding her father's killer.

CHAPTER TWENTY

"It's not too cold outside," Craig said as he dried the last dish. "Would you like to go for a walk? I have a few of your father's books that I'd like to take to school tonight."

"Including Chaucer's *Canterbury Tales*?" Emily was still chuckling over the discussion her father and Alice had had. Even though Father had always claimed to admire Chaucer, Emily and her sisters had suspected that was a ruse designed to encourage them to read the stories medieval pilgrims recounted for their fellow travelers. The antiquated language had made it a difficult task for all three of them.

"No, not that one. I don't think any of my pupils are ready for it."

"You and Alice would agree. It appears she and my father had a heated discussion of the book's merits. But, to answer your question, yes, I'd like to take a walk." Fresh air and Craig's company were an unbeatable combination after a day that had had more disappointments than high points.

Emily wrapped her shawl around her shoulders, knowing the night would be cooler than Craig had thought but not wanting to forfeit the change of pace . . . literally. Somehow the simple act of putting one foot in front of the other, particularly outdoors, often made her think more clearly. She hoped that would happen today.

They spoke of inconsequential things until they approached the schoolhouse. Then raucous laughter shattered the peace that had settled over Emily as she and Craig walked together.

" 'S big rock. Gonna make big smash." Though the words were slurred, Mitch's voice carried clearly through the still night air.

" 'S good idea, ain't it?" Harlan laughed as if he'd said something hilarious.

A second later, the sound of breaking glass told Emily and Craig the boys had hit their target. She recoiled in horror. The willful destruction of property was bad enough. What was worse was the realization that the only building close enough for the crash to be so loud was Alice's home.

Oh, Alice. You don't deserve this. No one did. Emily started to run at the same time that Craig dropped his bag of books on the schoolhouse steps and sprinted toward the sound. The scene was what she had expected. Shards of glass were all that remained of her friend's front window.

Emily said a silent prayer that Alice and Jane had been in the back of the house and hadn't been injured by flying glass, then darted a glance at Craig. His clenched fists revealed the depth of his anger when he reached the bullies who'd used rocks instead of words to wreak damage tonight.

"What do you think you're doing, boys?" Craig grabbed each of them by the shoulder and spun them around so they were facing him.

"Ain't boys. We're men." Though Mitch's words were defiant, he did not attempt to break free.

"Men don't destroy someone else's property."

Harlan continued laughing, pausing only to say, "Who's gonna stop us?"

"I am. I imagine your parents and the sheriff will be interested in seeing what you've done."

"What's going on here?"

Emily turned at the sound of Sheriff Granger's voice. With his office directly across the street from Alice's home, it

315

wasn't surprising that he'd heard the noise and had come to investigate.

Craig released his hold on Harlan to let the sheriff restrain him. "It appears these boys" — he emphasized the word — "have been drinking something stronger than sarsaparilla. A night in your cell might help them realize the error of their ways. Would you like me to help you get them there?"

"I'd be much obliged." Sheriff Granger turned to Emily. "And I'd be obliged if you'd check on Mrs. Patton. Tell her I'll be back to board up her window."

Surprised that Alice hadn't opened the front door, Emily knocked on it. A few seconds later, Alice unlocked it and peered out, her wet hair telling Emily she'd been washing it while the boys were hurling rocks. One of Emily's prayers had been answered.

"What happened?" Alice's gaze shifted, and she stared in horror at the glass littering the floor. "Who broke my window?"

"Let's go to the kitchen and sit down." Not only might Alice catch cold, but Emily suspected her legs might give way from shock. She put her arm around her friend's waist and led her to the back of the house.

When they were both sitting at the kitchen table, Emily began her explanation. "I'm

316

not sure how they got the whiskey, but Harlan and Mitch are drunk. They seem to have thought it would be fun to throw rocks at the library." Emily refrained from calling it Alice's home, not wanting to increase her friend's distress. Anyone would be upset that their home, which should have been a sanctuary, had been breached, if only by a rock. A woman alone with a baby would feel even more vulnerable.

"What if Jane or I had been there?" Alice began to shake, the magnitude of what had happened beginning to register. "We might have been hurt."

"But you weren't," Emily was quick to reassure her. "As soon as he has them locked up, Sheriff Granger said he'd board up your window. I'll get someone to clean the mess tomorrow. A good sweeping will make a big difference."

Alice nodded, but her face was ashen, and her trembling only increased. Clearly, Emily's attempts to comfort her were falling short. Though there was no longer any danger, Alice was still reeling from what had happened.

"Why don't you pack a bag for yourself and Jane and spend the night at Finley House? You know I have plenty of room."

Alice gripped the edge of the table, seeking comfort from the solid surface. "Are you sure you don't mind? I don't like leaving my house, but I don't feel safe here." She shook her head to emphasize her fears, then frowned as a drop of water hit the table. "What a sight I must be!" Her frown deepened as she ran her fingers through her hair and began braiding it. "I couldn't go out like this."

Alice had just finished securing the braid around her head when heavy footsteps announced the sheriff's and Craig's arrival. Under other circumstances, they would have knocked and waited to be invited inside, but tonight they simply entered the building and followed the light to the kitchen. Both men's expressions were solemn, but Emily saw regret in Craig's while the sheriff radiated anger.

"You don't need to worry, Mrs. Patton," the sheriff told her. "The boys are in jail. I'm on my way to talk to their parents. As soon as that's done, I'll work on your window."

"I'll take care of that." Craig stood in the kitchen doorway. Though Emily knew the danger had passed, she found reassurance in his presence. Craig was a man who'd protect women, not harm them.

"I imagine Mr. Miller has some empty

crates at the saloon. I can break them apart and use the wood to cover your window." Furrows formed between Craig's eyes. "I'd insist the boys do it, but they're in no condition to do much tonight."

The sheriff nodded. "What they need is a trip to the wood-shed they won't forget." The way he flexed his arm suggested he was volunteering to administer the discipline.

Though Alice nodded in agreement, Craig's expression said he disagreed. "I'm not excusing them. What they did was wrong, but the real problem is how easy it was for them to get the whiskey. Mitch wasn't making a lot of sense, but he kept talking on the walk to the jail. It seems Harlan's father doesn't lock his storeroom. The boys stole a couple bottles from the saloon after school and spent the rest of the day drinking in the park."

And neither mother had come looking for her son when he missed supper. Emily wondered what the boys' life at home was like and whether that was one of the reasons they'd become bullies.

"I don't think it was personal," Craig said to Alice. "It seems your house was the closest one when they decided it was time to make some noise."

As she recalled Mitch talking about the

smash the rock would make, Emily realized that noise, not destruction of property, had been their objective. In their drunken state, they might not have recognized that one would cause the other.

Craig's explanation appeared to reassure Alice.

"I'll make sure Jason Miller keeps his storeroom locked and his son under control." The sheriff's voice left no doubt of his determination to do his job. "You don't need to worry, Mrs. Patton. You're safe, and this won't happen again." He turned to Craig. "Let's go, Ferguson. We've got work to do."

When the men left, Alice locked the front door, ignoring the gaping hole where the window had been and the easy entry it gave to her home. "I've changed my mind, Emily. I'm going to stay here tonight."

Though Alice's voice was steadier and color was returning to her face, Emily wasn't certain that was the right decision. "Are you sure?"

"Yes. It's my home, and I'm not going to let two hoodlums drive me out of it. What you and I both need right now is a cup of tea."

When Craig had finished boarding up the window and returned to the kitchen, Emily repeated her invitation to spend the night at Finley House. As she'd expected, Alice refused again. "I'll be fine, and Jane will be happier if she wakes in a familiar place. I don't want her to be confused."

It was a valid concern. Emily gave her friend a hug, then accompanied Craig outside.

"It's been a long time since I was so angry," he said as they headed home. "I thought Mitch and Harlan were outgrowing their foolishness, but I was wrong."

Emily wasn't certain people outgrew being bullies. Her experience with George suggested they simply learned to conceal their true nature until they were thwarted. Then they vented their rage on whoever was closest.

"You handled your anger differently than most men would have."

Craig paused and turned to face her, the moonlight revealing his somber expression. "Because I didn't advocate beating the boys? You know I don't believe violence is the answer. I expect Mitch and Harlan to pay for the repairs, and I'm going to insist they apologize to Alice, but Jason Miller is equally to blame. Doesn't he remember what young boys are like and what happens when they give in to the lure of strong drink?"

Emily shook her head. "Not just boys. Grown men too. Mr. Miller and my father had more than one discussion about the effects of selling whiskey for half price on Saturday afternoons. Too many men took advantage of it and were in no condition to attend church the next day."

She sighed, remembering the number of Sundays when women brought their children to services without their husbands. "Father tried his best to get Mr. Miller to stop, but he never did. As a result, there was no love lost between them."

The words were no sooner out of her mouth than Emily realized the implications of what she'd said. "I wonder if he could have been the one who killed my father. Mrs. Carmichael didn't say anything about seeing him that day, but she wasn't on the Albrights' porch after noon. He may have come later."

Craig inclined his head in agreement. "It's possible. I'll talk to him."

"If you've come to complain about my boy, don't waste your breath."

Though Craig had met the saloon owner several times, this was the first time the man hadn't bothered with a polite greeting but had launched into what sounded like the start of a tirade when Craig entered the building. Fortunately, since it was only mid-afternoon, the saloon wasn't crowded. Jason Miller and a young man whose position behind the bar made Craig assume he was an employee were the only people besides two men seated at a small table, apparently engrossed in a conversation.

"The sheriff was here last night and again this morning. And if you're wondering why Harlan didn't come to school today, it's because he was sicker than a dog. Serves him right for drinking my best whiskey."

The man's disgust seemed to say that the loss of the whiskey bothered him more than his son's drunkenness and the destruction of the library window. If this was the way his father treated him, it was little wonder Harlan spent so much time with Mitch. For all his faults, Mitch was loyal to his followers.

Craig gave Jason Miller a long, appraising look. The man was about his height, with hair and eyes almost the same color as Craig's, but the similarities ended there. Miller was a decade or so older, his face bearing the creases of time, his midsection paunchy from too much drink and too little exercise.

"I'll expect Harlan back in school tomor-row," Craig told the boy's father. Mitch had come to school but had spent most of the day moaning while he rested his head on his desk, his bleary eyes leaving no doubt of the reason for his moans.

The saloon owner's shrug said his son's education was of little importance.

"Harlan wasn't the reason I came," Craig told him. "I wanted to talk to you about Reverend Vaughn."

When Miller's employee grabbed a bottle and headed to the table to refill the men's glasses, Miller leaned on the bar. "Sure you don't want a drink? First one's on the house."

When Craig declined, Miller's lips curved in scorn, although Craig wasn't certain whether it was because of his abstinence or the saloon owner's opinion of the minister. Miller's next words erased any confusion.

"That old busybody? He was always med-dling in other folks' business, trying to tell us what we oughta do. He made himself a bunch of enemies."

That was consistent with what the mayor had told Emily. The question was, who were those enemies? "It sounds like you might have been one of them."

"Nah." Miller shook his head. "I didn't like him and thought he should mind his own business, but I didn't wish him any harm."

Though the words rang true, Craig wasn't through. "Any idea who might have?"

The saloon owner straightened his shoulders and glared at Craig. "What are you getting at? The preacher killed himself. Everyone knows that."

"His daughter doesn't think so."

"Emily? She's wrong. She didn't see what he was like after his wife died. He was sobbing like a baby when he read her funeral service." Miller shook his head again. "That was the last time I saw him, but it's not something I'll forget."

"Then you didn't talk to him the day he died?" It was a long shot, but Craig had to ask.

"How could I? I'm here every day, eight to midnight. They're mighty long days, but a man's gotta do what he can to make a living."

"And you never leave, not even to eat?"

"I already said that. If you don't believe me, ask Zach." He crooked a finger to summon the man. "Zach, when's the last time I left this place for more than five minutes?"

"Never." Zach thought for a second. "No,

wait. That's not right. You left me in charge when you went to Mrs. Vaughn's funeral."

"What about after that?"

"Nope. Never."

Like the saloon owner's, Zach's words rang with truth. Jason Miller might be a poor father, but he wasn't a killer.

CHAPTER TWENTY-ONE

"This was a day for apologies." Alice smiled as she buttered a piece of corn bread.

Emily was reassured by her friend's apparent recovery from last night's ordeal. She'd stopped by the library when it opened and had discovered half a dozen women inside, sweeping, dusting, mopping — doing everything they could to erase the previous night's damage. The window was still boarded up, leaving the room dark, but the library was returning to normal.

This was Sweetwater Crossing at its finest, its residents banding together to help one of their own. The townspeople might not approve of either Craig's teaching Beulah or Emily's defending her, but Alice had never done anything to warrant their disapproval, and so they'd given her their support.

Craig raised an eyebrow. "Both Harlan and Mitch apologized?"

"Plus Mrs. Sanders. I didn't expect that. This was the first time she and I exchanged more than two sentences, but she seemed genuinely upset that Mitch had been involved in breaking my window. She even offered to pay for the new one." Alice dipped her spoon into the stew Emily had prepared for tonight's supper. "I don't see how she could do that. Everyone knows she doesn't have much money. Folks think that's why she —"

"Careful." Mrs. Carmichael interrupted, her eyes darting toward Beulah, who'd leaned forward, clearly intrigued by the conversation. Noah, bored by the adults' discussion, was attempting to make a mountain out of corn bread crumbs.

When Alice said nothing more, Beulah spoke for the first time since they'd started eating. "Are you okay, Mrs. Patton? I saw your house." Her shudder confirmed what Emily thought: the girl was more nervous than usual tonight. No one had discussed the broken window at breakfast, but it would have been a major topic at school, and Craig had said that a number of students had walked by the library during recess, perhaps to assess the damage.

Giving Beulah a reassuring smile, Alice

said, "I'm fine, and so is Jane. No one was hurt."

"Okay." Beulah glanced at the baby, who was happily playing with a stuffed sock. A second later, she frowned. "Mitch and Harlan are bad boys."

Though Emily wanted to agree, she remembered what Craig had said last night and shook her head. "What they did was wrong, but they're not necessarily bad boys."

For a second Beulah appeared confused. Then she nodded. "Okay." Turning to Alice, she asked, "Did Mitch's mother do something bad?"

Alice hesitated before saying, "She apologized. That was very good."

"Okay." Apparently satisfied, Beulah returned to eating.

When the meal was over and Beulah had volunteered to read Noah a story, Alice turned to Emily. "That was awkward, wasn't it? Sometimes I forget that Beulah listens so carefully. I'm glad Mrs. Carmichael stopped me before I said anything more about Mrs. Sanders's gentlemen callers."

"That's gossip, isn't it?" Emily had heard stories but had dismissed them as nothing more than rumors.

Alice shook her head. "As far as I can tell,

it's true. Cyrus told me he saw men going in and out of there at all hours of the night."

Though she wondered how Cyrus had known that, Emily wouldn't ask. The logical explanation was that he'd seen the widow's visitors when he was walking to or from the saloon. Emily could only hope that was before he and Alice married.

"I heard some people were urging your father to denounce her." Even though Beulah was no longer in the same room, Alice kept her voice low.

"You know he didn't believe in public denunciation."

"That's true" — a shrug accompanied Alice's response — "but people were becoming adamant that he should."

As she remembered seeing an unfinished sermon on Father's desk, Emily wondered what he'd planned to say. Was it somehow connected to Mrs. Sanders? Did she know about it, or was it only coincidence that she had visited him the day he died? Those were questions Emily would ask tomorrow.

Two hours later, she closed the book and smiled. As Emily had hoped, reading had helped her relax enough that she'd now be able to sleep. She reached for her nightgown, then dropped it as the unmistakable sound of a girl's screams rent the night. Hoping it was only a nightmare and not physical pain, Emily raced across the hall, her heart pounding with fear. Moonlight streamed through the window, revealing that Beulah was awake and sitting up in bed.

"Don't hurt me! Don't! Don't!" The shouts continued.

The look of terror on Beulah's face broke Emily's heart. It might be nothing more than a nightmare, but Emily knew all too well the power nightmares could exert. It was likely they were even more debilitating for Beulah, who might not be able to distinguish between a dream and reality. As it was, the child had endured more shunning, humiliation, and ostracism in her short life than anyone should, and now she was frightened beyond all reason.

"It's all right," Emily said as she sat on the side of the bed and wrapped her arms around the girl who'd become so dear to her. "You're safe. No one will hurt you."

Beulah covered her eyes to block out the images that had frightened her. "Bad boys," she sobbed. "Throw rocks."

So that was what had triggered the dream. The nervousness Emily saw at supper had escalated, sleep turning it into a full-fledged nightmare. "It was only a dream, Beulah.

331

You're safe here." Emily continued to stroke the child's back, hoping the action and her words would soothe her.

"I'm scared."

"I know you are, but it wasn't real. It was only a bad dream. You're safe. I won't let anyone hurt you."

Though color had returned to Beulah's face, she was still trembling from the nightmare's aftermath. Knowing Beulah wouldn't be able to sleep for a while and that she needed a distraction, Emily rose. "Would you like to help me make some cocoa?"

The girl's eyes brightened. "Yes, ma'am."

"Put on your wrapper, and we'll go downstairs."

Half an hour and two cups of hot chocolate later, Beulah was calm enough to sleep. Once she had her settled in bed, Emily returned to the kitchen and began heating water to wash the pans.

"More dishes?"

Startled, Emily dropped the pan, splashing soapsuds onto the counter. She'd been so engrossed in her thoughts that she hadn't heard Craig's footsteps. "Beulah had a nightmare, so we made cocoa."

Craig nodded. "The cure for everything that ails a child. Is she better now?"

"I think so. She dreamt that boys were

hurting her." A quick swipe with a towel cleaned up the soapy mess. Emily could only hope that the cocoa cure had been equally effective.

"I'm not surprised. She was nervous at school and kept glancing at Mitch. There was no mistaking her fear." Without asking, Craig picked up another towel and began to dry the cups and saucers.

Emily appreciated the help. More than that, she appreciated Craig's presence, because he was the one person who could tell her whether the concerns that had gripped her while she was trying to comfort Beulah were real or simply a reaction to what had happened tonight.

"First Lizzie and now this. It makes me wonder if we made a mistake encouraging Beulah to attend school."

If he was surprised by her words, Craig gave no sign. "It was no mistake," he said firmly. "Beulah's stronger than we realize. She'll recover from this."

Emily wasn't so certain. "I hope so. The effects of nightmares can linger."

"You sound like you've had your share of them."

The words popped out before she could censor them. "I lived one for almost a year."

■ ■ ■ ■

Craig stared at Emily. The anguish in her eyes left no doubt that she regretted saying what she had and that she hoped he'd ignore it. Perhaps he should, but he couldn't because he felt compelled to ask, "Do you want to talk about it?"

She turned to lean against the counter, making him wonder if she needed its support. "No. Yes. I don't know."

The uncharacteristic dithering revealed the depth of Emily's pain. Craig pulled a chair out from the table and urged her into it. Only when they were both seated did he speak. "Rachel used to tell me that talking helps."

That had been a difficult lesson for him to master. While he found it easy to stand in front of a classroom and talk about facts, expressing his feelings had seemed wrong. If it hadn't been for Rachel's persistence, he would have kept his deepest thoughts bottled up inside him.

Emily's eyes were dark with remembered pain. "It's not a happy story."

"I didn't expect it would be. Nightmares aren't happy." And the way she twisted her wedding band made him suspect he'd been wrong in believing her marriage had been as happy as his and Rachel's.

As if she realized how much her nervous gesture revealed, Emily folded her hands on the table and stared at them for a long moment. Finally, she raised her eyes and met his. "I haven't told anyone, not even Louisa. I didn't want anyone to know what a horrible mistake I made. They thought he was perfect."

His stomach churning at the confirmation that what he'd feared had been true, Craig clenched his fists, grateful that he'd kept them in his lap where Emily couldn't see his reaction. "Your husband?" By some small miracle, his voice did not reveal the anger that surged through him.

"Yes. George. Louisa claimed he was like a prince from a fairy tale. Joanna didn't say much, but the way she looked at him told me she agreed. Even my parents were charmed. As for me . . ."

Emily lowered her gaze for a second, trying to marshal her thoughts. "I couldn't believe such a handsome man would choose me over both of my sisters."

One thing Craig's parents had taught him was that all of God's children were special in their own ways, and Emily was more special than most. He wanted to enumerate the ways, but now wasn't the time. Instead, he contented himself by saying, "I haven't met Joanna, but I'd definitely choose you over Louisa."

"That's because you saw Louisa at her worst. Both she and Joanna are more talented than I am. Louisa's a born healer, and Joanna's a gifted musician. George didn't pay a lot of attention to Louisa, but he'd sing while Joanna played the piano. I thought he fancied her and wasn't surprised. What did I have to offer him?"

A lot. Craig started to protest but stopped when Emily seemed determined to continue her explanation. He'd encouraged her to talk; the least he could do was listen, even though every fiber of his being urged him to contradict her.

"I was just as surprised as my sisters when George asked for my hand. I couldn't believe my good fortune. I thought I was the luckiest woman on earth, because my dream of becoming a wife and mother was coming true. It was only after we were married that I learned why George chose me." She paused, clearly unwilling to admit the reason, then said, "It was because I'm a blond."

Craig made no effort to hide his surprise. "What does the color of your hair have to do with who you are as a person?" The whole idea was nonsensical.

"It was simple," Emily said. "George had blond hair and blue eyes. He believed that if his wife did too, he'd have blond children. He'd seen how men bred horses and thought the same principles worked for people." She sighed. "That's all I was to him, a broodmare."

"You must be mistaken. No one would choose his wife that way." Craig had loved Rachel for her kindness and the way she filled the empty spaces inside him, not for the color of her hair or eyes.

The look Emily gave Craig was so filled with pain that he knew she believed her appearance was the only reason she'd been a bride.

"George did," she said firmly. "He didn't care about me. He only cared about the sons I would give him, and when I didn't . . ." She closed her eyes and shuddered.

As the memories of how Emily had shied away from him at first, how she'd cried "don't touch me" and fled when he'd kept her from falling off a chair, how the thought of pupils being caned bothered her flashed through Craig's brain, he realized what had happened. Emily's husband had hit her.

337

More than that, he'd beaten her.

Rage, deeper and darker than anything he'd ever known, filled him. Though he knew violence solved nothing, if George Leland were still alive, Craig wasn't sure that he wouldn't have resorted to violence to show the man what it felt like to be a victim.

"I prayed and I prayed," Emily said, her voice little more than a whisper. "I prayed for a baby because having children was my fondest dream. I prayed that George would understand that sometimes it took a while. I prayed that my family would come for a visit because maybe then I could go home with them. None of my prayers were answered."

She was silent for a moment. "One month when George was angrier than usual, I was afraid he'd kill me. The next day I saddled Blanche and left. That was the worst mistake I made." Tears began to roll down Emily's face. "George found us and took us back to the ranch. When we got there, he made me watch while he removed one of Blanche's shoes and trimmed her hoof so much that it began to bleed. Afterward, he told me if I ever tried to leave again, he'd do even more to her."

And so she'd stayed, knowing she might

be beaten again but unwilling to be the cause of an innocent animal's pain. No wonder Emily had described her life as a nightmare. No wonder she was adamant about not marrying. Her husband had been a monster.

Craig took a deep breath, trying to subdue the anger that flooded through him while he searched for a way to comfort her. Emily was good at comforting Noah and Beulah and even Mrs. Carmichael. Now it was her turn to be comforted, but Craig's fury that men like George Leland existed was so strong that he found himself at a loss for words. Finally, he said, "Not all men are like that."

Emily nodded as she brushed the tears from her cheeks. "I know, but all men want children, especially sons. No one wants a barren wife."

Craig's anger turned to sorrow as he realized the depths of the wounds Emily had sustained. The physical ones were bad enough, but her husband had done more than that. He'd made Emily doubt her value as a person. George had belittled her, and she'd believed him. He'd made strong, caring, wonderful Emily feel that she was less than a woman, all because she had not borne him a son. The man was an idiot.

Only an idiot would have failed to recognize what an extraordinary woman Emily was. Only an idiot would have failed to love her as deeply as Craig did.

He blinked, shocked by the thought that had taken residence in his mind and at the same time warmed by the realization that it was true. He loved Emily. He couldn't say when it had started, when gratitude and friendship had become love. All he knew was that he loved her with all his heart.

Rachel had been his first love, and deep inside, Craig knew that Emily would be his last. He also knew that this was not the time to tell her. She wouldn't trust words when she was so vulnerable. He could say that Emily's being childless didn't matter to him, but since he already had a son, his words would hold little weight. She needed more than words. She needed actions to help her heal, to show her that he wasn't like George, to show her that he loved her. Craig didn't know what those actions would be, but he did know that he loved Emily and that he wanted her to be his wife.

He placed his hands on the table, then moved slowly, not wanting to alarm her. "I'm not most men," he said as he laid one hand on top of hers. To his delight, Emily did not flinch.

It was twelve hours later, but the memory of what had happened last night was still as vivid as if only seconds had passed. She had told Craig the truth about her life with George.

Emily rolled out the final piecrust and laid it carefully on top of the peach filling. Though she'd vowed to herself that no one would ever know of George's cruelty, she did not regret revealing it to Craig. The pity she'd feared had not come. Instead, she'd seen Craig's anger and sorrow and something more, something she'd been unable to identify the first time it shone from his eyes. All she knew was that it comforted her, telling her she was not alone, that what had happened was not her fault, that staying on the ranch to protect Blanche had been a sign of strength, not weakness. As the words had spilled out of her lips almost of their own volition, Emily had felt the weight she'd been carrying for so long begin to lift.

She pressed the piecrusts together and began to crimp the edges, her heart warming as she remembered Craig's words and the look that had accompanied them. It had been tender and filled with emotion, reminding her of the way Father used to look at Mama, like she was the only woman in the world, and in that moment, she'd been filled with hope. Hope that Craig didn't view her as damaged or lacking. Hope that maybe one child was enough for him. Hope that dreams did come true.

Craig wasn't like any man she'd ever met. He wasn't as handsome as George, but what was inside him was more than handsome. It was honest and honorable. And those qualities, added to everything else that was Craig, made him irresistible.

Even before what happened last night, thoughts of him had become Emily's constant companions. As she scrambled eggs, she found herself dreaming of eyes the color of melted chocolate. While she hung laundry out to dry, she wondered whether Craig would be content to live in Sweetwater Crossing for the rest of his life. When she watched him swing Noah into his arms or ruffle his son's hair, she asked the most difficult question of all: Would Craig be content with only one child?

On its heels came the other question: Would that be fair to Noah? The boy wanted a sibling. He deserved one. But Emily could not give him one. And that was why, no matter how close she had felt to Craig last night, Emily knew she needed to accept that her dream of a husband and children was only that, a dream. What was paramount now was finding her father's killer.

The place to begin was his desk. While the pies baked, Emily opened the top drawer and pulled out the papers she'd stashed there. There it was, the sheet headed "August 20 Sermon." She'd only glanced at it in the past, but now that she stared at the paper, she saw that what should have been a full page of notes was nothing more than a Scripture reference, John 8:1–11.

Unlike her father, Emily did not have major portions of the Bible memorized, and so she opened his well-worn Bible and found the passage. It was the story of Jesus with the scribes and Pharisees and the woman taken in adultery.

Emily nodded slowly at the familiar story. Father had used it as the basis for sermons in the past, asking the congregation to ponder verse 7. If she closed her eyes, Emily could almost hear him reading, "He that is without sin among you, let him first cast a stone at her" and asking whether anyone sitting inside the church could honestly claim to be without sin. Perhaps he'd planned to preach about that again. But as she continued to read, Emily saw that another verse had been underlined, the darker ink indicating that it was a more recent annotation.

"Go, and sin no more." Was Alice right? Had Father bowed to his parishioners' demands and planned to address Mrs. Sanders's sins, or had he summoned her to discuss them? Was that the reason she'd visited him that morning? There was only one way to know.

"Emily Vaughn. No, it's Emily Leland now, isn't it?" Mrs. Sanders's face registered her surprise. The woman's hair was almost as dark as Craig's, but her eyes were hazel rather than chocolate brown. Had her parents named her Hazel because of them? Emily wouldn't ask. That was not why she'd come here.

"I didn't expect to see you." Mrs. Sanders's almost diffident tone made Emily suspect few women visited, undoubtedly the result of the gossip.

Emily held out the still-warm pie plate. "I brought you a peach pie. I thought you and Mitch might enjoy it." Another of Mama's lessons was the insistence that her daughters not visit relative strangers without bringing a small gift.

Mrs. Sanders smiled as she inhaled the

aroma of peaches and spices. "Thank you. We certainly will." She appeared to be inspecting the crust. "Your parents always said your piecrusts were the best they'd ever eaten."

It was Emily's turn to be surprised. Her parents had never told her that, although Mama had encouraged her to teach Joanna how to make flaky piecrusts.

"You must think I've lost my manners. Come in, come in. I'll cut us each a slice." The widow led the way into her small but immaculate house, gesturing to the table.

"No, thank you," Emily said as she took a seat. "It's all for you and Mitch, but I would like to ask you a few questions."

Mrs. Sanders's smile disappeared, replaced by narrowed eyes. "About my son or about the rumors you've undoubtedly heard of men coming here?"

Though Emily was surprised that Mrs. Sanders would even mention the men, she shook her head. "Neither. My questions are about my father." When the widow relaxed, Emily continued. "I heard you visited him the day he died, and I wondered what kind of mood he was in."

"I wish I could tell you. It was a difficult day for me. I was worried about Mitch because I'd heard him and Harlan talking and knew they had some kind of mischief planned. I tried to find my son, but he'd disappeared." She shook her head in obvious disapproval. "It's hard to keep track of him, particularly on a Saturday. I thought I'd heard him say 'Vaughn,' so I planned to go to your house to make sure he wasn't bothering anyone in your family."

She turned her right hand so that Emily could see the recently healed scars on the palm. "I would have gone to your house sooner, but I tipped over the teakettle and scalded my hand. It took a while before I could put on gloves."

And no lady would go out without them. Emily stared at the woman's hand while Mrs. Sanders continued her story.

"When I arrived, there was no sign of him. Your father wasn't in his office, so I looked around the first floor. No one was there." She met Emily's gaze and said, "I'm sorry I can't help you."

"And I'm sorry you hurt yourself." Though it wasn't impossible, Emily doubted that anyone with a badly injured hand would fashion a noose and hoist a grown man off the ground, even if she had the strength to do it.

It was almost ironic that the injury George had invented in his efforts to keep Emily's family from contacting her had happened to someone else, but the scars were unmistakable. And while it was possible that Mrs. Sanders had hurt herself on a different day, Emily did not believe she was lying. Her story rang true, leaving Emily only one conclusion: Mrs. Sanders hadn't killed Father.

CHAPTER TWENTY-TWO

Craig stared out the schoolhouse window. Though his eyes registered the sight of a third girl playing tag with Beulah and Susan during recess, his thoughts were focused on Emily. The woman he loved was amazing, stronger than anyone he'd met — male or female. Some would laugh at the thought of a woman being stronger than a man, and it was true Emily couldn't match his physical strength, but she possessed something far more important: inner strength.

She'd survived what sounded like a horrible marriage without any help from her family. Craig recalled Rachel speaking of a woman whose husband's cruelty seemed equal to George's. That woman — Lily was her name — had sought sanctuary with her parents. Even though some in the town had claimed Lily's husband was justified in disciplining his wife any way he chose, her parents had refused him entry to their home. They'd protected her, but Emily had had no protection. Most amazingly, she hadn't expected any. If that didn't prove Emily's strength, he didn't know what would.

And then she'd come back to Sweetwater Crossing only to discover that both her parents were dead. That would have been enough to make most women — most people, he corrected himself — rail at the unfairness of life, but Emily hadn't done that. Instead of sinking into self-pity, she'd thought only of others. She'd offered him, Noah, and Mrs. Carmichael a home; she'd volunteered to make meals for the widow's friends and Alice; she'd given Beulah a room so she could attend school. The woman was truly selfless. And he loved her. Oh, how he loved her.

This morning when they'd sat at the table together, he'd imagined how different the day would have been if they were married. He could have wrapped his arms around her while she was scrambling eggs and stolen a kiss after she put the bread into the oven to toast. Even with Mrs. Carmichael and Beulah present, he and Emily could have shared smiles as they recalled private moments. More than anything, he wanted Emily as his wife, but first he had to woo her.

It was too soon to ask to court her. He doubted she'd accept gifts, even if he could find something as unique as Emily herself, but there had to be a way to show her how much he valued her. What could he do for her?

When Susan led Beulah and the other girl toward the swings, Craig nodded, as pleased by the thought that had popped into his head as by the evidence that more children were accepting Beulah. There was one thing Emily wanted above all else: to clear her father's name. That would be the first step. It would be an unconventional wooing, but Craig knew that if he could help her exonerate her father, the next steps would be easier.

He squared his shoulders as resolve filled him. Somehow, he'd find the answers Emily sought.

"The chicken fricassee smells delicious," Mrs. Carmichael said as she entered the kitchen Friday morning. "I hope you made enough for yourself and Noah."

Emily turned and smiled at the widow and the boy who was holding her hand. "Of course. We need to eat too, don't we, Noah?"

When Noah nodded his agreement before picking up the wooden truck that had become his favorite toy, Mrs. Carmichael gave Emily a piercing look. "You don't need to eat in the kitchen. Betty and I want you to join us."

"Are you certain? I don't need to tell you that Noah can be rambunctious."

"That might be exactly what we need. Now that it's only the two of us, it seems all we talk about are Clara and Lottie and how much we miss them. You and Noah would give us something different to discuss."

"Like Noah wanting to pick the peas out of the sauce?" Over the past week, he'd developed an aversion to anything green and had refused to eat beans, peas, and spinach.

The widow shrugged. "We might be able to convince him peas are delicious."

"It's worth a try."

"Then you'll sit with us. I'm glad." Mrs. Carmichael glanced at the door to the dining room, her eyes narrowing, perhaps imagining four settings on the table. "The diversion will be good for Betty and me."

And for Emily. This had been a trying week, a week that had been made even more complicated by her late-night confession to Craig. While she couldn't regret it, since sharing the story of her life with George had eased her pain, she continued to wonder how it had affected Craig. She felt that the road they'd been traveling had taken an abrupt turn, leaving the destination unknown.

There had been no more warm and comforting looks, making Emily wonder whether she had imagined that Craig harbored special feelings for her. He hadn't referred to their conversation, although she'd caught him looking at her with a speculative expression, all of which left her more confused than ever and totally unprepared for the discussion they had Wednesday evening while they did dishes.

"How can I help you prove your father was killed?" Craig spoke so calmly he might have been inquiring about tomorrow's supper menu.

He was calm, but the question took Emily by surprise. "You believe me? I thought you weren't completely convinced."

"I am now." He dried another plate, then turned to face her, waiting until he had her full attention before he continued. "Your story about the knots rings true, but it's more than that. I trust your instincts. You may not have been here for the past year, but as the eldest, you knew your father better than your sisters. If you believe he would never have killed himself, I believe it too."

Tears of gratitude, relief, and something she couldn't define welled in Emily's eyes. "Thank you." Craig was the first to trust her unconditionally, and that meant more than she could express. The trust was wonderful, but what filled Emily's heart with an unexpected warmth was that somehow he had realized how important finding Father's killer was to her. Only when she'd done that would she be free to begin the next chapter in her life.

"My plan is to talk to everyone who came here that day," she told Craig. "I've already spoken to Alice and Mrs. Sanders, but there were others. Even if none of them killed him, they might have seen or heard something that would point to whoever put that noose around Father's neck."

Craig nodded slowly. "It's a place to start, but you know no one will admit to being a murderer."

"I know that, but I still have to talk to them. That's why I visited Mrs. Sanders today."

"What did you learn?"

When Emily finished her explanation, Craig raised an eyebrow. "Did you believe her?"

"Yes."

"All right then. Who's left?"

"Chauncey Clinton and Adam Bentley." She'd left the men for last, knowing it would be more difficult to approach them. While she had made countless trips to the mercantile, it would still be awkward to ask Mr. Bentley about Father's final day. Talking to Mr. Clinton would be even more difficult.

"Clinton's a rancher, isn't he?"

"Yes. He and Father were at odds when his son died." Emily could still recall the shouts emanating from Father's office. "When Chauncey Junior killed himself, Father wouldn't bury him in the cemetery. Mr. Clinton stopped attending church that week and told anyone who'd listen that Father was wrong. After that, he spent the time we were worshipping standing by his son's grave. As far as I know, he didn't speak to my father again, so I don't know why he would have come to the house that day."

"I see." The look Craig gave her told Emily he understood just how painful it would be for the rancher to talk to her, the daughter of the man who'd hurt him so greatly. "It would probably be better if I spoke to him."

Emily let out a sigh of relief. "I have to admit that I was dreading seeing him."

"Then I'll do it. Do you want me to talk to Mr. Bentley as well?"

It would be easy to agree, but Emily didn't want to relinquish all responsibility to Craig. "I can do that. I need to go to the mercantile soon."

As he stacked the last plate in the cupboard, Craig said, "You've got a good plan. If the men can't help us, we'll figure out another way. Between us, we'll find the answers."

The way Craig kept saying "us" and "we" reassured Emily as much as his offer of assistance. She'd been prepared to do everything alone, but the search would be easier with Craig on her side. It wasn't simply that he'd talk to Mr. Clinton. Just as important was the knowledge that they would discuss whatever they learned and, if needed, devise a new plan. Working together would lighten her burden and make a difficult task more pleasant.

"Thank you, Craig. I hope you're right, because I hate knowing Father's buried in unconsecrated ground. He wanted to be next to Mama."

"And he will be. You and I'll see to that."

Craig placed his hand on Emily's shoulder and gave it a little squeeze. Perhaps he meant it to be comforting, and it was, but it was more than that. His touch sent tingles of warmth down her spine and made her long for things that could never be.

"So you agree you'll eat with us?" Mrs. Carmichael's question brought Emily back to the present.

"Yes. Noah will be excited."

He was. And, as she had predicted, he began picking the peas out of the fricassee sauce.

Mrs. Locke gave him a look that might have intimidated a less audacious child. "I'm surprised to see you doing that, young man." The last of Mrs. Carmichael's widowed friends was taller than many men, with what Mama had called large bones. Perhaps it was because of her size that she held herself with an almost regal air, one that was highlighted by her silver hair arranged in a coronet and the gold-rimmed spectacles perched on her nose. Right now, she was peering over the spectacles at Noah.

"Don't like them." He placed two more peas on the side of his plate.

"As I said, I'm surprised. Little boys do things like that." Mrs. Locke emphasized the adjective. "Young men eat what's put in front of them."

Noah's eyes widened. "Me man." He stared at his plate, seeming surprised by what he'd done. A second later he stirred the peas back into the sauce and began to eat with apparent relish. It was all Emily could do to keep from laughing.

"That young man is the grandson I wish I had." Mrs. Locke's smile faded a bit as she looked at Mrs. Carmichael. "It was a tragedy that your son died in the war, but at least you and Harry had eighteen years with him." She helped herself to another serving of peas as she continued. "James always said he didn't blame me, but being childless broke both of our hearts."

The amusement Emily had found in the widow's skillful manipulation of Noah vanished, replaced by the knowledge that despite her attempts to convince herself otherwise, being barren was something no man could overlook.

The two widows chatted for a minute before Mrs. Locke turned back to Emily. "Are you planning to attend services on Sunday?"

"Yes, of course." She tried to push aside her unhappy thoughts. "Why do you ask?" No matter how many in the congregation shunned her, Emily would not forfeit her chance to worship as part of a community.

"I wanted to warn you that there might be more unpleasantness. Doc told me everyone he's seen recently has complained about not having a regular minister. The mayor does his best, but . . ." She left the rest of the sentence unsaid.

"They blame me."

"I'm afraid so."

Mrs. Carmichael frowned. "That's nonsense. Betty, I hope you set Doc straight."

A shrug was Mrs. Locke's first response. "I tried, but he said he wasn't the one who needed to be convinced. It was everyone else."

Emily wasn't surprised. The congregation had been floundering before Reverend Dietrich arrived, and now they were once more without an ordained pastor.

"Good boy, Noah." Mrs. Carmichael smiled as he cleaned his plate.

"Me man," he corrected her.

"Yes, of course. You're a good man, Noah." The widow's smile faded as she returned her attention to her friend. "I can see there's only one thing to do. We need to help the elders find a new minister." She was silent for a second. "I'll ask Craig whether he knows anyone, but tell me, Betty, what did Doc say about your lumbago? I assume that's why you consulted him."

"It was. The pain was something fierce

yesterday morning, so he gave me some salve to put on it."

"Did that help?"

"Oh yes. Doc Sheridan is a miracle worker. He can do anything."

Mrs. Carmichael shook her head. "Except find us a new minister."

CHAPTER TWENTY-THREE

"Our prayers have been answered."

Craig saw the way Emily's shoulders relaxed as they headed home from church. Though Noah would normally have accompanied them, this morning he'd announced that he was a man and would stay with Mrs. Carmichael while she spoke to her friend. When the widow agreed, Craig had offered his arm to Emily, relishing the time alone with her.

"Mrs. Locke claims Doc Sheridan is a miracle worker," Emily continued, "but the real miracle worker is God. He knew we needed a minister, and he's sending one."

The announcement had caused most of the congregation to applaud, though applause was not a normal part of the service.

"He sounds very different from Pastor Dietrich." Craig had listened carefully as the mayor extolled the man's credentials. "Younger, unmarried, the son of a minister, with glowing recommendations from his last three churches."

"I was surprised that the elders would choose someone who's only looking for a temporary position."

Craig agreed with Emily. That part of the announcement had been as unexpected as the speed with which they'd found a new minister. "I wonder if the elders are trying to avoid repeating their mistake in not checking Pastor Dietrich's references more carefully."

Emily shook her head. "The only mistake they'll admit to is letting the Dietrichs live with me. That's why they arranged for Pastor Grant to stay with the Albrights."

Craig had no complaints about that arrangement. As much as he hated to think he suffered from jealousy, when he'd heard the new minister's age and bachelor status, he'd found himself worried about sharing the house — and Emily — with him. Ministers were often encouraged to marry, and who was better suited to be a minister's wife than a minister's daughter?

"Their house may not be as large as yours," he told Emily, "but the Albrights have room for him."

Unlike most of the Sunday Houses, theirs was designed as a full-time residence.

361

"That's true, but it stings a bit, knowing so many people blame me for the Dietrichs leaving."

And the criticism, combined with the way her husband had berated her, had left Emily vulnerable. Craig had made it his mission to bolster her spirits and convince her that she was both valuable and valued even if it meant repeating things he'd already said. Perhaps, like many of his pupils, she learned from repetition.

"You did the right thing when you defended Beulah." When Craig saw hope light Emily's eyes, he wanted to continue, but as they approached the cemetery, he spotted a man standing next to the two graves outside the fence. "Is that Chauncey Clinton?" Based on what Emily had said, it almost had to be.

"Yes. I thought he might have come to church now that Father's no longer there, but he seems to be continuing his practice of spending Sunday mornings at his son's grave."

Though he'd have preferred to stay with Emily, Craig didn't want to miss this opportunity to speak with one of the men who'd visited Joseph Vaughn the day he died. "Will you excuse me?"

"Of course. And thank you. I know you're

doing this for me."

Approaching the rancher was only one of the many things Craig wanted to do for Emily. As she continued on her way, he crossed the street. Seeing the man's bowed head, he waited until Mr. Clinton's prayer ended before he approached him, extending his hand in greeting.

"We haven't been introduced, Mr. Clinton, but I'm Craig Ferguson."

The rancher's auburn hair was liberally threaded with silver, and lines bracketed his eyes, but his smile was genial and his handshake firm. "The schoolmaster. What brings you here?" Other than the clothes that hung on his frame as if they'd been made for a larger man and his presence outside the cemetery, he could have been any rancher, but both of those told Craig the man's grief had yet to subside.

Craig gestured toward the grave that had yet to be covered with grass. "The man who's buried next to your son. His daughter's having a hard time believing he killed himself."

Clinton nodded. "We never want to believe someone we love would do that." He reached down to lay his hand on his son's small stone marker. "It's been two years since Junior pulled the trigger on that shotgun, and even though I'm standing here looking at his grave, I still can't believe it. I keep thinking about that day and blaming myself."

This wasn't what Craig had expected to discuss, but he wouldn't stop the man. The more he knew about Chauncey Clinton, the better. "Why do you say that?"

The rancher's eyes held the same pain that Craig had seen so often when he'd glanced in a mirror. "I should have listened to him when he said he was unhappy. I thought it was a passing mood, so I told him to be a man and accept that life isn't perfect. An hour later, I heard the shot." Clinton's lips moved as if he were trying to hold back a cry. "I hope you never see anything like that."

Craig had no trouble imagining the grief the man had felt at the loss of his son. If something happened to Noah, Craig knew he'd be devastated. And if he believed he'd been somehow responsible for Noah's death . . . The thought was unbearable.

"It's not the same," he told the rancher, "but I watched my wife fall to her death. To this day, I wonder if I could have prevented it." Logic told Craig he wasn't responsible, but in the darkest hours of the night, logic fled, and he was left with the horrible fear that somehow he should have realized Rachel was in danger and come home sooner.

Clinton inclined his head in understanding. "Then you know how it feels to wake up every day and wish you could turn back the clock."

"But we can't, so we have to go on the best we can." Unlike the rancher, who appeared to be alone in the world, Craig had Noah and, if everything went the way he prayed it would, the hope of future happiness with Emily.

Clinton's shrug said that going on, as Craig had called it, was not easy. Then he gestured toward the second grave. "You said you came here because of him."

"Him and you," Craig clarified. "I heard you saw Pastor Vaughn the day he died." Since the man hadn't spoken to him in years, Craig had no doubt he would recall that day. "Did he say anything that made you think he'd take his own life?"

A quick shake of his head gave Craig the answer he'd expected. "I never could figure that out," the rancher said. "Folks knew he and I had words — angry words — when he refused to bury Junior in the cemetery. I'm not proud of my part in that. I said things I regretted as the months went by."

The man pursed his lips, as if trying to rid himself of an unpleasant taste.

"It took me too long, but I finally realized the preacher did what he had to. More than he had to. Even though he wouldn't allow Junior to be buried in consecrated ground, he gave him a Christian burial. I wanted to set things straight between us, so I went to tell him that."

This time a small smile lit the rancher's face. "Pastor Vaughn's a good man. Was a good man," he corrected himself. "He accepted my apology, and we talked for a while about forgiveness. He seemed to be in good spirits other than complaining that his leg hurt more than usual. He was wounded at Gettysburg, you know." When Craig nodded, the rancher continued. "I felt better after we talked, and I could see that he did too. That's why I was shocked when I heard what he'd done. I can understand why Emily doesn't want to believe it. If I were in her shoes, I wouldn't either." Clinton turned pensive again. "I wonder whether Adam said something to upset him."

"Adam Bentley?"

"Yeah. He came in just as I was leaving." The rancher fisted his hands. "It's possible Adam came looking for forgiveness just like me. Lots of folks say he overcharges them. I can't say it happened to me, but I'm not real good at checking prices. I expect folks to be honest."

So did Craig, even though he knew not everyone was. As he bade the rancher farewell and headed toward Finley House, he reflected on what he'd heard. Just because someone had visited the minister after Clinton didn't mean the rancher couldn't have come back later and killed Emily's father, but his story had the ring of truth. The last time Chauncey Clinton and Joseph Vaughn were together was in the minister's office.

The man's apparent honesty had swayed Craig, but what convinced him was the rancher's past and his still-fresh grief. Craig couldn't imagine him wanting another family to endure what he had after his son's death. If he'd meant to kill Joseph Vaughn, he would not have disguised it as suicide.

Chauncey Clinton was not the killer. That left Adam Bentley, who may or may not have been cheating his customers.

Emily tried not to frown as she approached the mercantile. Adam Bentley was the last person on her list of people who'd talked to Father that day, the last one anyone had seen enter the house. She'd known the man her whole life and found it hard to believe he'd killed her father, but Father would have been the first to say you never knew what was inside a man's heart. Like several of the other parishioners who'd come to Finley House that day, he and Father had been on opposite sides of an argument.

Before she'd left Sweetwater Crossing, she'd heard Father chiding Mr. Bentley for raising prices during a year of poor harvests when farmers were struggling to feed and clothe their families. Though he admitted his costs hadn't increased, Mr. Bentley declared his right to make a profit any way he could. Father didn't raise his voice, but Mr. Bentley's shouts were loud enough to be heard throughout the house. They disagreed, vehemently, it seemed, but surely that wasn't a reason for murder. Even if the story Craig had heard was true and Mr. Bentley was cheating people, the shopkeeper knew Father well enough to realize there would be no public denunciations.

Try though she might, Emily could not imagine Mr. Bentley murdering anyone. Bracing herself for what she hoped would be a more pleasant encounter than the one she'd overheard, Emily entered the mercantile.

"Good morning, Emily. What can I get for

you?" Mr. Bentley tipped his head in greeting, sending a shock of light brown hair tumbling over his forehead. Though his store sold Macassar oil, its owner apparently did not use it.

Emily smiled as she pulled an invoice from her reticule. "I found this among my father's papers and wondered if you could explain it." The description had been maddeningly vague, saying only "special order."

Mr. Bentley studied it for a second, then nodded. "Ah yes, the blue china vase." Though his words were ordinary, he appeared uncomfortable. "I rushed the shipment as much as I could, but it arrived too late. I doubted your father would want it, but I couldn't return it."

If the invoice was vague, Mr. Bentley's explanation was equally obscure. "I'm confused. Could you start at the beginning? Why did Father want a blue china vase? Mama already had one." It was the only gift her mother had from Emily's father, her first husband, and was one of her most prized possessions. Though she rarely used it for flowers, she kept it on the bureau in her bedroom.

The shopkeeper met Emily's gaze, his eyes a lighter shade of brown than Craig's, his expression almost condescending as he said,

"That one broke. According to your father, your mother lost her balance and knocked it to the floor. He said she was heartbroken. When he came here to find a replacement, he told me he'd pay anything. I thought I could get it before she . . ." Mr. Bentley paused, obviously not wanting to complete the sentence. "Unfortunately, it took longer than I'd expected and didn't arrive until that Saturday. I didn't want your father to have to come here to pick it up, so I took it to him."

"What did he say?"

For the first time since she'd asked about the invoice, Emily saw Mr. Bentley relax. "He thanked me. He said even though it wasn't the original, he felt like I'd brought him a piece of Prudence. It was the happiest I'd seen him since he buried her."

If the story was true — and Emily suspected it was — Father had had one fewer reason to have killed himself. When she found the vase, she'd keep it in her own room until Louisa and Joanna returned. The three of them could decide whose it should be.

"Can you think of any reason my father would have wanted to die?"

Mr. Bentley's face registered his surprise at the blunt question. He hesitated for a

370

moment before saying, "Those first few days after your mother died, he was like a lost man. I wondered if he might will himself into the grave."

When Emily gasped, the shopkeeper shrugged. "Doc said it happens more often than folks realize. Someone just loses the will to live. But the way your father smiled at that vase wasn't like a man who was contemplating suicide. That's why I was so shocked when I heard what happened. The Joseph Vaughn I knew wouldn't have done that. Something bad must have happened after I left."

Everything Mr. Bentley said confirmed what Emily believed: someone had killed Father. But who? It wasn't anyone she or Craig had questioned. They'd reached a dead end.

"I know you're discouraged," Craig said when Emily recounted her conversation with Adam Bentley. They'd finished the dishes and were standing in the kitchen, spending a few minutes talking as they did most nights. "I'm disappointed too."

It wasn't that he wanted to believe anyone in Sweetwater Crossing was a murderer, but he wanted Emily to be at peace, and the only way that would happen was to discover who'd killed her father.

"I feel like a failure," she admitted, her voice breaking on the final word. "The only good thing that happened today was that I found the vase. Father had placed it in the back of a desk drawer."

"You're not a failure," Craig said firmly. This was what he had feared, that Emily, who'd shouldered her family's problems, would view her conversation with Bentley as a defeat.

"We've reached what appears to be an impasse, but it's not the end. The answers are somewhere, and we'll find them."

Craig wished he were as confident as he sounded. The truth was, even though he'd told Emily they'd devise another plan if the first one didn't reveal the killer, he had no idea what the next plan should be. All he knew was that Emily needed comforting tonight. And so, though he knew she might shy from his touch, he took a chance and wrapped his arms around her waist, drawing her close to him.

"It'll be all right, Emily. You're not a failure. Together, we'll succeed." Perhaps if he said the words often enough, she'd believe them.

She was silent for a moment before she tipped her head up and gave him a weak smile. "Thank you." And then, to Craig's immense satisfaction, she rested her head against his chest. It wasn't a romantic gesture, but it made his heart sing, because it told him Emily did not fear his touch. She trusted him.

Thank you, God.

Emily dipped another piece of chicken in the seasoned flour, then laid it with the others. It was too soon to start frying it, but she wanted to have everything ready before Noah and Mrs. Carmichael returned from their afternoon walk. As much as Noah enjoyed fried chicken — it was one of his favorite foods because he could eat it with his fingers — he was too young to help her prepare it, no matter how often he asked. Emily smiled, anticipating the way he'd giggle when he realized what she was cooking.

It was easy to please Noah, and that made her feel like less of a failure. For, despite Craig's reassurances and the wonderful moment she'd spent in his arms, a moment when her cares had disappeared and she'd believed they would succeed, Emily had spent most of the day wondering if she'd ever be able to restore Father's reputation. Perhaps making Noah giggle was all she'd accomplish today. If so, she needed to accept that and consider it a success.

She was washing her hands when she heard the front door open. Perfect timing. She could spend a few minutes playing with Noah before Beulah came home from school. Maybe that would boost her spirits.

"No cry, Mcar. No cry." Instead of the happy chatter and giggles she normally heard, Noah's words were little more than a wail. What on earth could have happened to make Mrs. Carmichael weep? The widow had been careful to hide her grief from Noah, not wanting him to be affected by it.

Emily rushed into the hallway. It was as she had feared. Something was horribly wrong. Noah clung to Mrs. Carmichael's hand while the widow seemed to be staring sightlessly, tears streaming down her face.

"What's wrong?" Emily hurried to the older woman's side and wrapped her arms around her. "What's wrong?"

Mrs. Carmichael looked up, her face contorted with grief. "It's Betty. She's dead."

CHAPTER TWENTY-FOUR

The night was cool but not unpleasantly so, with only the slightest of breezes as Emily and Craig strolled toward the bridge, the full moon lighting their way. It was Friday evening, the first time they'd walked in a week, the first time they'd come this way alone in far longer than that. Noah was asleep, Alice and Jane had left, Beulah had returned to the ranch for the weekend, and Mrs. Carmichael had retired to her room as soon as supper was over, overcome with grief.

Perhaps sensing how much she needed to escape the house and the pall that hung over it, once Noah was in bed, Craig had suggested they walk. Even if the weather had been unpleasant, Emily would have agreed, because she relished the opportunity for uninterrupted time with Craig. He'd been her bulwark this week, providing support when she needed it.

"I wish there were something I could do for Mrs. Carmichael," Emily said as they reached the corner of Creek and Center and turned north. "You should have seen her when I served lunch today and it was only her, Noah, and me in the kitchen instead of her and her friends in the dining room." Emily paused and looked directly at Craig. "It was horrible. She didn't cry — she tries so hard not to do that in front of Noah because she knows it upsets him — but she looked devastated."

Craig nodded. "It has to be difficult for her, burying her three closest friends in such a short time."

"I told you how she worried something awful would happen to either her or Mrs. Locke on December 6 since her other friends died on the sixth of October and November. She wasn't prepared for another death only two weeks after Mrs. French's."

A frog's croak was followed by a small splash as it slid into the creek. An owl hooted. A rodent scurried through dry leaves. It was an ordinary night for them and for most of Sweetwater Crossing's residents, but it was far from normal for the widow.

Emily stopped and looked up at Craig. Though his expression was somber, she took comfort from his presence and the knowledge that he would do everything he could to help her.

"She keeps saying, 'I don't understand,' and I don't either. Nothing makes sense, Craig. The women weren't ill. Mrs. Locke complained about her lumbago last Friday, but lumbago doesn't kill anyone."

"No, but old age does. As far as anyone knew, my grandmother was healthy, but she dropped over dead one day." Craig shook his head and urged Emily to resume their walk. "I know you're troubled tonight, and it's more than Mrs. Carmichael's grief that's weighing on you. You loved your father, and you don't want to abandon the search for his killer."

"I don't." Emily said a silent prayer of thanks that Craig understood her. Knowing that she was not alone made the difficult times easier to bear. "I have no idea who could have killed Father. It was hard to believe that Alice or Mrs. Sanders could have done it. Even before I knew about Mrs. Sanders's injured hand, I didn't think she or Alice had the strength to lift him. I also couldn't imagine Mr. Bentley being that angry. He never struck me as a violent man. That left Mr. Clinton. I didn't know him well enough to say whether or not he was capable of murder."

"Almost anyone is, given enough provocation."

They'd reached the bridge and by unspoken consent stood next to the railing. Only a few inches separated them, making them close enough that Emily could feel the warmth emanating from Craig. Like the words he used to reassure her, his nearness brought her comfort.

"I believe Clinton's story," Craig told her. "If he'd wanted to harm your father, he would have done it soon after his son died, when his anger was the strongest."

That made sense. Why would a man wait almost two years if he wanted to wreak vengeance?

"That leaves us without any suspects." Emily used the plural pronoun deliberately, wanting Craig to know she considered him an essential part of her search. And he was, for without his support, she might have given up in despair.

"Once Mrs. Carmichael left the Albrights' porch, there was no one looking at the house, so I have no way of knowing who else came." Emily stared at the water flowing beneath the bridge, wishing it held answers. "I don't want to abandon the search, but I don't know what to do next."

They had spoken of a second plan, but Emily had no idea what that could be. The future was darker than the creek's water.

"Maybe this is the time for trust." Craig's voice was soft, almost tender, as if he were trying to convince her. "I know you want answers. When Rachel died, I kept asking why. Why had she been so foolish? Why had God let her die? Why had he left me to raise Noah alone?"

Those were the questions Emily would have asked, had she been in a similar situation. "Did you find answers?" She had found none when she tried to understand why she had misjudged George so badly, and now as she tried to learn the truth about her father's death, she once again had nothing but unanswered questions.

Craig shook his head, confirming what Emily suspected. "Not at first and not all of them, even now. It wasn't easy, but I finally had to accept that I might never know why my wife died. That's when I realized I needed to trust God when he said he'd make everything work out."

Though he didn't quote the verse, Emily knew which one he meant. "Romans 8:28. That was one of Father's favorites, along with Jeremiah 29:11." She gripped the railing as she thought about what Craig had said and the peace she heard in his voice when he explained the decision he'd made. For it was a conscious decision. Emily knew that.

"You're right. I need to trust God. It's what my father would have wanted me to do, but it's difficult. So very difficult." She wanted to be the one who discovered why Father had died, and it felt like defeat to admit she couldn't do it.

"I know." When Craig laid his hand on hers, the warmth that made its way through the fabric of their gloves comforted her as much as his words had. "Trust was a slow process," he admitted. "At first I was so mired in the past that I failed to appreciate the present. It's only since I came to Sweetwater Crossing that I've begun giving thanks for each day. I learned to find pleasure in the ordinary parts of my daily life. Now, for the first time since Rachel died, I'm looking toward the future."

Emily had stopped believing in a happy future when she'd failed to give George the son he wanted, and even when hope of a future with Craig and Noah had taken root inside her, she had done her best not to water the seedling. What she wanted was less important than what Noah needed. Still, she couldn't stop herself from asking,

"What do you see in your future?"

"You."

Emily turned and stared at him. Was it possible she had been right when she'd thought he might harbor tender feelings for her? Craig had claimed he wasn't like George, that having sons wasn't the reason he'd married, but he also said he wanted Noah to have the siblings he'd longed for. Surely he hadn't forgotten that she was unable to bear children.

"Me? What do you mean?"

Craig lifted her hand and cradled it between both of his. "This isn't the way I'd planned to tell you, but I admire you more than anyone I've met."

Admiration, not love. Emily's spirits, which had soared toward the stars, plummeted.

"You're strong; you're courageous; you're caring. I know it's too soon to say anything more, but I want you to know how much I esteem you and that when I think about a future without you, it seems bleak and lonely."

As the words registered, disappointment threatened to overwhelm Emily. Craig esteemed her. He didn't love her. She should have realized that he saw her as a friend, nothing more. She should take comfort from the fact that being esteemed was better than what George had given her. And yet, though she told herself to be as strong as Craig claimed she was, Emily wanted nothing more than to weep over dreams that would never come true.

"I admire you too, Craig." By some small miracle, her voice remained steady. "You needn't worry. I'll always be your friend." She feigned a shiver. "We'd better go home before it gets any colder." Or before she succumbed to tears.

What a fool he'd been. Craig was still berating himself the next morning as he wiped Noah's hands and face after breakfast. It had been more than twelve hours, and the ridiculous words he'd spoken still reverberated through his mind. Had he really said he admired and esteemed Emily? There was nothing wrong with that — anyone would want to be admired and esteemed — but it was hardly the way to tell a woman he wanted to court her. He'd have to find a way to make her forget the silly words that had somehow come out of his mouth. Right now, though, he needed to keep Noah entertained.

He smiled at his son. "Do you want to go for a ride?"

As he'd expected, his son grinned. "Yes!" he shouted and moved his hands, pretending to flick a horse's reins.

For the past week, Noah had insisted he was old enough to have a pony. He wasn't, of course, but Craig hoped a ride would satisfy some of that longing. Ten minutes later, he settled his son in front of him on Horace and wrapped an arm around him. "Let's go, pardner."

"Pardner." Noah grinned again as he tried out the new word.

Noah was still grinning and bouncing up and down as they headed west. It wouldn't be a long ride, because Craig knew how cranky his son would be if he missed either lunch or his afternoon nap, but he craved a change of scenery and a chance to clear his head as well as an opportunity to indulge Noah's love of horses.

The day couldn't have been more perfect, with a few lazy white clouds drifting across an otherwise faultless blue sky. His son was excited, and Craig's mood had lightened. Not even the sight of a woman approaching could spoil the outing.

"Good morning, Mrs. Neville," he said as he recognized the rider.

The former schoolteacher pulled her horse to a stop next to his and wrinkled her nose in apparent displeasure. "Now, Craig, haven't I told you you should call me Gertrude? Where are you headed?"

"No place in particular. Noah and I just needed some fresh air."

She shrugged, her disbelief apparent. "I'm on my way to help my parents prepare for the new minister's arrival and thought I'd stop in to see Emily. How is she?"

Annoyed with me, and justifiably so. Craig wouldn't admit that to anyone, so he answered honestly, "She has her hands full trying to console Mrs. Carmichael."

This time his predecessor nodded. "It's such a shame, losing all her friends like that. I remember my father saying it wasn't the same when Clive Finley didn't come back from the war. The three of them who remained hated that empty chair, and now there are only two: my father and Doc Sheridan." She shook her head. "You don't need me talking about gloomy things. How are your pupils now that little troublemaker Lizzie is gone?"

"Better. It seems that a night in jail had an impact on Mitch and Harlan. Their pranks have been fewer and less cruel."

"I hope that lasts." She didn't seem convinced that it would. "What about Beulah?"

That was a happier subject. "She won't

ever be my star pupil, but she's making progress. Best of all, she's happy."

"Which means you're doing a good job. I had my doubts at first, but you're turning into a fine schoolmaster. You should be proud."

Perhaps he could take pride in Beulah's progress, but Craig wasn't proud of the way he'd bungled the conversation with Emily.

"Ooh, he's good looking." Alice pinched Emily's arm to get her attention.

It was Saturday, December 2, and the townspeople had gathered to welcome their new minister. Emily had seen him arrive yesterday, but once he'd entered the Albrights' house, he hadn't emerged. Gertrude had explained that her parents were arranging a small supper for him Friday night so that he could meet the mayor and the church elders, but today would be his introduction to the rest of the congregation. And tomorrow was his much-anticipated first sermon.

Emily tried not to shudder as she looked at the man who'd caught Alice's attention. Pastor Grant was the same height as George. Like George, he was blond and probably had blue eyes. Like George, he had a square chin. Emily shuddered again. It was unfair to judge a man based on physical attributes, but she couldn't help being wary.

"He reminds me a bit of George," she admitted.

Alice's smile widened into a grin. "And he was almost as handsome as the new minister. I hope Pastor Grant decides to stay."

"You know he only agreed to stay for six months. Gertrude said he wants to return to his family in Louisiana." Gertrude, whose father was one of the elders, had more information than most of the town.

Alice's enthusiasm dimmed. "Oh. I wonder whether he has a sweetheart there."

Emily studied her friend, trying to understand her reaction. It wasn't like her to sound so flighty, but Alice's moods had been less predictable since the night Harlan and Mitch broke her window. She'd admitted that she worried about living alone and wondered if it was time to marry again. Could she be considering the new minister as a possible husband, even though she hadn't spoken a word to him? "Surely you're not going to ask him if he has a sweetheart."

Alice's smile turned mischievous. "No. I'll ask Craig to do that. That man has a way

with words."
Words like *admire* and *esteem*.

CHAPTER TWENTY-FIVE

"Have you eaten there?" David gestured toward Ma's Kitchen.

Craig shook his head. "I haven't had any reason to. Emily provides all the meals for Noah and me." He looked at the building that stood opposite the school, wondering what had precipitated the minister's question. There was nothing noteworthy about the restaurant other than the savory aromas that sometimes wafted across Main Street, but perhaps Pastor Grant was merely making conversation.

For the past week, David — he'd insisted on the informality, saying he wanted them to be friends, not simply minister and parishioner — had joined Craig for his walk home after school each day, and they'd talked about everything from Craig's pupils' latest hijinks to possible subjects for David's sermons. Though the man was four years older than Craig and had a very different upbringing, they'd discovered an almost immediate affinity, making Craig wish David's stay in Sweetwater Crossing were permanent. He could use a friend like him.

"Why did you ask? According to the grapevine, you've had supper invitations almost every night."

David nodded, then rolled his shoulders to work out a kink before they started to walk. "That's one of the advantages of being a new minister: many in the congregation want to welcome me by breaking bread with me. The same thing happens when I announce that I'm leaving. In between, I fend for myself or, if I'm fortunate as I am here and live with a family, I eat with them."

All of which made Craig wonder why his new friend was curious about Sweetwater Crossing's restaurant. Mrs. Carmichael said that while no one's meals surpassed Emily's, Lorena Albright was a good cook. David should have no worries about being fed and no reason to frequent Ma's Kitchen.

Craig turned away from the restaurant and headed north on Center Street. There were still a couple hours before supper, and he had things to do.

"Emily said she asked you to join us tonight." When she'd mentioned it at supper yesterday, not wanting Beulah to be surprised when the minister arrived, Beulah and Mrs. Carmichael had seemed enthusiastic. Only Alice had said nothing, but that could have been because Jane was fussy.

"She did. I know you won't tell anyone, but I'm looking forward to tonight's supper more than any other meal I've shared."

The sparkle in David's blue eyes gave Craig pause. Was he interested in more than food? Did he, like George Leland, find blond, blue-eyed women attractive? Choosing to ignore that possibility, Craig said, "Emily's an excellent cook. I doubt you'll have eaten anything better than whatever she plans to serve. I should probably warn you, though, that my son's table manners leave much to be desired. Fortunately, he's gotten over his aversion to green vegetables." Craig still chuckled whenever he thought about the way Mrs. Carmichael's friend had convinced Noah to eat peas.

"I'm sure I've seen worse than your young man's eating habits." David's emphasis on "young man" told Craig he recalled the story he'd recounted and found it almost as amusing as Craig did. "I'll have to remember the widow's trick for getting young'uns to eat when I have my own. But, back to my original question: have you eaten at

Ma's Kitchen and do you think it would be the right place to take a woman?"

Though it was possible David was thinking of a way to repay Mrs. Albright for her hospitality, Craig doubted that. If he was, David would have planned to invite both Mr. and Mrs. Albright and wouldn't have been so concerned about taking a woman there. That narrowed the possibilities and raised the hackles on Craig's neck.

"You mean if you were courting her?" Perhaps it was because courtship was on his mind or perhaps it was David's expression when he'd mentioned his enthusiasm about tonight's supper that made courtship the only reason Craig could imagine.

David nodded. "The first step is getting to know a lady well enough to decide whether you want to court her."

Craig was well past that step. The months he'd spent living at Finley House had revealed Emily's many facets, and each revelation had deepened his conviction that she was the woman he wanted to court and marry. But this conversation was about David, not him.

"I suppose that would be fine," he admitted, hoping his lack of enthusiasm wasn't evident. "It's a public place, so there's no question of impropriety. Being seen there in the company of a single lady would, of course, raise all kinds of speculation."

"I realize that." A shrug accompanied David's words. "It's not easy being in the public eye. You must have the same problem."

They turned right onto Creek, Craig's steps slowing as his eyes registered the obvious neglect of what had been Mrs. Adams's house. The grass needed mowing, and a crumpled piece of paper was caught in one of the rose bushes that lined this side of the house. The next time Mitch and Harlan misbehaved, he'd have them work on this yard. Thinking about improving a dead woman's property was easier than continuing a discussion of courting.

"You're right," he told David. "Folks expect me to marry again and give Noah a mother, especially when they learn how long it's been since Rachel died." Though it didn't happen as often here as it had in Galveston, more than one well-meaning woman had stopped him after church to introduce him to someone she was certain would be the perfect mate for him.

"But you're not courting anyone." David sounded surprised.

"Not yet." Courting Rachel had been simple, but Emily wasn't Rachel, and Craig wasn't certain how to start. Maybe inviting her to dine at the restaurant would be a good first step, unless she was the woman David fancied.

Craig fixed his gaze on his friend. "You sound like someone's caught your eye."

"You could say that. The moment I saw her standing in the crowd, I felt drawn to her. I can't explain it other than to say that I felt that a magnetic force was bringing us together and that she was the one woman in the world for me."

Craig let out a soft whistle. What he'd felt for Rachel had not been a force like the one David described, but that was natural, since he'd been a young boy. It was true that Rachel had caught his eye that first day of school, but it took years before either of them acknowledged their mutual attraction. And with Emily, the attraction had been like a seed, sprouting then growing slowly but steadily. "That's more than catching your eye."

They'd reached the Albright house, but instead of heading toward the front porch, David stopped and gazed across the street at Finley House, a wistful expression on his face. "The problem is, even if she feels the same way, we have some huge obstacles to overcome. She'd have to be willing to leave

Sweetwater Crossing."

"Or you could stay. Based on everything I've heard, the town would welcome you as its permanent minister."

Craig tried to tell himself that he was wrong and that Emily was not the woman with the magnetic force, but the way David was staring at her home made him fear he had correctly interpreted his friend's interest. He and David were alike in so many ways that it made sense that they'd both realize how special Emily was, but oh how he hated the idea that David might want to court her.

David shook his head and continued staring across the street. "Sweetwater Crossing's appealing, but it's not where I'm meant to be for the rest of my life." He shifted his weight from one foot to another, as if uncomfortable with the discussion. "I don't know how much you know about me, but my father's a minister and his father was before him. My family's what some people call a pillar of the community. They even named the town Grant Landing in honor of my grandfather."

Craig hadn't heard that. All he knew was that David had come from Louisiana.

"Pa's getting up in years and wants to retire from the ministry, and the town's asked me to take his place."

"Then why are you here?"

Tearing his gaze away from Finley House, David faced Craig. "Because I wanted to learn how to lead a congregation where no one has expectations based on my name. That's why I became an interim pastor for three other churches. This is my final one. When my six months are over, I'll go home. The question is, if this woman is indeed my helpmeet, will she want to go with me?"

"That would depend on the woman. If she loved you, she might be willing to uproot herself." Emily had done that once. If she was the woman David wanted for his wife, would she do it again? Would she find the idea of a fresh start more appealing than a life here in Sweetwater Crossing with him and Noah? The prospect soured Craig's stomach.

Emily looked at her apron, chagrined by the knots in its strings. Tying knots was a nervous habit she'd thought she'd banished ten years ago, but it had resurfaced this afternoon. The cause wasn't difficult to find.

She knew she shouldn't be nervous about her dinner guest simply because he reminded her of George. She'd listened to two of his sermons and had been impressed by both his sincerity and his knowledge of Scripture. Using simple but powerful words, he'd helped the congregation prepare for Christmas, now less than two weeks away.

Other than the physical resemblance, David Grant was far different from George, and his preaching was far different from Pastor Dietrich's. If that weren't enough to convince Emily she was silly to harbor any misgivings about the new minister, Craig had said the two of them had discovered many common interests and that he considered him a friend.

She trusted Craig. Father would have said he was wise beyond his years, the proof of which was Craig's advice to enjoy the present and look forward to the future rather than dwelling on the past. That had been exactly the counsel Emily needed.

It hadn't been easy, but she had finally accepted that she might never know the truth of Father's death and that it might not be in her power to clear his name. Instead of worrying about that, each night Emily searched for — and found — at least two good things that had happened that day and gave thanks for them. To her surprise, that simple act filled her with contentment, made sleep come more easily, and caused her to wake filled with anticipation of another day.

Her contentment had increased, but she would be happier when supper was over and her guest had left. She'd invited him because it was the right thing to do and because she'd hoped that having him here would help Mrs. Carmichael. Though the widow did her best to hide her grief, Emily knew it was deep and tried to find ways to distract her, even if only for an hour or two.

When she heard the knock on the front door, Emily slipped off her apron, patted her hair, then hurried to greet the visitor.

"Welcome to Finley House, Pastor Grant."

The man's smile was warmer and more sincere than George's had been, confirming Craig's opinion that he was trustworthy. "Please call me David, and I hope you'll allow me to call you Emily. I'm here as a friend, not your minister."

The words weren't simply warm; they were disarming. "Thank you, David, and of course you may call me Emily." She gestured toward the parlor. "Would you like to wait here until supper is ready?"

Though she'd expected him to agree, he shook his head. "I don't want to impose, but I'd like to see the rest of the house — at least this floor. I admire it every time I look out my window and have been trying to imagine which rooms are where and what they look like."

Most men Emily knew wouldn't have been interested, but it appeared Pastor Grant — David, she corrected herself — wasn't most men.

"Certainly." She led him into the parlor. "This is obviously the parlor." When he'd seen the formal seating arrangements and the marble mantel, she opened the sliding doors to the next room. "This was designed as a library, but my father used it as his office."

David's eyes lit on the tall bookcases, and he ran his hands over the embossed spines on several volumes. "Being surrounded by all these books must have inspired some sermons."

"It did. It was also a way my father reached out to a number of his parishioners. He enjoyed sharing his love of reading and would lend books to people who expressed an interest." Emily looked at the man who was taking her father's place for six months and smiled at his obvious fascination with the library. "You're welcome to borrow anything that catches your fancy. As you may have discovered, my father owned more books than you'll find in the town's library."

"You may regret that offer," he warned

her. "The last three towns where I served had nothing to compare to this."

"Father would have been happy to know someone appreciated the books, but we'd better continue with our tour." She led David into the dining room. "I'm sure you need no explanation of this room. The others are ordinary — the kitchen, pantry, laundry."

She'd expected him to dismiss the working rooms, but he surprised her by saying, "May I see them? I'd like to see where you create those delicious meals Craig has told me about."

"Did I hear my name being taken in vain?"

David shook his head as Craig and Noah entered the dining room. "Hardly." When he crouched so that he was Noah's height and extended his hand for a shake, David rose in Emily's estimation. Mama had claimed you could tell a lot about a man from the way he treated children, and the minister's greeting left no doubt that he valued them.

"You must be the young man who lives here."

Noah grinned and pumped the minister's hand. "Me man."

Before the boy could say anything more, Mrs. Carmichael and Beulah arrived. As was often the case around relative strangers, Beulah remained a few steps behind the older woman, unsure of her welcome.

Though etiquette dictated that he address Mrs. Carmichael first, David moved toward Beulah and extended his hand. "Hello again, Miss Beulah." His broad smile coaxed her forward, though she hesitated for a second before she shook his hand and uttered a soft hello.

When Beulah tugged her hand loose, David turned his attention to the widow.

With the introductions complete, other than Alice and Jane, who were unexpectedly late, Emily once again addressed David. "If you still want to see the kitchen, it's through here."

"I do." He followed her with Noah close on his heels, despite Craig's attempts to keep him in the dining room.

"As you can see, it's an ordinary kitchen with an ordinary stove and ordinary cupboards."

"But something extraordinarily delicious is simmering." David gave an appreciative sniff, then took a step back when the door opened, revealing a harried-looking Alice with Jane in her arms.

"I'm sorry I'm late." Alice's face was red, perhaps because she'd been hurrying, and she averted her eyes from the minister, instead focusing on Emily. "Jane was fussier than normal."

When the baby whimpered, Noah laid a hand on her foot. "Be good, Jane." Jane giggled in response.

David flashed a wry smile at Craig. "Your son's already charming the ladies. I wonder who taught him that."

As Craig shrugged, apparently uncomfortable with his friend's comment, Emily turned toward Mrs. Carmichael. "Supper will be ready in five minutes. Would you show everyone to their seats?"

To Emily's relief, the meal went well, though Alice was uncharacteristically quiet. Noah was on his best behavior, perhaps because of the presence of a stranger, and Beulah spoke more often than usual, encouraged by David's questions. As she watched the kindness he bestowed on the girl so many shunned, the last of Emily's concerns about the new minister disappeared.

"This was the best meal I've had since I arrived in Sweetwater Crossing. Craig was right when he sang your praises," David said as he forked the final bite of pecan pie. "Thank you, Emily. You're a gifted cook. I wish I could persuade you to go back to

Louisiana with me and teach my sisters. I hate to say it, but their talents do not extend to the kitchen."

Surely it was only her imagination that Craig appeared annoyed. David was merely being polite. When no one else spoke, Emily asked the first question that popped into her brain. "How many sisters do you have?"

"Two, both younger." David let his gaze move around the table. "How about you?"

Craig was the first to respond. "No sisters or brothers."

"Me neither," Alice said.

"I had one brother, but he's gone," was the widow's contribution.

"And you, Emily?"

"Like you, two sisters, both younger."

"I haven't met them, so that must mean they don't live here," David said as he poured milk into his coffee.

"They're both traveling. Louisa's visiting a friend's family in Cimarron Creek, and Joanna is studying music in Europe."

David's eyes darkened with understanding. "And you miss them. I know I miss my family, even though there were times when Ruth and Rebecca drove me crazy."

"I do miss them." As she pronounced the words, Emily realized how much she longed for her sisters' company. It had been close to a year and a half since they'd all been together, since they'd shared laughter and love as well as the occasional disagreements and disparaging remarks. Though she couldn't bring either of them back before they were ready, she resolved to try to bridge the distance between them by writing letters to both of them tonight, even though it wasn't her usual day to do that.

"Family is important," she said.

While the others nodded their agreement, Craig did not. Instead, he looked at her with an expression that, if she didn't know it was ridiculous to even think it, she would have called annoyance.

CHAPTER TWENTY-SIX

"How does it feel to have two admirers?"

Emily blinked in surprise as Mrs. Carmichael's words registered. Craig and Beulah had left for school, and Noah was playing quietly on the floor while she and the widow drank their second cups of coffee.

"Two admirers? What do you mean?"

Mrs. Carmichael's raised eyebrow said she questioned Emily's surprise. "Surely you know that Craig is interested in you and not simply as his landlady."

There was little point in denying it, and Emily realized she would appreciate some motherly advice, or what David had called a different perspective. "He did say he saw me as part of his future."

The widow's smile turned triumphant. "I thought so! He's a fine man, and he'd make a fine husband, but now you have a choice. David couldn't keep his eyes off you last night. He'd glance at Alice occasionally, but each time he'd turn back to you."

"That's because I was his hostess. He was merely being polite."

"I'm not so sure. The man looked interested."

"You must be mistaken, and even if you aren't, I have no interest in him."

An hour later, Emily was dusting the parlor when she heard furious knocking on the front door.

"Alice." Her friend's face was flushed, and a scowl marred its normal prettiness. Most alarming of all, Jane was not with her. Alice had been adamant about not leaving her daughter alone after the night Mitch and Harlan broke the window, yet she'd broken what she called her cardinal rule.

"What's wrong? Shouldn't you be at the library?"

Alice stepped into the house, her posture rigid. "I closed it for an hour. The patrons can wait, but this can't. I thought you were my friend."

"I am." Surely she knew that.

"Then why were you flirting with David last night?" Alice's voice broke, and tears filled her eyes. "You know how I feel about him."

What Emily knew was that Alice had found him attractive, but that was before she'd even spoken to him. Her friend had said nothing more since that day, making Emily believe it was simply a passing attraction to an undeniably handsome man. Alice's silence last night had confirmed that belief, leaving Emily bewildered by her current mood.

"I wasn't flirting," she insisted. "I was simply being a good hostess. And I assure you that I have no romantic interest in David."

Doubt clouded Alice's eyes. "Are you sure?"

"Yes." Only one man stirred Emily's emotions. "But it's clear that you do. Tell me why you feel so strongly about our new minister." Emily led the way into the parlor and gestured toward the two comfortable chairs that flanked the fireplace. "What happened? I know you think he's handsome, but there must be more than that to have you so concerned when another woman talks to him."

This time Alice nodded. "Oh, Emily, I've never felt like this, not even with Cyrus. That first day when my eyes met David's, sparks flew between us, and in that moment, I knew he was special. More than that, I knew he was the man I was meant to marry." She paused to take a breath, then asked, "Did you feel that way about George?"

"No." As painful as the memories were, Emily forced herself to think about the first time she'd seen George. There had been no sparks, but there had been something. "I was attracted to him." Perhaps more than that, she'd been flattered that he chose her over her sisters. "At the time, I believed what I felt was love, but now I realize it was only infatuation." She hoped that what Alice felt for David was stronger and deeper than mere physical attraction. "Do you think David feels the way you do?"

Alice leaned forward, clasping her hands as she said, "I thought so. When we talked after church both Sundays, his eyes sparkled and he made me feel special, but after last night, I'm not sure. It was you he talked to."

Emily refused to tell Alice that Mrs. Carmichael thought the minister was attracted to her. That would only hurt her friend. Besides, the widow must have been mistaken. "You were quieter than usual. Maybe that worried him. Also, some people find it difficult to talk to the person seated next to them." Although he'd had no trouble conversing with Beulah, who'd been seated on his other side. "I think it was most likely a case of him being polite. There's one way to find out."

"Ask him?" Horror crossed Alice's face. "You can't mean that."

"Don't worry. I wouldn't do that, but I can invite him to supper again. Next time you need to talk more. That's the only way you'll know whether the attraction you feel is real." And the only way Alice could avoid possibly making a huge mistake.

If she and George had spent more time talking, Emily might have realized that his interest in her was based on her appearance rather than who she was, and she would have been spared months of pain.

"It's real. I know it is." Alice rose and wrapped her arms around Emily. "Thank you. You're a good friend."

"Do you think the ladies would join us for supper at the restaurant?"

Craig almost smiled at his friend's question. Normally there would have been a greeting when he left the church and joined him, but today David simply blurted out what was obviously on his mind.

"Ladies?" Craig pretended not to understand.

408

"Alice and Emily."

Was there a reason that David mentioned Alice first? Perhaps it meant nothing, but the possibility raised Craig's spirits.

"Emily invited me to supper again," David continued as they headed north on Center Street. "I thought she might enjoy an evening without cooking and Alice might enjoy some time without her daughter. I heard Mrs. Carmichael say she'd be happy to care for Jane occasionally."

Both were valid reasons. The question was, which one was most important to David? This time he'd spoken of Emily first. "The food won't be as tasty and tongues will wag, but it's a good idea. You've seen that meals at Finley House can be hectic." Even though Noah had been well behaved, he'd spilled a glass of milk, and Jane had demanded attention during dessert.

Craig's friend kept pace with him. "I'm glad you like the idea. I thought by having you and Emily there, tongues wouldn't wag as much. Or if they did, people wouldn't know whether to speculate about you two or Alice and me."

Alice. David wanted to deflect attention from himself and Alice. Relief washed over Craig, surprising him with its intensity. "Then Alice is the woman who caught your eye." His worries, his irritation, and yes, his jealousy had been unfounded.

"Of course. I don't know whether I have a chance with her, but I need to discover whether those sparks were real." David paused and looked at Craig, his expression speculative. "Surely you didn't think I meant Emily." When Craig said nothing, not wanting to admit how mistaken he'd been, David nodded. "I see. You're unsure about her feelings for you. Don't worry, Craig. She looks at you the way my ma looks at Pa — with love in her eyes."

Craig could only hope that was true.

CHAPTER TWENTY-SEVEN

"I'm so excited." Alice clasped her hands together, perhaps to keep from clapping them. She'd already ignored Emily's offer of a chair, preferring to pace from one side of the parlor to the other while they waited for David and Craig.

"I think I was right," Alice continued. "I think David felt the same spark I did. Did you notice that when he and Craig invited us to supper, he was looking at me?"

Emily nodded. "I noticed that." She'd also noticed that Alice was wearing the new dress she'd been saving for Christmas. Looking at the dark green poplin that highlighted Alice's eyes made Emily smile because it solved a problem. Now she knew what she could give her friend for Christmas. She wanted everyone who'd be sharing Christmas dinner with her to have a special gift, something she had made for them rather than something she'd purchased at the mercantile. Mrs. Carmichael, Craig, Noah, even baby Jane had been easy, but until she'd seen the dress, Emily had had no idea what she could give Alice.

"I wouldn't say I saw sparks," she told her friend, "but I did see the way David grinned when you accepted his invitation. I'm surprised his face didn't hurt from that grin. Mama would have said it was about to split his face."

Craig had appeared pleased by the plans for supper at the restaurant too, but his response had been more subdued, something Alice, who'd had eyes only for the minister, hadn't noticed. But Emily had, and the two of them had shared a look that was almost conspiratorial.

"They should both be here soon," she told Alice. Craig was reading a story to Noah, since it was Saturday and Beulah wasn't here to do that, and Mrs. Carmichael had taken Jane to the kitchen, where she was heating the soup Emily had prepared for their supper.

"She doesn't need to see you leave," the widow had told Alice. "Noah and I will keep her occupied."

The knock on the front door stopped Alice's pacing, and she settled into one of the chairs, pretending she hadn't been counting the minutes — perhaps the seconds — until David arrived.

"Come in, David." Emily greeted her guest. "We're waiting for Craig to finish reading to Noah."

She could have been speaking Greek for all the attention the minister paid to her. He managed a polite smile, but his eyes lit at the sight of Alice. There was no mistaking either his attraction to her or the strength of her response. Alice had not exaggerated in describing their reaction to each other as sparks.

"You look beautiful."

The compliment turned Alice's cheeks a rosy hue and broadened her already wide smile. "Thank you." She smoothed an imaginary wrinkle from her skirt, then looked up again. "I wanted to wear something special tonight."

As David shook his head, Emily noticed that he'd had his hair cut since she'd last seen him. Alice wasn't the only one taking extra pains over her appearance. "It's not the dress," he said. "You'd be beautiful in rags."

The man was smitten. Emily turned at the sound of muffled laughter and shared another smile with Craig. "Are you ready?"

He nodded. "I thought Noah might protest, but he's thrilled that Mrs. Carmichael promised he could help feed Jane."

"He might not be so excited if she spits up when she burps," Alice cautioned as she reached for her cloak and moved closer to David.

The minister bent his arm, inviting Alice to place her hand on it, then led the way out the front door, leaving Emily and Craig to follow.

"They look happy together," Craig said as they strolled down Creek a few feet behind the other couple.

"I've known Alice my whole life, and I've never seen her like this. She's almost giddy."

Craig placed his hand on top of the one Emily had laid on his crooked arm. "David would probably hate being described that way, but he seems giddy too. The question is, how do you feel about them as a couple? I suspect you have mixed feelings, knowing that if they marry, your friend will leave."

"I'll miss her," Emily admitted, "but I can hardly complain, can I, when I left her to marry George?"

"You returned." Craig squeezed Emily's hand. "And for that, I'm thankful."

She was thankful for the gesture, which did not feel as if it were meant to comfort her, and the way his words sent tendrils of warmth down her spine, once more igniting dreams of the future she wanted. For this one evening, she would pretend those dreams might come true.

When they reached the restaurant, fragrant aromas, a crowded room, and Mrs. Tabor greeted them. "I've saved my best table for you," the woman who now ran Ma's Kitchen said as she led them to a table near the potbellied stove. Like her mother before her, Mrs. Tabor was heavyset with brown eyes and a snub nose, though her hair had not turned gray prematurely as her mother's had. Tonight she wore a dark gray dress, a white apron, and a welcoming smile. "I thought you might appreciate the warmth, being as it's cooler than normal today."

When they were seated, she continued. "Your choices are roast beef and fried chicken."

After they'd placed their orders, with Emily and Alice choosing the chicken, the men the beef, David engaged Alice in a discussion of books, challenging her opinion that *A Tale of Two Cities* was Dickens's best work and insisting that *Bleak House* was superior.

Emily, who'd watched the exchange with amusement, turned to Craig. "I suppose you prefer *David Copperfield.*"

He shook his head. "The only Dickens book I liked was *A Christmas Carol.*"

An interesting choice. "Because of the message?"

"Because it was short."

Emily was still chuckling over his response when their meals arrived.

Alice took a bite of the chicken, chewing carefully as she evaluated it. "It's better than it used to be, but not as good as when Ma was here."

"Mrs. Tabor isn't Ma?" David seemed surprised.

"No, that was her mother, Lillian Webster. She died last summer." Alice turned her attention to Emily. "It was a week or two before your father's death. Very sudden. No one expected it, even though Ma was getting up in years. She used to tell everyone that working here kept her feeling young and healthy." Alice cut another piece of chicken. "I think hers was the last funeral your father performed."

There was nothing Emily could say to that, and so she concentrated on enjoying her meal while Craig and David debated the merits of insisting students read books by both Jane Austen and Charles Dickens.

"Good evening, Doc." Mrs. Tabor's voice drew Emily's attention to the man who'd just entered the restaurant. "Your usual table is waiting." She led the town's physician to a table with a single place setting in the far corner of the room. Once he was seated, she walked to Emily's table. "Is everything all right?"

Emily nodded. "The food is delicious." And it was.

Mrs. Tabor raised an eyebrow, disputing Emily's assertion. "That's a high compliment coming from you. I know my cooking isn't as good as Ma's or yours, but it fills people's stomachs. I don't know what that poor man would do if I closed my doors." She inclined her head toward the doctor. "He's been eating here every day since his wife left. He even takes extra food home with him each Saturday so he has something for Sunday supper. I guess he'll have to order twice as much next week, being as I won't be open on Christmas."

A wave of regret washed over Emily. "I should have realized that he was lonely." She'd heard rumors that Doc's visits to the saloon were no longer limited to Friday nights but hadn't paid much attention to them.

"Hungry too," the restaurateur added.

When Mrs. Tabor left, Emily looked at her companions. "If you'll excuse me for a

417

minute, there's something I need to do." She walked to the doctor's table, taking the unoccupied chair so he wouldn't feel the need to remain standing after greeting her. "I hope you'll accept my apologies for not being a good neighbor. My father would be ashamed if he knew I'd neglected one of his closest friends."

Doc Sheridan stared at Emily, his expression inscrutable.

"I can't undo the past months, but I will do better in the future. I hope you'll come to Finley House for Christmas dinner."

Surprise and something else, something that might have been uneasiness, flitted across the doctor's face before he nodded. "Thank you. I'll look forward to that."

"Crim." Noah hopped from one foot to the other, making Craig's efforts to dress him twice as difficult as usual. He couldn't blame the boy, though. What young child wasn't excited on Christmas morning?

"Yes, son. It's Christmas." And this year's celebration would be unlike any in the past. It was his and Noah's first Christmas in Sweetwater Crossing; the first time the minister who read the nativity story from Luke was a friend, not simply a man of the cloth; the first time Craig had been trying to court a woman.

He took a quick breath as he attempted to tie the red ascot around Noah's neck, urging his son to stand still. In another hour, he'd discover whether he'd chosen the right gift for Emily. He'd known it couldn't be too personal, since they weren't engaged or married, but he wanted something more than books or candy, and so he'd spent close to an hour in the mercantile, trying to find the perfect item for the woman who occupied so many of his thoughts.

"There you go." Craig lifted Noah so he could see his reflection in the mirror over the bureau.

"Open prent." Noah was still finding s's impossible to pronounce, forcing Craig to interpret his speech.

"We'll open presents after breakfast." Emily — wonderful, thoughtful, generous Emily — had expanded her invitations, saying that Alice, Jane, David and the doctor should spend the entire day here. She planned to serve breakfast before everyone went to the parlor with its festively decorated tree to open their gifts. Craig's primary responsibility was keeping Noah occupied until breakfast was ready.

When he heard Mrs. Carmichael's door closing, he took his son's hand. "All right,

Noah. We can go now." Noah shook off his hand and scampered toward the staircase. "Careful. You don't want to fall." Craig doubted he'd ever overcome the fear of people falling to their death, but he forced the disturbing thoughts away. Today was a day to celebrate birth.

The widow waited at the bottom of the stairs. "Look at you two."

Noah patted his carefully tied ascot and pointed toward Craig. "Match."

Though Craig rarely wore ascots, when he'd seen red ones in a variety of sizes at the mercantile, he'd bought one for himself and another for Noah.

"So I see." The widow smiled her approval. "Very dapper."

"Dap?" Noah was obviously puzzled by the word.

"It means handsome," Craig explained.

"And both of you are," Emily said as she entered the hallway. "Merry Christmas." She hugged Mrs. Carmichael and murmured a compliment on the widow's attire.

It was Emily who deserved the compliments. Her dress of a deep red, almost wine-colored fabric made her blond hair seem even lighter and drew attention to the faint color in her cheeks. Without a doubt, she was one of the prettiest women Craig had ever seen.

Perhaps his son agreed, because he raised his arms. "Hug me." When she complied, giving Noah a little tickle that made him giggle, he patted Emily's arm. "Hug Pa too."

The widow chuckled as Craig and Emily stared at each other for a second, unsure how to proceed. Then, when Noah tugged on her hand, Emily took a step closer to Craig and slid her arms around him. It should have felt awkward, especially with an audience, but it didn't. Instead, it felt so natural that Craig wrapped his arms around Emily and drew her even closer, savoring the sensation of her body next to his, enjoying the fragrance of her perfume and the silky smoothness of her dress beneath his fingertips. It was only when the widow's chuckle turned into a full-fledged laugh that Craig broke away, putting distance between him and the woman whose nearness felt so right.

"Merry Christmas, Emily," he said softly.

They were spared further awkwardness by the knock on the front door, and a moment later David entered, accompanied by Alice and Jane. It wasn't coincidence, Craig was certain, that they came together. Unless he was mistaken, David had stood at the front window of the Albright house, waiting for

Alice to approach.

"Let's go into the dining room," Emily said when she'd taken their coats. "Doc should be here soon."

Within ten minutes, they were all enjoying what Emily called a simple breakfast of scrambled eggs, bacon, and cinnamon rolls. It might be simple, but it was one of the best meals Craig could recall. Perhaps it was because today was a special day; perhaps the memory of the moment he'd held Emily in his arms had colored everything. Craig didn't know, and he didn't care. What was important was that he was spending Christmas with the woman who'd captured his heart.

When they'd all cleaned their plates, Emily rose. "Dishes can wait. Presents can't."

Noah giggled and started to push his chair back, his eagerness to open gifts overcoming the manners Craig had tried to instill. "Prent for me."

"That depends." Craig wiped the bacon grease from his son's hands. "Were you a good boy?"

Noah nodded, then shook his head. "Good *man.*"

Biting back her smile, Emily led the way into the parlor, where a small pile of gifts sat beneath the tree. "We'll start with Noah."

Though Craig had placed several items for Noah next to the tree, Emily handed a different box to his son. Within seconds, Noah had ripped the wrapping from it.

"Hor, Pa. Hor!" He shrieked in delight at the sight of a stuffed horse that must have been Emily's answer to Noah's demand for a pony of his own, one that could share his bed.

"I see. Remember what a young man does next?"

Noah nodded as he clutched the toy to his chest. "Thank you, Em."

"I hoped you'd like it."

Mrs. Carmichael studied the stuffed animal. "That's fine workmanship, Emily."

Craig stared at her. "You made it? Is there anything you can't do?"

As Emily's glance slid to Noah and Jane, sorrow filled her eyes, making Craig regret he'd asked the question. How thoughtless of him!

"This is for you." She handed him a flat oblong package. When he opened it to reveal a heavy denim bag embroidered with his initials, she said, "I thought you could use it to carry books. Your satchel always seems to be overflowing."

423

"You're right. It is, and this is perfect." He could only hope she'd enjoy the gift he had for her half as much as he did this one. His wasn't handmade or particularly expensive, but when he'd seen it, he'd pictured her using it.

The other gifts Emily had chosen revealed the same thoughtfulness she'd put into his satchel: handkerchiefs with a handmade lace edging for Mrs. Carmichael, an embroidered bib for Jane, a fancy collar and cuffs that Alice insisted on wearing immediately, a copy of *Bleak House* for David. Other than the gift for the minister, each one had involved hours of work, making Craig wonder where she'd managed to find the time. Did the woman ever sleep?

"I wasn't sure what you needed," she said as she handed the doctor a small package, "but I hoped you'd like this."

Doc's expression when he saw the meerschaum pipe was almost reverent. "I can picture your father holding this," he told Emily. "Joseph rarely smoked it, but he had it with him every time the four of us met all those years ago." He lowered his head for an instant, then met Emily's gaze. "Thank you, my dear. This is a welcome reminder of happier times. Now, open your gifts."

She smiled at the length of calico from

Mrs. Carmichael, the bottle of perfume Alice had chosen, and the box of candy from the doctor, her responses making each of them believe the gift was exactly what she'd most wanted. How would she respond to Craig's?

"This is from Noah and me." Craig handed her the box that Adam Bentley's wife had wrapped for him. Slowly, she removed the wrapping paper, then pulled the first item from the box.

"Oh, Craig! How did you know?"

"You turned what could have been a sad occasion into a happy one," Craig said as he dried another plate.

The day was almost over. Noah was already asleep; the guests had left, and Mrs. Carmichael had retired to her room, leaving Craig and Emily alone for the first time all day. Even though they were doing nothing more than washing dishes, Emily was savoring the moment.

"Wonderful food, perfect gifts, good company," Craig continued. "This was a Christmas none of us will forget."

Least of all Emily. Even though she told herself that receiving gifts was not the most important part of Christmas Day, her heart overflowed with happiness whenever she thought of what Craig had given her. She was certain she'd never told him how much she wanted a piece of fine china, but somehow he'd known.

"I wanted it to be a festive day."

"You succeeded, but I still think you should have accepted Alice and Mrs. Carmichael's offer to do the dishes."

"And let them be the first to wash such a beautiful gift? Never! Besides, I was hoping you'd help me christen it." And then she'd do more than thank him again; she'd tell him how much it meant to her.

Craig raised a questioning eyebrow. "You want to christen a tea set?"

"What else would you call its first use? If you don't want tea, I can make coffee or hot chocolate."

"And have you tell me it was sacrilege? No, ma'am, I can't do that. Let's have tea."

When the last of the dishes had been washed and dried and the tea was steeping, Emily placed two of her new cups and saucers on the table. "I haven't seen this pattern before," she said, admiring the tiny flowers that rimmed the saucer and decorated the sides of the cups and the teapot.

"Mrs. Bentley told me it was the first time she'd ordered it. She wanted bluebonnets, but this was the closest she could find."

"Forget-me-nots. When I first saw them in one of Father's books, I thought they were beautiful. This is the perfect pattern and the perfect present." Even without the tiny blue flowers as a reminder, Emily knew she would never forget this Christmas or the man who'd given her such a special gift.

"I don't know how you guessed, but I've always wanted a china teacup. I was sure tea tasted better in china, but my parents weren't ones to splurge on things like that. Mama insisted the flavor was the same whether the cup was made of crockery or china or tin."

Emily poured the fragrant liquid into both of their cups and took a sip. "Mama was wrong. And now I have more than a single cup. I have a whole tea set. Thank you, Craig. You couldn't have chosen anything I would have liked more."

"Rachel would have agreed with you. Her parents gave us china as a wedding gift." Craig wrinkled his nose. "I would have preferred a new ladder."

Though Emily laughed at his response, her mirth faded. "Special days like today must be difficult without your wife." She had no such thoughts about not spending the day with George — last Christmas had been a painful one because she'd discovered she wasn't carrying his child the night before — but memories of a lifetime of Christmases with her parents and sisters had ambushed her at unexpected times today, making her wish for one more day with all of them together. Surely Craig had experienced the same longing.

Instead of the pain she'd expected, his face radiated peace. "This Christmas has been much easier than last year," he said, "and that's thanks to you. You've given me hope for the future."

He placed his cup back on the saucer, then rose to stand next to her. "I bungled this the last time by using the wrong words, but I'm determined not to do that tonight. I said that I admire and esteem you. I do, but those feelings pale compared to my other feelings."

Craig paused for a second, and this time she saw, if not pain, at least regret in his expression. "I loved Rachel with my whole heart. I never thought I'd feel that way again, and I don't."

Emily bit back a gasp. Why was he telling her this? Why was he spoiling what had been a surprisingly happy day? Though she wanted nothing more than to flee, she couldn't, not with Craig standing so close to her, blocking her way. She closed her eyes, not wanting to hear his next words.

"My love for you is different from my love for Rachel, but that doesn't mean it isn't as deep or as true. It is."

Emily's eyes flew open, and she looked up at him, wanting to believe what she'd heard but knowing that, no matter what he said, they had no future together.

"It took me a while to understand what had happened," Craig said, "but I finally realized that my heart has expanded to encompass my love for you." He reached forward, capturing Emily's hands between his. "I love you with every fiber of my being. I want to share your life and have you share mine. Will you marry me?"

Oh, how she wanted to say yes! The hope that had burgeoned deep inside her was making its way through her body, urging her to tell Craig how much she loved him, that there was nothing she wanted more than to be his wife. But she couldn't.

"I want to," she said, choosing her words carefully, "and I know you think you want to marry me. I don't doubt your sincerity, Craig, but marrying me would be a mistake that you'd regret. Noah wants a brother or sister, and you want him to have at least one. I can't give you that."

When Craig started to protest, Emily held

up a cautioning hand. "You may not think it matters today when we're caught up in the wonder of celebrating Jesus's birth, but one day it will matter."

He shook his head and squeezed her hands. "That won't happen."

Though his voice rang with certainty, she shook her head. "You can't be sure."

"I *can* be sure, and I am. If we want more children, we can adopt them."

The one time she had told George that, he'd answered with his fists. "It wouldn't be the same," Emily told Craig, repeating George's words.

"Do you mean to tell me you don't love Noah even though you didn't carry him beneath your heart?"

The sharpness of Craig's question took Emily by surprise. "No, of course not."

"Then why would you believe I'd be unable to love another man's child? You're not being fair, Emily."

His argument was meant to sway her, but though it was tempting to agree with him, Mrs. Locke's words about the heartbreak of a childless marriage still echoed through her brain. Emily couldn't take the risk that she and Craig would both be miserable when the reality of her barrenness destroyed his hopes for the future.

"I'm trying to protect you," she said. "I want you to be happy. Not just today, but five, ten, fifteen years from now."

Furrows formed between Craig's eyes, and for a second she wondered if they were caused by anger. When he spoke, his voice was calm. "I will be happy if you marry me." He paused long enough to raise her hands to his lips and press a kiss on her fingers. "I can see you're not ready to accept my proposal. I wish you were, but I respect your need for more time."

When she started to tell him that time wouldn't make any difference, he shook his head. "I'm not willing to accept your refusal. Think about it, Emily. Pray about it. I won't rush you, but I will ask you again and again and again."

"The answer will always be the same."

Craig managed a small smile. "I'm determined to win you, and I won't accept defeat. You shouldn't doubt my patience and my powers of persuasion."

"Powers of persuasion? What do you mean by that?"

"This."

He pulled her to her feet and wrapped his arms around her. For a second, all he did was stare into her eyes, his expression so filled with love that Emily wanted to weep

431

from sheer joy. Then, as slowly as if they had all the time in the world, he lowered his lips to hers.

CHAPTER TWENTY-EIGHT

Emily smiled as she tied the ribbon on Alice's birthday gift. The last time she'd wrapped presents was for Christmas, a day that had been marked by many firsts: her first Christmas since her parents' deaths; the first one she'd shared with Craig; the first time Doc had come to Finley House as her guest, not her father's. But most of all, she remembered December 25, 1882, as the day Craig Ferguson had kissed her for the first time.

And what a kiss it was. His lips were firm but tender, tantalizing her with gentle touches that promised greater delights if only she'd say yes. His hands moved slowly, tracing patterns on her back and sending sparks of longing through her. There was no need for words, for each touch, each kiss showed her the depth and breadth of Craig's love. He would cherish her. He'd protect her. He'd do everything in his power to ensure her happiness. All he asked in return was that Emily marry him, that she agree to be his wife and Noah's mother.

For the briefest of moments, she was so caught up in the wonder of being in Craig's arms that she almost said yes, but then reality intruded.

"It's too soon," she said as she broke the embrace.

When a sweet smile of satisfaction lit Craig's face, Emily realized what she'd done: she'd opened the door, even if only a crack, admitting she hadn't completely dismissed the possibility of marrying him.

In the six weeks since then, Craig had kept his word and persisted in trying to persuade her. The man was persistent — no doubt about that — and Emily could feel her resolve weakening, but so far she had managed to resist by focusing her attention on Alice. She wanted her friend to be happy and would do everything she could for her.

If all went as planned, Alice would be both surprised and pleased by the small party Emily had arranged to celebrate her birthday. Emily had asked Gertrude to join them and charged her with convincing Alice to close the library at lunchtime and bringing her to Finley House.

Emily had invited Mrs. Carmichael to join

them, but the widow had declined, saying she'd prefer to care for Noah and Jane. "It should be just you girls," she'd declared. When Emily later recounted the story, Gertrude laughed, but she obviously was delighted that someone still considered her a girl.

Emily hoped Alice would be equally delighted by the cream-colored nightgown with its intricately smocked bodice she'd made for her. Unless she was mistaken, it would become part of Alice's trousseau. Everyone in Sweetwater Crossing knew David was courting her, and while there had been speculation over Emily and Craig's accompanying David and Alice on nightly walks and occasional suppers at Ma's Kitchen, Emily informed anyone who asked that they were there for propriety's sake.

Most appeared to believe her and turned their attention to the more interesting question of whether David would return to Louisiana at the end of his six-month commitment or whether Alice would convince him to make this his home. The townspeople were hopeful that Alice's persuasive powers in addition to the prospect of a new parsonage would keep the minister in Sweetwater Crossing, but Emily knew how unlikely that was.

Though the new parsonage, constructed of limestone so that fire was less of a threat and considerably larger than the one that had been Mrs. Carmichael's home for so long, would attract many, David was adamant in his insistence that Sweetwater Crossing was only a temporary assignment. Knowing her friend would probably be leaving made Emily even more determined to make Alice's final months in Texas happy.

"We're here!" Gertrude called as she pushed the front door open. "I don't think she believed my excuse, but I got her to come."

Emily hurried into the hallway to greet her guests. While Gertrude wore one of her Sunday frocks, Alice's dress was a simple gray calico that she'd told Emily was easy to launder if Jane spilled something on it.

"Happy birthday, Alice." Emily led them to the dining room, where a carefully frosted cake sat on the sideboard.

Alice's eyes widened, and her grin was infectious. "You remembered!"

"Of course I did. It's February 6, isn't it?" Even though this was the first time she'd prepared a birthday meal for Alice, Emily had celebrated with her friend each year except the last one. "How could I forget that you were born exactly six months before me? You're an old lady."

"I'm simply older and wiser."

Emily laughed as Alice completed the banter they'd repeated each year for as long as either of them could recall. They were older now, but were they wiser? Emily hoped so.

She was still laughing when Mrs. Carmichael entered the room with Noah at her side. "This young man and I have been looking forward to some time with Jane," she said as she took the baby from Alice's arms. "We want you girls to have private time the way my friends and I used to." Mrs. Carmichael blinked rapidly, trying to hold back the tears that often came when she spoke of her three closest friends. "Come along, Noah," she said. "Jane wants her food."

"Me too!"

"This is wonderful." Alice gestured from the cake to the table set for three. "You've thought of everything."

Emily shrugged. "I tried. Now, please be seated, and I'll bring in the food."

Though she smiled when she saw the baked ham, scalloped potatoes, and green beans, Alice's smile faded a second later. "You remembered all my favorite foods. Oh,

Emily, how can I leave? Louisiana's so far away."

Emily's question about whether she and Alice were wiser as well as older was answered in part by Alice's hesitation. Unlike Emily, who'd been so infatuated with George that she'd scarcely considered what moving away from her family would mean, Alice was wise enough to recognize potential problems.

Before Emily could reply, Gertrude did. "It sounds like our minister asked you a very important question."

"He did. Last night."

"And how did you answer him?" Gertrude had never been one for subtlety.

"I said I'd tell him tonight. I think I know what I'm going to say, but I wanted Emily's advice before I made up my mind." Apparently oblivious to Gertrude's annoyance that she was not being consulted, Alice fixed her gaze on Emily, her green eyes radiating confusion. "What do you think I should do?"

Emily was the last person who should be giving advice about matters of the heart. She'd made a huge mistake in marrying George, and now, even though she had a wonderful man wanting to marry her, she was unable to leave the shadows of her past failures behind.

Because she'd married George, she had missed her parents' last days on Earth, and the once close relationship she'd had with her sisters appeared to be permanently fractured. For, though she continued to write to both of them weekly, Emily had received no further letters from either of them, not even an acknowledgment of the Christmas gifts she'd sent.

Knowing Alice was waiting for an answer but unable to give her one, Emily responded with a question. "Do you love him?"

It was the right question, for Alice's face lit with happiness, leaving no doubt what she should do. "Yes. More than I thought was possible."

"Then there's only one possible answer."

"But it means leaving you and everything familiar. Sweetwater Crossing is the only home I've ever known."

Though Gertrude had remained silent during the brief exchange, she placed her fork and knife back on her plate and looked at Alice. "If the man I loved had asked me to go to China with him, I'd have done it. If you need more advice, look at Emily. She left her family and friends when she fell in love with George. I'm sure she didn't regret it."

But she did. Emily had lost so much as a result of one bad decision — her innocence, her family, her dreams of a happy future. She wouldn't tell either Alice or Gertrude that. Instead, she said, "My situation was very different from yours, Alice. I hardly knew George before we married and didn't realize we had different expectations, but you and David have spent more time together. You won't be marrying a stranger. There won't be as much of an adjustment."

Alice nodded as if she understood, and perhaps she did. Perhaps she remembered that when she'd recounted amusing stories from her marriage, Emily had not shared any from hers. Perhaps she realized that Emily grieved more for what her marriage could have been than for what she'd lost. But perhaps she was simply responding to Emily's statement that she would not be marrying a stranger.

"I want to say yes. My heart tells me to say yes." And so did the sparkle in her eyes.

"Then do it." Gertrude's words were emphatic. "If there's one thing I've learned, it's that life is short and we shouldn't waste a single day."

"You're right. I will marry David, but I still hate the thought of leaving you." Alice forked three green beans. "We'll have to make the most of the next four months. And who knows? Emily and I may both be married again before June."

Gertrude narrowed her eyes and studied Emily. "So the rumors I've heard are true, and you and the schoolmaster are courting."

Emily shook her head, wondering whether she should try to change the subject but realizing that Gertrude would not permit that. These were her friends. She might as well be honest with them. "We aren't courting. Craig asked me to marry him, but I refused."

Alice's reaction was immediate. "Are you crazy?" Ignoring the good manners her mother had instilled in her, she waved her fork at Emily. "The man loves you, and unless I'm sorely mistaken — which I don't believe I am — you love him too."

"I do." There was no reason to deny it.

"Then why did you refuse him?" Gertrude's tone was the one Emily remembered from her school days, the one that made pupils quake.

"I'm afraid his love will die."

"Nonsense. True love doesn't die. Why would you even think that?"

Though Emily knew Alice had the same question, she faced Gertrude as she replied,

"Because I can't give him children."

Gertrude shook her head. "Just because you didn't have a child right away doesn't mean you can't ever have them. Sometimes it takes a while." She paused, and her lips curved into a secretive smile. "I wasn't going to tell anyone yet, but Thomas and I are expecting a baby in August."

"What wonderful news!" Alice clapped her hands. "You've made my birthday celebration even better. Now all I need is for Emily to agree to marry Craig."

But despite Gertrude's encouragement, Emily wasn't convinced. She and George had been married longer than Gertrude and Thomas, and they'd certainly tried to have a child, only to be disappointed again and again. Alice and Gertrude were fertile. Emily was not.

She fixed a smile on her face. "I'm happy for you." Gertrude had been a good teacher, and she'd be a good a mother.

Her former teacher grinned. "So you see, Emily, anything's possible."

CHAPTER TWENTY-NINE

"I hear congratulations are in order." Craig clapped his friend on the shoulder when the minister joined him for their afternoon walk to their respective homes.

"They are indeed." David was beaming, his whole demeanor more relaxed than Craig had ever seen it. "Alice accepted my proposal last night. I know it wasn't an easy decision for her, and that makes her acceptance all the sweeter."

As happy as he was for his friend, Craig couldn't help feeling a pang of regret that Emily hadn't been as easy to convince.

Pushing those thoughts aside, he smiled at the man whose dreams were coming true. "Have you set a date for the wedding?"

Though Craig hadn't thought it possible, David's smile broadened. "The last day of March. It's the first Saturday after Easter." He slowed his steps and fixed his gaze on Craig. "I'd be honored if you'd stand

443

by my side."

"The honor is all mine." And it was. In the short time he'd known David Grant, the man had become the brother Craig had always wanted.

"Perhaps you'll be asking me to return the favor before I leave."

If dreams came true, if prayers were answered. "Perhaps, but don't count on it. Emily's more stubborn than any woman I've ever met."

David nodded, then laid a comforting hand on Craig's shoulder. "Patience and persistence, my friend. Those are the keys."

One of the good things about dusting was that it gave her time to think. One of the bad things about dusting was that it gave her time to think. Today Emily wasn't certain which was dominant. All she knew was that she couldn't get Craig out of her mind. That had been happening more and more often in the three weeks since Alice and David announced their engagement. Craig had warned her that he was patient, and he was, but he was also persistent, doing everything he could to persuade her.

He was wooing her, but not with flowers, books, and candy, the traditional courtship gifts. Instead, Craig continued to give her far more valuable things. Gentle touches that warmed her blood and showed her he was nothing like George. Thoughtful gestures like picking up the mail on rainy days so she didn't have to venture out in inclement weather. Kisses so sweet they made her want to swoon. And — more powerful than anything else he could have done — deliberate efforts to make her an integral part of Noah's life.

Each night they tucked him into bed together, alternating reading his bedtime story. Each morning Craig lifted Noah so he could kiss Emily before breakfast. Each afternoon he encouraged Noah and Beulah to recount their day's adventures in the kitchen so that Emily could participate.

Craig was a clever man, a determined man, his every action designed to make Emily feel like part of his family, to show her they had no need of another child to be complete. He'd mounted a carefully plotted campaign meant to wear down her resistance, and it was working. Her doubts were diminishing, her fears were lessening, her love was growing.

And at the same time, she'd discovered a new sense of peace. She hadn't expected it, but it had crept up on her, happening so slowly that she hadn't been aware of it until the day she realized she no longer felt the need to prove that Father had not taken his life.

She had opened her father's Bible, not seeking anything in particular, but when she'd seen the verse about God's ways being different from man's carefully underlined, she had felt peace wash over her. God knew the truth about Father, and that was enough. It was time to put the past to rest and move into the future.

Tonight when Craig repeated his proposal as he had on the first and fifteenth of each month, Emily would give him the answer he sought. Today was the first of March. Agreeing to be Craig's wife was the perfect way to celebrate the beginning of a new month.

"I'm hot. Mr. Ferguson sent me home."

Emily turned to look at Beulah as she entered the kitchen an hour before school ended. The girl's face was flushed, her eyes were glassy, and she wobbled as she walked. Alarmed that the child who'd remained healthy even when Noah had caught a cold and given it to both his father and Mrs. Carmichael was so visibly ill, Emily moved to Beulah's side and laid a hand on her forehead.

"You are hot," she told her. "That means

you have a fever." It was probably nothing serious, but Emily would take no chances with the girl who'd become so dear to her. "I want you to lie down while I get some cold compresses." That's what Mama had done when one of them was feverish. "Now, off to bed with you."

It was a measure of Beulah's discomfort that she did not complain but simply headed toward the stairway while Emily retrieved some soft cloths and poured cool water into a basin.

She was about to leave the kitchen when Noah burst through the door. "Where Beulah?" he demanded.

"She's not feeling well." When Noah pouted over his pal's absence, Emily pointed to the plate of cookies she'd put on the table. "That means more cookies for you." With the boy mollified, Emily turned toward Mrs. Carmichael. "I'm not sure what it is, but Beulah has a fever. We'd better keep Noah away from her."

"Does she have spots?" the widow asked. "When I was in the mercantile the other day, I heard several women say their children have measles."

"I didn't see any on her face, and Craig hasn't said anything about his pupils being sick, but I'll check Beulah for a rash."

There was none, which was reassuring, but Emily's concerns grew when hours of applying cold compresses did nothing to reduce the fever.

"Should we fetch her parents?" she asked Mrs. Carmichael.

The widow was silent for a moment, then shook her head. "If she's not better by morning, I'll ride out there. Right now, you're doing everything you can."

Craig seconded her advice when he returned from school. "I sent her home early because I was afraid it was contagious, but children's fevers rarely last long. At least Noah's never did."

But when midnight arrived and Beulah showed no signs of improving, Emily feared they were both wrong.

"Any change?" Craig asked. Though Emily had insisted he needed sleep and that she would keep the vigil, he'd come to Beulah's room almost every hour, perhaps realizing Emily needed comfort almost as much as Beulah did healing.

Emily turned from the girl who'd refused all food, saying she hurt too much to eat, and who'd continued to moan in pain. If Louisa were here, she'd know what to do, but Emily had exhausted her limited knowledge of healing.

"I think you'd better fetch Doc Sheridan."

Though she'd spoken softly, not wanting Beulah to hear the worry in her voice, the girl sat up in bed, her face contorted with fear.

"No!" she shrieked. "No doctor. Bad man."

This was more than fear. This was panic. Was the fever causing Beulah to hallucinate?

"No! No! No!" Beulah continued to shriek, her terror increasing with each cry.

"It'll be all right." Emily sat on the side of the bed and wrapped her arms around Beulah, trying to comfort her. "You're sick." She stroked the girl's back, hoping to ease the sobs that were wracking her body. "I've done everything I can, but now we need the doctor to help you get better."

"No!" Beulah clutched her upper arm and shook her head violently. "He'll poke me and I'll fall dead."

So that was why Beulah was so distressed. Doc must have given her an injection, and all she remembered was the pain, not the healing it brought. Though she was surprised by the intensity of Beulah's reaction, Emily knew some people dreaded injections. She'd never liked them, but her father had said he'd grown accustomed to them, that the momentary sting was the price he paid for relief from pain.

"You won't die," Emily said firmly.

"I will. I will. He'll poke me and I'll fall dead just like your pappy. I saw him." Beulah shuddered and covered her face to block the memory. "Bad man."

Emily felt the blood drain from her face as Beulah's words registered. Was it possible? Surely it couldn't be. When Craig laid a hand on her shoulder, she turned and saw her thoughts reflected in his expression.

"What did you see, Beulah?" Craig asked.

Uncovering her face, Beulah looked up at Emily. "Your pappy was in the barn. The doctor poked him, and he fell dead."

The barn. Though she might have blamed the fever for Beulah's story and dismissed it as nothing more than a seriously ill patient's raving, the addition of that one detail made Emily believe Beulah was recounting something that had happened.

Her thoughts returned to the day she'd arrived in Sweetwater Crossing when she'd seen Beulah running. At the time, she'd thought the girl was late for something, but perhaps she had been running from a sight that had terrified her. If Beulah's story was true, Doc had killed Father, probably with an overdose of morphine, then made his death appear to be suicide.

As far as Emily knew, Beulah did not lie or even exaggerate stories. That meant Doc was the man who'd ended Emily's father's life and destroyed his reputation. But why? Why would Doc have killed one of his closest friends?

It made no sense.

CHAPTER THIRTY

"He won't admit it, even if he did it."

Emily looked up from the eggs she was cracking to nod at Craig. He must be as exhausted as she was, since neither of them had slept for more than a few minutes while they struggled to soothe Beulah and lower her fever, yet he'd insisted on staying with Emily while she prepared breakfast.

One of their prayers had been answered, and Beulah's fever had broken an hour ago. She was weak and continued to clutch her arm occasionally as if she feared an injection, but the fever and the headache it caused had subsided. Both Emily and Craig had agreed there was no question of Beulah's attending school today. Instead, Emily would keep her in bed until it was time for her mother to take her back to the ranch.

"I'm struggling with the idea that one of my father's closest friends and a man the whole town trusts could have killed him."

Emily nodded at the evidence that God's ways were indeed different from man's. How often had Father told her that God would always answer her prayers but not always in the way she hoped? *"Sometimes he says yes. Sometimes he says no. Sometimes he says not yet. The last one is the hardest to accept because it means we have to be patient."* And Emily was not a naturally patient person. But Father was right when he said she would receive an answer, even if it took a while.

Father had also said that God's timing was perfect and that there were no coincidences. Yesterday was proof of that. It was only after she had finally accepted that she might never know who'd killed her father and had been at peace with that that she'd been given the answer. For Beulah's revelation was a gift, a gift from God.

"I never considered Doc Sheridan," she told Craig, "but I believe Beulah. The story is too strange for her to have invented it."

Craig refilled his cup and took a swig of coffee. "I don't think Beulah invents stories. Her imagination isn't that strong."

"Which means Doc did it." Emily cracked the last egg, then began to beat them with a fork. "For months I've wanted to know who killed Father, but now that I do, I almost

453

wish I didn't. Doc always seemed like such a good man. It's hard to believe my father was mistaken in believing he was his friend."

She paused and looked at Craig. "The Bible says the truth will set us free, but I don't feel free." The burden that had lifted yesterday was back, leaving her feeling there was more to do.

Craig's expression said he understood. "That's because you have no proof."

"And no reason why he would have done something so horrible. I may have one answer, but now there are more questions." Emily gave the eggs one last beating, wielding the fork with more force than necessary. "Even though I believe Beulah, Doc will deny all wrongdoing and the sheriff will believe him."

"Which means we have to find the proof."

With the eggs ready for scrambling, Emily started slicing bread to toast. "There must be some." If they could prove the doctor was a killer, perhaps he would reveal his reasons. "My father used to say that Doc kept the most meticulous records of anyone he knew. When Louisa was trying to convince him to train her as his assistant, she offered to help with the record keeping, but he was adamant that only he could do it properly."

Emily thought about the first day she'd taken Noah to the doctor's office. "There are two books. He entered information about Noah's symptoms and his diagnosis in one and used the other one to record the type and amount of medicine he gave me."

"Then we need to find those books. If Beulah's right, Doc would have dispensed a large quantity of morphine the day your father died."

"True, but we can't simply stroll into his office and ask to see his records."

A faint smile crossed Craig's face. "We can go when he's not there. Mrs. Tabor confirmed what I'd heard, that Doc goes directly from the restaurant to the saloon every Friday."

Emily matched Craig's smile as hope filled her heart. "How fortunate that today is Friday."

The sun had set by the time Craig and Emily made their way toward the doctor's office. For most people, it had been an ordinary Friday in Sweetwater Crossing. Despite his lack of sleep, Craig had conducted the lessons he'd planned, saying only that Beulah was too ill to come to school. Fortunately, by the time Mrs. Douglas arrived, she'd recovered from her fever and was acting like nothing extraordinary had occurred the previous night.

Craig wished he could be as calm. Though he knew Emily was as anxious as he to read the doctor's records, he kept their pace slow enough that anyone who saw them would think this was their usual evening stroll, even though Alice and David had not accompanied them. When Craig had told David he wanted some time alone with Emily, the minister had smiled, saying he and Alice needed to discuss their wedding plans and would do that in the Finley House parlor with Mrs. Carmichael as their chaperone.

"The building will be locked," Emily had said when they'd planned their evening, "but I remember Doc's daughter saying he kept a key under a rock by the back door for the nights when he came home late. For some reason, he never wanted to carry keys with him."

If the rumors were correct and he often returned inebriated, perhaps he feared losing his keys and being locked out.

The key was exactly where Emily had predicted, allowing them to enter the doctor's office without anyone seeing them. And, since shutters covered the windows, they could light the lantern Craig had brought without worrying about being discovered. So far, everything was going smoothly. He prayed that would continue.

Craig gave the office a cursory glance, not surprised that the layout resembled that of the doctor's office he'd visited in Galveston. Glass-fronted cabinets filled with assorted bottles and vials lined the back wall along with a small bookcase, while an examining table and desk occupied most of the other space.

A bit surprised that the doctor hadn't locked his desk, Craig opened the top drawer and pulled out two books. "Are these the ones you saw?"

"Yes." Emily's voice was little more than a whisper. "The blue one is for patients, the red for medicine."

"Which do you want to read?"

She hesitated for a moment, then held out her hand. "The medicine." Perhaps she feared that seeing her father's name in the doctor's records would be painful.

Before she opened the book, she turned and gasped. "That's what was missing. The day I brought Noah back for his checkup, something seemed wrong." Emily pointed toward the top shelf of the cabinet filled with bottles. "One of the morphine bottles was missing. Now another one's gone. There used to be three."

It was what they'd surmised. Now they needed the proof of what Doc had done with large amounts of morphine.

"Let's see what his books tell us. Your father died on August 19, didn't he?" Craig began leafing through the patient records. "There's an entry for that day. 'Joseph Vaughn, pain from war wounds.' "

Emily's eyes widened, making Craig realize she had been harboring a hope — no matter how improbable — that the doctor had not killed her father.

"Doc claimed he didn't see Father that day, that he didn't know that his leg was hurting more than usual, even though Louisa said Father complained about it."

"He could hardly admit to what he'd done, could he? I'm surprised he wrote anything in his books."

"So am I. Let's see what's in this one." Emily turned a few pages in the red book, then frowned. "It says Doc dispensed six grains of morphine that day."

"That sounds like a lot." Craig didn't claim to be an expert, but he knew morphine was a powerful and potentially deadly drug, and while Beulah had no way of knowing what was in the injection, she had claimed it acted quickly, either killing Emily's father or rendering him unconscious.

"There must be something in this office that tells us what a normal dose is."

Emily rose and walked to the bookcase, studied the titles for a few seconds, then pulled a well-worn book from the second shelf and handed it to him. "You read it. I don't think I can."

Knowing she was still hoping for a way to prove the doctor's innocence, Craig studied the table of contents. It took only seconds to find the entry he sought. "If he gave your father the full six grains, there's no question about it. Doc meant to kill your father. Even three grains is lethal. The book says a dose that large is only to be administered when the patient is in extreme pain and near death because there's no way to counteract such a large dose."

Emily bit her lip in an apparent effort not to cry out. "Father said people become accustomed to morphine, so it takes more and more to relieve pain."

Emily, sweet Emily, wanted to believe the best of everyone. Even now when the proof was in front of her, she sought a way to exonerate her family's friend.

"It's still too much. Much too much. Let's see what Doc gave your father the last time." Craig turned a few pages, searching for another entry with Joseph Vaughn's name. "There it is. He saw your father on July 28."

Emily looked up. "That's odd. I expected you to say August 2 because there's an entry for three grains of morphine that day. July 28 is only half a grain."

Craig's mind began to whirl. "August 2?" He consulted the book again. "There's only one patient listed that day: Lillian Webster, suffering from rheumatism."

"Ma Webster?" A note of incredulity colored Emily's voice. "As far as I know, she never suffered from rheumatism."

But the doctor had given her a massive dose of morphine. Craig hated the suspicion that had begun to grow. "Didn't Alice say she died suddenly last summer?"

"Yes. Everyone was shocked because she hadn't been ill."

"If the records are right, and we have every reason to believe they are, Mrs. Webster wasn't ill. She was killed."

Emily gripped the chair arms, obviously reeling from the implications. "Then Father wasn't the first."

It was almost unthinkable that the doctor, a man who'd taken an oath to do no harm, had deliberately killed at least two people. "Let's hope there weren't others. What does your book say? Are there any large doses of morphine after August 19?"

Emily's expression was troubled as she scanned the book. "October 5."

Craig found the entry in the patient book. "Clara Adams, gout."

Emily shuddered. "Mrs. Carmichael found her dead on the sixth. Oh, Craig, I'm afraid to keep looking."

"You know you need to."

She turned a few more pages. "November 5."

"Charlotte French, cough."

"I'm the one who found her." When Emily's gaze met his, Craig saw both horror and determination in it. "If I'm right, there'll be an entry for November 20." She turned a page and nodded. "Another three grains of morphine."

Craig wasn't surprised by the entry in the patient ledger. "Elizabeth Locke, lumbago."

The evidence was damning.

Emily stared at him, her eyes glistening with tears. "I don't want to believe it, but I have to. For some reason, Doc killed all of Mrs. Carmichael's friends, and he kept records of what he'd done, just like normal house calls." She shook her head, perhaps trying to clear her thoughts. "Why would he do something like that, something so evil? Didn't he realize he was hurting others?

461

Mrs. Carmichael was devastated by her friends' deaths. She kept saying they weren't sick enough to die."

"They weren't." But that hadn't stopped the doctor. "Were there any more large doses after that?" Craig doubted she'd find any because there'd been no funerals since Mrs. Locke's, but they needed to check.

Emily turned each of the clearly written pages, searching for suspicious entries. "No."

"That's good, but it doesn't mean he won't kill again. The man has killed at least five people. I suspect that if we look at earlier records, we'd find other cases of deliberate overdoses of morphine."

Though her reluctance was clear, Emily flipped back a few pages. "There was another three grains on May 15."

Craig searched for the same date. "Myron Brattle, fractured femur. No one — and I mean no one — needs that much morphine for a broken leg."

Emily shuddered. "Poor Mr. Brattle. He was such a nice old man. I can't believe Doc killed him." She shuddered again. "We need to stop him," she said as she closed the book but kept a tight grip on it. "I wonder whether the records are enough to convince the sheriff. I'm afraid they won't be because he and the doctor are good friends."

Craig shared her concern. "I doubt Sheriff Granger will want to believe he's been so mistaken in his crony. Look at how hard it was for you to believe your father's friend could have killed him. The sheriff will probably accept any explanation Doc gives him."

"We need more proof. We need to catch him before he kills someone else." Emily voiced Craig's thoughts.

"I agree, but right now we'd better leave. We don't want him catching us here." There was no predicting what the man might do if he realized someone had discovered his secrets.

Craig and Emily replaced the books, being careful to leave everything in the doctor's office the way they'd found it, then locked the door behind them, neither one speaking until they were back on the street. Craig hoped the casual pace he and Emily adopted as they returned to Finley House would convince anyone who spotted them that they were simply enjoying a stroll. The reality was far different.

Though Emily kept her head high, he could feel the tension in the hand she'd placed on his arm. For his part, though he didn't know Doc Sheridan well, he felt like he'd been betrayed. As the town's physician, Doc should have been worthy of trust, but tonight's revelations had destroyed that trust.

"I keep thinking about the people Doc killed," Emily said, her voice low but filled with pain. "Other than my father, they were all older people who consulted him about minor illnesses. Even a broken leg shouldn't have been serious. I cannot imagine why Doc would have killed them, but the only way I can see us uncovering his reasons is to set a trap."

They'd reached the corner of Main and East Streets. In the past, they would have turned north onto East, but when Craig looked at Emily, she shook her head, and so they continued on Main Street.

"When you say set a trap, do you mean have another person, probably an elderly woman since most of the people he killed were women, call the doctor, and we'd be there to see what happens?"

"Exactly. I wish we could convince the sheriff to accompany us, but I'm afraid he'd say something to Doc."

"I agree. It's a good plan but a risky one, especially for the older woman. Are you thinking about Mrs. Carmichael?"

Emily frowned. "I know she'd agree, but I don't think it would work out. We'd have to be hidden where we could see him and stop him before he could inject the morphine, but there's nowhere to hide in her room."

"We could be on the verandah."

Emily drew her shawl closer around her shoulders as she said, "Nights are still fairly cool. That means Doc might be suspicious if the door were open."

It was a valid and important consideration. Emily would leave nothing to chance in her search for the truth.

"You've thought of everything," he told her, still amazed at how quickly she'd devised a plan. "I can almost see your mind whirling, and that makes me believe you have someone in mind."

"I do. Beulah's grandmother. She's old. I don't know that she has any serious illnesses that have made her consult Doc before, but that might not matter."

"What about the location?"

"Doc makes house calls farther away than the Douglas ranch."

"That wasn't what I meant. Is there a good place to observe but not be seen?"

"Yes." Emily's voice was firm. "I was invited inside the house the day I asked Beulah's parents if they'd be willing to send her to school, and the grandmother took me into her room. It's almost perfect, Craig.

The room was once used for storage and has a large cabinet."

"Big enough for both of us?" No matter how courageous Emily was, he wouldn't let her face a murderer alone.

She paused, tipping her head to one side, considering. "I was only thinking of myself. You could be outside the room, listening."

"Or I could be inside the cabinet and you could be outside."

"I want to be there. I need to be there." Stubborn Emily wasn't going to concede anything.

"So do I. I've lost the first woman I loved, and I have no intention of letting the last woman I'll ever love put herself in danger. If we can't both be there, we'll have to find another way."

Emily was silent for a moment. At last, she nodded. "It would be a tight fit, but I think we could do it."

Relief and what felt almost like exhilaration flowed through him. He couldn't discount the danger, but it was exciting to realize that he and Emily would work together to unmask a killer and protect Sweetwater Crossing's residents.

"Will the Douglases agree?" he asked. "After all, there's risk involved."

"I think they will, and as long as we warn

Beulah's grandmother not to let the doctor near her with a syringe, she should be safe."

"Your plan just might succeed." Craig laid his hand on top of Emily's and squeezed it. "You're an amazing woman, Emily Leland."

CHAPTER THIRTY-ONE

Emily did not feel amazing. What she felt was squashed and more than a little apprehensive as Craig pulled the cabinet door shut. Mrs. Douglas's quilt cabinet was smaller than she remembered, and even with the shelves removed, she and Craig barely fit. The cramped conditions were trivial compared to her worry about what might happen next. Fortunately, so far, the plan had proceeded flawlessly.

When Emily had gone to the Douglas ranch on Saturday and explained her suspicions, all three Douglases stared at her, shocked by the idea that the doctor could have done such heinous things.

"It wasn't a nightmare." Beulah's mother was the first to speak. "I thought Beulah was only dreaming when she told me a bad man had poked someone and made him fall, but it wasn't a dream at all." She blinked furiously, trying to hold back her tears. "My poor girl! I should have listened to her. Maybe we could have stopped him sooner."

But who would have believed Beulah? Rather than hurt her family by saying that, Emily continued with an explanation of the proposed plan, ending with, "If you don't want to take the risk, I understand."

There was a moment of silence as the three Douglases exchanged looks.

"He cain't be allowed to continue," Helen Douglas declared. "I'll do whatever ya say." And so she agreed to play the starring role in the drama Emily and Craig had developed.

Her son nodded. "I agree. The man is evil. We need to do anything we can to stop him."

Following the script Emily had outlined, the Douglas family did not attend church on Sunday. Monday morning when Mrs. Douglas brought Beulah to school, she stopped by the doctor's office, claiming her mother-in-law had been too sickly to come into town for services yesterday and asking him to visit the ranch tonight.

"It may be nothing serious," she told the doctor, "but Mother Douglas is getting up in years, and I worry about her."

According to Mrs. Douglas, Doc nodded

solemnly, then took a blue bottle from the cabinet and placed it on his desk. "I may need this," he said without explaining what the bottle contained. "I'll follow you back to the ranch."

Mrs. Douglas gave him the response Emily had suggested. "I'm sure it's nothing urgent, and I know you must have other patients to see today. Why don't you come late this afternoon? That way you can stay for supper after you treat Mother Douglas. I'll make my pecan pie."

The doctor agreed, perhaps persuaded to delay his visit by the prospect of a piece of the pie that was generally acknowledged to be the best in the county.

Not wanting anyone to see them leave town together, Emily had ridden to the ranch half an hour before Craig dismissed school. Now here they were, crammed into a cabinet that wasn't designed to hold one much less two adults, peering through the holes Beulah's father had drilled in the middle of the ornately carved panels and waiting for Doc Sheridan to arrive.

"He's here," Craig whispered as the back door slammed and Mrs. Douglas led the doctor toward her mother-in-law's room, speaking more loudly than normal to give everyone as much warning as possible.

"Do you want me to stay with you, Mother Douglas?" she asked when she'd ushered the man Emily knew had killed so many into the room.

"That won't be necessary, Mrs. Douglas." Doc gave the older woman no chance to reply. "I prefer to treat my patients privately."

Though Beulah's mother nodded as if she agreed, Emily knew she and her husband would be on the other side of the door, listening to everything that happened, prepared to intervene if Craig or Emily called for help.

When the door closed, Doc moved toward the bed. "What seems to be the problem, Mrs. Douglas?" His voice sounded sincere.

"I got terrible pains in my innards." Beulah's grandmother punctuated her words with a groan. "I can't keep nothin' down. Ain't never felt so bad."

Emily thought he might have made a pretense of examining his patient, but the doctor simply nodded. He removed his coat, hanging it on one of the hooks in the wall, then reached into the black bag that he'd placed on the bureau. "You were wise to call me. Pain like that must be stopped." He pulled out a syringe and one of the blue bottles Emily recognized as the ones he used to store morphine.

Even though she'd expected it, seeing the doctor so calmly preparing to administer a lethal dose of the powerful drug made Emily shudder. She wanted to stop him now, but Craig shook his head, urging patience.

"So much pain." Beulah's grandmother was playing her part well, her writhing in pretended agony making it difficult for the doctor to touch her.

"It'll be all right." Doc's voice was designed to soothe his anxious patients. On another day, it might have soothed Emily, but today she knew what he intended, and nothing could soothe her.

"The Lord put me on this earth to stop pain," the man who'd betrayed his oath to do no harm continued. "He showed me what I had to do when my grandmother was ill. He told me she'd lived her allotted three score and ten years and it was time for her to meet her Maker."

Emily clapped a hand over her mouth, trying to muffle her gasp. Craig had speculated that if they'd had time to review earlier entries in Doc's books, they would have found other killings, but this was worse — much worse — than she'd expected. By his own admission, the doctor had killed his grandmother.

"I don't want you to suffer, but you've lived as long as God intended." Slowly and deliberately, Doc filled the syringe, then approached the bed. "Just close your eyes, Mrs. Douglas. This will sting for a moment, but then it'll all be over."

"It's over right now!" Craig flung the cabinet door open and sprang toward the doctor while Emily raced to the bed, determined to keep Doc from harming Beulah's grandmother. Though Craig had a pistol strapped to his hip, he and Emily had agreed he'd use it only as a last resort. They needed answers, and Doc might be more forthcoming with them if he thought he was still in control.

The doctor's normally ruddy complexion paled at the sight of Emily and Craig, and for a second he was speechless. Then he brandished the syringe like a weapon, pointing it at Craig's neck. "Don't come any closer, or I'll use this on you." When Craig remained motionless, Doc's gaze moved from him to Emily. "What are you doing here?"

"Stopping you from killing another innocent person."

Clearly confused, the doctor looked from Emily to Craig, then turned an accusing look at his patient, who was now sitting up in bed, no longer exhibiting any signs of pain. "You were supposed to be alone."

"Well, I ain't. And you ain't gonna kill me like you did them others." Helen Douglas might be over seventy, but she hadn't lost any of her feistiness.

"How did you know?" This time Doc fixed his gaze on Craig.

"Your records made it easy to trace what happened."

Emily couldn't imagine why he'd kept such incriminating records. She would have thought that a murderer would have tried to hide the evidence, but it seemed the man she and many others in Sweetwater Crossing had trusted with their lives was proud of what he'd done, that he truly believed he was acting on God's command.

Doc shook his head before turning his attention to the syringe, as if trying to decide what to do with it. "No one was supposed to figure it out. The only one who knew was Joseph."

Emily nodded slowly as the last piece to the puzzle slid into place. No matter how much he valued Doc's friendship, Father would never have condoned murder. Though he would not have denounced his friend from the pulpit, when Father had chosen "Go, and sin no more" as the subject for his sermon, he must have hoped it would persuade Doc to stop the killing, to confess what he'd done, and to accept the punishment. But Doc hadn't allowed Father to live long enough to deliver that sermon or to tell the sheriff what he knew if the doctor refused to admit his guilt.

"What I don't understand is why you did it." Though her heart was pounding with alarm, Emily managed to keep her voice calm. "Why did you kill all those people?" There'd been murderers since Cain and Abel, but this was the first time she had confronted one.

The doctor's gray eyes gleamed with fervor. "It was their time. The Bible says a man is meant to live only seventy years. God gave me the power to do his will."

Helen Douglas gripped Emily's hand, her trembling fingers telling Emily she was as horrified by the doctor's apparent madness as Emily. They were getting the answers, and they were almost as chilling as the killings themselves.

"Killing innocent people is not God's will," Craig said as he inched his way toward Doc, intent on getting the syringe away from him.

Emily said a silent prayer that he'd be successful, but the doctor, realizing that Craig wanted to disarm him, took a step backward. "You don't understand."

"No, I don't." Emily tried to draw Doc's attention away from Craig, hoping that a momentary distraction would give Craig the opening he needed and her the answers she sought. "You killed my father, and he wasn't seventy." She infused her words with anger, trying to keep the doctor's focus on her.

What appeared to be genuine sorrow clouded the older man's expression. "He was the hardest, but I had no choice. Joseph was out walking and saw me leaving the saloon. I'd had more than my usual amount of whiskey that night, and it loosened my tongue. Before I knew it, I'd told him what I'd done to Ma Webster." Doc's lips curled in a sneer. "Your pa said God would forgive me if I repented, but I couldn't do that. How could I repent when I was doing the Lord's will?"

Doc shook his head, silently saying there was no possibility. "When I woke up the next day, I knew Joseph had to die. I couldn't let him interfere with my mission."

His mission? Emily stared at the man who'd been one of her father's closest friends, the man who'd killed him and then tried to make it look like suicide. How could he believe God sanctioned murder when the

Bible said clearly, "Thou shalt not kill"?

"You know you have to stop." When Craig took another step toward the doctor, he moved backward again, keeping the same distance between them. Doc wasn't going to make this easy. In the time it took Craig to unholster and fire his pistol, the doctor might hit him with the syringe.

"When the sheriff hears what you done, he's gonna lock you up." Helen Douglas released her grip on Emily's hand and wagged a finger at the man who'd planned to kill her. "You'll be hanging from a noose afore the week's over." She was taunting him much as Emily had, trying to give Craig an advantage.

"Never!" Doc's gaze darted from Helen to Craig to Emily then back to Helen before he began to unfasten the cuff of his sleeve. "You don't understand. None of you do. I had to do it. Don't you see? I had to!" His words were clear, but his eyes betrayed the madness he'd kept hidden for so long.

When no one responded, he shook his head, then started backing up as he tugged his sleeve over his elbow. "I had to do it. Just like I have to do this." Moving so quickly that no one could stop him, Doc plunged the needle into his arm. "I can't let them shut me away like they were going to do to my grandmother. She wasn't crazy, and neither am I."

"You are crazy." Beulah's grandmother climbed out of bed and glared at the man who'd been responsible for so many deaths. "I reckon you're crazy as a rabid skunk."

"Why you old . . ."

Before Doc could complete the sentence, the door flew open, the force knocking him to the floor.

"Are you all right, Mother?" Mr. Douglas raced to his mother's side, his wife only a step behind him.

"I'm fine. He ain't."

No, he wasn't. As the doctor tried to scramble to his feet, Emily saw the fear in his eyes.

"I'll take him to the sheriff," Beulah's father announced.

Doc shook his head. "Not while there's a breath in this body." Though he seemed slightly unsteady, there was no doubting the man's determination.

"He's going to die, probably before you could get him into town. There's no antidote for that much morphine." Craig's voice was as firm as if he were teaching a class.

Mr. Douglas nodded. "Then I'll fetch the sheriff."

"Mother Douglas and I will go with you,"

Beulah's mother said. "We need to tell Beulah that the bad man is done hurting people."

To Emily's surprise, Doc was silent until the trio had left. Then he said so softly she almost didn't hear him, "I'm not bad."

But he was. He'd killed her father, Mr. Brattle, and at least five elderly women. "How did you do it?" she demanded. "How did you persuade Father to let you treat him in the barn?" The man she remembered would have insisted on receiving the injection in the library.

Doc swayed, then reached for the edge of the bureau to steady himself. "No persuasion. Forced him." The words were beginning to slur, and Emily could see the effort it was taking for him to pronounce them. "Found him with that horse of his. Grooming." There was a pause as the doctor appeared to have forgotten the story he was relating. "Knew he had to die. Pressed his neck. Made him dizzy. Gave him morphine. Fainted."

Emily heard Craig's quick intake of breath and knew he'd had the same reaction she had, relief that her father hadn't suffered. Perhaps Father hadn't even realized who was killing him. But there was still one more question.

"Why did you hang him?"

"Couldn't . . . let . . . anyone . . . guess . . . happened." As Doc's breathing became irregular, each breath more labored than the previous one, he leaned against the bureau in an attempt to remain upright. "Saw . . . rope . . ." Whatever else he was going to say was lost as he slumped to the floor.

As Craig knelt beside the doctor and felt for his pulse, Emily stared at the man she thought she'd known. Had anyone in Sweetwater Crossing realized what was behind the calm exterior he'd presented to his patients? Was there anyone who knew the truth about his grandmother's mental state? Was it possible he'd inherited a sickness from her? She'd probably never know.

"He's gone."

Emily nodded as Craig's words registered. The danger was over. There would be no more killings. Her father was exonerated. She had the answers she'd sought.

Tears welled in her eyes. She ought to be relieved, not overwhelmed with sorrow, but it was sorrow that filled her heart, sorrow and deep regret. So many lives had been cut short; so many people had questioned why death had taken loved ones before their time; so many people had mourned the loss of their families and friends. There was no undoing that.

The grieving would continue, and it wouldn't be limited to those who'd lost loved ones. Doc's family would bear the burden of what he'd done. Like Emily and her sisters, Phoebe and her mother would face the shame of a burial outside the cemetery. They might even be shunned because of Doc's actions. Emily's heart ached at the thought of what might happen to them once the truth was revealed, and she found herself speechless.

"This time it really is over," Craig said as he rose.

"At least for him." Emily felt a moment of sympathy for the doctor, realizing how tortured he must have been. Despite his claims that he was doing God's will, she'd seen genuine sorrow on his face the day Father died and knew he'd had at least a fleeting regret that he'd killed his friend. Had he been equally distraught after Mr. Brattle's and the elderly women's deaths? She'd never know.

Emily nodded slowly. "What he did was wrong, but now we have the answers."

Most of them.

"We have the answers." Craig repeated Emily's words as they rode away from the

Douglas ranch. The sheriff had arrived more quickly than Emily had expected, his face solemn as he stared at his friend's body.

"You were right about your father. He didn't tie that noose." His lips quivered with emotion. "I had no idea what Doc was doing."

No one had.

Though the sheriff had suggested she and Craig remain until the Douglases returned, Craig had insisted it was time for him and Emily to leave, perhaps because he'd seen how her limbs trembled with the aftermath of the scene in Helen Douglas's room.

Even now, an hour after Doc had slumped to the floor, Emily was still reeling from what she'd seen and heard. Though she'd been in no danger, she knew the image of the syringe and the madness she'd seen in Doc's eyes were indelibly etched on her brain.

She tugged on Blanche's reins as she tried to make sense of the thoughts that were whirling through her. Craig might not have the answers, but she knew he'd listen. "Do you mind if we stop for a few minutes? I'm not ready to go back to Sweetwater Crossing."

His eyes filled with sympathy, Craig helped her dismount. "I'm almost afraid to ask how you're feeling."

"My thoughts are in a jumble," she admitted. "I thought I'd be happy or at least relieved when I proved that my father hadn't taken his own life, but I'm not. I'm saddened that Father's life was cut short and hope he died so quickly that he didn't realize his friend had betrayed him." For that would have hurt him unbearably.

Craig slid an arm around Emily's waist and drew her close.

Comforted by his nearness and the knowledge that he understood her better than anyone, Emily continued. "I'm also sad that Doc carried such horrible secrets." Even a man as troubled and misguided as Doc Sheridan must have had moments when he recognized and regretted his actions.

Craig nodded. "When we saw the records, I was filled with anger and wanted Doc to pay for his sins. And when I saw him pull out that syringe and point it at Beulah's grandmother, I wanted nothing more than to see him with a noose around his neck, realizing everyone knew what he'd done and that his time on Earth was coming to an end. But when I listened to him rant, I realized he's been paying for his sins for years. We'll never know what got him started on the wrong path, but I feel sorry for him."

The sun was beginning to set, turning the sky a brilliant orange. Another day was ending, a day unlike any Emily had experienced. It had been filled with worry, with fear, with sadness. But now as she stood with Craig's arm around her, she felt the heaviness begin to lift, replaced by the hope that had buoyed her when the month began. Today was a day of endings. Perhaps it could also be one of beginnings.

Emily turned to face Craig. "I told you my feelings were in a jumble, and they were, but now they're making more sense. I'm happy that I can restore my father's reputation and have him buried next to my mother." She would write letters to Joanna and Louisa tonight, telling them what had happened and reassuring them that the father they'd loved had not been so overwhelmed with grief that he'd taken his own life.

Craig's brown eyes reflected understanding. "That's what you've wanted from the beginning. I can only imagine how relieved you must feel now that you've accomplished that. Relieved and maybe even satisfied."

Once again, he understood her better than anyone she'd ever met. "A little of both, I think. Most of all, though, I'm filled with hope."

Craig's arm tightened, drawing her closer, and she heard his breath hitch. "Hope for what?" The question was simple, but the fervor in his voice set her spirits soaring.

Emily's lips curved upward as she said, "Hope for the future. You were right when you told me how important it is not to live in the past but to appreciate each day and look forward to the future. I'm ready to do that now." She could not undo the past and correct the errors she'd made, but she did not have to remain mired in the past either.

As a gentle breeze heralded the dusk, Emily fixed her gaze on Craig, praying he'd accept what she was offering. "I can't predict the future. I can't promise you a child, but I hope you still love me. I hope you still want to marry me. And even though my first marriage was barren, I hope Gertrude was right and that you and I may be able to give Noah a brother or sister."

Craig's eyes glistened with emotion. "Oh, Emily, you wonderful, wonderful woman. I don't need another child to make my life complete. All I need is you and your love." He paused for a second. "Do you love me?"

She nodded. "More than I knew was possible. It took me a while to conquer my fears of marriage and disappointing another man, but when I look back, I think I've loved you almost from the first day I met you."

The day she'd returned to Sweetwater Crossing had been one of the most painful of her life, a day of endings, but Craig's arrival at Finley House had marked the beginning of a new chapter of her life, a chapter that was now filled with hope.

"For a long time, I was too stubborn and too frightened to accept that love, so I kept inventing excuses that would keep us apart. When I finally admitted how deeply I loved you and how much I wanted to share your life, I started planning how to tell you, but then Beulah was so sick and . . ."

"And all of this happened." Craig gestured to the road behind them. "That's in the past. Now it's time to build a future. A future together." He studied Emily's face for a moment. "You spoke of hopes. I have hopes too. I hope this is the last time I'll ask this question. I hope you'll give me a different answer today. Will you be my wife and Noah's mother?"

Her heart so filled with love that she feared she'd be unable to speak, Emily nodded. "There is nothing I want more."

The smile that lit Craig's face warmed her with its intensity, chasing away the last of the shadows that had kept her from recognizing love. "Then, my dearest Emily, there's only one thing to do."

"What's that?"

"Set the date."

She shook her head. "Soon, Craig, soon, but right now there's something else we should do."

Emily smiled at the question in his eyes.

"This," she said as she tipped her head up and pressed her lips to his.

AUTHOR'S LETTER

Dear Reader,

Thanks so much for journeying to Sweetwater Crossing with me. I hope you enjoyed getting to know Emily and Craig as well as the other residents and that you're looking forward to the next book in the series, this one featuring Louisa and a man who's literally thrown into her path.

Louisa has her future planned, and living in Sweetwater Crossing isn't part of that plan. You know the adage about the best-laid plans, don't you? Yes, Louisa's go awry. Though she's reluctant, circumstances force her to return to Finley House for what's supposed to be no more than a week. Josh Porter's life isn't that well planned, but he's working on it . . . until his horse catches his leg in a prairie dog hole.

Have I intrigued you? If so, turn a couple pages, and you'll find a sneak peek at their story.

I'm often asked what inspired a story. In the case of the Sweetwater Crossing trilogy, the answer is family relationships. I've always been fascinated by the role birth order plays in both our personalities and how we deal with our siblings. Perhaps that's because I'm the oldest of four children; perhaps it's simply curiosity. Whatever the reason, I wanted to tell the stories of three sisters, all very different, not only because of their birth order but because they're part of what we'd call a blended family.

And since nothing is perfect, not even in a picture-perfect town like Sweetwater Crossing, I created a few not-so-admirable characters to add to the conflict. You've already met one, but there are more to come.

While you're waiting for Louisa and Josh's book to be released, I invite you to read my earlier books, if you haven't already done so. Since Louisa's story starts in Cimarron Creek, you might want to begin with that trilogy, because it'll give you the opportunity to meet the people who become her mentors: the town's doctor and its midwife. Austin comes to Cimarron Creek in *A Borrowed Dream,* and

Thea's story is *A Tender Hope,* but you won't want to miss the first book, *A Stolen Heart.* Be warned, though. My editors said that story made them hungry for chocolate.

You'll find information about these and other books on my website, www.amanda cabot.com, as well as a sign-up form for my monthly newsletter. I've also included links to my Facebook and Twitter accounts along with my email address.

It's one of my greatest pleasures as an author to receive notes from my readers, so don't be shy.

Blessings,
Amanda

ACKNOWLEDGMENTS

John Donne is famous for saying, "No man is an island," and no author is, either. While writing a book is for the most part a solitary task, it's not done in a vacuum. Sometimes it requires help from friends to turn an idea into a finished product. I've received assistance from so many people over the years I've been writing that it would take pages to list them all, but today I'd like to thank three women for their contributions to this book.

Award-winning author Sarah Sundin, who's also a retired pharmacist, took time away from her own writing to answer questions about morphine in the nineteenth century. Thanks to her, I avoided making some major mistakes in the critical final scene with Doc. Many thanks to Doctor Sarah. Any mistakes you find are mine, not hers. And, if you haven't read Sarah's books, I encourage you to pick one up today. Her tales of World War II are unforgettable!

Kathy Flinchum has been my go-to resource for information about horses ever since she pointed out a glaring error I'd made in *Summer of Promise*. (If you're curious, it's that the cavalry would have had geldings, not stallions, at Fort Laramie.) I appreciate her willingness to answer questions, most of which show my total ignorance of all things equine, and to offer plausible explanations for various plot points. Thank you, Kathy!

Vicki Crumpton has been my editor since 2007 when she acquired the Texas Dreams trilogy, but she's been much more than that. She's also been my champion and my cheerleader, doing everything in her power to advance my career and ensure that my experience at Revell has been overwhelmingly positive. That's why when she announced her retirement, my first response was, "You can't do that!" As much as I hate to say goodbye to Vicki, I wish her a long, happy, and healthy retirement and give thanks for the many years she provided insightful editing to make my books the best they could be. It's been a privilege to be one of Vicki's authors.

ABOUT THE AUTHOR

Amanda Cabot's dream of selling a book before her thirtieth birthday came true, and she's now the author of more than forty novels as well as eight novellas, four nonfiction books, and what she describes as enough technical articles to cure insomnia in a medium-sized city. Her stories have appeared on the CBA and ECPA bestseller lists, have garnered a starred review from *Publishers Weekly,* and were finalists for the ACFW Carol, the HOLT Medallion, and the Booksellers' Best awards.

Amanda married her high school sweetheart, who shares her love of travel and who's driven thousands of miles to help her research her books. After years as Easterners, they fulfilled a longtime dream when Amanda retired from her job as director of information technology for a major corporation and now live in the American West.